A Londoner, Tom Barling has worked for the national press, in advertising, as an art director and a TV producer. For many years he ran his own production company producing commercials and animated films, mostly for the American market. His previous novels include *The Olympic Sleeper*, *Goodbye Piccadilly*, *Bikini Red North*, *Terminate with Prejudice* and *The Smoke*.

Also by Tom Barling

THE SMOKE

and published by Corgi Books

God Is An Executioner

Tom Barling

CORGI BOOKS

GOD IS AN EXECUTIONER

A CORGI BOOK   0 552 12813 9

First publication in Great Britain

PRINTING HISTORY
Corgi edition published 1987

This book is set in 10/11pt Century.

Corgi Books are published by Transworld Publishers Ltd.,
61-63 Uxbridge Road, Ealing, London W5 5SA, in Australia by
Transworld Publishers (Australia) Pty. Ltd., 15-23 Helles
Avenue, Moorebank, NSW 2170, and in New Zealand by Transworld
Publishers (N.Z.) Ltd., Cnr. Moselle and Waipareira Avenues,
Henderson, Auckland.

Printed and bound in Great Britain by
Cox & Wyman Ltd, Reading

This book is respectfully dedicated to all my friends in Californian law enforcement. In particular to:
Frank Bridges, Chuck Elliott, Billy Farrington, Roger Kelley, Bob O'Sullivan, Tony Palmer, Clay Sanderburgh, George Smith, Roger Wilson, and Jack Whitehouse.
They live the fact I write fiction about.

'The figure of Justice has had such a rough voyage from France to Indochina that she has lost everything but her sword.'

Ho Chi Minh

'Whether the French like it or not, independence is coming to Indochina. Why, therefore, do we [Americans] tie ourselves to the tail of their battered kite?'

Raymond B. Fosdick

'Let us remember the main purpose of American foreign aid is not to help other nations but to help ourselves.'

Richard M. Nixon

CHAPTER ONE

Matthew Pepper tossed in haunted sleep.

He dreamed assault helicopters out of the night and sweated into his pillow as the choppers swept him across the darkness of the Iron Triangle, the defoliated 'White Area' north of Cu Chi.

The sidegunner pointed out the abandoned 'Ann-Margret' observation bunkers at the edge of the Fil Hol rubber plantation, and opened up on the dark forest for the hell of it. The Cav 4 Pathfinder marked phoney drop-zones with parachute flares to fool Charlie, and the lead choppers sprayed Gatling rounds at nothing to keep him underground. The heavy bombers had already earthquaked the area and the sting of HE still hung in the air.

'Central Casting' might say their USAF B52s couldn't neutralise the underground VC bases from the air, but the whole damned world and his dog knew they could pancake Mount Everest to peanut brittle if they wanted to. But that was Central's way of *not* saying they wanted Hanoi to know their CIDG (Civilian Irregular Defense Groups) Spooks could double-zap Charlie in his own boondocks any time they chose.

Like now. A last vicious whack at the VC even though Tricky Dicky was talking about pulling out.

The briefing back at 'Saigon on the Hudson' had been held in a Quonset hut around blown-up reconnaissance photographs taken with heat-sensors and infrared bioptics, and Pepper's Spooks had made the CIA Pogues look like wimps from Wimpsville. A skinny captain had used his pointer as he described mission objectives as boringly as his dry voice could make them, and it was left to smooth old Luther Cash to sum it all up for Pepper and Taylor over cold Buds.

Cash knew history and politics. In the tunnels he let Pepper and Taylor take the lead. He said:

'Charlie's been building tunnels since before Dien Bien Phu, when they dug under the French perimeter, and came up at the Foreign Legion every whichway. Charlie's built two-hundred miles of inter-connecting tunnels right under our noses, and means those mothers can come up into the middle of our base and supply camps any time they choose. Could be that explains why so many Grunts went ''Missing in Action'' without even joining a patrol. So, despite Operations Crimp and Cedar Falls, and the Tunnel Rats from the 25th going in after them, it comes down to us making those bastards bleed, is all. Jerk Charlie off in his own toilet.'

Taylor had belched and reached for another Bud.

'You believe that, I've got a bridge I can sell you. You go for this sorry scenario, Pepper san?'

'Just go with the flow, buddy . . .'

Pepper sweated beside his sleeping wife and sat on his helmet in the gunship.

Cav 4 choppers settled in their own rotor dust and hostile fire came from spider holes off to Pepper's right. Tracer and grenades blew yellow holes in the night and a flamethrower torched a stand of palms on the northern slopes of the main hill. Crisscrossing beams of candle-power and volatile smoke made wild and surreal patterns in the moonless sky as if some ethereal Dali had learned to paint on infinite velvet with primal light.

'Go, you *mothers*. Go-go-*gooo* . . .' the sidegunner screamed.

Charlie hung D-10 mines and friction fuses in the treetops near probable landing zones, and triggered by rotor-downdraught, they blew helicopters out of the sky like toys.

'*Gooooo* . . .'

The pilot wanted to be back amongst the stars.

Pepper's Montagnards spilled from the Chinook and made their ducking run to the muster point where Zulu's radioman swapped call-signs with Cash's Bravo and Taylor's Able. Screams came from a collapsed bomb-shelter the Zulu Spooks had found. The wiry Khmer Pepper called Pizza Man showed his betel-stained teeth and mimed throats being cut.

The Viet Cong had punished Pizza Man's village for 'deviance' after the Tet Offensive, and every male above age zero had had their hands severed at the wrists for accepting food and medication from a forward patrol of Marine Grunts. The women and girl children had been raped and drowned in a buffalo pen before Charlie torched the whole ville and slaughtered the livestock down to the last hog. Pizza Man hated Charlie for that, and he'd just as soon see every last VC dead rather than bother with prisoners.

Pizza Man was a perfect Spook so long as you didn't have to watch him work.

Pepper's Montagnards were harder to swallow. They made a ritual out of decapitating their prisoners, and played a complicated game of headball wearing necklaces of severed fingers. Pepper had cut that out, and let them collect ears when time allowed. That way, Central got its precious 'body-count', the Montagnards had trophies to strut about, and Pepper sold the ears through a mercenary for a century a pair and pocketed half.

The Montagnards respected Pepper on several counts. He could live off the land as readily as any of them, and only used opium to keep them company. His brain wasn't muggled by pot-roaches, coke or horse, or any other hallucinagents most forward-line Grunts shotgunned their heads with. Mostly they liked him for the golden buddah necklaces he gave them. And for honouring their feast days with gifts of tobacco wrapped in traditional red cloth.

Pepper rolled his face in his pillow and hugged the earth as the empty Chinook rose to lose itself above the treeline.

Cavalry helicopters blatted above their own searchlights and the hill shook as a cache of shells went up in a sudden thrash of foliage and streamers of flame. A quarter-pound charge took care of a booby-trap at a tunnel entrance, and Able's M79s blooped grenades into spider holes as Bravo's 66-Millimetre chopped up incoming Kalashnikov fire. The gunships were minutes away from withdrawing their covering fire, and Pepper was reminded of Luther Cash broaching another Bud in a spray of foam as he said:

'When those Cav babies pull out is when we field-test our undershorts. Man, Charlie-Victors have been born in those tunnels. They've even got hospitals and bomb-factories down there – you guys saw how the heat-sensors picked up the images. Even keep stripped-down 105s down there. Water-traps that keep CS gas from getting into the main tunnels, and cute tricks like bubonic rats and snake-traps to keep us amused. There's gotta be slopes down there who never even saw the light of day. That means mamasans and babysans . . .'

'And all that baby-killing shit we do so good,' said Taylor.

'And twelve-year-old Lucy Congs who'll take your head off without a "sorry-bout-that",' said Pepper.

And after nods all round they drank too much to stay drunk and dried out for a week before the choppers took them into Cu Chi.

Pepper's Kit Carson scouts had marked the ingress tunnels with luminous flags, and Pepper hunkered down for a final equipment check. His Montagnards painted their faces ochre and oiled their naked torsoes to keep the chiggers out of their skin. Pepper hoped they couldn't see his skin crawl through the countdown seconds as sweat and insect-repellant stung his heatrash.

Pizza Man had a flashlight tied off to the shaft of his short stabbing spear and his issue belt was heavy with throwing knives. The grenades in his pouch were for booby-trapping the dead VCs they'd jam in tunnel bottlenecks to give Charlie the kind of headache he liked handing out to the Rats of the 25th.

Pepper checked his flashlight, silenced burp-gun and ammo clips, his tungsten-carbide stiletto and hip packs. One hip-pack held stun-grenades, the other, nerve-gas cylinders. And it paid not to mix them up in panic. No respirator in the world could save your brain if that gas so much as touched your skin. That was scratch one Spook. You were untouchable. Even in death.

Pepper didn't think about that too long. He'd be fine.

The radio confirmed Able and Bravo green for go.

'Give them a likewise.'

Pepper heard the Gatlings quit as the gunships peeled off to find some safe sky. The silence got edgy until he said,

'Let's do it,' and turned his Spooks into ghosts with a pump of his forearm.

Pepper brought up the rear. Rolled down a channel between earth and wicker gabions. Wallowed in mashed palm fronds. Elbowed into a communications trench beyond a spider hole, and felt his way downward when he wanted to scramble back to fresh air and honest sunlight.

Wanted to swallow Buds and breath through a Chesterfield. Watch a girl's hair bounce when she laughed. Thinking like that would get him dead fast. He lost all sense of time and direction as he worked down the stinking shaft.

Charlie lived in his urine and ordure like an animal, but his tricks got cuter all the time. He used recorded sound to distract incoming Spooks. Drew them into traps and cul-de-sacs with the clatter of kitchen woks or nurses tending babysans. Anything to convince roundeyed Yankee he's homed in on a soft target instead of a pit lined with poisoned punji-sticks. A blind spider hole where Charlie waited to spear you through a false wall. A loose trapdoor that dropped you into a hole where spiders the size of your face covered the walls. Or tripwires fed bamboo stakes into your lap.

Training with PsyOps at the classified SAWTOC (Special Asian Warfare Training and Orientation Center) complexes had been rugged. Guys had lost their marbles over it, but nothing's like the real thing.

Pepper listened to nothing with stink coming at him from three directions. He risked a torch flash and found himself at an intersection tall enough to stand up in. Central had some-how got it right for once, and he listened for his Montagnards before he moved. He wouldn't hear them but he listened any-way. Sliding down over the lip of the small shaft he had wormed down, he dropped on to a ramp of packed earth and straightened up. There was just him, sour air and the plop of water seepage, and the three tunnels sloping down into darkness.

Pepper smelled Charlie just as his flashlight drew fire.

He kicked left and AK47 rounds gouged the wall where he had been. Clay fragments spattered everywhere. Pepper skidded into a sudden dip that plopped him into a water-trap without the chance to take air. He ducked under the bend and swam. Swam not knowing how deep or long the trap was, and came up years later, gagging on stale urine as he trod water, checking for tripwires with his flashlight. There were two, and he negated them with bamboo plugs. Hung primed grenades beside the Coke-can mines and hauled himself into the tunnel beyond. If Charlie came up behind him, he'd have enough time to see the flash that tore his head off.

Pepper followed his torchbeam around a series of curves. A rat ran across his back to drop into the water-trap. Another bared teeth at the beam and scuttled away into a hole. It was a cache of rotten rice, and Pepper bit on nausea as he passed it.

Then Charlie surfaced and triggered Pepper's grenades.

Pepper forgot about traps and covered ground. Blast and earth blew him into a skid as the tunnel behind him collapsed. Pepper rolled on hard slats. Worked out he was sprawled across a bamboo trapdoor just as it tore apart under his weight.

All directions were down. Pepper lost skin in the shaft before gravity slammed him into a swarm of arms and legs and startled Vietnamese. His flashlight came on by itself. Cots showed in the erratic beam as men sat up reaching for boots and weapons. It was a dormitory, and Pepper hauled the torch in by its lanyard before it got him killed.

A bayonet cut through his hip-pack and nerve-gas cylinders rolled between naked feet. Fear triggered Pepper's burp-gun and faces disintegrated in flickers of muzzle gas. He kicked and elbowed himself away. There were too many faces screaming at him. Too ready to capture a running dog for the Hanoi TV cameras.

Pepper fired another clip as he rolled.

Figures jerked. Impaled on the darts of gunfire.

Pepper's leg kicked high as a round punched through his boot. The flashlight flickered out and he scrambled through clay and stale water, knowing his wounded leg would stiffen if he didn't keep moving. Knew hookworms would cost him his foot if he didn't fill his boot with sulfa powder. Knew nerve-gas would kill him if the VC mistook the canisters for regular grenades.

The hole in his foot felt bigger than his mouth.

A paraffin lamp turned the dormitory into a glare of over-brightness. Pepper lobbed a grenade and saw men scatter before flash and concussion tossed them every whichway. The lamp blew apart in a spurt of violet and Pepper skidded into a passage with a duckboarded floor. VC in a parallel chamber told each other where he was. Pepper got his back into a niche that stank of body waste. Hoped he could spray the mothers before they swamped him. Then a muddy hand clamped his mouth and good old Pizza Man's voice was in his ear.

'Sitting tight, Pepper san. We bac-bac Charlie damned pretty.'

Oiled bodies crawled over Pepper, and he heard Montagnard spears go home. There was one honest scream and a bubbling snort through severed vocal chords. The rest died in unnatural silence. Pepper counted off a slow century before using his flashlight on the earless bodies. Pizza Man grinned his red grin and wiped his spear off on the nearest dead buttock. A sight as risible as it was obscene.

'Bac-bac them focking A-1, Pepper San. Able and Bravo come from there.'

Pizza Man pointed down the dormitory but he eyed Pepper's shredded boot.

'You want to join them Able, Bravo mothers?'

'When we've rigged for boom-boom.'

'Hookay.'

Pizza Man gave Pepper's boot a long last look and began wiring grenades to the corpses. Pepper avoided putting pressure on the dead VCs, there was enough stink coming from the bodies as it was.

'Charlie's Last Trumps' as Luther Cash called the escape of internal gases. He and Taylor worked hard to get the phenomena logged in writing at the compulsory debriefs. Just for the hell of goosing the Saigon Pogues with boys' faces and degrees in medieval potty training.

Pepper always left the verbal funnies to Cash and Taylor. He just liked to look crazy behind a ten-day beard, and empty sacks of ears out onto the Pogues' desks to watch their faces

13

turn to spit-and-sawdust before they pulled rank or a faint. Then the Spooks went into their favourite diatribe – Vietnamese who banked kickback by the suitcase and let American Grunts die for them. How the dock police helped 'accredited' Americans, Australians, and imported Koreans coin millions selling PX goods straight from the harbour, untroubled by Customs.

And all in the name of good old American Free Enterprise, Baby.

In the end Taylor would be yelling in Chinese, Cash would smash typewriters, whilst Pepper bit the heads from felt pens and spat them into desk drawers. With the debriefs ended in anarchy, the Spooks would get the hell out of Saigon. Nuzzle Buds in a piece of country nobody wanted to fight over that afternoon. After the beer they'd reach for the Jim Beam and Branchwater. Get stinking enough to discuss the next raid into Laos or Cambodia.

Pepper's rapid metabolic rate got him drunk quickly and sobered him up just as fast. He burned alcohol too fast to stay brewed, and he stared into the night as Cash and Taylor snored or had bad dreams. Nobody saw Pepper's ghosts march in the small hours. But that was before the Long Beach Vets Hospital with the rats and crazies for company. Long after the tunnels and the face-off with hijackers on the Cholon Road.

'Go time, Pepper san.'

Pepper left the syrette of morphine zipped in his pants. Pain was better than losing edge, and Pizza Man would finish Pepper if the Khmer thought he couldn't hack it. Spooks who didn't keep up got left on the backtrail with his tags missing. Bringing bodies back wasn't a club rule.

Pepper showed his Montagnards the tripwires and led them back to the dormitory where Cash and his Bravo Khmers worked on the best way to bring the roof down. They'd heaped bodies in a cage of cots and Luther Cash marked the corpses with Bravo playing cards. PsyOps figured Charlie should know who to fear, and the cards made it simple for him. Well, that was the theory.

An Able runner reported that Taylor had an egress tunnel secured, and had his men deployed to cover withdrawal.

Pepper gave the runner a one-hour ETA and sent him back.

Cash chewed a green cigar.

'Looks like your pirates get the ear-count again, Matt.'

Pepper decided not to unlace his boot. A shot foot blew up like mashed eggplant.

'How'd your ordnance forage go?'

'You never saw the likes. More GI 'quipment than you see in a month of Sunday markets in Saigon. Ain't no need to bring stuff down the Ho Chi Minh Trail when Charlie's cousins can boost what they need from Uncle Sam right here in the South. Back there's more Bouncing Bettys than I've seen hot geishas. And the D-10s are wall to wall. When that blows we'd better be long gone. Let's take some air and take us a Cav chopper to the nearest bar, huh?'

'Sure.'

Pepper knew he could make it out. Blood oozed from his boot as slow as lubricating oil on his old man's lathe. Back in his machine shop in Des Moines. Pepper hadn't thought of his father in years. A bad thing to do. He would have crossed himself if the dream hadn't been shredded by a pistol pressing his face back into the pillow.

The darkness was Pepper's bedroom. The tunnels were history.

His hand was in the warm hollow where his wife usually slept. His right foot ached as it did in damp weather, and the silencer against his top lip smelled of oil and spent cartridges.

'Anything sudden and it ends here, mister.'

The voice was young and hard and local. From the Falls or Orangefield. Politics didn't colour an accent, and Pepper wondered if he'd traded one bad dream for another.

Then he saw his wife in torchlight and, for a moment, Donna looked like a Lucy Cong he'd blasted in the tunnels. A forearm clamped her throat and a revolver bit her temple where the freckles gathered in summertime. Pepper knew he was awake and made himself lie still with knotted muscles.

'Nothing sudden,' he agreed. No shake in his voice.

'Out of bed slowly. Down the stairs. Got that, chief?'

Chief? thought Pepper.

That was pure Belfast and went with pints of stout in bars where jukeboxes played songs of rebellion to minds attuned to treason.

Out on the landing, Pepper measured himself against the Irish gunman. Found he topped the yellow skimask by comfortable inches.

The man covering his wife was six-feet plus, and matched Pepper's eyeline when they weighed each other across the living room. A third and shorter terrorist with a machine-pistol could have been feminine. There was something about the sway of the hip.

Pepper stood in a draught. Cutting through the french-windows he'd planned to weatherseal that coming weekend. He smiled to reassure his wife, but Donna's eyes were just blue holes in her face. The tall terrorist's breath stirred her hair. A specious intimacy that tightened Pepper's scrotum.

'You're Matthew Pepper. Development Director of BelTech Aerospace.'

It wasn't a question. Someone had done their homework.

'Answer the man.'

The Irish one twisted knuckles in Pepper's side.

'Uhhh . . . yeah.'

'And a turncoat Irish-American who refused to subscribe to The Cause at last year's Boston Rally.'

Pepper blanked off the pain in his side. Remembered the women and collection tins under golden slogans and green banners. Their dogma and blind patriotism had vaguely amused him.

'Not so funny now, eh, Jose?'

The tall terrorist could have read Pepper's mind. His accent didn't gel. Like a Slav or Balt had learned English from foreign radio programmes. The kind of American-English the Russians broadcast propaganda in.

'Now you pay, you whore's melt,' said the Irish one.

Pepper saw where things were going and steeled himself.

The effeminate one moved to show Pepper his son. She had Max perched on the leather recliner in the window bay.

His face was puffed with sleep but his eyes were alive with curiosity. He and Pepper had just discovered Rudyard Kipling's novels of India, and *Kim* had fast become Max's favourite. He liked to play the memory game. Remember how many kinds and colours of pebbles there were on a tray before Pepper covered them with a cloth.

Donna thought Pepper had turned Max into a perfect police spy before his ninth birthday. Thought it immoral and probably illegal. She made it a joke but she looked troubled. Pepper just hoped Max wouldn't crack wise and anger the terrorists.

'If you're looking for ransom . . .' Pepper started.

The tall terrorist laughed.

'Money, Pepper? Where would you get the long green?'

The question hung fire and dried Pepper's mouth. The tall terrorist's mask sucked in against his face and laughter punched out through the ribbed wool. No humour in it.

'You're flat broke, Pepper san. Up to your tush in mortgages. Schoolfees and insurance. Bank loans and like that. Hell, you couldn't make a time-payment on an aspirin until the Pentagon comes through with the big bucks next fall. The US military loves those neat little gizmos you miniaturise for Uncle Sam. And beat the Japs and IBM to the punch. Magic little guidance-systems you can mass-produce for cents and get paid grands apiece for. You got the cash-flow problem, not us. Maybe we should slip you a couple of sawbucks.'

A handout at gunpoint was almost funny. A glance at Donna and Max killed Pepper's half-smile stillborn. The tall terrorist let Donna sag at the piano and her elbow struck a dischord as he said:

'Here's how this goes down, Pepper. It takes the individual keys of three directors to open the security vaults at the BelTech plant. Including the safe behind the phoney Matisse in your office. That's the one we want cracked. Our bingo box. That takes your key, Sean Collin's key, and Corny Taylor's key. I dial their home numbers. You tell them to meet you at the plant in one hour from now. Make it sound convincing. Got it?'

'Got it,' said Pepper.

'Collins is a pussy-cat. He'll jump whatever you tell him. And Taylor'll go along with his old 'nam buddy. They act cute- oh, you show them this ·38. Ain't loaded with ought but blanks. But they don't know that, right?'

'Guess not.'

Pepper sensed the sneer under the mask. Wondered if they knew his laundry number. Wanted to smash the face under the red wool.

'You so much as hiccup out there, I'll waste momma and sonny in a hot second.'

'I know it.'

'And know this: two more of my guys are in your Merc right now. You drop them where the service road from the A2 hooks off into BelTech. Park in your regular spot. No deviation. Make pleasant with the duty-guard as usual. We'll have you bugged, so no cute dialogue. Once your co-directors are in your office, you neutralise them. Open the safe and bring the package out of the plant. Boogie back to your car, pick up my guys and hand them the package. When I know you've brought me the right stuff, we take off. Leave you here in the arms of your everloving. After we've cut the phone and put you bye-byes with a soporific.'

Pepper was sick at the thought of being drugged.

The tall terrorist hummed as he dialled Sean Collins' number.

'On your way, mister.'

Conservative in poplin and grey charcoal, Pepper went down ornamental stone stairs to the rear garden. Bitter wind came in at roof-height to toss the pines enough to shed cones into the shrubbery. Heavy dew silvered the lawn, and false-dawn haloed the crown of Woodbury Forest as a heron beat toward the reservoirs beyond Carn Hill.

Pepper reached the garage tucked under scotch pines.

The Mercedes ticked over and puffballs of exhaust rolled with groundmist. The smell of rain came from North Carn, and Pepper remembered Taylor saying:

'You would buy a house on the crossroads where all the weather in the world meets to be bad-tempered.'

'Get in and drive.'

The voice could have been black and a pistol came over the back seat. They had disconnected the interior light.

Pepper took the A8 south and turned off through Newtown-abbey to the A2 coast road. The army had a checkpoint east of Tory Town and Pepper's heart lurched as he waited in line to filter left. The Irish sea sprawled beyond Belfast Lough as he edged toward the roadblock, chopping waves wild under black barrows of cloud.

'What now?'

Pepper didn't turn his head.

The men muttered and the offside door opened.

'Well find you, man.'

Pepper saw two men duck away through incoming cars in his rearview mirror. A horn blared and Pepper jerked the Mercedes forward. Gained control and hugged the car ahead. Anything to stop the clown behind leaning on his horn. Then he coasted past soldiers who recognised his number plate. A sergeant he'd drunk cocktails with pointed him out to a first lieutenant with a young moustache and old eyes. Belfast did that to officers. Pepper stalled to let a lorry cross the line of traffic. Wiped off his face and thought of blue voids to calm himself.

A corporal leaned over the car behind.

'What else you get for Christmas then, Paddy? Waking us all up with your bloody beeping. Let's have you stood out here with the rest of us bloody morons. Insurance and licence. And them hands of yours nice and visible.'

The levelled AFN denied the banter. An army patrol had been ambushed in Cregagh that morning. The snipers had stood a nursing mother and baby in the window to cover their escape. Not caring who got added to the list of martyrs murdered for The Cause.

Waved on, Pepper drove across a ditch of rubble that deterred rush hour traffic using the BelTech road as a short-cut to the B90. A bright sabre of sunlight cut through cloud as Pepper parked, and the glass face of the plant became a sheet of radiance as he pushed inside. Sullivan the ex-RUC man saluted smartly and walked Pepper to the elevator with squared shoulders. Still missing rows of smart coppers at morning inspection.

'A soft day but for the wind, sir.'

Sullivan brought the lift up the shaft. Irritated that the weather couldn't be regimented like constables.

Pepper told him to expect Collins and Taylor. Earned himself a salute and went down to Level 3 where the air was double-filtered and inaudible sonics killed virus bugs. The plant could provide zero-humidity to suit the robot machines, and with two-thirds of the complex below sea-level, its pumps drew saline water from the Lough and purified it for the cooling processors. Pepper drank some from a fountain and let himself into his chrome and white office. Sat at his desk without smoking.

And limped back into the tunnels.

Pizza Man found the Able runner and finished what the VC had started. The crucified body drooped on the bamboo stakes as if glad it was all over. They had gouged out his eyes and skewered them on the punji stick through his tongue. Pepper took his dogtags without reading off his name. The rear-echelon Pogues would give him back his identity when they typed him up. In the tunnels he was more useful as a nameless body. With his face and uniform gone he could have been a VC anyway.

Pepper told Pizza Man to rig the body for boom-boom and checked the tunnel ahead for D-5 anti-personnel mines. Charlie was primed to make the going bad now they had a fix on Zulu Company, and mining the tunnels would soften up the roundeyes.

Luther Cash chewed his green cigar over Central's roneoed map.

'Shit City, my man. South of here is earthquaked to hell, and north is a definite no-no. We retrace or keep going. And hope like snowflakes Taylor *has* consolidated rendezvous.'

'Corny Taylor's always there.'

'So was Kinney. Now he's back there with punjis through his eyeballs.'

Cash's face was greener than his cigar.

Pepper imagined leeches in his boot. Liver spots napalmed his peripheral vision and the foetid air stank of primordial sludge.

Cash said, 'John Wayne ahead. Or split and filter.'

Pepper shook his head.

'Only a bubble-brain would tell my pirates how to deploy. I'm for letting them loose and holding on to their tailfeathers.'

'Some plan, Eisenhower.'

Pepper forced a grin.

'Keep your chorus line in step, doll.'

Cash tried a smile that went nowhere.

'After you, general.'

Pepper moved his Montagnards ahead without lights, spotting for them through his infra-red nightscope. The matting floor had rotted to a fibrous mush and he had trouble keeping his feet. Smallarms hacked from somewhere above ground. Able minding the store or VCs suckering Zulu and Bravo into crossfire.

Pepper followed his forward screen along a concrete gallery and joined Pizza Man in a crater. Stars showed through what had been a bamboo and earth roof. How many Lucys had been in the bomb-shelter was anybody's guess. Now there was just visceral sprawls amongst the collapsed bamboo poles.

Pepper turned to call Cash. Heard – sensed a hammer hit a priming cap. Registered the whack and concussion and lay on his back spitting mud in ringing silence. Some dumb dead mother had triggered a D-5 and vapourised anybody within an eight-foot radius.

Pepper moved before his hearing came back, and his flashlight showed him a fresh red scar where earth dribbled onto what was left of three of his Montagnards. Going on would be stupid. They had to climb the crater and go overground. If Charlie *was* up there, it was a hell of a killing ground.

Pizza Man and the Kit Carsons went up first. Pepper waited for Cash as long as he dared, then followed them to the jungle floor to roll in groundmist and the stink of napalm. He sent a Carson to bring up the ingress guard and the radioman, and made a head count as he listened for incoming fire.

There was nothing but the wrong kind of silence.

Pepper jerked from reverie as the elevator pinged and opened.

Corny Taylor skimmed his case across a yard of Pepper's blond-oak desk. Leaned on spread hands to jut his chin. He had a shaving nick under his long nose and his electric necktie screamed at his pale grey suit. There were raindrops in his white hair and his eyes were cross and sleepy.

'Show contrition, you chucklehead,' he said. 'Blowing my night of wonderment with a set of jugs Ruben would have saved his Sunday-best sables for. And for what?'

'When Collins gets here, OK?'

Taylor shielded Pepper's note from the surveillance camera and read, *5 terrorists have Donna and Max at the house. They want prototypes. I'm bugged. Use Spook sign-language.*

Taylor scrawled *OK*. His fingers formed questions as he said:

'Ain't no never-mind to *this* child if the damned Defense Department don't sleep weekends. Three-months of laying siege to that special fox-lady went blooey when you broke her concentration. You and the Pentagon are as popular as Dallas on Kennedy's birthday.'

'Send her flowers. Send me the bill. Is it my fault they want me and the prototypes in Brussels soonest?'

'A posy won't bring that fox back, jack.'

Taylor watched Pepper's hands talk him through the events of the early hours. His own fingers were clumsy as they made ideograms instead of fists. They had discussed attempts at extortion many times. Recognised Pepper's family was the likeliest target. Now it had come. His three tours in Vietnam had been months of boredom punctuated by moments of sheer terror. Nobody was ever prepared, and for a moment Taylor wished he wasn't involved.

The feeling passed when Sean Collins bustled in. A clean joke at a stag night. His moon of a face as innocent as blancmange. He took a chair, crossed a leg under notepad and stylus, and said:

'Checkpoints. Did I keep you both?'

'How could you? We're too expensive.'

Taylor kept dislike out of his voice. Turned his back and fed fresh water into the percolator.

To become eligible for a Development Board grant, Pepper and Taylor had needed an Irish partner. Collins' legal background and political connections had made him the obvious choice. With the spectre of De Lorean still haunting Northern Ireland, two Americans promoting a high-tech plant set to employ less than fifty men at a cost of five million plus was, in the words of the first minister Collins approached, 'As unwelcome as a colony of termites in milady's bustle'. Only an underwriting from a Lloyds consortium, the carrot of a NATO contract if the project killed off a similar French operation, had earned BelTech the green light.

Collins had proved invaluable during those early months. But on the eve of the first real audit in two-years, a different picture had emerged. The London accountants had called Taylor just before the weekend, and Taylor had planned to brief Pepper at their regular Monday morning meeting set for tomorrow. Bogus claims paid over to the construction companies had skimmed a quarter-million from the company accounts, with the probability of a similar figure leeched from the production budgets. The finger pointed at Collins.

Taylor watched the percolator bubble and said:

'Sean, Matthew has to demonstate our protos to some NATO think-tank in Brussels tomorrow. That means the first flight out today. Adopting a low-profile, there's no need for security to go with him. Since only we three know he's carrying the protos, there's little chance of outside agencies acting against him. Agreed?'

Collins lit a Gallagher Blue and leaked smoke into his lap.

'You're security, Corny. Sure I'm only your man for pouring oil and mixing drinks for the bewildered. A simple PR man with nothing to offer on the subject. And those NATO Sandbaggers will screen Matthew's flight. They always do.'

Taylor's smile was as bleak as arctic sunlight.

23

'You and your mother's poteen both,' he said as if it meant something.

Pepper sensed the animus and refused to be distracted. Nothing must alarm the terrorists listening over the bug inside his shirt.

'Keys then, guys.'

Taylor kept his on a platinum neckchain with a crucifix and a Star of David. Asked about the odd trinity he would say, 'To confuse witnesses at the morgue.'

Collins produced his key from somewhere, and Pepper brushed the revolver in his waistband when he took his key from his waistcoat. He swung the Matisse aside. Punched his personal code into the safe's sensors and fed his key into the triple lock. The disarming light stayed neutral until all three keys were inserted, then deepened to an unblinking red.

'Sequence starts,' said Pepper.

Taylor made the Alpha keyturn and amber lights came on with an electronic twitter.

'Alpha keyed. Yours, Matt.'

Pepper made the Beta turn and lights flowed down the spectrum to deep orange. Flicked to crimson with a bass murmur, and paled to neutral ready for Collins.

'And open sesame.'

Collins turned his key with a flourish. The lights died and alarm klaxons screamed in high register. The steel panel didn't slide aside. The safe beyond didn't iris open. There was just panic and noise.

Taylor's yell was lost in rising wail and the lights pulsed like disco strobes. Soaked by a scald of sweat, Pepper dropped his key as Taylor cannoned Collins into him. Taylor hissed through spittle. He barged Pepper aside to cuff Collins a second time. Collins slammed across Pepper's desk. Sprawled on the far side, mewing in his throat like a beaten cat.

Pepper threw Taylor away from Collins and grovelled for his lost key. Found it somehow, and tried to negate the electronic time-lock that automatically sealed the safe for twenty-four hours. Knew it was useless. Collins had deliberately broken the proper sequence. Taylor was up and stalking Collins. His hands stiffened for a Naked Kill.

Needing Collins alive, Pepper blocked Taylor's forward jab with his shoulder. Bilious numbness spread as his deltoid absorbed the blow. Liquid lightning burned his spine and his legs turned to rubber. Going down on his knees he fired the revolver close to Taylor's face to back him away. The gun bucked and an overhead strip exploded to shower them with shards of glass. Taylor went back and down. A bright red gash in his chin spattered blood on his shirt and across the polished floor. His mouth gaped and his jaw hung at an odd angle as his eyes rolled to white.

Nausea swilled in Pepper's stomach.

He fell twice trying to reach Taylor. To stop him drowning in his own blood. Pepper was staunching the wound with the tail of Taylor's shirt when a swivel chair smashed across his back. There was black on black and pain on pain. He went across Taylor in a forward roll. Flipped on his back to freeze Collins midway through a second swing, the gun supported with both hands. Black tides lapped his eyes and Collins was a triple-image in the wavering light.

'Why, bastard? *Why?*'

Pepper's question was a tear in silk.

But Collins was bringing the chair down again.

Pepper fired at the central image. Spun all three to the floor with a shot to the right pectoral. Collins and the swivel skidded into a potted yucca and crashed into the glass partition shattered by the same bullet. There was a squeal and a brittle snap. The sheet-glass guillotined down as Collins jerked three heads forward to stare at Pepper. The glass blade sheered through his necks like a knife through cabbage. His look of surprise was still there when one of the heads rolled across the floor to fetch up against Pepper's foot. One blue eye closed in an amused wink.

Pepper kicked it away and fell back into a rush of nothing filled with sirens.

Pepper went back to the edge of the crater in Vietnam.

Pizza Man pointed out the VC mortars zeroed in on Taylor's position.

'Issa bigga fook-hup, Pepper san. Then USAF flyboy mothers shoulda bac-bacced them slopes to dick-cream. Very bad for Able-Taylor san. Very godshit badder for us.'

And the radioman dropped to whisper:

'Able just don't answer, sir. Must be holding dead ground down there. Which is a Grade-A double-eagle bollix. The map marks that compass-bearing as high ground. Not a knoll in a goddamned valley.'

Suspicion grew like cold stones in Pepper's mind.

'And how come Charlie's got the balls to show himself above ground like that? They ain't just Charlies neither. Those are regular North Viet troops with uniforms and topees and everything. Deployed as ground forces. Not hiding in spider holes and drawing us into their moving minefields like Charlie.'

'All got throats don't they?' said Pizza Man.

'If we can get to them,' said Pepper. 'Why are they holding fire if they ain't watching for us to rendezvous with Able? Cream us all before we scatter into their Bouncing-Betty fields? They *let* us come in here.'

'Now Bravo don't answer, sir,' said the radioman. 'Just went off the air in the middle of a song.'

Pepper lay on his back. Swore at his shot foot for misting up his mind.

'We go down there, we're between a rock and a hard place.'

'Godshit harder,' said Pizza Man.

'Central's handed us the shaft, guys,' Pepper said. 'There was something screwy about this hit from moment one. You get the feeling this is like how Charlie and Delta didn't come back from Laos last month?'

'Hell of a flyer,' said the radioman. 'But I'll buy it, sir.'

'With confederate bonds, Willy,' Pepper said to draw a grin.

'Yessir.'

'We go down there. Open order.'

Pizza Man shadowed Pepper as he hobbled toward the nearest mortar crew.

Pepper lost fifteen men before he reached what was left of Taylor's command. Got nothing but silence when he called up the Cav choppers. He was trying to raise Cash when the mortar barrage came in with pinpoint accuracy. The few of them who could still walk lost themselves in the boondocks for the long march home.

CHAPTER TWO

The strands of medicated fog mixed past and present into the same confused dream. Pepper smelled jungle corruption when he was strapped to a stretcher, and he gagged on hospital astringence when he buried Taylor and himself in river mud to wait for nightfall. There had been a ring of British soldiers in the plant lobby when Sullivan took his revolver away, and a VC patrol had stopped on the Mekong foreshore to smoke Chinese tobacco as they joked about a Lucy Cong who claimed descent from the goddess sisters Trung. She called herself Trac Nhi, and would not marry until her ancestors showed her a suitable groom in a vision. The VC had laughed together in the gathering dusk, and one of them had stood on Pepper's hand before defecating near his buried face.

When they had gone, Pizza Man came out of the bush to stew banana sprouts with the bats he had netted, and Pepper used his last cigarette on the leeches feeding on their bodies. Taylor was delirious by then, but he walked when he was told to and kept his wild talk to a mutter during the night marches.

Days and nights had melted together and Pepper carried Taylor when they crossed rice paddies on what might have been the twelfth evening. Pizza Man and the eleven Montagnards went into a 'friendly' ville for brown rice and never came back. The sporadic gunfire lasted no time at all, and Pepper dragged Taylor west the moment he heard the first fusillade of shots. The moon came up to show black pyjamas combing the hills behind him, so he kept to the dykes and floated Taylor behind him when he had to swim. By then Pepper understood Taylor's crazy talk, and was using it himself when they stumbled across a US patrol boat beached on a mudbar.

Manned by six black Grunts from Texas, it had been stooging about for a survey team that had gone ashore and not returned. Pepper said they wouldn't and didn't need to use his gun to make them haul the boat back into deep water.

The cruise down to Vinh Long had been a hazy drift of heavy rock and marijuana smoke, and jumping choppers across to Saigon had been a milk run. They had holed up in a small ficky-fick hotel on Tran Hung Dao Street until their minds were straight and Taylor could keep food down, and when they had cashed their MPCs (Military Payment Certificates) with the Ameen Brothers on the corner of De Tham Street they let Command know they were alive with an obscene phonecall. That brought a CIA seersucker to their hotel with enough hardhat-goons to take Hanoi, and cuffed together for the fast ride to the shuttered house on the outskirts, Pepper and Taylor played dumb for the man with two noses who interrogated them about the tunnels and their days in the bush. Pepper didn't tell him about the Chinese surgeon who had worked on his foot for a $1,000, but he asked about Luther Cash a couple of times, and Taylor said he had too, but the man with two noses never answered; he just wrote in a black book with a gold pen and kept the same questions coming in the same sequence, day after day after day.

The civilian brass finally passed them over to the shrinks for psychiatric reports, and when they'd put enough square pegs in round holes, and run out of perversions to stammer through, their files were stamped for immediate release from all front line duties. The man with two noses gave them his best shot on the last day, and had them flown to the Veterans Hospital south of Long Beach for thirty days of observation. After a month of keeping company with goony-bird paper-tearers, cold-turkey crazies and paraplegics medicated into silence, they were out on the street with their severance checks and nowhere to go but ape.

Thumbing up through the Big Sur to Monterey, Pepper and Taylor splurged out on a motel in the redwoods to watch the whales sound on their way to their breeding grounds in the north, and met Luther Cash by chance in the restaurant bar.

Cash had kept his army crop and most of his tan, and must have been carrying the best part of a fifth of bourbon on his breath before they called the first round.

Six months had passed since the tunnels, and Pepper had to know how Cash got himself out of the crossfire. But Cash got them into a brawl with a surfing convention of hippies over nothing at all, which brought the blues in black-and-whites and a night in the local chokey. Cash wasn't with them in the cells or in court, and they were released when their fines were settled anonymously. Talking about it on the way to Oregon just made it crazier.

Fog drifted Pepper to Belfast in a cocoon of pain.

Taylor might have leaned over his hospital bed to whisper about Collins defrauding the company, but Taylor's jaw was wired and the words came out all bitten off. Asking Taylor's night-shadow about Donna and Max sent him scurrying, and morning brought a cop with a drone of questions that reminded Pepper of the man with two noses. Pepper hauled a punch at the sneering face, wrenched his mashed shoulder against the straps, and lost more time putting himself back together. After that there were always men watching him, so Pepper watched back to learn their schedules. He was about ready to move when they got him dressed and took him by car to his house.

The unmown lawns glistened with dewed cobwebs and Max's garden swing hung motionless. The front door stuck as it always did, and his private mail had been opened, read by the police, and laid out in neat piles on the hall table. The heating was off and the house smelled of gathering neglect. The kitchen radio wasn't humming commercials to itself, and Max's erector-set didn't form fanciful hazards down the staircase. In the living room, Donna's careful flower arrangements wilted in green water, and the drapes had been drawn carelessly aside.

The man in charge kept his raincoat on and invited Pepper to get comfortable in one of his own chairs. He lit a long and thin cigar and sat at the piano where Donna had sagged with an empty face. He plumed bitter smoke through his clamp of a mouth and almost lost his narrow eyes in crowsfeet staring at

Pepper as his men stood where they wanted with blank looks.

'My name is Maycroft, Mr Pepper,' he said. 'I thought our talking here might prove a shade more informal than facing each other across an office desk. Telephones ringing, knocks on doors, that sort of thing.'

Pepper glanced at the recliner where Max had perched. There wasn't the slightest pucker to show he'd ever been there. Pepper's neck bristled and his shoulder throbbed from Taylor's blow.

Maycroft saw Pepper wince and said:

'You know, if I hadn't seen the videotape and had the surgeon verify the clinical damage, I'd never have believed a bare hand could have impacted human tissue with such devastating effect. Special training, I suppose.'

'What have you people done about locating my family?'

'Enough to satisfy me.'

'Which means what?'

'Exactly that, Mr Pepper. You've talked at length about five terrorists being here in this house. Perfect models of description in their way, and yet there isn't a shred of physical evidence to bear out your word that they ever existed except in your imagination. No fibres from their clothes. No skin particles or hair samples. No hand or shoeprints in any of the rooms you say they were in. Nothing in your Mercedes. Nothing anywhere. How do you explain that?'

'They were thorough, is all. They vacuumed through. Cleaned off the door handles, wore surgical gloves, stuff like that. Didn't you check the Hoover or the garbage sacks? Talk to the neighbours? The soldiers on that roadblock? And where in blue blazes are my wife and kid if they weren't abducted?'

Maycroft scratched his tuft of a moustache with a thumbnail.

'We've been just as thorough as your ''terrorists'', Mr Pepper. The RUC and security forces here in Ulster have to be given our special problems. We use the most sophisticated equipment and advanced forensic techniques as a matter of course here in the province. We took several hundred samples from the house and grounds, analysed the dust and lint in the two vacuum cleaners you have, cross-matched them with the polishing and cleaning cloths your wife and her daily keep in their work-baskets; took samples from the S-bends in the kitchen and bathroom, and took fresh vacuum samples from all the carpets and curtains in the house. We did find some fibres we couldn't match up, but the simple reason for that is: those articles of clothing are no longer here in the house.'

'Sure thing, Sherlock. And means that Donna and Max didn't walk out of here naked. They had to be wearing something when those animals took them away to God knows where.'

'That did occur to us. But it doesn't explain why every stitch of your family's clothes are gone, does it? All the wardrobes upstairs are empty except the one with your things in, Mr Pepper. So tell me: How were things between you and your wife? Generally, I mean?'

'Up and down like any marriage. But at bedrock we were fine and dandy. Hell, *are* fine and dandy.'

'You hadn't quarrelled recently? Over money, perhaps? Your son or another man or woman?' Maycroft shed ash into a ceramic dish and looked interested.

'Nothing serious. Except maybe that one time Max left the garden hose running and washed out some border plants I'd just bedded in. I paddled him for that, and Donna and I had words about it. We both got steamed, but that's all. It was over in seconds.'

'And wasn't enough of a reason to make her leave you?'

'Are you kidding, you mother?'

'Is that meant as a ''no'', Mr Pepper?'

'That's a resounding negative, Maycroft.'

'And she didn't make a scene at the local store when they refused further credit for groceries? Or at the garage when one of your joint personal cheques came back marked ''Refer to Drawer''? Or in several other places where your rocky financial position had become common gossip amongst the locals? And didn't she resent the fact that your son might have to leave his private day school at the end of this current term because you couldn't meet the proposed 15 per cent increase in fees?'

'We both did. But I applied for a bank-loan to cover that.'

'And were refused. A letter from the bank to that effect is with the other mail in the hall. I took the liberty of reading it.'

'Which is more than I did.'

'But more to the point, your wife had. But you knew that from the note she left you.'

'Note? What note?'

'The one you found when she and your son had gone. The one you tore into pieces and threw into the refuse sack before you met Collins and Taylor at the plant with such tragic results. There never was a NATO meeting scheduled in Brussels was there? You were going to sell your prototypes for enough ready cash to bail you out of the crushing financial straits you found yourself in.'

Pepper's sour laugh had no substance. Through the window he could see where they'd dug the flowerbeds for bodies.

'I blew away a partner to steal my own prototypes over a lousy two grand overdraft? Eat mine, you turkey.'

Maycroft bled smoke in a stream and looked wise.

'You shot Taylor in the face before you shot Collins, remember? And we aren't talking about your paltry overdraft at the Linen Bank of Ulster. We're concerned about the whereabouts of the $400,000 missing from your company.'

Taylor talked through wired jaws in Pepper's mind and he kneaded his torn deltoid, trying to think through a welter of confusion as Maycroft kept talking.

'That's the amount your own auditors account as missing to date. The details of your long-term embezzlement are all in the late Sean Collins' notebooks and diaries, and have to be the most probable reason for him stopping you from pilfering your own office safe. Given that, don't ask us to give any credence to your story about your ''terrorists'' handing you a gun loaded with blanks. A man with your specialised arms training would have known otherwise, and would have turned that same weapon on them, had they existed.'

'Corny Taylor must have told you real different, bubble-head.'

'You seem very sure of that.'

'Does bacon taste of pork?'

Maycroft looked bleak and passed Pepper a sheet of folded A4.

'Refresh your memory with this.'

Pepper unfolded the photostat and recognised Donna's sloping hand through stains and sellotaped repairs. It read:

Dear Matthew,

I'm taking Max away with me. Pa has arranged for us to fly home to Oregon. That last filthy row over Max's schooling was the last I can take. (Obliterated) through being a tumbleweed and Max deserves more than either of us has provided. (Obliterated) glad the final decision has been made and (Obliterated) wasn't enough for us, was it?

Donna.

Pepper skimmed the facsimile onto the carpet and scrubbed his face with a sweating hand.

'That isn't Donna speaking. She doesn't even *think* that way. They must have made her write that. Left it for you guys to find.'

Maycroft tutted in a tumble of smoke.

'They dictated it. She wrote it. They tore it up and buried it in the kitchen rubbish for us to find, is that it? And then took your wife and child away with them, yes?'

'What else?'

Maycroft leaned forward.

'Just this: your wife caught the New York flight with your son and eight pieces of luggage on which she paid excess baggage. They were quite alone. No terrorists. No guns at their heads. They waited on stand-by at Kennedy for five hours before they caught the shuttle to Portland. Our friends over there even traced the cab-driver who drove them to Wapinitia. And he remembers the boy talking about seeing his grandfather for the first time.'

Pepper's head pounded and swam. Maycroft could have been the man with two noses for all the sense he made. Donna had been estranged from her father since before the wedding, and only sent him a card every Christmas because Pepper kept him on their list.

'Donna wouldn't have done that. Ask Taylor, he knows better than anybody how it was between my wife and her father.'

'What Mr Taylor may or may not know is entirely academic. He took himself off over a week ago. Absconded. And I must say, he covered his tracks better than your wife did.'

Pepper could only blink. Either Taylor had been at his bedside two nights before, or he and his wired jaw were just another unreal fragment of the recent mad mosaic. He must have wondered aloud because Maycroft said:

'You talked to Taylor when?'

Pepper no longer knew and said so.

Maycroft thumbed his moustache, his smile remote.

'So sure and yet so confused. The classic response of the congenital liar. My humble view is that you'll earn the maximum sixteen years for this little lot, Pepper. All right, lads, get him on his feet. It's time to trot down the station for the formalities.'

Pepper pushed a supporting hand away and climbed through the stratosphere to his feet. Maycroft killed his cigar in tendrils of red fog and Pepper withdrew inside himself to stop the floor coming up at him. His torso went into controlled spasm as he hypervented to drive the pain from his left shoulder. The world was lost in shades of red glass and Maycroft talked too slowly to be understood.

One of Maycroft's men moved to catch Pepper as he swayed and took a forearm across the windpipe. He was a loose rag doll when he hit the floor, and a rapid handthrust to Maycroft's temple wiped his face clean before he draped himself across the piano.

Pepper spat used air and lost the third man with a knee to the crotch and a hard hipthrow. Dead flowers showered as the body smashed a vase against the wall, and the last man drew his Ruger ·33 through crimson glue.

Pepper used a violent upward twist to pull the gunarm from its socket and bounced the policeman's hair into chaos with a rising knee. The revolver spun on the carpet and the body skidded away across the recliner. The flailing legs kicked glass

35

from the window and hooked themselves over the sash before going limp.

Pepper ate glucose in the kitchen and changed his clothes in the bedroom. When he had stripped the unconscious men of their cash and warrant cards he drove Maycroft's unmarked car to the border. He didn't use the rearview mirror. There was no pursuit.

Maycroft's hand fluttered on ebonised wood with a life of its own and wouldn't stay in focus when he ordered it to respond to the pain over his eyes. It fumbled at his temple and a surge of nausea made him jacknife to vomit over the revolver on the carpet. Being on his hands and knees in a yawing sea intrigued him as much as Fleming's arm hanging all wrong as he tried to slap Salter awake with his good hand.

Maycroft learned to stand without falling and found Mahan hooked up in the window when he looked for the telephone. Dialling was a clumsy affair, but hearing the Duty Officer report his official car abandoned at the border near Fivemilestown cleared his mind enough to give his status and ask for assistance.

The dusk was deepening and he couldn't read his watch in the failing light. There was a rail-link into the Republic where his car had been left and Pepper must have caught a train down to Dublin. Maycroft had found the light switch by the time an ambulance and two army ferrets threw gravel up the drive.

The first SAS man through the door whistled at the wrecked room and holstered his Browning when his rear cordon came up the ornamental staircase from the rear lawn.

'One man did this?' he asked with professional interest.

Maycroft's nod upset his stomach again.

'Didn't even see him move.'

The SAS man took Maycroft's arm to steady him.

'The bathroom's this way, old chap.'

Maycroft issued orders between heaves over the bowl.

Early rain spotted the pavements when Pepper left the small commercial hotel on East Bridge Street before the morning papers arrived, and he breakfasted on bacon, eggs, wheaten soda and very sweet tea before strolling along to Belfast Central Railway Station. He bought a platform ticket and left Mahan's warrant card under a seat on the Dublin train for the cleaners to find before checking the bookstall newspapers for his picture with headlines. A bomb in Londonderry bannered the front pages and he wasn't even a squib in the Stop Press.

Acting drunk for the taxi-driver who'd brought him up to the maternity wing of the Balmoral Hospital from Fivemilestown, Pepper carried a bouquet and football boots for the wife and newborn son he'd invented, and had been generous with five of Maycroft's tenners. Dumping the flowers and boots on a startled matron in Casualty, he'd caught a bus into Belfast and spent the night at the hotel using Salter's ID and Visa card. When the morning rush-hour had died down he walked to the Irish Tourist Information Office on Castle Street and hid behind a folded London *Times* to watch for the right man.

It was almost noon when a man roughly the same height and build as himself asked about the Abbey at Assaroe near Ballyshannon. Pepper followed him back to his hotel and was right behind him when he let himself into his room. Eight seconds of even pressure to the tourist's carotid artery rendered him unconscious, and it took Pepper eleven minutes to decide what to do with him for the next twenty-four hours.

When Pepper left Taylor's apartment an hour later he was Charlie Moone from Phoenix, Arizona, and brown hair dye made him five years younger.

Maycroft discharged himself from hospital after fourteen hours sleep and had an RUC man drive him to his office where he quizzed the Evidence Officer over a hair-sample a second forensic sweep of Pepper's house had turned up. It was bleached blonde with a dark root and was long enough to have come from a female head. Caught up in the bathroom venetian blinds with a scale of dandruff, it had been identified as Caucasian, and the skin-sample had come from the same head. It wasn't Donna Pepper's hair although it had been washed with her shampoo and conditioner. It was evidence of a sort, and left Maycroft cautiously ambivalent where he had been completely certain of Pepper's guilt before.

He was going through Pepper's first hospital statement when the man he'd posted outside Taylor's apartment came on the line. Maycroft put him on the amplifier, kept his thumb on Pepper's verbal description of the female terrorist holding his son at gunpoint, and said:

'Speak to me, Hunter.'

'I think . . . Pepper was here . . .'

Hunter sounded worse for drink.

'You only *think?* I've got him placed firmly on the Dublin Express with good circum-physical evidence, and you only *think?*'

Hunter swallowed around something inedible.

'It was just a glimpse . . . fraction of a second. He's so . . . *fast*. Must have been five, maybe six hours ago. Caught me from behind on the stairs. Came to hung up in a cupboard by my ankles . . . tied to an ironing-board with sheets and a clothes-line . . .'

Maycroft touched his swollen forehead and silently commiserated with the whine in Hunter's voice. He used his red telephone to send a mobile to Taylor's flat and buzzed his Duty Officer. Hunter mumbled through a set of pips and Maycroft made him repeat himself.

'There's another man here, sir. A civilian. Mr Charlie Moone from Arizona . . . tied to a bed by a man answering Pepper's description. Took him out at his hotel. Took his clothes, credit cards, everything. Moone thinks he heard Pepper book himself through Heathrow to Los Angeles. Using Moone's name.'

From his knowledge of airline schedules, Maycroft knew Pepper could easily have made his connection in London, and calculated the evening Pan Am flight to LAX would be about two hours out over the Atlantic.

'Got him,' Maycroft told his Duty Officer.

'Only if it isn't another false trail, sir.'

Wishing he could have the 747 diverted to Belfast, Maycroft used his High Priority Code to order the plane back to Heathrow, planning to be there with an armed squad to bring

Pepper off. He allowed himself a smile, until the bleached hair came back to worry him.

Driving to the airport, his carphone informed him that Pepper's seat had been taken by a stand-by passenger, and ordered him to report to London in person 'Most Immediate'. He caught the next flight out.

A 'Green Parrot' Wessex of the Queen's Flight flew him from Heathrow to a USAF base in Suffolk where he was told to wait in a hangar skimmed by landing aircraft. A hour later a car brought him the company of two Foreign Office smoothies, a crumpled SIS agent, and a 'retired' USN Admiral Maycroft knew from his days in Hong Kong. The Admiral signed FO documents, the SIS agent seconded Maycroft to American Intelligence and, when everyone had shaken hands, Maycroft and the Admiral were left alone.

'Hullo, Gus,' Maycroft said without warmth. 'Still cloak-and-daggering for Uncle Sam?'

The Admiral offered Maycroft a White Owl from a leather case without taking one himself.

'Advisor to the White House and the Security Council on Internal Security. Got me a hot potato needs your special talents.'

'On a carbohydrate-free diet, Gus?'

The Admiral laid flame to Maycroft's cigar and nosed the bloom of fragrant smoke.

'Can't even smoke those beauties. Heart.'

'You were never issued with one, Gus.'

'Stow it with your unstencilled sea-gear, Maycroft.'

The Admiral listened to an aircraft land with reverse thrust. Waited for quiet and said:

'BelTech was a covert CIA operation that nobody told Langley about. Set up by some damned offshoot called the Executive Bureau. Pepper and Taylor didn't even know they were being funded by The Company. Hell, I never even *heard* of the Executive Bureau until two days ago, and I got that from the man in the Oval Office *himself*. He's burned, and I do mean pissed about it. It's got so's he don't trust any of our agencies further than spitting distance. And that man

39

don't spit never. Now I have to clean house for him. And that puts old Gus way out on a limb, and you're way out there with me.'

'You must have called in a lot of favours to get me, Gus.'

'All there were and some. I need results here, friend. This gets screwed up I won't even rate as a toilet attendant in a laughing academy. You screw up, nobody's ever heard of you *both* sides of the pond.'

Maycroft snorted smoke and sarcasm.

'Best to get the niceties out of the way, Gus. Now let's have the bottom line before I die of cold and boredom.'

The Admiral conjured a red folder from inside his raincoat.

'I pulled the files on Pepper and Taylor. They both did two straight tours in 'Nam. Took a year off in Kyoto, Japan, then went back to Indochina for a third tour. Got invalided out at the same time, went on the bum for a while, got into electronics together, and finally turned up in Belfast to start BelTech. There's no way either of them knew about the CIA connection. That puts them both left of left-field.'

'And innocent?'

'That's for you to find out, brother.'

'Then Pepper's family was abducted by terrorists.'

'Sure, sure . . .'

The Admiral shrugged that off as if it meant nothing.

Maycroft held his tongue as an aircraft screamed overhead and dopplered away with a bass roar. Nodded and said:

'Tell me about Kyoto, Gus.'

The Admiral toed oil on the concrete.

'There's some kind of religious order down there that goes in for all that physical and mental control. Kind of monk-warriors. Not just Ninja, more like your European paladins. Errant knights. Pepper and Taylor joined the order as students. Maybe even earned their dans or whatever.'

Maycroft touched his tender forehead. Said, 'Pepper did', and remembered his Chinese sergeant taking him to a building in Hong Kong where eight members of the Bamboo Tong sat in their ornamental chairs like wax effigies. Dead from single blows to the bridge of the nose. A small square of green silk on each head sewn with a chop in the shape of a running horse. The Chinese sergeant saying: ''One man made this kill. A Ninja from Kyoto. They are vapour to ordinary men. They kill for honour, not yen.''

Maycroft looked the Admiral in the eye.

'You were there, Gus. Remember?'

'Sure . . . sure . . .'

'If Pepper finds those men he'll kill them, Gus. And anybody else who gets in his way. That rather includes me, doesn't it?'

The Admiral wiped oil from his patent shoe.

Said nothing as aero-engines whined on tarmac.

'Talk to me, Gus. There's more to all this than you're saying. You don't want me to wet-job Pepper and Taylor. You want me to what?'

The Admiral rapped the file against his teeth.

'Find out who'll *try* is all. Follow Pepper where he leads. Let him bird dog for you. Where would you go if you were him?'

'After my wife and son of course.'

The Admiral looked sly.

'And if that trail should lead to the Executive Bureau, and a certain man in a certain office on Pennsylvania Avenue . . . Well, that Ruger you're packing looks well oiled . . .'

'But a suicide would please all the more.'

The Admiral spread his hands.

'Discretion's your middle name.'

'Who is he, Gus?'

The Admiral opened the file and turned to a bromide of a man with a deformed nose. Split at the bridge by some rare birth defect, ugly strawberries of flesh grew out from each nostril.

'Him. He was Pepper's Case Officer in 'nam. Had a hand in all those early PsyOps programmes. Ran tests on service personnel to find their mental breaking points. All that's classified material though. Even I can't get near it. This I can tell you though: Pepper was the only guy didn't knuckle under. Could be our friend here's holding some personal grudge against Pepper. No telling with a guy has an IQ you couldn't measure without shooting for the moon.'

Maycroft thought back to Pepper muttering under sedation.

'The man with two noses?' he asked aloud.

The Admiral closed the file with a snap.

'Oregon or bust,' he said.

'Carte Blanche, Gus?'

'What else? The FBI in Portland will have the red carpet out for you. But you trust no mother. Except old Gus here of course.'

Maycroft's smile was feral.

'Of course,' he said with quiet insincerity.

Wearing western boots and a simulated hangover, Pepper boarded a charter flight at Gatwick and slept all the way to New York without a single bad dream. Charlie Moone's dollars got him all the way to Portland where he hung around the terminal for a cabdriver who remembered a woman and a small boy who wanted to go to Wapinitia.

CHAPTER THREE

Sammy Washbourne was a tanned side of ham with a chuckle that bounced his belly all over his lap. He wore a campaign medal on his old wicker Panama, and he'd been hacking cabs since Truman fired MacArthur for wanting to extend the Korean War to mainland China. He recognised Pepper's snapshot of Max, but he wasn't nearly so sure of the Polaroid of Donna.

'Unless she lost some pounds and forgot how to smile like that.'

'Could be she did,' said Pepper.

'And could be you helped her.'

Sammy met Pepper's eyes and held them.

'Could be you're right.'

Sammy liked that and said so.

'Climb in alongside me, son. Saves me using the rearview to see what you're up to back there. Had me a freak this time last year. Figured to shake old Sammy down, and I got me a seven-inch souvenir in my thigh to prove it. Now only ladies and kids get to ride behind me. Guys sit alongside.'

Sammy spun his cab out into thin traffic and gunned onto the eastbound highway. He had a way of staring without being rude, and took his time looking Pepper over as he drove.

'What happened to him?'

'The freak? He got States Farm after they dug my shells out of him.' Sammy patted the steering wheel. 'Me and the Duchess here were off the road for most of two months. About as long as it took to wheel freak-oh into court for a wrist-slapping. She your wife?'

'I surely hope so.'

43

'Preacher married legal? Hell be commonplace if I didn't think that was plain unconstitutional in most states nowadays. You can smoke if you want. Just so you don't take 'em out one at a time like a dentist.'

Pepper lit two Camels and passed one across when Sammy had passed a truck hauling bathroom furniture.

'Lucky you found me, son. Ain't but me and one other independent who'll hack down to Wapinitia with just one fare up. They got them damned microbuses now. Wait until they got a full load and take them hell-for-hoohah packed in like roosters, baggage and all. You following just her, or her and the kid both?'

'Can't break up a matched set.'

'Just spinning my wheels to pass the miles, son. You ain't the first asking about the little lady and the kid. Had me a Federal doing just what you're doing now. 'Cept he took my word for where I dropped them off. Chewed dental gum and showed me his gun inside his drip-dry jacket. Made a big deal out of buying me a MacDonald's coffee, and called me ''Pop'' like I was a stuffed-and-mounted goony bird in some medicine show. Jeee*zusss*.'

Pepper blew smoke through the opened window and felt Sammy watching him some more. The tyres purred on the road-surface and the passing trees were turning with the fall. The high ground was a haze of purple and sage, and the sky was heavy with white galleons of cumulus.

'She'll rain come morning,' said Sammy. 'Your name's say-what?'

'Charlie.'

'Like hell you say, but it'll serve. They looking for you too? Seems that Federal made it sound that way without using the words.'

'You asking or telling?'

'Don't turn mean on me, son. They're watching for you like you been watching for me. I took a couple of turns around the park before I picked you up, and made damned sure that other independent I told you about knew what was going down. I could have tipped the Fed right there at the airport if I'd a mind to.'

Pepper kept his face smooth.

'There has to be a "why" for that.'

'Sure. You want to listen while I drop a dime on you.'

'Like you said, it passes the miles.'

'And there's forty-odd to burn. There was this family from out of state. Turned up here looking for their son whose Volks camper showed up three months after he went missing on a vacation trip. The kid was eighteen and straight, and they got worried when he didn't show up at home or back at college for the start of the new semester. Only thing was, his credit card was being used all over Oregon, and the kid hadn't phoned home once a week all that time. And seeing as missing persons is Federal, they tried the local FBI. Got an answering service and nothing else. So they hired an ex-homicide cop who'd gone private, and he found the Volks being driven around by an ex-con who said the kid sold it to him before boogying off he didn't know where. The con's high on angel-dust or PCP and doesn't shake down worth a damn. He even has the kid's stuff in a sack in his garage and says the family can have it, they collect. If the kid didn't want his junk it wasn't never-no-mind to him.'

Sammy flipped his butt away and stabbed two fingers at Pepper for a fresh smoke.

'The cop traces the route of the gas stations where the kid's card had been used, shook down a couple of people who'd dummied up on the local law, and got positive IDs that proved the kid hadn't been in the Volks when the ex-con and his lover-brother gassed-up using the kid's card. The private cop takes what he has to the Feds and gets yawned at. He gets onto the family, and they come up with the bucks to keep the cop digging. He goes back over the route and pinpoints the body-shop where the kid had picked up the con and his buddy, and had some work done on the Volks transmission. Turns out the mechanic moonlighted the job without telling the boss, pocketed the dough, and dummied when the law questioned him. The cop goes over the route the kid and his passengers took that first day, and gets an eye-witness to swear the kid isn't in the camper or anywhere around when the con and his buddy park up at an overnight picnic ground. This sends the cop backtracking, and he finds the kid's body dumped in a river. He's tied to an ice-box missing from the Volks and, with a body, the law gets real interested. That's when the local Fed came out from under a rock to smile for the TV as he took credit for busting the case. That's the boiled bones of it, Charlie, but enough for you to get the idea why Sammy Washbourne hates those mothers' butts to perdition and back.'

'It doesn't tell me why you're taking a chance I'm no crazy.'

'Your Kodaks mainly. See, that lady in your picture wasn't never in my cab, but the kid was. I could've told the Federal that. If he'd asked. But he was just going through the motions as if old rubes like me gave him terminal constipation. Man, I was at Pork Chop Hill when them Chinese came at us waving black flags 'cause only one in five had rifles. And the only time I saw guys like that Federal was back in Seoul using their peckers on ficky-fick girls when they weren't busting combat troops on R&R for being improperly dressed.'

'You can't live with old wars, Sammy.'

'I hear your mouth, son, but your eyes tell it different. Is your wife a natural blonde?'

'Sure.'

'Show me that Kodak again.'

Sammy held Donna in his knuckles at the top of the wheel and puffed his cheeks at her.

'Worth turning all the rocks in the union for. Wouldn't give the other bitch a tumble if she was pinned all over with thousand-dollar bills.'

'You'd better be sure, damn you.'

'You think old Sammy's eyes are blind glass balls like that medicine show goony bird's? Think I can't tell butter-coloured hair from bottle-blonde? And that gal in my hack weren't no American neither. And the kid was all goofed-up. Didn't say a word. She allowed it was jetlag and chest-medication made him sleepy, but that kid was souped to the gills. She kept hauling him up straight when his legs slid off the seat like he just had to be seen. A natural mother would have held him in her lap, seems to me. Or let him sleep stretched out on the seat.'

Pepper sighed deep in his chest and the Camels he was lighting wouldn't stay in the flame. One was scorched black by the time Sammy pulled onto the parking lot of a concession diner to take them from him.

'But the Fed said Max talked about seeing his grandfather.'

Sammy got a cigarette smoking in Pepper's mouth.

'*She* talked about the kid seeing his mother's old man.'

Pepper gnawed his fist to hold the world steady.

'You look like garbage, son. Damned if I shouldn't have fed that to you smoother. Me and my mouth. How long's it been between bites, son?'

'Four days and some. Ran out of dough outside Roseburg. Hitched up on a logger with a guy whose idea of conversation was spitting at the roadsigns.'

Sammy's gentle chuckle rolled his belly.

'Should have saved that chorus of Hallelujah for Wapinitia, Charlie. Or had you planned to duck out on me at the other end?'

'No, I've got dough stached in old man Clayton's barn.'

'Knowed you for a country boy. My daddy kept his roll down a well until brother John used it to see the world. Heard he got himself killed with the Foreign Legion at Dien Bien Phu. You ever serve in that neck of Indochina?'

'I did it one time.'

'Pegged you for a Vet. Coffee or stronger'll do you no harm, son. You wanna lean on old Sammy?'

'I'll make it.'

Pepper levered himself out onto hot blacktop as if it was silvered by ten-degrees of frost.

The glass was falling when Pepper got into the high trees from a storm ditch and climbed a slippery pine to give himself a view of the Clayton property. Mount Hood wore cloud off to the north and cool winds from Canada tossed the thunderheads into tall boils of white and blue over the hills.

Sammy was parked on the old McFee place, and had burned

the miles at speed because he knew where to slow for the smokey traps. He'd laced Pepper's coffee with bourbon from a brown bag and fed him a Blue Riband special with double-fries and pecan pie, and told him all he could remember about the woman and the boy. Donna's father had helped her up to the house with the eight pieces of luggage and been short with Sammy when he'd offered to carry Max.

Pepper allowed time to saunter and reverted to using the clock in his head to mark its passing. The jays would scold anyone coming up through the sloping woodland behind him, and Pepper watched ants forage pine-resin from the ripe cones all around him as he became a natural part of the landscape.

The Clayton place had lost its manicured look. The chicken coop was silent and there were deer tracks in the vegetable garden where old Man Clayton's setter should have been snapping at flies. The red A-framed house had faded to a dull rose and lichens spread their red and gold pennies across the shingled roof. The picket fence leaned and flaked, and couche-grass from the overgrown and unwatered lawn had invaded the path up to the front stoop. An axe rusted on the chopping stump, and the bleached barn leaned into the hill harder than ever. Ring doves cooed together on the telephone feed to the house and the window curtains did not stir. Pepper dropped onto the carpet of needles and circled the property twice before climbing into the barn through an unfastened rooflight.

Ben Clayton's ancient pick-up was parked inside the double-doors and his workbench and lathe where shrouded by a yellow tarp. Pepper's old saddlebag was up in the rafters where he had left it, and when he unrolled the poncho inside, the money and the shell-boxes had soaked up a little oil from the hand-guns. He worked the action of the stocked ·38 Savage, broke the seal on a box of factory loads and fed the revolver with brass-jacketed hollowpoints. As an added precaution, he loaded two Ezy-Loders with soft-nosed shells. Satisfied he could get them from his pocket without fumbling, he un-wrapped the Tunnel Gun.

Only about seventy of the specially-adapted Smith & Wessons had been issued by the Limited Warfare Laboratory in Maryland before they were withdrawn for contravening the 'allowable' weapons section of the Geneva Convention. A six-shot snub-nosed double-action ·44 magnum, it fired stainless steel segmented bullets with the spreading range of a shotgun, and tore a man up with less noise than a child's cap-pistol. Pepper had bought it from a 25th tunnel rat for the price of twenty ears, and posted it home in pieces with a hundred rounds of ammunition. When he had loaded it, he fed it into his clamshell shoulder-holster and climbed down to check out the pick-up.

The hard Turtle Wax shell had grown a veil of dust and chaff, and a web thick with flies hung from one of the door mirrors. A month-old newspaper yellowed on the front seat and the keys were in the ignition.

Pepper was searching the immaculate engine for extraneous wires when the extension telephone bell rang in the yard. He froze, and the ring doves skimmed away with soft hoos of alarm. After a slow count to twenty, Pepper blessed Sammy for dialling the number from a toll booth, and knew he'd let it ring until Pepper lifted the receiver inside the house.

Pepper crossed the yard with the sun at his back. He climbed the front stoop and used one of Ben Clayton's chisels on the landing window. The squeal of the rising sash was lost in the clamour of the bell, and Pepper ducked inside to crouch and listen. The house listened back. Far thunder brawled in the distant hills and wind chased pine needles across the yard. Pepper drew the Savage from his belt and turned the nearest door handle.

There was nothing in Ben Clayton's spartan bedroom to show he'd ever been anything but a self-contained widower for twenty years. The bed was as brown as the walls, and the Indian rug on the polished boards was the honeyed tan of Pueblo sandstone. His seed catalogues and car manuals made a small library between ebonite bookends on pine shelves, and Donna's graduation picture smiled next to the rack of briars he hadn't used in fifteen years. Apart from his dressing gown hooked over the wardrobe and a desiccated blowfly on the sill there was nothing else in the room but dead air.

The landing closet held brooms and a pail, and the guestroom was under sheets. The bathroom was small, neat, and smelled of medicated soap. There were no tights or panty-hose on the drying line across the tub, no creams or lotions on the glass shelf, and no toothbrushes in the holder. Just Ben's dentifrice tablets in the cabinet with his cutthroat Charleston Blue and shaving block. His leather strop hung beside the handbasin and a drowned black beetle floated in the toilet.

Pepper steeled himself to open the last door.

Donna's bedroom was still a shrine. The bed had a frilled white canopy with matching pillowcases and her dolls from many lands lay on the quilted bedspread waiting for her to return. Mr Muggins, her one-eyed bear, sported a Kennedy button and lounged in a baby-chair in his Uncle Sam suit. Donna's bronzed baby shoes were on the sideboard with her porcelain animals, and her diplomas were in frames on the flowered walls. The dressing table had a skirt of flounces, and the heart-shaped mirror was fringed with pictures of her growing from kindergarten to college. She dribbled in a sandpit, showed a freshwater bass to the camera, ate a double-cone on a ferris-wheel, and looked shy in her first formal dress.

And in an oval of silver ivy, Donna the Sphinx. The closed face she wore when she was mad at the world and was too cross to talk to it. The last face old Ben must have seen the morning she had walked out for good.

Donna had talked out her hurt when she and Pepper knew they were serious about each other. She had stumbled through the last weeks in old Ben's house as they snuggled together in a sleeping-bag high in the Blue Mountains. Pepper had let her talk herself to sleep and brought her down to face her father with the news of their marriage plans. Old Ben had looked empty and treated Donna like another shadow in the room. He'd been pleasant enough with Pepper so long as Donna wasn't mentioned. They'd fished the lakes, shared beers when the bass weren't running, and talked football around the TV when the weather wasn't ghosting it up. But he and his pick-up went missing on their wedding eve, and he stayed away until they'd left for Europe.

Stale perfume made the closeted room as oppressive as a desert tomb. Pepper's eyes stung, and he pictured old Ben religiously dusting off toys and mementoes as he relived the happy times before Donna saw his paternal affection warp to the brink of the incestuous when she brought the first boy to the door.

Pepper closed the room away and went down the stairs with the Savage ahead of him. He was in the hall before he caught the faint cloy of spoiled meat through the cling of old scent. The potplants were on their last legs and junk mail had bred all over the mat. The telephone kept up its persistent ringing and eight pieces of luggage he'd last seen in Belfast made an unmatched huddle in the centre of the living room.

Multicoloured wires webbed out from the suitcases to link the ground-floor windows and doors into a defensive grid, and Pepper touched nothing until he'd traced the contact points and circuit-breakers. A secondary system protected the suit-case locks, and time crawled as Pepper armed himself with a mental blueprint. He neutralised the cellar door with a bridging circuit of kitchen foil and flex from a table lamp.

By then he was shaking, and he let the kitchen faucet run over his neck and hands before using the kitchen phone to tell Sammy what he wanted him to do next in a shock of sudden silence.

That done, he went down into the cellar to look at the bodies lying on the dirt floor. They had been there a long time and Ben's face was a black mass of corruption. Maggots writhed under his shirt to simulate breathing, and the girl sprawled beside him held the hole in her stomach with bloated grey claws. Most of her face was under a toss of bleached hair, and the teeth bared by rictus were too long and uneven to be Donna's. There was nothing else in the cellar but apple sacks and two playing cards marked with the Bravo flash.

Pepper looked as long as he could, then reset the circuits and waited for Sammy to come up the hill on foot.

The Duchess hated the steep track up to the Clayton place, and Sammy wedged a rock under her back wheel when he parked under cottonwoods stunted by altitude. He checked the shells in his Model 60 Smith & Wesson and took it up the hill with him for the company. Pepper had sounded all used-up over the phone, and Sammy knew he'd been right to drop an insurance dime on Gene Summers back at the taxi rank.

The Blue Mountains were loaded with Vets who couldn't hack family or city life after Indochina, and a man had more chance of getting kissing-close to a sixteen-hand bull moose than of buddying up with one of those solitary mothers. And Pepper could call himself 'Charlie' until glaciers ran through Hades if that was his bag, but it didn't change the way he moved or thought – or stopped Sammy Washbourne from knowing his face from the time he'd brought the Clayton girl home to marry up with her. Sammy had seen Pepper and old Ben fish the Deschutes that same spring, and had recognised him straight off when he'd hailed the Duchess back at the terminal.

Sammy's boots slipped on smooth rock and he stopped to mop his neck with his lucky horseshoe handkerchief. He was close enough to pick out the barn and the chimney of the house, and he knew this was about the spot he'd dropped the woman and the boy most of three weeks before.

Sammy had made a couple of other calls before letting the Clayton number ring, and had confirmed that old Ben hadn't been seen down at the store or the liquor mart in all that time. Ben going off was no real surprise to anyone, but Sammy had the gut-feeling that this time was different.

He plodded up the hill under lowering cloud and wished his store-bought shorts didn't bundle up when he walked any distance. Lightning fluttered in the distance and tambours of thunder rolled over the brow in a scurry of wind and leaves. Sammy kept climbing with his head down, and found the money Pepper had left for him in the mailbox. When he had counted it he turned to the house to shout, and saw the landing curtains dance in the open window.

'Too damned generous, son. Me and the Duchess could lay up for a week on . . .'

Sammy got no further.

The ground shuddered out of the horizontal and he sat

heavily in a blast of hot concussion. Rock and shale bit his buttocks as he was slid backwards, and the roof of the red house hurled itself into the air in a rising flash of white heat. Weather boarding flew outward with long spits of brilliant flame, and splintered before spearing into the trees. There was a storm of dust and burning ash as dark smoke boiled around him to steal all the breathable air. Sammy retched to fill his lungs and gulped nothing but heat.

Lacerated by whirring and invisible debris, Sammy rolled into a ball to protect his face and belly. Sound was lost in a monumental clamour, and a second shock-wave threw him bodily away.

There was a spinning memory of being lighter than air, of skidding and landing winded in a stew of leaf-mulch, mud and whipping branches. Sammy floundered in the storm ditch with pine cones dropping all around him. A boot and sock had gone. A dead jay flopped onto his belly and his shirt was full of needles. Somehow his hat had stayed on his head and the money was still in his fist.

'Hot goddamn,' said Sammy.

And when he looked over the edge of the ditch the house had gone. A fat brown cloud rolled in the air above the stripped trees, hesitated as it gained height, then shredded as the wind blew it to tatters out over the highway.

Sammy stumbled through the wreckage and called Pepper's name until the rain swept in. Then he limped down the hill in a downpour that turned the track to a river of mud.

Sammy did some real swearing when he found his cab.

The Duchess was buried in fallen branches and a balk of timber studding had taken out the windscreen on its way through the driving seat. Sammy earned splinters trying to pull it free, and was sucking a torn thumbnail when men in flak-jackets came out of the cottonwoods with levelled M16s. Somebody in charge gave orders through a bullhorn and a riot-truck showed yellow heads through dollies of dancing rain.

Made to 'assume the position', Sammy was spread across the hood of his cab whilst they took his Model 60 and called his license through for verification. Turned to face a SWAT lieutenant with a bromide of a younger Pepper in uniform, Sammy was asked to put a name to the face.

Sammy said, 'Say what?' as if his ears were clogged when he saw Hood the local FBI man behind the lieutenant. Hood was trying to stay dry in a showerproof designer-anorak, and his hair was as soaked as his shoes. He looked at Sammy as if he had a nametag on his big toe, and talked fast to a tall grey man with an accent you could engrave glass with. Hood called him Mr Maycroft with the deference a drummer saves for the Chamber of Commerce, and pointed at Sammy as if he had Chairman Mao tattooed in red neon on his forehead.

'If it ain't the answering service,' said Sammy. 'Looking for headlines, Agent Hood? You want we should wait up for the TV?'

Hood drilled Sammy's chest with a manicured nail.

'You brought Pepper up here, Washbourne. That's giving aid and comfort to a fugitive.'

'That guy?' Sammy began to shake with cold and reaction. He felt like Pepper had sounded on the phone.

'Was this man in your cab?'

'Maybe. You'd want what with him?'

'To take him into custody,' said the SWAT lieutenant, biting off an expletive.

Sammy laughed and hurt something deep in his gut.

'You'll need a doggy-bag to do that, son,' he said.

And he was still laughing when they put him into the ambulance.

CHAPTER FOUR

It was his tenth dawn in the mountains above Thief Valley.

The sky finally ran out of rain and a cold lemon sun hung in a wash of luminous cloud. The liquid hammering petered out, and the high gorges roared with downfalls of flash-water. Tumbling out and down from the long bald ridge above Three Stone Peak, the creaming freshets cascaded into spray and fell into the lower terraces as drifting banners of fine white smoke. A pair of eagles wheeled in the early thermals, and faint rainbows formed pastel arches in the glittering humidity below them.

The dry cave was in the lee of a high granite shoulder that knuckled out from the ridge and fell sheer into the silvered metal overcast. A natural chimney took the smoke from Pepper's fire and lost it in the rock faults near the summit. He had hunted in the rain, and had used the long days to cure his catch over charcoal and oak-chips. He had two clay-baked raccoons, smoked fillets of salmon, and a month's supply of jerked deer meat. He spent hours straight-lifting rocks to enhance his muscle-tone, and greased his young beard with the mountain-tallow left over from coating the Savage. He no longer used tobacco or allowed himself coffee. Smell carried for long distances in the high-country, and could attract men as readily as it frightened the game. With the skies clearing, he had to cross the swollen lakes before a helicopter caught him in the open. The game trails on the far shore were invisible from the air.

Pepper worked rapidly. He had collected beer cans, cigarette butts and other junk from an abandoned campsite in the valley, and he scattered it about the remains of the fire. To kill the

55

smell of smoked fish, he broke a bottle of cheap deodorant against the rock wall and dropped the broken glass into the embers to destroy any fingerprints. He defecated near the entrance and wiped himself off with a page torn from a sports magazine like any city redneck, and obliterated his bootprints with quick whisks of a pine branch. When he was satisfied with his efforts, he shouldered his pack and climbed the sheer rockface to the summit so as to leave no tracks on the down-slope. Then he drove a crampon and used a dead-man's hitch to abseil down to the forest floor. A single jerk brought the rope down after him, and he went into the brooding trees to find old Ben's dog.

Thin and footsore, Sultan had shown himself about ten miles out from the Clayton place. He had bolted the raw rabbit-liver Pepper had fed him, and licked Pepper's hand when the last pellets were dug out of his shoulder. The shotgun wound raking his back had healed to an ugly black pucker, and Sultan growled with raised hackles when he sniffed Pepper's gun.

Pepper carried the dog all the rest of the first day, and he greased his paws when they dry-camped for the night. After two days, Sultan could keep up with Pepper's easy lope, and backtrailed often to sniff the wind for pursuit. He sneezed to warn Pepper when his keen ears picked up an aero-engine, and he pointed at game without flushing it when Pepper set night-snares. Pepper rewarded him with the last of his milk, and built the dog a shelter when he left him to climb the ridge to the cave. Each night, Pepper had taken Sultan squirrel meat or cured fish, and treated his scabbed neck with salted water and honey. Kept dry and warm under a bower of fern and saplings, the dog's condition had improved with the weather.

To bring the dog, Pepper snapped his fingers, and Sultan came out of nowhere with a quiet sneeze of greeting. He took the strips of jerked deer-meat without snatching, and followed Pepper down to the shoreline of the lake.

The rain had toppled a tall silver birch, and it lay in the water in a long red stain of disturbed mud. The outer current was trying to carry the birch out of slack water toward the falls below Three Stone Peak. Ignoring the chill, Pepper stripped off and stowed his clothes and backpack inside his poncho, waded out and tied the bundle to the birch under the cover of leaf-bearing branches, and pushed the tree out from the shore, content to let the current carry him across the chopping grey water. Sultan sneezed twice before plunging in, and had a good shake when Pepper hauled him up onto the trunk. Swimming alongside, Pepper guided the birch towards a point just above the rapids, and they were well into the middle of the lake when the helicopter skimmed in from the west.

Hood got Maycroft out of the shower to answer his call, and told him he'd be picked up within the hour.

'About time,' said Maycroft, and got dressed. Oppressed by the brilliant yellow walls of the motel room and the piped music in the coffee shop, Maycroft had long despaired of being entertained by television, and his smoker's cough had roughened in the chill damp of the mountains. Hood had been up in Washington State for some sort of briefing, and Maycroft's attempts to interrogate Sammy Washbourne had become a diatribe against Hood's 'answering-service', and an interminable anecdote about a college student being dead for two months before anybody took any notice.

Maycroft lit himself a White Owl and tried to find a radio station with more to offer than commercials and folksy news items that made him think the world ended at the edge of town. He settled for a music station playing Mozart, and lay on his bed to fret about the months his men would spend in Intensive Care after Pepper's attack.

An SAS colonel had given Maycroft a fast verbal lesson in unarmed combat at Belfast Airport, and Maycroft's neck crawled from cheerful descriptions of how to break bones, gouge eyes and ruin tendons with nothing but the bare hands all the way to Heathrow. The use of ballpoints, tongue-depressors and drinking-straws as lethal weapons stayed with him all through the flight to LAX and on the shuttle up to Portland, and just reminding himself of the techniques used in the Naked Kill made him queasy.

Maycroft had served in Malaya, Cyprus and Aden before

being seconded to Belfast; and was no stranger to terrorist butchery in all its forms, or to the brutal and effective ways of breaking a suspect during interrogation. He had threatened to bury devout Moslems and Buddhists with pig-offal to make them betray other members of their cadres, and knew the efficacy of the urine bath on a fastidious man, but the ease with which Pepper, and for that matter Taylor, could maim or kill a target turned his hardened stomach to water.

Hood had convinced Maycroft that Pepper would be hard to take alive by screening a classified CIA training film of CIDGs operating in Vietnam, and Maycroft instinctively knew nobody really wanted Pepper to face a long, expensive and widely reported trial, and that included the Americans he liaised with. They just didn't use the words.

Maycroft strapped his Ruger ·33 on over his flakvest and made a face at himself in the bathroom mirror.

'A grey face, greyer hair, and a grey mind to go with the grey areas you wallow in,' he told himself, and had his waterproof on when Hood hammered on his cabin door to take him out through rotor-turbulence flattening the grass verge of the motel parking lot to the Sikorski S-72. The helicopter took off with a fast forward tilt and was blatting east with a three-knot tailwind before Maycroft got strapped in beside Hood and the six-man SWAT team in their black coveralls. The smell of their hamburger and fries breakfast turned Maycroft's stomach as much as the fast ascent, and he sucked on the last of his Rennies as Hood showed him their flightpath to the Blue Mountains on a plasticated map.

'This low cloud'll burn off, and if our boy's anywhere in this region we'll pinpoint him with the 'tronics aboard this sucker. She's fitted with heat-sensors, infrared spotting scopes, and you name it,' said Hood. 'We've tracked polar bears in the snow, and flushed wolves out in Alaska with this 'quipment. You can pick those mothers out up to three-miles off against the snow. Put a dart or a bullet into them sweet as maple surple.' Hood slurred his words and pawed Maycroft's shoulder, winking at each point he made as if he had an eye affliction. 'Old Pepper better throw in his hand the moment he gets the

58

option over the loudhailer, and that's in stereo at eight-hundred watts a channel. Sounds like the Wrath of God coming down on you, my Brit friend. And those side-mounted Gatlings throw out two-thousand rounds in a burst. Turns a man to raw chuck in a hot second.'

Maycroft turned away from the bourbon on Hood's breath. The FBI man was tight and looked as if he planned to stay that way. Whatever he'd been told in Seattle had made him reach for the bottle with both hands. The SWAT team swapped in-jokes over cartons of milk, and the Sikorski rose through powdered haze to skim the low scallops of cloud piling in against the foothills below.

The Sikorski's turbofans went to full forward power just as Hood leaned across to say something more. Maycroft gave him a vague smile of discouragement, glad that the rising vibration and engine-noise made serious conversation impossible. Hood nuzzled a hipflask and watched the SWAT marksmen load their automatic rifles. Every fifth round was a tracer to mark their lines of fire, and teflon-coated shells cleaned their weapons during action. Their faces had closed down for the business in hand, and they showed less emotion than tellers weighing nickels in a country bank.

Maycroft knew a shooting party when he saw one, and stared out of a sideport to avoid eye-contact.

A scudding sun turned the watercourses to radiant platinum snakes, and misty autumn trees stippled the valleys with ragged mosaics of rich fall colour. The Sikorski's shadow chased across pale russet hills where massed pines pierced the smokey haze with evergreen spears, and sudden outcrops of rock rose to rake the brightening sky. Off towards the Blue Mountains, clots of grey scud bearded a false horizon, and clouds of cumulus sailed in armada above distant peaks.

Maycroft was jolted from a light doze when the Sikorski went into a forward dive. His stomach slammed the roof of his mouth and he swallowed to relieve the pressure on his ears. The Sikorski yawed and sideslipped into a deep canyon, using its contour beam to keep exactly a hundred-feet above the ground. Maycroft unbuckled and went forward, ignoring whatever

Hood was trying to tell him. The pilot followed a twisting course over tumbles of landslip, boulders and fallen trees, and dropped to fifty-feet where ice-melt waterfalls fell into boiling brown rapids. The canyon sides fell away and the Sikorski sped across a lake where the rising waters had drowned a wide area of woodland. Maycroft glimpsed deer bound for cover as the Sikorski made a hard rising turn, banked steeply, and skimmed a flat sheet of water between high wooded peaks.

Maycroft grabbed a headset to hear what the crew were saying.

The navigator had dark blips on his infrascope which marked the deer, and the head-sensor showed a small patch of body-warmth in the water ahead. He gave the pilot co-ordinates and counted off the shortening range in metres as the weapons-system laid digits and a target-grid on a plexiglass screen. The turbofans whispered into silence, and the rotors cut the forward speed to four-knots as the Sikorski made a slow purring pass over an uprooted birch gliding toward an angry series of falls.

'Contact positive,' said the navigator. 'Lifeform ident.'

Maycroft caught a flash of red fur before the Sikorski went into a tight upward turn.

'Dogfox, would you say, Guppy?' asked the pilot.

'Just some dog is all,' said the co-pilot.

'Secondary echo in the water,' said the navigator.

'Still only a goddamned dog. Sorry-looking sonbitch too.'

'Your mother's ass, Guppy,' said the nagivator. 'That there secondary was a positive-positive.'

Guppy the co-pilot raised a single digit.

'You and your 'tronics. If we were navy we'd have side-scan sonar. Then we'd be certain-sure 'bout water-echoes, my man.'

The pilot turned to make a second pass and armed his guns.

'Arming now. Let's get another visual before we cut loose on a lost mutt.'

'Dog,' said Guppy.

'Fox,' said the pilot. 'Ain't but three-centsworth of meat on that crittur.'

'Listen, captain, sir: don't you know a wet dog loses a good two-thirds of its size? Had me a chow one time . . .' said Guppy.

'Positive on the secondary,' said the navigator. 'Got us a live one in the water.'

Maycroft knew the late Ben Clayton had a setter, and heard Hood pass that information through his throat-mike.

'Arming for a run,' said the pilot. 'Buckle down, guys. And let's see if we can't bring the secondary target to the surface.'

'You have weapons-control, captain.'

There was quiet satisfaction in the navigator's voice as he confirmed the gunnery co-ordinates on the pilot's visual display.

The rockface of Three Stone Peak came up too fast for Maycroft. The pilot made a sharp climbing turn at the eastern edge of the lake where the rapids creamed over steep terraces, and made his strafing run with the sun at his back. Maycroft had just spotted the birch when the Gatlings opened up with gaseous belches of yellow flame. White water erupted in parallel lines across the birch before a wall of violent spume hid it from sight. Tinder, bark scales and leaves fell back into the water spouts, and the Sikorski went through a fog of spray before turning in its own axis.

Maycroft saved himself from pitching over the pilot's headrest by catching hold of a grab-bar. Somebody said 'Asshole' through his headset and told him to take a bucket seat and to belt himself in. It was Hood. Maycroft pushed him away and kept himself upright as the Sikorski slammed into a hovering mode.

Riddled and chopped apart, the remains of the birch showed through falling vapour. The root boll bobbed just below the surface, the main trunk turned in an eddy, and the head of the tree swept into the long blue tongues of current running for the first waterfall. The setter was swimming for an inlet above the rapids where a mudbar had formed against a cat's-cradle of rock and old pine trunks.

'Give me a reading on the secondary, Nav,' said the pilot.

'Split reading, captain. He's gone deep, or he's into the rapids.'

Guppy said, 'Goddamned 'tronics. Three variations in water-temperature, you've lost a nuclear submarine in a jacussi.'

The pilot went to vertical thrust to gain height and said:

'Or he's swimming under the dog.'

'Earns a big aye from me,' said Guppy.

'Nav?'

'Can't give you a positive negative, cap.'

'Let's buy it, cap,' said Guppy. 'And what say we set the SWAT cats on that mudbank and stooge around up here? Cover the situation both ways?'

'You read that, Lieutenant Conway?' asked the pilot.

'Affirmative and Wilco,' said the SWAT lieutenant. 'We are "Go" status back here.'

'*Something* went over them falls,' said the nagivator.

Guppy sprung the sidedoor seals.

'Watch for the green light, lieutenant.'

'Affirmative.'

Maycroft stripped off his headset and started to the rear.

'Leave it to the SWATS why don't you?' said Hood.

'Isn't that your Ansafone ringing?' snarled Maycroft.

Pepper trod water until the Sikorski made its strafing run, then he used his pack as ballast to go deep. There was nothing he could do for Sultan. Sinking into the silted darkness under his pack, he used it to screen his diminishing body-heat from the Sikorski's electronic sensors. Judging himself deep enough, he kicked out for the southern shore and dribbled air to maintain negative buoyancy.

Sudden hard concussions battered his senses as heavy-calibre shells drove the birch down at him in a stew of debris and cannon-trails, and the erratic undertow plucked him off-course. Bowled over and over by the tumbling waters, he was dragged against the rising bottom. Invisible rocks flayed his back and an unseen something numbed his right foot. He released more precious air and tried for more depth, but there wasn't any.

The current was filled with stinging rubble, and a cage of birch branches hooked down to trap him in a whirl of stripping foliage. Pinned to the bottom by the upended tree, Pepper lost the last of his air, and felt the freezing turbulence become a warm and blind womb. He was drowning and it didn't much matter. He clung to his pack and conjured Donna and Max to embrace them one more time. They came across sunlit grass with smiles and tans, and wanted him to swim in the Pacific breakers with them. He blew them a bubbling kiss and nail-heads of pain savaged his spine. His roar was as loud as the brawling water, and the will to breathe came back in a wild upsurge of light and air and coughing. He broke surface and fell back with full lungs, sad he was alone again.

The birch had been veered across boulders creamed by fast waters, and it rose up to spill Pepper across waterworn hardness to the brink of the falls. Pepper floundered through a roaring spill into the full bore of the downtwisting cascade. Flung outward and down, he was plunged into a deep granite sink and the hissing waters drew him down into the heart of a spiralling scour. He swallowed water and lost skin from his elbows and knees in the swilling eddies. Slammed around for a century of seconds, he was battered and whipped by whirls of shale and birch wands.

Pepper swam toward green brilliance, and burst into dull sunlight shadowed by a granite overhang. His pack dragged him down for another decade, and he kicked into the outer surge to break the surface again. This time he hurled his pack onto the overhang, and saw it lodge in a cleft thick with self-planted fern before he was sucked back into the icy maelstrom.

Without the weight of the pack to stabilise him, Pepper was a toy in the water, and there were no handholds on the slimy sides of the granite sink. His scrabbling hands stripped the algae off in black streamers of stinking gelatine. Pepper let himself sink, found the bottom with his feet and kicked hard, boring up through the race with outstretched arms. His torso cleared the tow and luck jammed his hand into a crevace as his left knee found a shallow ledge. A long pull jacknifed him over the overhang, and he rolled onto his back to listen to the Sikorski hover over the southern shore, out of his sight.

Resting was unthinkable, and he opened his pack to lace

on his boots. Wearing nothing else, and leaving the Savage behind, he climbed a broken fault in the cliff face, hoping to get to the high ground before the SWAT team were deployed.

Maycroft hung in the hydraulic winch harness until the mud came up to bury his shoes before he punched the release to send the cable back up to the Sikorski. The S-72 swung away to hover over the lake, and Maycroft minced through black mire to join the SWAT team. Lieutenant Conway had crossed the mudbank as if he sprinted on concrete, and he was clearly impatient with Maycroft's slow progress. His men were deployed in a half-circle waiting to see if the dog came out of the lake alone.

The setter came ashore through the brush above the falls, sneezed as he shed water in a wide arc, and growled with bared teeth at the guns levelled at him. When he had shaken himself enough he lay down to lick his paws, his brown eyes watchful.

Conway used hand-signals to send his men into the trees.

'So much for Pepper swimming under the dog.'

'If it was Pepper.'

'Anything on that secondary?' Conway asked the Sikorski pilot over his handset.

'Negative in the water. If he went over the falls that's bingo in spades,' Guppy's distorted voice said, and the pilot cut in to add: 'We'll gain height to get a reading down there. Can't hover directly overhead. Too close to the mountain to keep rotor clearance. Over.'

'Wouldn't you know it,' said Conway. 'Out, flyboy. Keep this channel open.'

'Wilco, ground.'

'A dilemma, lieutenant,' said Maycroft.

Conway unslung his rifle hardfaced.

'You may be limey brass, Maycroft, but you're just a civilian playing tag. Hood had the good sense to stay airborne, at least. Leave that BB-gun in its holster and stay close to my ass.'

Maycroft was a Bisley gold medallist, and wasn't about to squabble mindlessly with a shavetail-louie loaded with gung-ho badges and shiny weaponry. He employed his best brown drawl with a smile.

'Press on, m'dear fellow. I'll linger hereabouts and compose a few lines of dactylic verse on transatlantic co-operation whilst you work murder in yon dank shades.'

'You'll stay here?'

'Beached like the old duffer I am? Why not?'

'Your decision.'

Conway padded off to lose himself in the crowding pines.

Maycroft gave himself an unlit cigar and walked up onto firmer ground to clean his shoes with a handful of dead fern. The dog watched him without seeming to, and sniffed the air for scent, one ear cocked. Both ears came erect when Maycroft lit a match, and Sultan sneezed when the cigar smoke blew toward him.

Maycroft sat on a log to hum a Verdi stanza, ran pine needles through his fingers and changed to a Bizet overture when he inspected a bush with trefoil leaves. The setter bit something on his flank and Maycroft had gone when he looked back. The pines dripped solemnly and long minutes passed.

Sultan sneezed twice and raised his head to stare intently at the outcrop above the falls. His tail wagged once, then he lay his head on his paws and pretended to doze. It was enough for Maycroft. He cut east through the trees and followed a mossy rise up into the broken high ground, breathing smoke in a continual fragrant stream and humming the overture from *The Gondoliers*. He made a mess of breaking through a tangle of undergrowth, came close to falling into a fissure, and breathed hard when he took a seat on a terrace above a wide clearing with his back firmly turned to the defile cutting down from the outcrop above the rapids.

'Excellent,' he told himself, and watched his shadow fall into the clearing below him, forming and reforming as the sun played hide-and-seek with the clouds. The falls and the Sikorski's rotors purled together, and a breeze fidgetted in the pinetops. The forest floor steamed, Maycroft's shadow came and went, and his cigar died in his mouth. He unloaded his Ruger to a Bach sonata, laid it well out of his reach, and sat very still with his hands clasped in the middle of his back. For a brief moment his shadow had two heads, and he spoke without turning around.

'They'll shoot on sight, Pepper. This is a head-hunt. You're to be a body that conveniently resisted arrest. You have enemies in high places who find you as embarrassing as highly soiled linen. So, before we're interrupted, let me try some names on you. The woman who kidnapped your son and ended up dead in your father-in-law's cellar? Charlotte Stoller, and not a nice lady. Enough of her teeth survived to crosscheck with Interpol and FBI records. Cuban trained, and one-time mistress of a sweetheart Ukrainian we know as Felix Kolki. He kills for pleasure and talks "American" like a character out of a B-movie. You'd remember him if you'd met him, I'd say. Your small Irishman is probably Danny Rourke. A provo gunman with four members of the security forces to his credit. The negro in your car has to be Jackson Tibbs. A Black Panther before he joined the Loonie Left and became an "Anti-imperialist", whatever that may mean. The man with him was probably a Japanese Red Guard called Than Nghu. He sprayed Lod Airport with machine-gun fire before settling down to political assassination. We know he shot an Austrian diplomat in Rome last spring, and took a crack at an Israeli in London a month later. A mixed bag of nationalities with a Libyan Paymaster. They're a new breed – freelance terrorists, motivated as much by money as by ideology.'

Maycroft rolled a fresh cigar into his mouth and let it bob there as he talked to the silent presence behind him.

'Those five animals don't come cheap. Somebody went to enormous expense to set up this elaborate operation with you as the target, which prompts more questions than I have answers.'

Pepper breathed warm feathers against Maycroft's neck, and water dropped onto the stone from his beard. Maycroft kept his eyes on his melting shadow and kept talking.

'You must have trodden on some very powerful toes down the line, and I'm tempted to believe BelTech was just an elaborate CIA front. Was it set up to goose the French arms companies? They don't shrink from using their agents to slap wrists, but I don't see them dealing with Libya or the IRA in this fashion. Unless Sean Collins was more than a NORAID paymaster, and badly miscalculated your . . . ability to violent action? Did you know funds from your company found their way into IRA coffers? Almost three-quarters of a million according to our money boys. But perhaps that was a side-issue, eh? And could it not be that the CIA in its infinite wisdom chose this way to punish you for past misdemeanours in Indochina? Somebody up there doesn't like you, Pepper. Somebody very powerful indeed.'

Pepper's sigh could have been a zephyr of breeze. Maycroft turned his head very slowly and stared into haunted blue eyes.

'Come back with me now. They can't shoot through me to get you, old son. But they'll kill you if you make a run for it.'

Pepper bared very white teeth and smelled the wind.

'The Cambodians called our marines "elephants". Crashing about in the bush and stinking the place up with their after-shave, cigarettes and chewing gum. The Cong could smell them coming; smell them because they were meat-eaters and used scented sprays, smoked grass and snorted coke. A man on drugs stinks, Maycroft, just as much as a sleeze on the bottle. I can smell the men in black from here, so you tell them to back off before it's too late.'

Maycroft nodded, stiff with tension he tried not to show.

'I know that from Malaya, we turned vegetarian for a week before we went out on forward patrol against the guerillas. I did have to lay on my clumsiness a bit to bring you to me, you know.'

Pepper said nothing as he read the forest with narrowed eyes.

'Come down with me, Pepper.'

'No way, not now.'

'Give me a name, damn it. Who's behind this?'

Pepper's laugh was a feral snarl.

'Ask the man with two noses.'

Pepper blurred away into rusty fern and was gone.

Maycroft threw himself flat. Silenced gunfire clipped leaves and snarled into the rocks. Tracer spat yellow trails and ripped across the glade inches above Maycroft's head. The Sikorski came in overhead to thrash the treetops into dance, and the loudspeakers bellowed orders in loud stereo. Black figures zigged across the clearing and Maycroft let himself fall into the depression where Pepper had crouched, swearing royally as he scraped his face on thorn. Then he hugged the ground as the Gatlings tore the trees on the upper slopes to defoliated kindling.

'Bloody fools,' he told himself. 'Bloody, bloody fools . . .'

The temperature dropped at sundown and a crescent moon rose through snow flurries in a bright halo of ice crystals. The forest crackled under a rime of frost and the ground froze hard.

Sultan lay where the men in black had staked him out, and watched the red dots of lazer-sights pan across the clearing. Ice had formed on the setter's coat, and he shook with cold and thirst. He had licked the moisture from all the frosted leaves he could reach, and his stomach growled as he gnawed at the steel line around his neck.

The spoor of the men in black came on the turning night wind, and he sneezed when he caught Pepper's elusive scent. It had come down from the outcrop at the dark of the moon; lost itself amongst the gun-raked trees that still stank of cannon-fire, and appeared again amongst the men buried in leaves to the north of the clearing.

Pepper smelled of green woodsap and river water, quite different to the men in black who gave off sharp auras of chemicals and gunsmoke. He circled slowly without sound, working to the west with short halts next to each of the camouflaged men. Sultan's ears pricked at the sound of a sighing grunt and a brief thrash of limbs. Then there was silence again, and Sultan exercised his teeth on the wire cutting into his neck.

The moon reached its zenith and more snow drifted down.

A body rolled in fern and air rattled in a constricted throat.

Somebody went across the clearing in a crouching run and slammed to a halt against nothing. He spun before hitting the ground, and his face fell into a patch of moonlight with blind upturned eyes, a green wand growing from his throat. Then Pepper was there. He pulled the wand from the man's neck with a quick sucking jerk, untied Sultan, and sent him into the trees with a finger-snap before trussing Conway's body with the steel rope.

'Burning for burning,' he said softly. 'You should have listened to the limey, kid. He told you and that FBI lush to leave well alone.'

Pepper stared up at the stars and rubbed his aching shoulder. The Sikorski would return in the morning, by which time he planned to be thirty miles north of the river. There was no going back now.

He melted into the frozen darkness and let Sultan lick his hand before making for the wooded heights and the snowline of the Blue Mountains.

It was noon before the 240-Roberts team brought the last body down to the clearing where Maycroft and Hood had found Conway's remains. Hood was green from a hangover and hadn't bothered to threaten his face with a razor that morning. He went off into the pines every now and then, and came back smelling of bourbon, lit cigarettes that made him cough, and refused to look at the row of green bodybags when he finally said:

'This gets a blackout, Maycroft. These guys got killed in a fall on a training exercise, okay? We weren't even here, so you saw diddly-squat. They should have followed orders. Should have just chivvied Pepper along, not laid for him thinking he'd come back for the frigging dog. Six of them dead from twigs for chrissake. Twigs.'

Maycroft bit on his rising temper and crushed Hood's arm.

'Chivvied Pepper along to where? To what purpose?'

'Classified, Maycroft. Let go of my frigging arm before I have you decked.'

'You'll answer, or by thunder I'll ruin all your careful dentistry, you imbecilic toad.'

Hood paled when Maycroft thrust his face close.

'All *right*. Washington got onto Seattle. Seattle gave me the heavy finger. Somebody close to the Oval Office wants Pepper and all those other boondock-crazy renegades together for one last big pop. What the hell more can I tell you? You don't question an anonymous White House source, my friend. The phone talks in your ear and you jump to it. Over and out.'

Maycroft threw Hood back a step.

'What kind of people are you?'

Hood wiped off his flask.

'The man wants his house cleaned, we clean house. Conway and his guys got themselves dead for not following orders, and this child ain't about to boogie down *that* particular boulevard. Okay?'

'Who's the man with two noses?'

Hood belched and laughed at nothing. Took a long last draught of whisky and said: 'One of the seven things in the world I don't know, and you shouldn't want to. Wise up. Lighten up. Go the fuck home. That way you won't get shipped back to mamma in a box marked "Unsuitable for Viewing".'

Maycroft went off to throw rocks into the lake until his arm stiffened and he was capable of rational thought. Pepper had earned himself a reluctant ally.

CHAPTER FIVE

October died with the first snows and November was born in the teeth of a blizzard. Pepper's fever came with the first white-out, and he was plagued by wild notions as he excavated a snow-shelter for himself and the dog. Building a fire took the last of his awareness, and the flickering shadows on the white walls became ghosts crowding in to haunt him. When the flames died, Sultan crawled into Pepper's poncho to warm the man raving through hallucinations.

Max dealt poker hands for Pizza Man and his Montagnards. They sat on a ring of skulls that called the plays as the dead Spooks anted-up with severed fingers. Donna poured tea from a silver service and the flowers she arranged were infested with centipedes and spiders from the tunnels. Her hair hung in shimmering golden bangs either side of a yellow skimask, and when Pepper lifted it away her face came away with it. Charlotte Stoller took her place to grin her dead grin with overlong teeth clamped on the golden buddah she wore on a chain around her mummified neck. She fell back into the cellar where Corny Taylor had found a trapdoor in the tunnel above his head. He lifted it to shoot the VC on the other side, but he was speared through the throat by a Lucy Cong who called Max to come and see her shrunken heads from many lands. Taylor got jammed in the trapdoor as he tried to squeeze through, his Tunnel Gun popping three times in succession before he fell back with punji sticks in his chest to say, 'Goddamn Vietnam', and tell jokes with no punchlines through a wired jaw.

Pepper screamed because Corny didn't bleed and watched him burn an oil-portrait of the man with two noses. But the man with two noses stepped from the frame when the flames melted the paint, and made notes with a gold pen that fired tracer to dazzle witnesses.

Luther Cash drank Buds and hit surfers as he accused Pepper of abandoning him to Charlie in the tunnels. His breath stank of blood and beer and Vietnam, and he read the man with two noses' notes in a language nobody understood. When he had put on a red skimask, he went off through the wall with the tall terrorist named Kolki who carried Charlotte Stoller over his shoulder.

Then the Master from Kyoto came forward to bow, his old yellow face seamed by all the knowledge in the world. He circled Pepper in the Mantis Position and called him to the quilted mat to practise the Naked Kill on blocks of Japanese hardwood. Pepper huddled where he was and made his apologies with a fluency he had never possessed before. The Master showed pleasure without changing expression and touched a hard palm to Pepper's forehead as though he were an equal. 'My sandals are yours, Pepper san. You merely have to return to The Way,' he said, and bowed into invisibility, leaving his pure white aura behind for a brief moment.

And Ben Clayton was there. Tangled in Donna's dress, he tried to kiss the face that wasn't there, his dead sockets running with tears as he pawed a mass of bleached hair, calling her name. But Donna was with Pepper under the poncho, and she licked his face with a rough dog's tongue as she told him she was alive somewhere beyond the snowline. Pepper just had to rest and find her when the storm had blown itself out. Pepper promised with Sultan panting close to his face, and the deepening snow muffled the shrieking winds enough for him to sink into oblivion.

The fever broke when Pepper let the nightmares go.

Only then did the dog leave him to clear snow from the mouth of the ventilation shaft, and kept vigil there until Pepper stirred eighteen hours later. By then it was night again, and they ate smoked fish together before digging themselves out to cover the last fifteen miles.

The man with only fifty Bravo playing cards had to be waiting for them in the Wallowa Mountains above the Snake River.

The old bear smelled Pepper on his backtrail and stood erect to grunt a warning before ambling down to fish the shallows of the Snake River. The horses stabled at the Firetop Ranger Station scented the bear when he crossed the snowfield below the firetower, and their whickers of alarm carried to Pepper as he waited for the bear to put distance between them.

The silence was as hard as the stars, and the ice crusting the shallows snapped under the bear's weight as sharply as pistol shots. Pepper watched the greyback hook trout onto the bank with lazy flicks of his paws, and passed downwind of him when he settled to feed. Sultan walked stifflegged until they left the bear far behind, then adopted his usual springing gait as if nothing had happened.

Deep in the trees, Pepper cut a deertrail running with the western bank of the Snake, and a family of porcupines he surprised stopped grubbing to bristle. Sultan gave them a wide berth and made water to mark his trail. Pepper dropped fresh snow over the small yellow patch, and brought the setter to close-heel when he struck west to follow a river spur into a canyon. Snow had formed deep drifts in the dykes cutting the river bank, and bitterns boomed at the first grey fingers of dawn from the thickets of frozen reed spiking the bottom land. The river stole light from the paling sky and steamed like a sullen run of oiled satin.

Pepper walked softly now, and his heightened tension transmitted itself to the dog. The canyon narrowed into a dogleg, and the path was a thin line of virgin snow between the foreshore and the trees, just wide enough to take two men abreast.

Pepper found the first mantrap between two pines. The crude crossbow was primed to slam two spears down the trail at waist-height, and drop their impaled targets into a tiger trap lined with sharpened hickory stakes. Pepper avoided the trip-wire trigger and came up short when he spotted the second hazard. A fish-hook spring buried in the snow would have swung a fifty-pound mudball studded with hardwood stakes

73

into his chest at killing force if it had been sprung. Pepper iced it up with water from his canteen and carried Sultan through a maze of baling wire hung with punji sticks and broken glass, a night-trap only a fool would have blundered into in daylight. He skirted another pit and set Sultan down when he reached a trellis bridging the river between sheer rock walls. White water creamed around the supports and the river surface was dimpled by whorls of undertow a strong swimmer would have had trouble living in. The water-smoothed rocks on the far side had no handholds, and wooden palings overhung the edge of the escarpment. Pepper whistled a six-note coda and sat down to wait for Annie or Willie Flatbush to show themselves.

Willy had been the radioman on Zulu's last raid, and had almost made it back to Cu Chi base before a Bouncing Betty took his legs off below the knee, and left him with one eye and just two fingers on his left hand. He had come home to Annie with nothing but nightmares and a morphine addiction she'd cold-turkeyed him out of. For months she hid his knives and guns and played her mandolin when he screamed and pleaded to die, and made love to him when the pain wouldn't let him sleep. For a year he sat in his wheelchair and watched the river and dreamed up ways of finishing himself in the neatest possible way. Then he learned to paint and fish with a handline, and study the birds and animals he used to hunt for pleasure.

Pepper was listening for the whine of Willy's electric chair when Annie showed herself on the far side. She had the olive skin and high cheekbones of her Cherokee mother, and her poncho was the green of dead foliage. Her pants were tucked into high boots and she held a twelve-gauge in the crook of her arm. Her black hair was scraped back under a brown stetson with a silver and greenstone band, and Pepper knew she could get a second knife in the air before the first had hit the target.

'Prettier than ever, Mrs Flatbush,' Pepper said in a carrying whisper.

'A face like ten miles of bad road and a temper to match.'

74

Annie said. 'If that ain't you, it's your double, Pepper san. Gotta be a long eight years and some.'

'That and more, Annie.'

Annie spread her weight and the shotgun shifted to keep Pepper at the centre of its scatter pattern.

'Years of cold nothing, then old faces turn up like hole cards at a Vegas table. Should tell me something. Except it don't, and it should. Right now, you and them others are about as useful to me and Willy as belly-gas in a bubble-bath. It ain't that you ain't welcome, except you ain't, and no offence.'

'Just tipping my hat, Annie.'

'Sure, like the drummer after the widow's cow. First Able Taylor san, now you. Got any more bad news back there, apart from that dog?'

'When was Corny here?' Pepper's back crawled.

'My question was down first.'

'There could be bad news behind. Maybe worse ahead.'

Annie nodded at that and watched for sudden bird flight in the far shore without taking her eyes off Pepper.

'Trouble always did come in threes down on the Nations,' she said. 'And Taylor hinted you'd maybe happen along. It was a month gone. He stayed long enough to hand me the worries, drank some white lightning, then took himself off to Flo Cordova's place. Flo's still up there on the ridge – digging tunnels and hiding out in the woods when he's spooked. Crazier than ever, and talking Armageddon when he talks at all – blasting into the ridge itself when he hits hardrock. Reckons it'll take an A-bomb to winkle him out of there, the crazy bastard. Willy had me chase Flo off when he wanted us to leave here and live in the tunnels with him. I thought Willy was gonna put a round up his third eye, he was so mad about it. Brought Willy's bad dreams back for a fistful of weeks. You bet I sure as hell chased Flo off.'

'You did right, Annie.'

'I know it. Now Flo's got all the company he needs. There's these motorcycle crazies who make it up here for the summer. A bunch from the 1st and 25th Infantry. Some of them stayed on we heard. A regular army of them nighthawking under the moon and sleeping days. When the wind's right we hear them shooting off at noises that come with the dark. Some scream, some don't. They're regular bedbugs, but they mostly leave us be. They'll sometimes sneak down and leave a rabbit or a deer haunch on our back porch, and have Willy paint up some dragon or wolf on their motorcycle jackets. One time they left Willy a hawk to nurse. This other time they left him three baby owls. Willy doctored them up and let them go. Except there's this one owl plain won't leave. Thinks he's people. Brings me a mouse now and then to show he can still do it, but he's just another bedbug who thinks he owns our barn loft.'

'Tell Willy "hello" for me, Annie.'

'You want to wait there? I could bring you some flour and bacon. Some coffee, maybe?'

'Can't use it, Annie. But thanks anyway.'

'Yeah, you look all leaned-down for something. Something I didn't plan to have you bring onto our property. Me and Willy like it fine on our ownsome. You ain't bedbug crazy, Pepper san, but you smell of meanness all the same. Willy always said there was something hanging fire in your gut, something you'd have to take out of your head and look at real close one day. Guess that day came, huh?'

'Willy can think what he wants. Just tell him "hello" like I said.'

'Me and this scatter-gun are talking, and I ain't done yet. Willy says there's something between you and Luther Cash too. Something that happened on the Cholon Road before that last raid. Like there was a hijack, and you and him was on different sides in a fire-fight. Willy sees clearer than most, Pepper san. He don't need no window or seaweed to forecast the weather, and he's sure you've got rain coming to you. Not the spit-and-miss kind, but the kind they built arks for back then and gone. Am I gonna see Luther Cash on your backtrail? Or is he by God ahead of you?'

Pepper had no idea and didn't feel the need to guess aloud.

'Something's out there,' Annie said. 'You feel it too.'

Pepper shrugged his pack straight.

'Like cold breath on my neck, Annie.'

'See you take your rain with you. Then I don't grudge you luck.'

'Whatever comes, don't you and Willy be here.'

Annie backed away with busy eyes.

'Where else is there?'

'Anywhere. There's a lot of country.'

'Not when you *belong* somewhere, Pepper san. But you don't belong anywhere, do you? Never did after 'nam. So you plain can't know how it feels to belong to what you stand on.'

Pepper took Sultan back into the trees and continued west without a backward wave, his spine pricked by sweat.

'Don't give advice you won't take yourself, Pepper,' he said to hear how it sounded in the forest silence.

The day turned to lead and diamonds at noon.

A gale tore the sky apart and avalanched snow from the ridge, throwing long walls of it down into the trees. Ice stiffened Pepper's beard and Sultan's coat was white with frost when they reached the pass cutting the ridge. The woods had closed in on the long climb to the foot of Flo Cordova's ridge, and the frozen ground had crackled underfoot as they struggled upward into a force ten filled with stinging snow. Scales of ice had sheered off the escarpment to smash into shrapnel on the lower buttresses, and Pepper was blown flat too many times to remember as he worked his way into the mouth of the pass.

If Hell was a place, Pepper figured this had to be it.

The gale had scoured the pass of drifts and there was no shelter until he and the exhausted dog crawled into a deep and downsloping fissure in the lee of an overhang. They huddled there to eat jerked meat without a fire, and watched the snowscape reshape itself like a slow white sea, rolling as ponderously as the black rags of cloud streaming out from the upper terraces.

Pepper used his nightglasses on the valley below and decided he and the dog were the only ones crazy enough not to have sought cover. He pictured Flo Cordova and his bikers snug in their bunker under the snow, maybe passing the bottle and drawing on muggles; talking Harley-Davisons and Presley, flower-power and Saigon whores, the merits of Remingtons and Ithacas, and how Buddy Holly died.

Flo, small and wiry with black holes in his face from grenade fragments, using his hands to relive Ho Bo Woods and the Iron Triangle. Putting names to dead faces, pouring kerosene over Charlie's rice caches, or throwing VCs out of the choppers to see them bounce because they sure as eggs wouldn't talk worth a wooden nickle.

Good-bad old days they couldn't go back to and couldn't escape from. Using hindsight to improve on what they did and what they had been. Damning the top brass and three administrations for their walk through hell before being dumped back into small town America without a parade or a 'sorry 'bout that'. Reminding each other how just as many veterans had suicided from drugs, booze or self-inflicted gunshot wounds as had died during ten thousand days of combat. The War That Never Was, except they'd been there. Bitter and proud and ashamed, and damned if they knew what to do about it.

Men from nowhere, going nowhere. Men who came awake with a wife or mother by the throat, who had come close to shooting a child seeking comfort in his parents' bed. Men who had killed in bar brawls because they knew no other way, had done time and preferred solitary confinement to killing again in their sleep.

Pepper knew them all without caring enough to join them.

Pushed back inside himself, he would stay alone until he found Donna and Max alive or marked their graves with somebody's blood.

The wind died as quickly as it had come and left a brooding silence. The snow settled in hasty flurries of powdery flakes and the light greyed down to a premature twilight. The valley was a monochrome postcard, and the coils of the Snake river were threads of black glass between white and whiter hills.

Pepper thought he saw the snow move and used his night-glasses. White shapes grew from the white blanket to become men in snowgear with whitened weapons. The first shots came in a fusillade of silenced pops and chased through the pass with flinty echoes. Charges blew out the outermost spider holes in shouts of red blast, and left black afterburns in the snow. An underground hootch blew apart, and bikes were tossed into the air with blazing tanks and spinning wheels. The helicopters came in then, and laid spotting beams where their heat-guidance systems located bodywarmth under the snow for the sappers to probe or lay more charges. The valley rocked with explosions and CS gas floated in the still air.

Pepper watched for two hours. Then he stowed his pack and took his guns and the dog down across the impacted snow.

Maycroft left Sammy Washbourne at the wheel of his rental car when he collected a package from the main Portland Post Office using a cover ID. Inside was a variable-speed recorder with a microwave output. It transmitted up to fifteen minutes of recorded speech as a high-speed blip in a burst of white sound only the receiver–consoles at Whitehall and GCHQ Cheltenham could decode. Programmed to respond to Maycroft's voice and palm-print, it fused itself to twisted plastic if tampered with by a third party.

Maycroft loaded his pre-recorded cassette into the machine, posted his plain language report to the British Embassy in Washington, and called the Duty Officer there to make certain it would be intercepted and read.

Using a second booth he dialled a local number where an automatic cheesebox redirected him to a Los Angeles house on Foothills Boulevard with a permanently open line to Whitehall. Any bugs on the line were fed white sound, and the numbers deleted themselves after a single transmission. The line established a satellite-link and fed more white sound back down the line once Maycroft's blip had been received.

Maycroft cleared down, wiped the tape, and had Sammy drive him to another public phonebooth across town. The relayed message from Admiral Gus came in as a high-speed blip fifty-seven minutes later, and Maycroft unscrambled it before going back to the car. The White House was advising the Los Angeles Sheriff's Department of Maycroft's imminent arrival, coupled with a 'request' to offer him any assistance he might need. Gus was pulling out all the stops.

Sammy had spotted two of Hood's agents in a parked tourer, and he asked Maycroft if he wanted them shaken. Maycroft gave him the location of his second car and told him to go ahead. Sammy lost the tourer with some fine driving and took the second car east, using back roads the snow hadn't blocked.

Maycroft passed Sammy a lit Perfectos Finos and poured thermos coffee into cups from a wicker hamper on the back seat. Sammy jerked his head at the hams and potted shrimp he glimpsed before the lid closed.

'You never got that box of goodies from no Lucky's market.'

'Fortnum & Mason's of Piccadilly. One may be in the field, but one doesn't have to pig it, you know. The diplomatic bag can carry more than documents and ordnance, and I like my little bit of comfort.'

Sammy's belly rolled with a chuckle.

'You talk prettier than a faggot in a TV soap opera, but I like your company, Maycroft. Or is there a first handle goes before Maycroft?'

'Not since Public School. I'm a natural surname person just as you're a natural Sammy.'

'Ain't that the truth, and I'll bet you was an officer too.'

'Just as you were a top sergeant before you decked a certain second lieutenant at Fort Baxter and were busted back to private.'

'I never told you that.'

'Files, Sammy, files.'

'And that man's army never lets you go. Damned if I know what I'm doing here anyhow. Driving some limey fuzz into the boondocks for no good reason.'

'I thought it wasn't the money.'

Sammy almost swerved on a tricky bend.

'Maybe it's a lot of things,' he said. 'Maybe because I'm Korea and that Pepper kid 's 'nam. Sort of a father-son-type-thing. I came home to a GI loan, and nobody spat on my uniform when I got off the bus. No hippies threw coke cans of pee out of a microbus at me and called me a pig-murdering

80

shithead. Granny ladies came around with cookies and lemonade, and the American Legion gave me a plaque and a dinner. Just maybe it's because I like the kid for being a loner like me. No, it ain't the money.'

'And your brother Melvin?'

'You meet him, you'll know Melvin straight off. He kept to the farm and counts his money. More like my old man than my old man was. He ain't the oldest, but he sure inherited for staying home to keep the pigs fed and the still producing. Made more money than King Croesus had gold buttons. He likes to fly though; keeps that 'copter of his gassed up and ready to go, day or night. He's crop-dusted with a tail-wind up his third eye that'd blow the ass-feathers off a Canada goose. He's a whisky drinking sonnabitch and hates the feds almost worser than I do, and that's going some.'

'Sounds a character,' Maycroft said dryly. 'More coffee?'

'Gimmee another of them high-tone smokes with the gold crest on. Character? Melvin? Shoot, you don't know the half of it.'

Sammy's grin lasted all the way to his brother's farm thirty miles from the Snake River, and they sat around the stove with a bottle of Maycroft's sipping whisky waiting for a window in the weather.

The helicopters peeled away, the white soldiers ran for cover, and Pepper went to ground to the wail of a 'fire-in-the-hole' klaxon. The sappers had fed what looked like bangalore torpedoes into the vent shafts above Flo Cordova's main bunker, and the effect of the computer-linked explosions was as devastating as FAE aerosol charges. The whole valley shuddered. Volatile gases expanding at 7,500 feet a second tore through rock and earth to throw up a lazy brown hump four hundred feet in circumference. White-hot blossoms of raw energy broke through the crust, the snow turned to steam, and a vast crater bottomed out under a short cloudburst of black rain. A corona of sizzling heat spread with the shock wave as a blinding ultra-violet sear, and scarred the surrounding area with dark furrows of tainted ice-melt.

Pepper threw himself across the dog to cover them both with his poncho. The ice in his beard turned to liquid in a brief summer wind of blast that sunburned his exposed skin. Bowled over twice, he came up running with Sultan at his heels, and sprang into the trees to zigzag to the nearest spider hole. The helicopters would be back, but the explosion had super-heated the ground, and their heat-sensors would be useless until the area cooled. Moving at speed was now more impor-tant than caution.

Sultan went ahead of Pepper when they crossed a shallow depression, and balked at leaping the far rim. He skidded to a halt with a sneeze, and lay still with his hackles up. Pepper crouched to listen before taking a quick look at the blood trail running from the spider hole. Somebody had dug themselves out and crawled north, leaving the dark smears of a serious stomach wound. Ordering Sultan to heel, Pepper followed the trail with his Tunnel Gun levelled. Fifty yards on, footprints came out of the bush to scuff up a bloodpatch before continuing north with deeper heelmarks, proof that the wounded man was being carried. Pepper trod in the same prints and slowed his pace.

He heard the sound of voices before he made visual contact. Flo Cordova lay with his back to a tree and the second man was packing his wound with a rough field-dressing. The second man had white hair and a soft voice, and he urged Flo not to talk, but the Mexican–American would have none of it.

'Nothing but talk left, Corny,' he said. 'They wanted you, and got me. Don't that beat all? They sure had it figured, didn't they? Blooped our spider holes to send us back down the tunnels, then World-War-Threed us with the nearest thing to a nuke strike. Those old boys down there didn't have time to kiss their butts goodbye. Came close to fooling them though. Real . . . close . . .'

'Easy, my man,' Taylor said. 'Save your strength . . .'

'Don't kid this Chicano, motherhead. I'm leaking out all over the snow. Must've been blown half across Oregon when that trapdoor fragged me in the gut . . .' Flo's cough was a light rattle that flecked his mouth with pink bubbles. The whites

82

of his eyes showed as quarter-moons and he punched the snow weakly. 'No more lies now, old buddy. Now I gotta talk straight-arrow. You guys should never have gotten out of that last raid. Would have told you then, but they never even told old Luther neither. And he was one of them. Never knew that, did you? Never knew he was a lodge-brother with them low-lifers back in Saigon. Trading off penicillin and pogo-sticks through the Chinaman to the NVA. Generators, gasoline, medical and surgical . . . you name it, they sold it . . .'

'Is this supposed to make sense to me, Flo?'

'I was their field-man, you clown. But I ran when they decided you-all was expendable. Did you and Pepper see Luther Cash blow that supply dump? The hell you did. Weren't none. That was old General Linh's headquarters down there, controlled the whole northern sector of the Iron Triangle. When you guys went on that raid the war was as good as over, and nobody working for the man with two noses was gonna stand still for that complex going blooey. It was too much too late, and you guys were dead meat. The Saigon Pogues were saving face, man. Leaving doors open for the future, you dig? Having you Spooks fragged was the deposit they paid to keep a back door open to Hanoi when the US-of-A pulled out the military and let the South go hang. Them VC knew every one of you Spooks by name – even had prices on your heads. You guys dead on Charlie's turf was Saigon's idea of a peace-offering to Uncle Ho . . .'

'Sweet God in Heaven,' Taylor said softly. 'Sweet Jesus . . .'

'I'll let you know if he's home when I get there,' said Flo. 'Guess I'll get to do some fast and fancy talking over all them villes we wasted and blamed on Charlie. We was the guys in the black hats, you know, and all in the name of mom and apple pie. 'Cept we was good at it, and liked it better than getting laid. I got me a hundred-some scalps to my name, so me and St Pete should have an interesting five minutes before he boots my duff downstairs. But what the hell, when did I ever get in anywhere through the front door . . .'

Taylor murmured comfort as Flo spat more bubbles onto the reddened snow, and Pepper moved closer without a sound.

He would sense white soldiers through Sultan's headturns and pricking ears.

The stink of chemical explosive was in the trees now, and the setter wrinkled his nose at it without taking his eyes from Taylor's back, his teeth bared in a silent snarl. Pepper's stomach rolled. The dog's reaction put Flo or Taylor behind the gun that had scarred Sultan's back.

Flo bubbled as he tried a laugh and said:

'You know what the mother-gag is, Corny? Saigon giving your scalps to Hanoi turned out to be a no-no in Washington. There was no way the administration wanted anybody talking to Hanoi. Not for a thousand-fucking-years. Them CIA Richmond Seersuckers just shredded their files, said ''ho-hum'', and ran off to South America to start themselves another war or three down there. So long as they can find themselves some rebels, commies or insurgents, they're as happy as humping hogs. The countries change, but the labels they use don't. I tell you, ''expendable'' is a right long word, but it comes with a short, sharp stick, Corny. And you guys got shafted with it.'

'You got that right.'

Flo sagged and a bony hand fluttered on his chest. His eyes lost light and his voice sounded younger when he found his father's ghost under a Douglas fir.

'Hey! You remember that last time I come home, poppa patron? In that sharp gold Chevvy-car the kids climbed all over and tracked up with dust? You grinning like I was the new President of Mexico, and done brought water to the village with a magic wand, huh? That muriachi band blowing its brains out like the twenty bucks I slipped them made me a champ? Me giving you that colour TV and wearing that suit with lapels wide enough for a million silver stars? Ratassed on tequila and happiness, and staggering like the King of Spain? Then tripping in dogshit, and that TV going way up in the air and straight down through the windscreen of that dumb gold Chevvy? Smashing to nothing but tubes and transistors? Me sitting in dog-doody, and you looking down at me with that knowing old peon's look of yours? And that band winding down like somebody pulled the plug on the stereo with everybody standing around too ashamed to laugh? You just looked at me real quiet and said: "God is an executioner, Chico. He kills foolish-show and pride." You remember that?'

Flo shuddered with closed eyes and opened them wide to say:

'And you dead these ten years, poppa. Never was here.'

'Easy there, horse,' said Taylor.

Flo sighed and bit on a knuckle.

'I'm right tired, man. You wanna finish this up?'

Taylor's headshake threw white hair over his forehead.

'No way, Flo. I'll get you out.'

'And take me where? Dead meat is dead, you motherhead. Do it before I yell "medic".'

Taylor seemed to look directly at Pepper. His teeth were bared and the scar on his chin was a scrawl of black crayon. His hand found the right place in Flo's neck, and his thumb went home with a quick stab. Flo grinned at nothing. His eyes rolled to white and his hands fell palms-up into the mush of red snow. His last sigh was the hiss of a slashed tyre, and he became a bundle of rags thrown from a moving car.

Taylor reached for his rifle as Sultan sprang forward with a hard bark. The snow behind Taylor was sitting up. Pepper's shot threw the white soldier back into the snowbank with a polka-dotted chest, and a second blew his respirator away with his automatic carbine. Sultan knocked Taylor to the ground and held him prone as green tracer glared through the air inches above them. Pepper fell back into the depression, pulling his Savage free with his left hand.

'I thought that was for me,' Taylor yelled.

'Almost was,' said Pepper, waiting for a target.

Maycroft chewed antacid tablets and wished he'd refused the last three white lightnings from Melvin's jug. Sammy and Melvin were at the controls of the red Gazelle, and lightspill from the radarscope tinted the cockpit and turned them into a matched pair of green buddhas. Melvin's chins vibrated as he flew through upfalls of turbulence below the mountain peaks, mangling country songs in a tuneless monotone. Maycroft thought him the worst singer he'd heard, and agreed when Sammy said: 'Melvin couldn't carry a tune in the bucket they used to put out the Chicago fire', but the fat man could fly.

Sammy had hunted the woods they skimmed at treetop height, and he gave his brother seat-of-the-pants direction to the stepped mesas running up to Cordova's ridge above the Snake.

'Hot rocks and Gila monsters.'

Melvin stopped riffing a middle-eight to swear, threw the Gazelle into a hard buck, hovered between two fingers of rock, and dropped into a canyon shaped like a run of overlapping meteorite craters. Maycroft saw the squadrons of olive-drab Chinooks in a holding-pattern over the snowfield ahead just as Melvin made the fast vertical drop and slammed them into a hover only feet above a narrow run of brown rapids.

'You see them mothers? Must be twenty-some,' said Sammy.

'Double the "and some",' Melvin said, comfortably drunk. 'Won't spot us lessen they're looking over their shoulders.' He punched through the radio bands and picked up pilot crosstalk, listening for any response that meant the Gazelle had been seen. 'Guess they're out to lunch far as we're concerned. You want I should get around behind them, Mr Maycroft?'

'If you can without drawing fire.'

'Does a "sooee" bring hogs? Ain't but one way to find out.'

Melvin and Sammy yelled face to face, and Melvin took the Gazelle in a low bank to the north with his skis brushing the pines. The Chinook pilots traded status reports and talked to ground-control in some sort of binary code.

'Goddamned robots talking numbers,' Sammy said in disgust. 'Don't even sound like men.'

Maycroft translated the codes into grid-references and the count-down to a rendezvous-time forty-three minutes away. Whatever had been going on down on the ridge was fast coming to a conclusion. They had only minutes to view the area from the air before the place swarmed with fast assault-helicopters. He had chewed a thumbnail down to the quick by the time Melvin had brought the Gazelle along the river to approach the ridge from the north, his skis inches above the frozen reeds.

Chemical fog rolled with the Snake and steamed in the dense forest. None of them spoke when they saw the scar in the trees and the two-storey-deep crater torn out of the snow. White soldiers massed on the western ridge, and ground-control was calling in the Chinooks for air-support against the lone intruder.

'That mean us?' Melvin asked Maycroft.

'We're the spare one at this wedding.'

Sammy pointed out a man running with a dog in his arms.

'That ain't no possum,' he said.

'Pepper,' Maycroft breathed. 'Can you get down for him, Melvin?'

'Only if'n you ask me,' Melvin went to full rotor-power and Sammy had his side-door unlatched.

'Run, boy, run.'

Lazy emerald fireflies climbed up at them and the pop of weaponry was a distant massacre of party balloons. Melvin dropped lower, used rudder to bring the Gazelle around to match the running man's speed, and bounced off the snow. The setter came in through the door with a sneeze and a thrash of legs and tail, and Sammy grunted as he caught a fistful of poncho, heaving Pepper across his lap. Maycroft got the dog back alongside him and had his face seriously licked. Melvin trimmed with gyros and rudder to compensate for the extra weight, and took off upriver at full revs. Maycroft hauled Pepper over the back of Sammy's seat, and stared when Pepper lay on his back to wink up at him. He had white hair and Taylor's crooked grin.

'Taylor?' Maycroft said. 'Where in blazes is Pepper?'

'Doing what he does best. Getting himself dead the fastest way possible.'

Melvin said 'Shoot', as a tracer-round punched through the fuselage above his head, and added, 'We ain't going back into that shooting gallery, Maycroft. What you got is what you keep.'

'Damned right,' said Sammy. 'They kill Pepper, I'll buy the headstone myself.'

Melvin flew west along a deep spur and passed the Flatbush place.

The house was well alight and rolled black smoke up at them.

'Flo was right,' said Taylor. 'God *is* an executioner. Except he's got two noses.'

The Chinooks had airlifted the main force out, leaving a small rearguard to clean up and talk to any TV crews who came in. The bodybag detail had eleven bodies 'cordwooded' in the snow, and a senior Federal with a clipboard checked the IDs of three dead white soldiers. He dangled dogtags from a thumb and stared at the third corpse with a low whistle.

'Got us a coloured boy in the winter woodstore here,' he told his black SWAT Sergeant through Camel smoke.

'Ain't you the ethnic one, Agent Hood,' the black SWAT Sergeant toed the bloody white coverall away from the belly wound and echoed Hood's whistle. 'Died real hard. Must've caught a blast in the tunnels.'

'Not in those clothes, and not wearing O'Keefe's dogtags.'

'Where's the bottle you been sucking on, Hood?'

'We've got three down and bodies to match, right? And that dead sonnabitch is Flo Cordova, the head honcho of this sorry bunch of misfits. Now d'you get it, you moron?'

'Why don't you tell me?'

Hood pulled his lower lip at the horizon where the Chinooks had disappeared.

'Ask yourself who flew out sitting on O'Keefe's helmet.'

The TV News anchor-man cut into the movie with a newsflash and cut away to a girl in a cute white-fur parka standing in a whirl of coloured lights bouncing from police helicopters. Taylor came out of Melvin's shower and towelled his hair as he sipped the drink Sammy had fixed for him.

'Earlier this evening,' the girl said, 'elements of an interstate and Federal force surrounded a commune of veterans here in the Blue Mountains after the abduction and murder of two neighbours, Willy and Annie Flatbush. Several hitchhikers had disappeared in the area over recent weeks, all young women, and one escaped to tell of an ordeal of repeated gang rape. A firefight ensued when agents arrived here, and the gang resisted until all of them were killed. More details in our regular morning broadcast. This is Moira Del Rey for CBS News . . .'

'That guy behind her,' Taylor said, dropping his drink.

'Agent Hood, the answering machine,' said Sammy.

'The hell you say,' said Taylor, losing his towel.

Maycroft turned to look into Taylor's suffused face.

'Corny . . . what in . . .?'

'That's good old Luther Cash, mister. Mr Cholon Road himself,' Taylor hissed. 'What the hell is going down here?'

Nobody had an answer to that, and they were still puzzling over it when bullhorns from outside ordered them to come out with their hands empty.

CHAPTER SIX

The Portland FBI agents met Cash at the airport with good and bad news, verifying what he already suspected. He reamed them out for losing Sammy Washbourne and Maycroft, and had them drive them to his office. Knowing his deep cover was probably blown, he locked himself in and dialled an unlisted Washington number on his scrambler. The voice-actuated recorder he used to log all such calls showed a red light as he waited for the familiar voice to come on the line, and the whisky died hard in his stomach as he kept his hands busy with a cigarette he didn't really want.

'Yes, Luther.'

The voice was as clear as imported Plymouth gin.

'We blew the Snake Pit.'

'I caught our cover story on the late news. It was crude enough to be believed since there will be no trial to complicate the issue further. Am I to congratulate you?'

'In part, I guess.'

'Never in part, Luther. You know that. All . . . or nothing. Now which is it?'

The voice stroked Cash's ear with cold fingers, and his knuckles squeezed white around the telephone when he said:

'The house-cleaning op was a hundred per cent effective, but there is a partial negative. Maycroft got into the Snake by chopper, and pulled Taylor out. My guys swarmed the Washbourne place and have all four men in custody. How do you want me to process them to you?'

'I want no such thing. I have other house-guests, as you well know, Luther. Am I to build yet another wing to my establishment to house the strays you tend to gather? You must make other more final arrangements.'

'Not with Pepper still out there.'

'One thing at a time, Luther. Mr Maycroft was a calculated hazard who might have proved useful to us. Now he's something of an embarrassment. A wet job, executive action, call it what you will, but do it, and nothing clumsy. I make myself . . .'

'Over the top. All we need do is hold him until . . .'

'You interrupted me, Luther.'

'I know, but . . .'

'You're doing it again.'

Cash wanted a drink. Just one to settle his stomach. He bit the webbing inside his mouth and poured himself a whisky in his mind. A golden, peaty scotch that blended malt and barley to sooth his throat and steady his hands.

'Better. You must learn self-control.'

'Yessir.'

Cash heard himself grovel and screamed silently as he mashed two noses with a mental fist.

'Private helicopters crash all the time. And in this weather . . . why not? See to it, Luther.'

See to it, Luther. Jump to it, Luther, Cash thought.

'Yessir,' he said aloud as the spool wound his submission onto the tape.

'That agreed, we can turn our attention to Pepper. You were so certain he would be drawn into your Snake River net. So confident . . . and . . .'

'I did. He was there.'

The phone sighed against Cash's face.

'Another interruption, Luther?'

Cash tasted his own blood as his molars ground through his inner cheek. He opened the drawer for his office bottle and tried to hook it out without the telephone picking anything up. The bottle wasn't in its usual place. He stared at the gap between the Thomas's Street Directory and his codebooks in disbelief.

Where the hell was it?

'You're listening, Luther?'

'Yessir.'

'Pepper clearly eluded you. How d'you explain that?'

Cash swallowed tobacco aftertaste.

'He took out one of our SWAT team on the Snake. Used a Tunnel Gun on him. Buried the body, and dressed Cordova's corpse in the white coverall. The dogtag checked out to Agent O'Keefe from Billings, Montana. The headcount on that Chinook checked out as full, so we had to assume Pepper had flown out aboard it. The local agents swarmed the Billing's landing field, and I-Deed all the guys aboard when they put down. Had them all assume the position until they all checked out A-Okay. Some turkey from our Seattle branch had boarded the wrong chopper. They were all unmarked, you know, and there were two other SWAT guys who goofed-up the same way. One from LA and . . .'

'I know. We monitored it from here.'

Then why ask me? 'There was no sign of Pepper. He took another chopper, I guess, or boogied off into the snow . . .'

'And is lost to sight. Is that your contention?'

'I guess so.'

'Won't wash, Luther.'

Cash denied that with a silent headshake. Heard the voice take breath and listen to him spill ash on the shag carpet as he tried another drawer. He crushed his Camel stub in an overflowing ashtray and tried to remember when he might have emptied his office bottle. The flights between Portland, Seattle and the Blue Mountains blurred together. He was sure he had filled his hipflask from the glove-compartment bottle for the flight to the Snake, so the office bottle should have been there in the first drawer. He couldn't think about finishing Maycroft without a long and hard swallow of amber fire. He ransacked a third drawer as the voice from Washington said:

'How simple you made it sound, Luther. How clever. Three birds with one stone, you said. And on the face of it, you were quite right. Finish Taylor, finish Pepper, and put an end to our "most wanted" terrorist group on neutral ground. All of them liquidated without our long-arm being anywhere in evidence. Another shredded file, and past errors rectified. But you badly underestimated Pepper, didn't you?'

'We *all* did, sir.'

'Some more than others, Luther.'

'I don't buy that.'

'How odd of you. You're the key to Pepper's version of the puzzle now, Luther. You. And who knows, perhaps you always were. Pepper must know it was you who sent that terrorist group against him in Belfast by now. You who had his wife and child abducted, and left his father-in-law dead at the end of a false trail. Fieldwork is a matter of having better ground-intelligence than the other fellow, and you signally failed to do your homework on the situation in Belfast.'

'Damn you,' Cash whispered with a drying throat. 'Damn you . . .'

He spilled the last drawer onto the floor and something rolled against his shoe with a dull chink. He knew it was a cracked tumbler without looking. He needed that bottle. It was a full fifth of true salvation.

'Petulence, Luther? When all we have is Charlotte Stoller dead whilst the rest of the group remains active? If Pepper hadn't reacted in his own particular way, and you had gotten the true picture of how BelTech was being skimmed for IRA funds, perhaps the British Security Forces would have swept the whole lot of them into their bag. It is always a mistake to settle old scores during a long-range operation, Luther, and you are guilty of that, aren't you?'

'You wanted it settled as much as me. Maybe more so, you've got a whole lot more to lose. You must have made millions out of those deals I set up for you. Man, you had Qui Nohn Port sewn up, had every Slope and Korean working that dock in your pocket. You should have nailed Pepper and Taylor when you had them in Saigon.'

'Irrelevent, Luther, and impossible. There were extenuating circumstances you were not privy to. And I don't plan to air them to you, not now or ever.'

No scotch and I've pushed him too far, Cash thought. Sweating seriously in his darkened office. 'Throw me more than a bone, *sir.*'

'Just who was it brought you out of the tunnels, Luther? Gave you nine years of security wearing two hats? Who was that, Luther?'

'You, but . . .'

'Precisely, and no buts.'

What's the use?

'Yessir.'

'Pepper is your affair now. Find him and finish it, Luther. Take a drink and use your grey cells. If Pepper finds you first, offer him a deal, you have the leverage for that.'

I do?

The voice from Washington could have read Cash's mind.

'His family, Luther. His family.'

'Yeah . . . yessir.'

'Let him come to you, Luther. And don't call me until you've downed the helicopter somewhere it can be found . . . in time.'

Cash held the burring phone and his recorder switched itself off. He dropped the scrambler onto its cradle and sagged in his old leather swivel with heavy eyes. His office bottle came into the spill of his desklamp, and he looked past it into cold blue eyes and the wide bore of a Tunnel Gun. He thought about screaming, but he wanted a drink more.

Pepper lifted the phone to reactivate the tape.

'Talk to me, Luther.'

Cash opened the bottle with the gun against his chin and didn't give a damn for his chances.

Maycroft came to with carpet fluff in his nostrils and heard Sultan sneeze for him. His stomach ached from the gunbutt that winded him, and a small hard egg throbbed behind his right ear. He eased his wrists inside the handcuffs and realised he lay between Melvin and Sammy. One of the agents used the kitchen phone with his hat tilted back and his riot gun trained on Maycroft's spine. Blows and questions had been filtering through the living-room wall for some time, and Maycroft heard

Taylor groan as he slumped in the chair they had tied him to. It would be Maycroft's turn next, and he hoped he could handle another beating. Sammy groaned in his own twilight, and Melvin's swollen nose leaked into the nubbed carpet.

A door opened and heels dragged before Taylor was dropped to the floor.

'Hardass,' said the agent with scarred knuckles and acne. 'Why don't we lose these guys in some swamp? They ain't but dumb strings of offal, Torreo.'

Torreo reset his hat.

'Portland calls the shots on this one, Baer.'

'Hood? That turkey?'

'That turkey has the clout, Baer. The closest you'll ever get to the man upstairs.'

'You want I should soften up the Limey some? Talks like he pees champagne and shits diamonds. I could turn him into cut-glass and warm beer, no sweat.'

'Sure, but don't kick the dog.'

'Why in hell not?'

'I like dogs, dimwit. And that's one good old boy, ain't you, babe?'

Sultan sneezed and let himself be patted.

Baer jerked Maycroft's head up by the hair and blew a moody stream of cigar smoke against his bruised cheek.

'Are you in the wrong place at the wrong time, schluck? Never did cotton to a man who can't drink his beer with an honest "cheers". Comes out "chuz" with you Brits. *Chuz*, Jesus. Can't even talk your own language.'

'Listen to the Kid from Brooklyn,' said Torreo.

'What's wrong with Brooklyn, turkey?'

'Nothing. If you're in Oregon.'

'You got that right.'

Baer let Maycroft's face hit the floor with a snort of laughter.

The back door opened to admit a keen draught, and somebody said, 'Bring them out. We found a perfect ditch. Six feet deep and long enough for four.'

'What about the dog?' said Torreo.

'Sure the dog. Why is every hardass in the department soft

on furry critturs? For that, Torreo, you can make it quick and painless for him yourself, okay?'

'Santa Claus,' Torreo sneered, hauling Melvin upright. 'This one oughta been born twins.'

'You seen the size of this Moby Dick I got here? More blubber than a school of whales.'

Baer lifted Sammy as if he were filled with air and man-handled him to his feet. The back door was thrown wide, and Maycroft shuddered as the nightwind stole his bodywarmth. Melvin and Sammy were dragged outside by Torreo, Baer and two other men, and Maycroft stole a look at Taylor. His teeth had cut through his upper lip and his eyes were pink gleams of anger in ripe wine grapes.

'How you doing?' Taylor mumbled. 'Should have resisted, Limey. Not tried . . . *talking*. You worrying your head about our civilian Tweedle-Dums has done them no good at all . . . Damn, but that Baer can hit . . .'

Maycroft clamped chattering teeth.

'Who are they, Corny?'

'Are you naive or what? They're anything they wanna be. Feds, State, Central Intelligence, you name it. Labels don't mean squat. Flo knew that, and he was one of them after he got outta 'nam. Did two years before he started digging holes in his ridge. There are more private armies working out of Washington than Rotary Clubs have class wheels. J. Edgar Hoover was a reactionary old manic, but he kept his guys in suits and ties and had them toe the line. He invented commies for his clean-cuts to hunt. Wasn't having them get tainted or raped going after organised crime . . . These apes are a whole new breed. Establishment mafiosi. There ain't any white hats any more . . .'

Maycroft kept nausea at bay with a supreme effort of will. Men were crunching back up the path. Torreo came in to coax Sultan outside, and Maycroft was lifted onto rubbery legs with Baer's smoky breath gusting in his face.

'Let's go, Chuz.'

Taylor was jerked to his feet with a shotgun at his chest, and he caught an agent in the face with a gobbet of bloody phlegm. That earned him three solid body blows, and Maycroft lost sight of him when Baer took him out into cold starlight.

Cars had been drawn up in line to throw their headlights into a ditch where Melvin and Sammy had been dumped. Maycroft was tumbled in beside them, and Taylor rolled down after him in a patter of earth and pebbles. Maycroft got his back against the side of the ditch and pushed himself upright to face the row of shotguns. He counted eight men throwing shadows down at him, and the plump of shells in the breeches turned his stomach.

'Any last words, Chuz?' Baer asked from the sidelines.

Maycroft had forgotten his Shakespeare, and he wished he had saliva to spit. He thought of his estranged wife, the son who had just passed out from Sandhurst, and the daughter who drowned in their garden pond when he and Elaine had lived in Esher. All the foreign postings after the divorce, and living out of suitcases in hotels. The occasional sexual encounters that left him ridden with guilt for betraying the wife he barely remembered. There had been one Eurasian girl who could have become something special, but she . . .

The shotguns opened up in exploding hammers of wildfire and turned Maycroft's mind to mush. He had no idea if his eyes were open or closed. The glaring muzzle flashes had burned into his optic nerves and blinded him with colours he had never seen before. A second volley crashed out, and he could taste burned powder and wadding on his arid tongue as he tried not to vomit. He kept his legs under him as long as he could, but they let him down onto the cold earth in an easy slide. He was grateful there was no pain, and lay still, waiting for infinite darkness to claim him.

'Bring them up,' said Baer. 'Let's deliver these assholes to Portland.'

Maycroft came back to life with a reluctance that shocked him, and he was still coming to terms with himself when he was bundled into a helicopter. The cigarette Torreo gave him tasted wonderful, and he drew on it with Sultan licking his chin.

Cash gave detailed instructions to his field agents and put the phone down to say:

'Now we wait. Satisfied?'

Pepper didn't even shrug. His face was a weathered mask under his greased beard, and his eyes borrowed light from the desklamp to shine like slivers of polished crystal.

'We were real friends once, Matt.'

'We got along is all.'

'It was more than that, and you know it.'

'There's another inch in the bottle if you need it.'

Cash grinned sloppily.

'Dunno much about alcoholics, do you? One shot can last all day. Another time, two bottles ain't enough. Some days I clean my teeth and the mouthwash coasts me through to supper time. I've been drunk for a week on my own breath, and gone from crisis to crisis without bending my elbow. Then, for no reason; on the clearest morning with nothing in my appointment book but blank pages, I reach for that bottle because all that tranquillity scares the fluff out of my navel. Thunder storms don't phase me a bit, but those clear spring mornings do it every time. Think you can take me without that gun between us, Matt?'

'Yes.'

'Guess I believe you.'

Pepper said nothing.

Cash scratched a nail against the Famous Grouse label.

'You shoulda come in with us when I offered, Pepper san. Right now, at this precise moment in time, I can buy you and sell you and give you back to yourself with a profit in it for me. We could run down to the bank this minute and make you richer by two million dollars cash money. Any currency, any bank you name, any country you choose. Tempted?'

'Blood money.'

'Money's green, Matt. The colour of spring. Killing me gets you nothing. You can't bank satisfaction.'

Pepper leaned into the light and almost smiled.

'You talk millions, Luther. But you can't buy what you need, you self-deluded pathetic bastard. You're still in the man's pocket. Or in a six dollar bottle. You can see out of your cage, but you're locked in all the same. You're like some bad women

I've seen, things are more important than people. They'd rather grab off an alimony check than make the effort to keep a relationship going. Most of them fall into a bottle, pop pills, or get themselves took by some big-shouldered guy with his fingers in their pocket book. You make love to a bottle, you wake up with a dead soldier. Get close to another person, Luther, you wake up holding hands with a smile on your face. Try buying that for yourself, and maybe I'd listen. But you can't. Look into your heart, Luther, you'll find nobody home. Hell, you were born dead. Emotionally stillborn.'

'Jesus,' Cash had paled. 'If that's what the mountains do for you, give me the city.'

'You'd only see the real estate, not the people. I kill you it won't matter. I'll only be finishing off what you and nature have already decided.'

Cash showed a palm that shook. Held it out like a pink shield.

'Blowing my sorry ass to hell won't get your family back. I can help you, but first you have to swear you'll deal.'

Pepper's face grew lines.

'They're alive?'

'So long as I am.'

'Where?'

'Oh, sure. I tell you and kiss my sweet ass goodbye. Nossir. First you listen, then we deal, okay?'

Pepper sat back into the shadows and his mesmeric eyes irised down to pinpoints.

Cash fondled the bottle as he gathered his thoughts, and laced his fingers with an apologetic belch.

'Donna and the kid can be gotten back, but only if you work *with* us. It's tell-all time, but you ain't gonna like it worth squat. BelTech was always a covert CIA operation. The only way you and Taylor got finance through the City of London was because the Richmond seersuckers put the dough through intermediaries there. All legit, and planned to keep the Brits happy with an important defence contract. Also, and just as important as far as the Pentagon was concerned, it screwed the hell out of a similar French project we wanted stopped.

We flew the flag in Europe to keep our NATO allies quiet, but Uncle Sam already had Silicon Valley down that research-and-development road five years ago. We were way ahead of Nippon and the Russkies, but it had to seem like we weren't – the reason Richmond came up with BelTech as a cover. They put you and Taylor in there, played up the importance of what you were doing, and hoped you'd show lights in an empty store.'

Cash lit a Camel with one already burning.

'But you guys cut corners and *improved* on the Silicon Valley product. Made it faster, cheaper, and smaller, and with ten thousand more modes, was it? Who remembers? What *was* important was, you guys were out there in vulnerable-land with a world-beater, and you had to be closed down and fast. We had to get your protos and plant back here to Silicon Valley, put it into production, and make it seem like you guys had screwed up. How to do that was the problem, and my outfit was handed the headache. Hitting you with a terrorist group seemed the only way. Hell, we were gonna pull you guys out and give you a new life, but those bought-and-paid-for terrorists of Kolki's had other ideas. They pulled the old switcheroo on us.'

Pepper watched Cash try to make eye-contact through the glare of the desklamp. He stayed well back in the shadows, so Cash sighed and went on.

'Okay, so I got to even an old score with you and Taylor. I wanted that worse than the next drink. I figured you guys owed me, even if it was nine long years down the road. I admit that freely, but I didn't know the goddamned IRA was already playing piano on your till. That guy Collins was supposed to be on our payroll. We slicked him into NORAID to make contact with Kolki's group, Matt. Those bastards were tailor-made for that kind of operation. They made it look like you'd run with the protos, and we nailed them on natural turf. They handed us your protos, we lost them over the side of the getaway trawler we'd laid on for them, and you and Corny did a little time in a Brit gaol before we brought you back home on the QT. Job done. Except Kolki's group split the scene

100

their own way. They took Donna one way, your kid Max another, and figured to get your gizmos out yet another. Seems they were gonna sell them off to the French or the Libyans, but Collins screwed them over that, and you put paid to him.'

'I wanted Collins alive.'

Cash shrugged.

'Another crazy who died for a lost cause. No sleep lost there.'

'Yours or mine, Luther?'

'Anybody's. I owed you and Corny Taylor lumps, but I wanted you guys back on my team. Back where you belong. With good old Luther and . . .'

'And who, Luther?''

'Nobody. Just me.'

'Like you got Flo and Willy and Annie back on the team?'

Cash blanched.

'You have to understand about that, Matt . . .'

'Do I, Luther? Like I should understand about Ben Clayton and the Stoller woman dead with Bravo playing cards on their chests? Like that, Luther?'

'That's a whole other crock of garbage. Listen . . .'

'No more, Luther. It's still you and the man with two noses versus the rest. Always has been. I could fish for a year with the worms in your head.'

Cash found the courage to thrust his chin and a finger forward.

'You want your woman and boy back? In one piece with unbent minds? Or d'you wanna hear they died screaming because you were too dumb to deal?'

Pepper was a dark sphinx that might have sighed. The silver eye of the gun stared at Cash like a deadly cyclops.

'I'm listening.'

'You won't regret,' said Cash. 'Man, we were headless chickens when Kolki's group split every whichway. We couldn't bring the Brits in without making mile-high waves either. But we had the Stoller broad covered from the second she and Max boarded the LA flight from Heathrow. Two of our agents took the same flight. They couldn't get a shot in, and drugging her was no-no. She didn't touch airline food, and she had the boy draped in enough plastic to take out *three* 747s. There was a hand-detonator taped to her palm, so there was no way of taking her out without losing your son and five hundred other passengers. We knew her luggage had to be dirty, but there was every chance her detonator was linked to that too, so she had us coming and going right up to the Clayton place.'

Cash lit another Camel from a long stub.

'We plastered the house with long-range bugs sensitive enough to hear cobwebs grow, and picked up nothing but breathing and bathroom noises. When we heard her take old man Clayton down into the cellar we swarmed the place. Going in through the ground-floor was out, and I got in through an upper window in time to hear her blow the old guy away. I hit that cellar door and pulled the trigger on her myself, Matt. That's when the dog got scattered, and took off while I was looking for your kid. But Max wasn't there.'

Cash bit on a yawn and spilled ash.

'The closest I can figure is that one of Kolki's people was already in the house before the Stoller broad got there. Probably Than Nghu, he's their explosives expert. He must have wired the house and taken off with the kid, knowing that Stoller could change her appearance and lose herself in any direction she chose. Except I changed her appearance for her, the bitch.'

'As a favour to me?'

'What else would you call it?'

'Doctor Suess written by a moron,' Pepper said. 'I was wrong about you. You've got three things going for you: Booze, money, and hatred. I haven't thought about the Cholon Road but twice since it happened, and here you are eaten up by it. You wouldn't do me a favour, Luther. You wouldn't cross the road to spit on my grave.'

Something squirmed deep in Cash's inflamed eyes. Gone almost before it had formed.

'So use that Tunnel Gun, you straight-arrow asshole. Go ahead.'

Pepper slowly shook his head, thinking back.

'You'd gone missing that day, so me and Corny drove up to see that French lady who married one of Diem's cousins. Drank her champagne and swam in her pool, ate dinner on the terrace, and drove back after dark. That's a spooky road at night, and we drove with our weapons drawn. All those transporters parked up for the night and flares popping off all the time. We came around a bend – we were tooling along fast in case Charlie decided to bang off at us from the paddies – and ran into a couple of trucks slewed across the road. At first we thought Charlie had lobbed in mortars or mined the road, but then we saw a bunch of Vietnamese MPs whaling the daylights out of a civilian, and their buddies slammed a couple of warning rounds our way to keep us off. I guess we would have if that civilian had been one of their own, a Vietnamese. But he was as American as Texas, and he went under one of the trucks pulling at his sidearm when those QCs opened up on him with automatic fire. That got Corny mad. He knocked one of them on his keester with a body-shot, and I sent the rest of them into the ditch with a full clip. That's when I saw *you* in the headlights, Luther. In *back* of those MPs, yelling at them to waste the sonbitch. And us if we kept coming.

'Corny took out the headlights so that civilian could make it back to his car and take off. And we followed him, stepping on the gas with rounds whacking off all around us. The back of that jeep was a sieve, and we put it down to Charlie when we reported back. We knew you were into some heavy deals out there, Luther, but blowing away a security man was over the hill and gone. Me and Corny figured the three of us were due for a serious head-to-head after that last raid. Facing you off before we went into combat was a definite no-no in our book.'

'Yeah,' Cash sneered. 'The war came first. The war was everything for you guys. The war was a crock of shit, and I wasn't coming home with a bunch of dumb medals and stories nobody wanted to hear. I was coming home fat-cat rich, and I did. I wanted you guys with me, but you were Eagle Scouts With A Mission. Gung-ho bedbugs who thought they were achieving something when it was less than nothing. The

Slopes hate all foreigners, us most of all. Worse than the French *or* the Chinese. All I did was claw back some of the dough the US Treasury poured in there. Hell, I was selling ammunition to Israeli agents in Cambodia, because there was an embargo on them in the open market. That was the reality of Indochina, not you guys playing Spooks in the boondocks.'

'And now you're drowning in a bottle.'

Cash cracked his knuckles.

'And you want your wife and kid back. All comes full circle, Matt. You would have been ace trading with them Slopes down on Qui Nhon docks. You'd have had them Koreans suiciding to keep up with you, and they were the slickest.'

'There were a couple of Chinese who could have taken them. Even you had to launder your money through the Dao Heng Bank of Hong Kong.'

Cash's eyes glazed.

'You knew about that too, huh?'

'I knew about that. You made dirty money and thousands of wounded grunts lay forgotten in medical slums back home. That's *my* reality, Luther. You prospered, and they rotted.'

'I didn't make the war, pal. It took three presidents to do that. I took a profit is all. And you guys, what did you do? Left me in the tunnels is what. There never was gonna be any head-to-goddamned head. I died back then, so pull the trigger. I'll be the first guy in history who got himself killed twice by the same man.'

'And you'd *love* me to make that a clinical fact.'

'Whatever,' Cash's defiance was already crumbling.

'Whatever,' he said again, tasting a lost flavour.

'You should have talked to Flo instead of murdering him. We all got dumped in the tunnels. You. Me. Everybody. I got lucky and made it out. Who made your luck for you, Luther? The man who left you in the tunnels was the only man who could have gotten you out. Think about it.'

'Don't hand me that, Pepper. I already bought the Brooklyn Bridge.'

Pepper flicked his gun at the phone.

'Yeah, from him.'

104

Cash's laugh was a cold scream.

'I *should* have hit you in the head on the Cholon Road, you mother. Then you *couldn't* have left me for Charlie. Fourteen days they had me. Fourteen days and nights. No sleep, nothing but bad rice for food, and watching them blow one of my guys away every morning at seven sharp. They saved me for last 'cause I was a brownbar, and made me smear myself with their dung 'cause they liked to see me all shitted-up. I just grinned and ate bugs off the wall – drank my own urine to stay alive. Laughed when them Lucy Congs peed over my head and hung me in a room full of centipedes as thick around as your pecker, and as long as two erections. And coming in any time of the day or night to put a gun to my head, just to see me wince every time the hammer clicked on an empty chamber. I lived through that because of you. I *still* live through that because of you. So don't tell me about the good life with marriage and kids and holding hands. I can't even *think* of touching a woman without all those Lucys coming back to me. Every broad I look at grows slanted eyes and makes me wet my pants. Your doing, Pepper.'

Cash shied in his swivel when Pepper slapped him. Shock teared his eyes and he sobbed without shame. A red light showed on the scrambler console and Pepper opened the line to say 'Hood' into the mouthpiece.

'Baer,' said Baer. 'I've got two live ones here at the airport, Hood. Chuz and Hardass. They've got CD status like you wanted, and they take off for LA just as soon as you clear the flight. You sure you don't want them surveilled?'

'I'm sure, Baer.'

'Your privilege. We bounced the Washbourne boys some. Left them at the farm with the paramedics pumping them full of sleepy-juice. I hope the man in Washington buys that. But like I say, a democratic slap in the mouth makes anybody a good citizen, right? And they'll wake up in about seventy-two hours wondering if they dreamt it all.'

'That's what I'm counting on. Where's Torreo?'

'He dropped off at an all-night Seven-Eleven to get some dog-chow for the mutt. He'll be along directly. You want I should stand down once I've waved Chuz and Hardass bye-bye? I'd sell my ass for some sack-time.'

'Take a seven-day furlough, you and Torreo both. Now put the Limey on.'

'You got it, and thanks, Hood.'

Baer said something indistinct and Maycroft came on the line with a tired 'Yes?'

'Expect a package of tapes at your safe house on Foothills,' Pepper said, hearing Maycroft recognise his voice. 'The "answering service" here kept records, and they make interesting listening. They were his insurance, now they're mine. And yours. You get Corny away with you, that's the price.'

'Meaning the safe house is no longer safe, and you learned that from these same tapes?'

'In one, Maycroft. You've got maybe forty-eight hours to clear US airspace. Do it.'

'Very civil of you, Mr Hood. I'll comply, of course.'

'My pleasure.'

Pepper cut the connection, took the tape from the machine, and dropped it into his pocket with the others he had found in a rack behind the wall panelling. Cash stopped gaping and threw himself at Pepper with surprising strength.

'You're killing us both, you crazy animal. You, me, your wife, and your ki . . .'

Pepper chopped Cash's hysteria off with a jab to the throat.

'We've got company, Luther.'

He made Cash look at the gun. A car door slammed. Feet hurried across the parking lot and faded around the corner of the building.

Pepper smiled in a silence as hard as a mute's scream.

The small hours had turned Portland into an abandoned morgue. Marbles of sleet bounced in the streets and razors of wind cut with cold precision. Torreo parked the limousine and took Sultan up to Hood's office by the back stairs. He had been on duty for thirty-six hours and he was close to dropping. Taking a real shine to the dog had been the only highlight of Torreo's day, and he hoped Hood's executive

106

kitchenette boasted a can-opener for the gourmet Mr Dog he had bought on 'special'. Torreo was past eating himself, and couldn't for the life of him see why Hood dragged him into the office when his motel was on the other side of town. Ten straight hours of mattress time was what he needed, not indulging some lush with clout in the department.

But then, working for the clandestine Executive Bureau had never made much sense to Torreo since he had been seconded to it. No written orders were ever issued, debriefs were by telephone, and Torreo had used so many aliases during his six-month tour he wrote the current one on his shirt cuff. Torreo preferred foreign service where he could goof-off to fish the Aegean from a boat with painted eyes, or picnic in the ruins of Ostia Antica with a willing Italian girl. To his mind, home postings were the pits of perdition, and Oregon was just a lot of scenery peopled by rednecks.

Torreo allowed Sultan to pull him up the last flight by his makeshift lead, and held the soggy paper sack together with a one-armed juggle when Sultan rushed him along the landing to scratch at Hood's office door with frantic paws.

'Smell somebody you know, babe?' Torreo asked, the significance of his question lost in numbing exhaustion.

The door was snatched open and Torreo glimpsed blue eyes coming at him before he reacted. His draw would have been fluid when he lost the cans if Sultan hadn't jerked him off balance. A handchop drove Torreo to his knees and his neck caught fire. His half-drawn Diamondback was taken, and Torreo saw Sultan clear the desk to sink his teeth into Hood's shirtfront. Dog, man and swivel went over in a thrash of limbs, and Hood squealed like a goosed secretary.

The blue eyes seemed to drive Torreo to the floor, and he lay there, knowing he was paralysed. For some reason he remembered what Maycroft had said when Baer tied him into the chair, grey hair plastered to his forehead and ice in his grey eyes. 'Hit away, Mr Baer,' he'd said with a mocking laugh. 'We're trapped in a playground of psychotic delinquents where push earns pull, kick earns bite, and escalates until violence becomes an end in itself. We're all on the bottom rung of this particular ladder-game, and you people don't even know the ground-rules. This is just another dead-end in another man's game, and none of you has a map of the labyrinth. Only one man has that, and he's in Washington.' Then Baer had knocked Maycroft insensible and asked Torreo what the hell 'Chuz' was talking about. Torreo hadn't known, but he was disquieted all the same.

Torreo found his voice as Pepper called Sultan off and Hood leaned himself against the window wall to whimper over his bites.

'And I thought that dog . . . was a pussy-cat.'

'He was . . . until Hood there killed his owner in cold blood.'

Torreo fought to stay conscious as Pepper stepped across him to gather Hood by the shirtfront.

'Than Nghu wasn't at the Clayton place, Luther. You were. You killed Ben and the Stoller woman, and let Sultan crawl off into the woods to die. You rigged the house with plastic and marked the bodies with Bravo playing cards for me to find. And you even had a Plan B ready just in case I didn't blow myself and the evidence away. You knew I'd go looking for Flo Cordova – make him show me the way to you and the man with two noses, and you figured to nail us both on the Snake. And if that failed, you had my son to bargain with. But who's got Donna, Luther? This Kolki character, or the man with two noses? The truth or the dog, Luther. Your choice.'

Cash moaned and tried not to touch his bitten chest.

'It's the same thing, for chrissake. Kolki *works* for the man with two noses. I swear I didn't know. Not until yesterday. And only because I intercepted Maycroft's last report to the British Embassy. It was plain-language, so I figured he wanted me to know. And not for my good health either. How long d'you think I'd draw breath if the man in Washington even *thought* I knew that? Ten short seconds, that's all.'

Pepper hissed through his teeth and let Cash slide onto his side. Cash sighed and said:

'You gotta get *him* and Kolki both, Matt. It's them or us now.'

'Us, Luther? Us? I'll give you a head start for the money

you offered me, after that I'll be at the end of every dark alley
you start down. And that's more than you deserve.'

'It's a deal,' said Cash. 'Thanks, Matt . . .'

Torreo took that with him into a spinning vortex with no
bottom, and it was still with him when he came back to find
he and the dog had the daylit office to themselves.

It was mid-afternoon. Torreo fought gravity as though it were
pre-set concrete, and nothing jointed the right way when he
stood himself up. He made the pink bananas that used to be
his fingers punch out the unlisted Washington number, and got
it to answer after the third attempt. Talking jangled Torreo's
inner ear and his voice was as frail as an octogenarian's bones
as he reported what had passed between Hood and Pepper.
The response was simple and chilling.

'Take executive action, Torreo. Publicly, and with extreme
prejudice.'

'Both of them?'

'Yes. Today. Most Immediate. Clear?'

It was clear. Torreo found his Diamondback on Hood's blotter and checked its load before feeding it into his shoulder
holster. He had two Thompsons in the car, and a sawn-off
Ithaca clipped under the dash. He woke Baer from a deep
sleep and gave him fifteen minutes to be ready to move. He
knew where the two men would be, and that was more than
enough edge. He fed Sultan some breakfast and coughed
himself awake with his first cigarette of the day. It tasted as
foul as his mood.

Pepper had trimmed his beard and wore one of Cash's suits.

Four hours sleep and a long scrubbing shower had taken
ten years out of his face, and he fed Cash a generous scotch
straightener before they kept their appointment at the Bank
of Nova Scotia. Pepper parked close to the entrance, and Cash
leaned heavily when he was walked into the Investment
Director's office.

Pepper shook hands with a plump silver man, sat Cash in
a chair facing a pristine desk, and explained his friend's frailty

109

as a 'hunting accident'. Herbert L. Poon told Pepper to call him 'Herbie', and had Cash sign a sheaf of withdrawal certificates as he talked about his own mishap with a twenty-pound pike up on the Canadian lakes the previous fall. He had lost his footing in the shallows and gotten tangled in his own line when the big fish drew him into deep water. About half-drowned, and colder than charity, Herbie slashed through the nylon with his fillet knife, floundered ashore a hundred yards down river, and clung to rocks until luck brought a game warden his way just before dusk. Now he wore a corset for his 'sprung' back, and had traded his fishing poles for a camera.

Cash left Pepper to nod at Poon's dreary catalogue of the nephews, nieces and grandchildren he had 'portraited', and sank into morbid reflection. Pepper had used the savage dog to milk him dry, and knew more than enough to sink the department; Cash included, if he went public. Cash knew he needed to put a mess of geography between himself and Pepper, and crossing into Canada by road made good sense.

His Porsche was too showy, even with false plates, so he meant to use the old Chevrolet he kept garaged by the bus station. The modified V-8 engine could cruise at 120mph and lose any mobiles sent in pursuit. He doubted the department would risk an APB through the State Police or the Highway Patrol, but it would cover the airport and all roads south. Fleeing north, he could go to ground in Vancouver or fly to Europe from Montreal. Once he got to Portugal, Cash could buy all the political protection he needed, and Pepper would create the perfect diversion. Cash only had to drop a dime on Washington, tell them Pepper knew where to find Kolki, and take off through Canada whilst the whole department swarmed Boston.

It would work. Damn it, he would make it work.

Cash felt more confident, and went through the motions of checking the two cases of used bills the vault guard brought to Poon's office. He was impatient to be outside. To breathe air that smelled of pine and snow, and hadn't been deodorised or convected through fans and ducts. The Algarve would smell of North Africa when the sirocco blew desert sands from Tangier across the Gulf of Cadiz. Goat bells would clank in the olive groves around his estate near Lagos, Cash would sip his sundowners as the sun drowned itself in the sea beyond Cape St Vincent; drink arak from an earthenware pitcher, and eat the octopus his housekeeper marinated in wine. The Lucy Congs never followed him there, and he could sleep dreamlessly without screaming awake to reach for a bottle.

Cash shrugged off Pepper's arm and took one of the cases out of Poon's office. He would make it alone, he decided. The lobby carpet was almost too springy to walk on, and the muted counter-talk was too loud for his sensitive hearing. Pepper could drop him at the garage and do what the hell he liked with the Porsche. Every agent in Portland knew it by sight, and Pepper could be picked up driving it. Wouldn't that be a thing? Cash thought. Pepper caught for a chicken-shit grand-theft-auto like some teenage dropout? His laugh became a cough that racked his bitten chest, and he knew he couldn't push through the revolving door unaided.

A guard started the door turning for him, and Cash let a woman coming in do the rest. He swayed in the cold and hypervented the stale air from his lungs. Pepper came out with the second case and got a hand to Cash's elbow before he overbalanced, turning him towards the Porsche.

Cash shivered and wished he was back in the warm as a fresh fall of sleet bounced around him. An Indian in a yellow mackinaw leaned on his broom to sneer up at the sky, and two women hung with shopping bags scurried for their Toyota. A black limousine came up the entrance ramp at speed and slewed across the exit with its doors opening. Baer's bulk identified him immediately, and Torreo threw himself from behind the wheel with the speed of a tired cat.

Cash wanted to melt into the ground, and keened in his throat like tyres on hot asphalt. He felt Pepper leave his side, and he backed into the Porsche feeling for the handle, his case held across his chest. Fear slowed anything down and Cash spacewalked through glue.

He saw the sawn-off come out of the skirt of Torreo's

raincoat to blow the rear windscreen into glitter-dust. The money-case punched into Cash's chest, and his exposed hand stung from sharp insect bites as it threw itself away from him. Pepper had gone over the hood of the Porsche like a tumbler, and reached through the driver's door for his Tunnel Gun. Exploding glass scattered with the sleet as Baer pumped his Thompson, and the Porsche rocked with the recoil.

Cash was skidded away on his back and wondered why most of his money fluttered in the air above him. Then he saw what had happened to his thighs and crotch, and tried to cover them with hands that spurted blood. Sudden agony killed his shame, and he lay full length to scream long and loudly with sleet pecking at his tongue.

Baer fired around the open limousine door, and Cash was swept with shot as a Porsche tyre collapsed around its hub. The Tunnel Gun snapped twice, threw sparks up around Baer's galoshes, and the multiple ricochets took his legs out from under him. His blotchy face hit the ground and a third shot blew most of his jaw away.

Torreo came forward pumping flame from the hip, ripping trim and shreds of upholstery from the Porsche. If Pepper fired back, Cash never heard the shot. Torreo simply slammed into nothing, pirouetted on tiptoe, looked haggard, and sat down on a leg that folded under him. He shrugged when Pepper kicked the sawn-off away, and muttered something too low for Cash to catch.

Pepper nodded and let Torreo fall on his side. He walked over to the limousine and threw his case onto the passenger seat before kicking the door closed. Baer crawled for the snowy verge in search of somewhere soft to rest, and Pepper narrowly missed him when he took the limousine out into the traffic. The Indian still leaned on his broom and the women clutched their bags by the Toyota.

The last thing Cash heard was a siren that would arrive too late for any of them. The spinning sky darkened as his eyes failed, and Cash was reaching for a long drink when his brain died.

Pepper booked Sultan into the Dogz-N-Katz Hotel for three

months. Posted a phoney parcel of tapes to Maycroft, and dumped Torreo's limousine at the bus station. When he had shaved off his beard in the restroom he took his bags to Cash's garage and drove the old Chevrolet to a Klamath motel where he rested up with a hooker he sent out for his meals.

All the Washington airports were socked in, and Pennsylvania Avenue was a silent traffic jam beyond the triple-glazed windows of the darkened office on the fourteenth floor of the Revenue Building.

The man occupying the office tapped his teeth with a gold pen and leaned into the glow of the TV commercials fronting a newsflash from Portland, Oregon. He had grizzled hair and the square face of a successful banker, and might have been handsome but for the rare birth defect that had malformed his nose. Where the fibro-cartilage should have formed a single bridge, it forked out and down from his nasal bone to form a deep cleft that separated his nostrils. All offers of corrective surgery had been refused by his fanatically religious parents, and by the time he had reached his majority and could have acted on his own behalf, he had learned to profit from the effect his appearance had on others.

Known as the 'Ugly Mandarin' by faculty and students alike during his college years, his natural reserve and clinical objectivity made him a brilliant loner. A perfect recruit from the Analysis Section of the CIA after his graduation with the highest honours. His rise in the service had been meteoric, and his promotion to Feasibility Analysis Officer at the age of twenty-eight made him the youngest to have held that rank during or since the Kennedy administration. His negative report on the proposals to invade Cuba and to assassinate Castro was a still, small voice neither Langley or the Oval Office advisers had wished to hear, for it was diametrically opposed to the current thinking.

Banished to Vietnam with the last of the 'military advisers' he was thought to have been safely neutralised by his estranged superiors, and his unwelcome reports were shredded the moment they arrived in Langley. Incensed, he made himself invaluable to the Diem regime, and continued to compile reports on mismanagement and corruption to reinforce his position.

As the American presence in South Vietnam escalated, so did the scale of corruption, and his outrage became a simmering hatred of both systems. From then on he gathered wealth with the same zeal he had expended on gleaning intelligence, and by the time Nixon had replaced Johnson in the White House he was beyond the control of the discredited hierarchy in Langley.

The last commercial faded and he turned up the volume.

The TV threw up a bright blue logo and the anchor-man talked over shots of a bank forecourt where bodies lay under black shrouds and yellow police tapes formed a cordon around a ruined Porsche. Two women gave conflicting views of what they had seen, and an Indian mumbled about gunplay before a TV reporter interviewed a local homicide lieutenant called Crosby.

Crosby identified one of the deceased as FBI Agent Walter Hood. A fine officer who had died assisting a John Doe citizen during an attempted armed robbery. That citizen had not yet come forward to assist the police in their enquiries. The unarmed perpetrators had both died during the shooting. And yes, it was the same Agent Walter Hood who had taken charge of the Snake River operation of the previous day. And no, the two incidents were quite unconnected. The anchor-man promised a fuller report during the regular evening news broadcast, and melted into a trailer for a popular sit-com.

The man with two noses killed the transmission and built his long fingers into a steeple under his chin, more than satisfied with the way his plans progressed.

Cash was an unmourned memory, Baer was no great loss to anyone, and Torreo would survive surgery to become useful now that the media had conveniently pronounced him dead. However, Maycroft and Taylor reaching the northern outskirts of Los Angeles had *not* been foreseen. Another reason for him to admire, however grudgingly, Pepper's ability to extemporise in the field, except that he had unwittingly put Taylor and Maycroft within reach of three of Kolki's men who were at a safe house in Watts. Activating them by telephone had been simplicity itself. The tapes Pepper posted to Maycroft had been intercepted, and a dummy parcel sent in its place. The thirty-six hours it would take for the dummy to reach Maycroft should be more than enough time for Tibbs, Rourke and Nghu to take executive action. And since Cash would have given Pepper Kolki's address in Boston, there would be no interference from that quarter. The man with two noses could turn his attention to more important issues.

Those tiresome tapes of Cash's might have provoked a Senate Committee of Enquiry had they reached the right quarter, and could have resulted in a public hearing before a Grand Jury with the attendant media circus; an expensive exercise in futility that had narrowly been avoided by prudent pre-emption. It was time for him to leave Washington anyway, for he had long ago tired of holding office there. And where he was going none could follow.

Except Pepper perhaps.

The man in the darkened office thought about that as he used an atomiser to clear mucus from his tender nostrils. Long hours in air-conditioning gave him sinusitis or nauseous migraines. Clear desert air kept the condition under control, and it would not be long before he would enjoy such an environment permanently.

He smiled at the thought and decided Pepper was no danger to him. If Pepper survived and kept coming, then keeping him at bay would be sport enough to keep him from becoming jaded in retirement.

He keyed his console to transmit his master tapes to his mainframe in Colorado and set them for automatic wipe when the transmission was complete. He cleared his desk of medication and personal items and took his private elevator to the basement car-park. Driving himself was a novelty he enjoyed, and he hummed as he pointed his classic Thunderbird towards the Anacosta Freeway.

The hooker returned from sending a parcel to Maycroft in LA to find Pepper gone and a thousand dollar bill pinned to the

115

pillow. For a guy who hadn't touched her she thought him generous. She and her pimp shot up with the best skag money could buy and forgot all about him.

Pepper reached San Francisco in time to take the evening shuttle to LAX, and lost himself in the late traffic on Olympic Boulevard.

CHAPTER SEVEN

The black panel truck turned off Foothills Boulevard at La Crescenta and parked in the tom-cat smell of eucalyptus trees on Franklin. The coolness was refreshing after the smog of the valley, and the night was clear enough to show stars. Deer down from the parched hills in search of water drank from a swimming pool, and a coyote raiding trashcans in the properties below Angeles Forest ignored the bay of a nervous guard dog. Music and charcoal-braised chicken drifted from a barbecue down the street, and latecomers bringing more beer slammed car doors with cheerful indifference. A deputy from the nearby police station swung into Franklin from Vista to check licence plates, and turned back onto the boulevard without stopping.

Jackson Tibbs lay along the seat of the panel truck until he was sure the deputy would not return, then went back to watching the house in the hollow beyond the eucalyptus trees. A big dun buck jumped the fence, and his does followed gracefully, their eyes dark and watchful as they crossed the road to lose themselves in the darkness of a storm culvert cutting down from the hills.

'Now weren't that a pretty thing?'

Tibbs earned a nod from Danny Rourke crouching in the back of the truck with the Uzzi machine-pistols.

'Never saw them outside a zoo before. What's happening at the house?'

'What should be happening? There's some sort of burglar alarm, and I figure they got the lights rigged to turn themselves on and off as if there was somebody home. No garbage in the trash cans, and that lawn ain't had a haircut in weeks. There're three phone lines running into that house, but there's no listing for that address. And that TV antennae and satellite-dish ain't for just hamming the airways. Looks to me they could talk to Mars on that thing.'

Tibbs licked his thick lower lip and fed himself a stick of Juicy Fruit. He was always tense before a hit, and wished he had Than Nghu to back him instead of the vitriolic Irishman. Rourke had the balls of an elephant, but he was a shootist first and a thinker second, and cruised the bars for girly action when he should be keeping his head straight.

Than Nghu had this small white bowl he stared into when he sought detachment, and Tibbs was sure Than's enhanced senses enabled him to hear the grass grow after an hour of meditation. Rourke just kept his guns clean and burned off excess adrenalin by sneaking something soft from a bar stool. No white bowls for Danny Rourke. A bottle of malt and a broad in heat was his bag.

Tibbs rolled his meaty shoulders and repeated his personal mantra inside his head. He liked women as much as the next man, but there was no way he was as pussy-whipped as Rourke. Danny seemed to be working off some deep-seated repression that had its root in his childhood, and Tibbs guessed the Catholic girls back in Dublin hadn't put it about like the quail he'd grown up with in Philadelphia. Philly girls with their cherries intact after fourteen had to have been hit with an ugly stick or be training for a nunnery. There may not have been enough chitlings, corn bread and okra to keep his belly from sticking to his spine, but a young stud with a ready smile could get himself jumped any night of the week.

'As natural as breathing,' Tibbs said aloud.

'What was that?' asked Rourke. 'You see something?'

'Just a lot of house and a sick yard,' said Tibbs, not yet ready to make a move. 'Easy there, greasy, you gotta long way to slide.'

'Sure and very ethnic,' Rourke sneered. 'I could grow a beard from all this waiting on yourself. If they're in there, let's for mercy's sake take them. If not, let's be waiting for them inside when they come back.'

'Hold ass, blood.'

Tibbs used a starscope to scan the house and yard, thinking that Than Nghu was different again. When he took a woman it was like he played chess. Every move was calculated, every response gauged, a cerebral ballet of juxtapositions where release was a silent shudder of gritted teeth until control came back and his mind blanked his face to an impassive monkey mask. One time in a Hamburg cathouse, Than had taken four women that way, then gone off with two more to make it under the stars on a rug with the temperature below freezing. And when he came back he wasn't even goosebumped. Then he asked for a boy, and broke up the bar when they couldn't get him one he liked. Hospitalisation for the kraut bouncers he took apart had cost a lot of bucks, and Danny Rourke had walked softly around Than after that. Even Kolki was polite to Than, and forgot to talk like a B-movie when he gave the Japanese orders. But then, something had gone out of Felix when Charlotte got herself blown away up there in Oregon, and Tibbs had never got it straight in his mind just how it had happened. It was a big question-mark, and he planned to get the truth of it out of Kolki when they all met up in Italy after this hit.

Tibbs changed the starscope for an infrared sight to locate body-heat images. Nothing registered in the yard or through the draped windows. The chimney stack was cold and only the merest trace of warmth from the central heating pipes showed as a black fuzz in the walls. Tibbs wadded the gum in his cheek and reached back for his Uzzi. Rourke slapped it into his palm with a grin and pulled his skimask down, his green eyes bright with malice. Killing the Englishman would be his pleasure, and he liked seeing the big Negro wrong-footed.

Tibbs was a meticulous planner. He liked to know where the cat slept and how long the target spent in the bathroom, but this contract had come up too fast for all that cerebral pencil-chewing, and suited Rourke where it disquieted Tibbs. Jackson Tibbs might have a lot of grey matter, but he didn't have Rourke's street-wise brand of opportunism, and the Irishman secretly despised him for it.

Danny Rourke had killed his first policeman at sixteen. He

had pulled a magnum from his sister's pram, squeezed the trigger six times, and turned the corner before the body hit the pavement. Gone before a crowd gathered. The baby had slept through the whole thing, and Danny's mother had cried when she burned the blood-spattered counterpane in the kitchen copper. But there was an extra chop on his plate for tea, and she'd kissed him goodnight for the first time in years. His father gave him his first taste of Irish as they watched the ten o'clock news, and the provos had spirited Danny away just minutes before an army patrol kicked in the front door. Three days later, Danny landed in Libya, and was shunted from one hotel room to another before they decided what to do with him.

Danny came up against sexual deviance for the first time in his life at a desert training camp a hundred miles south of Tripoli. The two Moroccans who raped him left him face down with a broken leg and concussion, and it took Danny the best part of two months to heal and catch them asleep. He sprayed them with a stolen Kalashnikov, spent six-weeks in a dugout cell that had once been a tomb, and might have died there if Felix Kolki hadn't bought his release.

Kolki flew him to Algiers for training with the PLO and a mixed foreign detachment from Germany, Japan and America. Danny slept through the indoctrination courses and shone at weapons training. He became the fifth member of Kolki's team when Charlotte Stoller's brother Christiaan was killed in Egypt by a Mossad hit squad headed by a woman known as 'The Black Rose'. Kolki's team tracked her to Sweden, and it was Danny who drowned her in a Stockholm hotel bath, and ransacked the room to make it look like a burglary that had gone wrong. Unfortunately for him, this enabled Mossad to claim the woman was an innocent tourist murdered by Libyan terrorists. This provoked Radio Tripoli into denouncing the hit as 'the work of political jackals in the pay of Israel', and as a 'crude attempt to blacken the name of Colonel Moammer Gaddafi, The Sword of God'; and the Purity Section of *Mukhabarat* ordered Kolki to 'cleanse his house of callow foxes' like Rourke. Their meaning was clear, the Irish 'deviationist' was to be liquidated immediately. Bowing to his own fury and pressure from Charlotte Stoller, Kolki flew his team to Italy, and negotiated all future operations for the Libyans through Syrian intermediaries.

Danny never forgot that act of loyalty, and suffered working with Tibbs and Than Nghu because of it. He had never taken to the Stoller woman, but he saw the light go out of Kolki's face when she died, and was touched by his grief. After this hit Rourke could say goodbye to the chocolate drop and the yellow monkey, go back to enjoying Italian girls with chests like the hills of Pompeii, ski with Felix, and spoil his mother with shipments of the Italian china figurines she liked so much. Being locked up with Tibbs and Nghu in that box of a house in Watts had gone on for too damned long, and he was ready to beat his buns out of California. Frank Sinatra scoobedood the closing bars of *Strangers in the Night*, and the smell of chicken made him hungry. He set his Uzzi to automatic fire and waited for Tibbs to nod.

The black man wiped sweat from his nose and winked.

'Bring your lucky shamrock, gobeen,' he said.

'And you say your mantra, blood.'

Rourke followed Tibbs down the drive and went over the fence without a sound, feeling completely alive for the first time in weeks. I was born for this, he thought, picking his way through ground ivy to the concrete walkway around the house.

Born for it.

Pepper drove with open windows to enjoy the lazy heat following him out of the San Fernando Valley. The rented Plymouth gave him a smooth ride through Burbank and he found the turn-off to La Crescenta first time. He parked on Foothills and ordered ribs at a Hungry Jack's on the north side of the boulevard. The sugar-cured meat was too sweet for his palate, and the tangy sauce tasted as phoney as liquorice ice cream. He pushed it away and fed himself club soda and bread rolls from the supermarket next door as he strolled up into Vista Court.

The dirt yard of the corner bungalow backed onto Maycroft's

safe house, and there was a locked wooden gate in the stone wall dividing the properties. Pepper prowled the length of the wall and climbed over where it keyed into a blind gable wall. He dropped into the sharp smell of lemon trees and crouched to let the surroundings come to him.

Muted conversation buzzed from the barbecue and coloured lights winked through a stand of cottonwoods. A coyote yipped in the hills and an electric guitar led violins into the sentimental ballad Donna played when she was in one of her private melancholic moods. The song floated her out of the darkness and her face hovered close to him. The huge eyes willed him to find her, and the soft mouth pouted in fun, teasing him. The lemons were for the rainbow trout she grilled the night she said yes to marriage and brought him into her sleeping bag for the first time. Pepper got the shakes as the fire streamed sparks up at the moon, the fish untouched on his plate, his hands all thumbs on the champagne he'd chilled in the river. Donna had popped the cork and held his face in her hands to make him look at her when she said:

'Yes is yes to everything, Pepper san. You're not the only one whose head's coming to a point from the need for kissy-mouth-touchy-body. Two boys have kissed me in my long and celibate life, and one got his hand to my knee before I slapped him down. His name was Clarence Milbeck. He had zits all over his chin, and hands as clammy as a dog's nose. He tore up my corsage, called me a dirty name, and drove home to his mother in tears. I laughed when I wanted to cry. He tore my flowers as if they were my virginity. Made me feel soiled, and I must have washed my hands a thousand times before I went to bed. Now you're here, you've had lots of girls, and you know everything I don't. I'm a blank page, and I want you to write on me. So make it good for me, Matthew. Make it good for both of us. Not some silly fumble in the back of your daddy's Buick with both of us turning into pumpkins from nerves. Don't make me laugh, and don't tear up my corsage, okay?'

'Okay,' Pepper whispered aloud in Maycroft's yard, lemon leaves brushing his face like Donna's hair once had. He crouched there when she left him, and long minutes passed before the night sounds came back. He heard a screen door open on the far side of the house and smelled Juicy Fruit on somebody's breath, the tang of Negro musk and the witch-hazel deodorant he had last smelled in his house in Belfast. He didn't need to see their faces to know who they were.

Tibbs neutralised the door alarm, sprang the double-lock with an upward twist of his adaptable key, and got his back against a washer-dryer in the unlit laundry room. Rourke went through a sliding door in a crouch and forward-rolled into the kitchen-diner. The coffee pot on the burner was still warm to the touch and there were cigar stubs in the ashtray next to the electric hob. Dishes drained on the sink and an electric clock ticked on a wall covered with the kind of paintings tourists paid too many pesos for in Tijuana. Tibbs covered Rourke as he went down the passage to check the bedrooms. A couple of the beds had been sloppily made and there were two sets of shaving tackle in the bathroom. Passports and TWA tickets lay on a sideboard with travellers checks, Henry Winterman cigarillos, and a can of gun oil. Rourke pointed them out without touching anything, and covered Tibbs as he took the lead back to the main lounge. They listened at the door for a count of twenty. Tibbs nodded, Rourke opened the door and Tibbs jumped through.

The room was long and had a fireplace. The walls were hessian and golden wood, and the furniture was low and worn and comfortable. A TV flickered in the far corner without sound and badly adjusted colour, and threw pastel shades out at the two men lounging in armchairs either side of a drinks table loaded with bottles.

Tibbs threw out a hand, too late to stop Rourke firing two short bursts.

The nearest figure sat up straight and folded forward to stab the carpet with stiff fingers, and the second man's head came apart like a broken vase. A toupee skimmed away like a soft frisbee and hung itself over a lampshade. The headless torso slumped sideways to leak sawdust onto the tufted carpet and kick a shoe against the skirting.

'Dummies, you dummy,' yelled Tibbs, backing away.

Rourke kicked the chairs over and had the gall to laugh.

'Sure they are, blood. Your infra-red would have blipped them if they'd been real, right? Now where are you going, you gutless . . . ?'

Tibbs sprinted for the open door thinking of sonic explosives actuated by sound. A stun-grenade blew the TV apart and pitched Tibbs into the heavy chairs around a Mexican dining table. Concussion blew him down a dark street in Philadelphia and he lay on the sidewalk wondering why all the jazz cellars were closed. Then he just lay there and thought nothing at all.

Rourke had time to open his mouth and close his eyes before he was hurled off his feet in a perfect swallow-dive. He tore through the window drapes and took most of the picture window glass with him into the yard. He skidded on cement, smashed a garden seat against a low stone wall, and was flipped into a thick bower of flowering shrubs to hang upside down. One of his ears bled and he had lost a lot of skin. His eyebrows and skimask were gone and his hair stank and smoked. A maverick nerve tightened his trigger finger, and he shot humming-bird feeders and hanging flower baskets from the eaves. A single ricochet whanged off into the night and Rourke fell out of the bower onto his head.

The night revolved in sixteen different directions and glared red when he couldn't take air into his impacted chest. The Uzzi fell somewhere and his head was a bloated gourd between his thighs. Moving was something other people did, so he stayed where he was.

The hell with it.

Maycroft wallowed in the jacussi with a blonde divorcee who had three husbands and numberless Universal screen tests to her credit. Taylor ate chicken with the host and his wife, and two young men in lavender held hands by the pool. A Mexican manned the barbecue pit and his sister circulated with a tray of drinks. A life-guard from Long Beach talked real-estate with some girls from La Canada, several couples smootched near the sound-system, whilst the downtown detectives assigned to Maycroft looked bored as they ate canapes with hands like shovels.

The divorcee thought herself perfect for 'aunt-type' roles in daytime soaps, appreciated Maycroft for being a 'maturer-type' man with a 'cute' accent, and nuzzled her Tom Collins like a lover's neck. Maycroft smiled at her between glances at his wristwatch and sips of gin drowned in lime.

The party had started in the late afternoon with guests coming and going like restless macaws. Maycroft had taken refuge in the hot tub after the umpteenth handshake. The blonde really was rather good to look at, however squiffed she may be. She was as brown as a raisin and her smile was genuine.

'And your acquaintances really do call you Chuz?' she asked.

'Invariably.'

'Even at school?'

'There I was Maycroft minor. My elder brother was Maycroft major.'

The blonde nodded into her drink.

'One of those military academy type-places, huh?'

'Something like that.'

'I just bet a gentleman like you knows your Queen Elizabeth.'

'Only from a distance. I've more chance of meeting *them* over here.'

The blonde laughed and said, 'Wicked, wicked, wicked. My second-ex went gay on our third anniversary. Announced it like he'd changed his brand of aftershave, and went off with most of my wardrobe. I heard he was stripping in Frisco, calling himself-herself Milady Sadie. Can you believe it? A marine biologist taking his jockey shorts off for guys? And he stuck me with tanks and tanks of arthropods, cephalopods and coelenterates, until I declared my own independence and dumped them all back in the ocean. My blow for ecology, may they take over the whole Pacific. I should have known he was a faggot when he got into hermaphroditism in molluscs, but you don't, do you?'

'Not readily,' Maycroft said with feeling.

The blonde scooped a fresh drink from a passing tray and asked Maycroft if he smoked.

'Cigars.'

'No honey, grass. Mexican Gold.'

'Not since . . . well, a long time ago. It made me sleepy, and people giggling at their own thumbnails isn't my idea of fun.'

The blonde grinned.

'I turn on, honey. You know, like amorous?'

'Ah,' said Maycroft.

'Find us some, Chuz, and we'll start a big secret in the shrubbery.'

'I'm wearing shorts. No pockets. Sorry.'

'Go ask Harry, he's a terrific host. I'd ball him good if I didn't like Carrie so much. Harry and Carrie, Harry Carrie. Sounds like something those crazy Japanese do, huh?'

'Doesn't it though?'

'You talk funny-nice, you know?'

Maycroft said he guessed he must and looked for an excuse to leave the jacussi. His watch just told the time and Taylor had his back turned. The blonde closed in to sample Maycroft's drink with her breasts pressed against his forearm.

'You're not so scrawny close up,' she said. 'But that drink rates a baby zilch on a scale of ten. Are you into guys, Chuz?'

'Only as bridge partners.'

The blonde turned tearful and solemn.

'You keep it that way, Chuz old sport. That *is* what you Brits say? Old sport?'

'Not since the advent of the mini-skirt. Now we're rather into "chum" and "buddy".' Maycroft's watch showed a red light and beeped softly. He asked to be excused, shrugged into his towelling robe and whistled to Taylor.

'You'll come on back, Chuzzy?' the blonde called.

'At the gallop, m'dear.'

'They in the house?' asked Taylor.

'As of fifteen seconds ago,' Maycroft made for the utility room and his clothes with Taylor pacing him.

'You going back to the blonde barracuda, Chuzzy?'

Maycroft pulled on his trousers.

'A woman,' he said, quoting Kipling, 'is only a woman, but a good cigar is a smoke. Now where's my bloody Ruger?'

126

'Under your towel, you grouch.'

An explosion slammed into the trees, bobbed the lights on their wires, and brawled off into the hills to set the neighborhood dogs barking. The young men in lavender shrieked as they fell into the pool, and the dancing stopped as the stylus jumped from the turntable.

'Think we rather overdid it,' said Maycroft. 'Let's go pick up the pieces.'

The downtown detectives were already running along Franklin with drawn revolvers.

Danny Rourke got his head out from between his legs and sat up to pick glass out of his jeans. Smoke drifted in the yard and flames flickered inside the house. The night was a vague wash of soft-focus and Rourke's head pounded with internal dischords. What might have been his Uzzi was picked up and he felt himself being lifted by the armpits. The face he looked up into was fuzzy and the features broke up when he squinted for focus. The hair might have been yellow, but Felix had bleached his hair once in Athens. Rourke wasn't fooled.

'Felix?' he asked. 'You . . . Felix?'

'Sure,' said Pepper.

Rourke's legs wouldn't support him and his toecaps trailed in the dirt as he was carried up the drive. Felix had come like he always did, and that was what mattered. Tough for Tibbs though. Rourke was convinced he'd seen the Negro's head fly apart like a shattered pot when he changed channels on the TV. Mossad must have found the Watts house and planted the bomb. There was something wrong with that, but Rourke couldn't think what. Felix would know.

'Dumb old Jackson Tibbs,' Rourke mumbled as he was lifted over the fence. 'All that worry, for what? . . . He can play banjo for the black angels in the big melon patch in the sky . . . spiriti sancti . . .'

Rourke found the black panel truck with his one good eye when Felix told him to, and was propped in the front passenger seat. He leaned against the glass side window to cool his face as Felix reversed away from the men running down Franklin with drawn guns. One of them fired a double cluster and jumped sparks from the road when his aim was spoiled by a man in an unbuttoned shirt. Rourke thought that funny until Felix took the corner on two wheels and he was pitched against the dash. His broken ribs grated together and just breathing drove knives into his lungs. The panel truck turned in its own length and powered downhill toward the Foothills intersection. Horns blared as Felix shot the lights at red, yelling for directions to the safe house.

'Not safe . . .' Rourke mumbled, but Felix was being thorough. He had to see if Tibbs was really finished. It made sense. Mossad mustn't take Tibbs alive. Rourke rallied to give Felix the route and watched the freeway become an endless grey ribbon of whipping lights and dull engine noise. If Felix held his hand the pain would go away. Rourke drifted into a doze trying to reach him.

Jackson Tibbs leaned against the overturned Mexican table with his useless legs out ahead of him and watched the fire eat the carpet around the smouldering dummies. The shimmering heat sweated him up and he longed for a cold beer. Something had broken in his back and he couldn't reach the refrigerator. He just hoped *they* came before the fire reached him. He had three full clips for his Uzzi, two grenades, and his Colt Savage. They'd know Jackson Tibbs had been here, even if there was nobody left to mourn him.

Poppa had keeled over reaching for a pool cue, and momma gave up the ghost waiting for a bed in the charity ward of St Cyr du Croix. His sister passed for white as a model in New York, had never picked up his messages from her answering-service, so the hell with her black ass. And the hell with Rourke too, at least he'd paid in spades for being fast, noisy and dumb.

Tibbs grinned at that and shivered despite the mounting heat. He must be weaker than he had supposed, and he hoped the mothers came soon. He primed a grenade, held it in his left hand as he aimed the Uzzi with his right, hoping there'd be white meat coming through the door. It'd be a hell of a final note if he went out blowing brothers away, even if they were Uncle Tomming it in service blues.

Tibbs shook his head as cold nausea climbed his belly and filled his arms with ice-water. The Uzzi sagged across his lap and his fingers wouldn't respond. The grenade fell to the floor and rolled out of reach. Tibbs stared at it without moving and counted off the seconds to detonation. Nothing happened.

'A goddamned dud,' he said through blue lips. 'Wouldn't you know it?' He was laughing when it blew his face away.

The black panel truck had gone, and Maycroft hoped his mobiles were in hot pursuit. The LA Sheriff's Department had a helicopter circling the area, and one of the downtown detectives read the vehicle's licence plate number into his car radio.

'Have the registered owner's address in a hot second,' he told Maycroft.

'You did see who was driving that rig?' Taylor asked.

Maycroft showed exasperation by slapping his forehead.

'Did I let chummy there get a clear shot? Give me *some* credit. That bloody man Pepper covers ground like an astronaut with the trots.'

The second detective listened to his handset and said, 'The SWAT team commander says there's a live one still in the house. They're ready to swarm when you give the word. We can't bring in the fire department until he's neutralised, and that fire is about to take out every house and tree in the neighborhood. There's been no rain for weeks.'

'False plates, Mr Maycroft,' said the second detective. 'But the truck's travelling south-west. They've got a pretty good fix.'

'That's something.'

Maycroft worried his lip as flames burst through the roof to reach for the eucalyptus trees. Greater Los Angeles was 254 square miles of urban sprawl with fifty-six inner cities. One helicopter and six mobiles was a small force to keep track of one vehicle, even if it did keep to the freeways. He had clearance to call on the Highway Patrol, but that wouldn't draw a smile from the Sheriff's Department personnel seconded to him. The Headquarters Captain of Detectives had summed up the Highway Patrol with a grunt and, 'They're just metre-maids with guns and traffic citations, is all.'

Maycroft snapped his fingers at the second detective.

'Tell them to swarm, but with extreme caution. I've seen what one man can do to a SWAT team tell them.'

'Yessir.'

'And get those fire-appliances rolling.'

'Yessir.'

The hard crack of a grenade came from the house, and glass showered across the yard. The detective's handset crackled and said, 'Scratch one target. Looks like the mother saved us some powder.'

'Get that confirmed,' said Maycroft.

'Affirmative,' said the handset. 'He's hamburger without the bun. Got yourself one Panther won't play jungle-ball again.'

Maycroft pushed Taylor into the back of an unmarked Plymouth and told the first detective to drive as fire-engines turned in from Foothills. What little control he had of the situation couldn't be allowed to slip away.

Taylor read his mind.

'I'll stay where you can see me, Maycroft. And Pepper's the best there is. He'll hack it.'

Maycroft faked a smile as he buttoned his shirt.

'He's safer than I was in that jacussi.'

Watts was an oven after the cool of La Crescenta.

Danny leaned against the mailbox until the night spiralled to a standstill, and kept his good eye on the house, willing it to stop fuzzing and rippling like an alcoholic mirage. The weather-boarding still flaked and the windows were all shuttered, just the way they were when he and Tibbs had left. As soon as the house stood still, Danny could move. Felix covered him from the panel truck, and all Danny had to do was bring Than Nghu to the door. Simple, except the cement path had grown dips and a camber, and the bird-of-paradise plants edging the scorched lawn pecked at his legs, trying to trip him.

Danny was trying to get up before he realised he had fallen. His hands had slapped the path and sweat from his hair spotted the cement between them when he shook his head to clear it. One of his shoelaces had come undone, and Danny carefully retied it to show Felix he wasn't really drunk at all. Let Than Nghu sneer his yellow sneer, Danny Rourke could hold his liquor with the best of them. Nobody could be better with fifty broken ribs, one eye, and a head the size of a Florida condominium.

Danny tried to remember which bar window he'd been thrown through as he got his knees under him. The fight had been over an exploding TV set, and must have been in one of those black joints off Lennox, because Tibbs had taken their side against Danny. Just another black brother yelling at him for changing channels.

Danny swayed upright and fell again. Getting there was more important than how he did it, he told himself, and followed his own trail of sweat to the front door on his hands and knees. The knocker was out of reach, the bell had never worked, and the pocket he kept his key in had been ripped away.

Danny worried about that as he rested.

Felix was nowhere to be seen, but he'd left the engine running. A helicopter passed overhead too high to be heard, and some drunks down the street bawled Spanish as they drove off in a squeal of hot radials. Danny held his head until the noise stopped scalding his ears, then scratched at the door to bring Than Nghu. Felix had taught Danny patience, and Danny didn't mind the long wait for Than to answer the door. He had more pain that he could handle for company.

Than Nghu showered the woman's musk from his hands and loins and sat on the rush mat before his portable Shinto shrine to oil himself. That done, he lit dragon-tails of incense and the small ceramic lamps, breathing deeply; first with one lung and then the other. For Than Nghu, control was everything.

Going naked into the void was an arrogance few would dare, but Than knew himself to be beyond the constraints of the ancient purists. He had learned to find his way to the heart of All Knowing with the aid of refined opiates, and his face was calm when he took the White Bowl Of Serenity from its black japanned box. He set the bowl between his crossed ankles, broke a phial of Peruvian cocaine into his right palm, and breathed it in with two quick snorts.

The drug burst in his mind and sent his body into sudden spasms. His head snapped back and his eyelids fluttered. His shoulders bunched and his pectorals hardened into plates of ridged muscle. His stomach sucked in against his spine to throw his lean torso into high relief. A surge of white vertigo brought inner serenity, and Than's torso relaxed as he bowed over the bowl with hooded eyes. His heart slowed to a murmur and his shallow breathing barely moved his chest. Only the big vein in his neck showed he was alive at all.

The perfect white concave softened under his stare, and milky iridescence spread from his face to consume the darkened room. Than's eyes blanked as he became one with the bowl, and his mind expanded into a vast ocean of pale white fire. Than and the bowl conjoined to form an aura he could contract or expand at will. He could taste colour, see odours, and smell emotion.

Brilliant dragons of cloud drew him from his body, and he saw himself squatting on the rush mat far below with incredible clarity. Every hair on his head was a black sapling rooted in creamy loam, and his skin pores were craters domed by beads of gleaming oil. His face was parchment stretched over bone, and his eyes saw nothing but the flawless porcelain. Than had achieved profound detachment, and could have pinched out his own life-force by simply willing it, a temptation all who crossed over into the void had to fight.

Than was the air his body breathed, the calcium in his bones, the gravity that bound his physical self to the earth. He existed on two separate planes, but the true essence of his being belonged to the void. He became one with the noble daimos and shoguns of the past, the thousand generations of samurai who swore eternal fealty to them, and was privy to the countless whispers that comprised the wisdom of All Knowing.

Than's enhanced senses brushed the outside world when the

132

panel truck coasted to a halt outside the house. The engine tasted crimson and the unburned exhaust gases were the texture of volcanic magma. Danny Rourke gave off a blue aura of pain when he fell on the path, and his consciousness was a guttering amber flame when he crawled toward the front porch.

Than dismissed the drunks as blurs of ochre stench as he probed the panel truck for Tibbs' ebony musk. He glimpsed the merest trace of his being in the upholstery a moment before he made contact with a stranger at the wheel. Than recoiled as he was seared by the taste of ultra-violet. Dry-ice burned his tongue and twitched his physical mouth in the darkened room below. Than's upturned palms jerked into fists as the stranger shimmered down the side of the house on rubber soles. The borrowed clothes tasted of Luther Cash, but the core of the man wearing them was as dense as molten lead.

Stunned by a corona as perfectly formed as his own, Than stayed in the void to soothe himself. He had brushed the same aura in Belfast. Then it had been a small seed-pearl of black light, locked away and forgotten. Now it was a hard negative shield he could not penetrate, and the black fist of starlight that was Pepper stank of malice.

Than's oiled body called him back from the void.

The scratch of Danny Rourke's nails was the grey of mouse-fur, and Than's heart quickened his blood. He reclaimed his eyes and rolled them to white to sever contact with the bowl. The white fire streamed away as feathers of cloud, and Than sat back into himself with his eyes locked on the lamplit shrine. He grew out into his fingers and toes and followed his spine up into his skull. He was back, and Pepper became an enemy at the back door of the house.

Than sat where he was and waited, content to let Pepper come to him. It would not be long, and Than was eager to test himself against a worthy opponent before taking the woman up forty rungs of The Ladder of Ecstacy. A fitting climax to a Naked Kill.

Maycroft had the detective park on a Pizza Hut forecourt when his mobiles lost the panel truck on the Watts downramp of the Harbour Freeway. Co-ordinated by the helicopter, the mobiles quartered the district, and Maycroft listened to their cross-talk on the car radio as Taylor and the detective eliminated the searched areas on a Thomas Street Guide. There were only five city blocks of the black residential area left.

'How long before the SWAT team can get here,' Maycroft asked.

'Fifteen, maybe twenty minutes,' the detective circled the unchecked area with a red stylo. 'If our targets are in that neighbourhood we're gonna need the men in black real bad. That ghetto makes Tijuana look like main street, Disneyland. It sports more bad hardasses to the square inch than an Attica cell-block. I worked undercover there one time, and man, that *was* one hard time. That's street-gang turf, they start fires to warm up a dull night and draw beads on the firemen when they come clanging up with their hoses. They're young too. Kids of twelve and fourteen mostly, but they'll shoot your ass off PDQ all the same. A blood past age twenty-five and still running in gang-colours is an old, old man. And white faces going in there better be connected or suicidal. Ain't no third way.'

'Nevertheless,' said Maycroft. 'I'd like us to get closer.' The detective's black face lined with concern.

'Okay, but it's doors locked and windows wound all the way closed. You *don't* step outta the car without my say-so. You stay low, and I do mean *low* in your seats. Those mother's can smell a cop-car ten blocks off, and that means drawing fire if we're spotted. Okay?'

'Sounds like outlaw territory.'

'The detective wiped sweat from his mouth and found first gear.

'You got that right,' he said.

A vague something touched Pepper's mind when he threw Cash's jacket into the panel truck and dropped to the ground. For a split millisecond he saw a hovering white disc of fire that became a dark afterburn and irised down to nothing, gone before he could blink. Pepper bared his teeth as the Irishman fell into the porch, knowing he had come to the right place. The probe came from the house.

Rourke mumbled boyhood gaelic and stank of wet bonfires as he scratched at the flaking front door. Pepper ignored him as he padded past, sniffing out what he couldn't see in the moonless night. Garbage cans formed a sour line, the locked garage was heavy with dead air and stale lubricants, and a recently repaired window gave off fresh putty and linseed oil.

Pepper halted halfway along the side path. A kitchen extractor leaked oriental perfume and man-odour into his face, and the mental probe came back for an instant, a sensation he hadn't experienced since the tunnels of Cu Chi. Another mind reached out to locate him, cutting the darkness with a strength of projection none of the Charlie Victors he'd hunted had possessed. Pepper felt it withdraw and change in a way that was new to him, and he wondered how that could be as he went up the back yard to see the upper floor more clearly.

The back lawn melded dried grass and mimosa blossoms with cat droppings, marimba beats duelled with distant sausa rhythms, and a LAPD helicopter bleached roofs with its searchlight four blocks to the south. Pepper felt the net closing in and rejected long-term considerations to concentrate on the house. There wasn't time for such diversions, and the compulsion to enter the house was far too strong to be ignored.

Pepper quelled a sudden need to strip off the rest of his clothes, and squatted quietly on the dead lawn, working his way through the house in his mind.

Old wooden shingles covered the roof, the chimney was stuccoed, and a downpipe located a bathroom for him at the left-hand corner of the top floor. Condensation on the window confirmed it, and a narrow landing window told him where the upper passage ran to meet the stairhead. A third shuttered window had to be a back bedroom and, because of the shallow pitch of the roof, the attic space could only be a low crawlway between the rafters. Access to it was through a square roof-light to the right of the chimney stack. Pepper had worked out the ground-floor layout from the panel truck, and was as sure as he ever would be of what to expect inside.

When he had located hand and footholds in the weather-boarded rear wall, he choreographed his coming moves in parts of seconds, checked that his guns were secure in their holsters, then flowed upright onto the balls of his feet. There was another scent inside the house, as weakly benign as the dominant male projection was malignant. Pepper put it aside with all the other extraneous signals when he cleared his mind, and moved forward to climb to the eaves without a sound.

He reached both hands over the plastic guttering, flattened his palms against the wooden shingles, and pulled himself onto the roof with his weight evenly distributed between his hands and toes. Still supporting himself that way, he inched up to the rooflight, kneeled up, and tore it open with a quick jerk. The rotten wooden frame sighed away from the bolts and hinges without snapping, and dusty warmth rolled out from the roof-space. A broken screw fell into the void to plop into a carpet of dust, and Pepper laid the rooflight aside with infinite care.

He dropped into the attic and a cobweb broke against his face. A black widow shone in the sweep of the helicopter's search-light as she scuttled for a dark corner where a dozen of her sisters hung like ebony beads. They bobbed in downdraught as Pepper ducked past them, feeling for the trapdoor with his knees, praying it wasn't bolted from below. The helicopter fluttered south and the darkness closed in again. Pepper was lifting the trapdoor when Rourke began to scream in high register, a keen falsetto that must have carried for three city blocks.

Pepper blocked out pity by recalling the gun at his head in Belfast. How the terrorist's breath had stirred Donna's hair as he let her sag against the piano she played minuets on. Max yawning to hide his fear, and the dead feel of his home when he was taken back there by Maycroft.

The screaming covered Pepper's drop to the landing. He made for the lightspill in the stairwell, his arms crooked and stiffened for close defensive aggression. He could smell the Japanese through incense, lampfat and coconut oil, and knew the kill must be personal. Not at long-range with accurate shooting, but face to face with his hands, Than Nghu's chosen weapons. That prospect reduced Rourke's wails to the fuzz of a drowning wasp. Nothing of any importance.

Pepper swayed to a halt, nailed to the spot by another smell. Closer at hand, and triggered by Rourke's screams, the benign scent flowed at him on a spurt of fear. Pepper found the closet with his nose and drew the bolts with hands that could bend metal. He opened the door to release foetid female musk and a feeble mew of fear. Blood gorged his face and his body swelled with raw anger as he watched his naked wife scrabble in her own waste to get as far into the stinking hole as she could.

Pepper dared not touch her. The fine grain of her skin was bruised and streaked with dirt. Than Nghu's nails had left long scratches on her shoulders and buttocks, and her swollen breasts were red with bite marks. Her split mouth bled and her blonde hair was grey with filth.

Pepper's silent bellow of rage started when Rourke's screams were chopped off, and he went down the stairs in a red mist, willing the Japanese to meet him halfway. The helicopter above the house meant nothing to him.

Than Nghu was one with the house when Pepper crossed the roof to tear the rooflight open, and the shingles were the sensitive scales of Than's outer persona. Than fell into the attic with the broken screw, and was one with the cobweb parting against Pepper's face.

Pepper's caution made Than bold, and he could not resist reaching for mental contact a third time. He needed to *feel* the novel sensation other men knew as fear for himself.

The crippling emotion was not new to Than, he had sensed it in others many times. He tasted its bitter root in Rourke and the woman, but its full effect had always been denied him. Until tonight. Contact with Pepper had brought home its truly enervating brilliance.

Drained by unreasoning inner doubts as black as graveyard worms, Than had truly *felt* his mind torn by naked weakness. If there was any real evidence of this fatal flaw in his psyche, then Than had found a new frontier to his All Knowing that must be conquered and controlled.

Than was about to reach for Pepper when the air above

137

the house came alive with rotor blades, and Rourke's mindless gabble rose to an ululating shriek. Aborting his probe with furious reluctance, Than wrenched himself inward to consider these new prime imperatives, losing Pepper and the oneness as he surged to his feet. The bowl was just a bowl at his feet, and he was sweating under the oil.

Than reached for the front door with quick strides, and his left hand opened it a millisecond before his stabbing right smashed through Rourke's oesophagus to break his neck.

The street was bleached by a hovering beam of candle-power, and a gale of rotor-wash bowled a garbage can between parked cars. Black residents emerged from their houses to stare at the sky, and a youth in gang colours cycled past with a rifle across his handlebars.

Than threw the dying body into the hallway and closed the door with his back. Drawing the last veil for Rourke when he deserved to linger in agony for eternity was an affront to Than's sense of honour. Rourke had not only brought Pepper and his pursuers to the house, he had cost Than his new taste for fear, and a last ascent up the Ladder Of Ecstacy with the woman.

Than regretted the loss of these pleasures almost as much as his need to finish Pepper at speed when he wanted to display his mastery at length. There was no time for finesse. Than must attack the boil of hatred coming down the stairs without opening ploys. He raised his metabolic rate to the Tenth Plane to give himself two minutes of hyper-speed, more than enough for six Peppers, and watched Rourke's last breath form a bubble of bile in his mouth without emotion.

Than's temperature rose to ten degrees above normal, and his heart-rate trebled. His world turned crimson as his eyes saw everything in the red wavelength of the light spectrum. The second hand of the kitchen clock slowed to an imperceptible creep, and sound was lowered to the deepest bass.

Than moved down the hall in the basic mantis position, ready to destroy Pepper with the eight arms of the crab on the bottom stair.

Pepper saw the white bowl in his mind as Than Nghu came

out of nowhere. The white orb threw out the eight arms of the crab, each arm aimed for a vital joint. Pepper flowed into the killing axis where the blows were born, too close to Than's core to be struck with accuracy.

Than's fists shattered a run of banister rails, and the pincers converging on Pepper's neck clapped together in thin air. The double-kick to Pepper's scrotum was deflected by turning thighs, and the hand-stabs meant to dislocate his knees splintered the bottom stair riser.

Pepper arm-lanced the crab dead-centre to rupture Than's midriff. Than blocked the move with an absorbent palm, and Pepper sprang into a genuflecting forward roll. It took him over Than's head and landed him in a hard ball in the living-room doorway. He blinked the white bowl away and slammed his palms against the architraves to skid himself further into the room. The carpet rucked under him and Than's heels landed where his face had been.

Than's crab became a scorpion, and his kick to break Pepper's ankles made the room shake.

Keeping to the Fifth Plane, Pepper snapped out of his foetal curl fast enough to counter four scorpion stings to ears, mouth and eyes, and skipped away from the ducking feint that would have rammed Than's foot into his chin. Pepper arched his spine to bow with the kick, and kissed the sole of Than's foot before numbing the ankle with a finger-flick, a gesture of contempt paid to a novice, and the first of a thousand humiliations he planned to inflict on Donna's behalf.

Pepper had thought her dead as many times since her abduction, and now she lived, her degradation at the hands of this psychotic must be paid for, cut for cut, burning for burning. Pepper laid Donna's wounds over Than's naked body in his mind's eye, meaning to mark him in the same way. By smashing Than's bodily pride, Pepper would bring him down to the mud of the sty. Death for the Japanese would only come after total humiliation, and by his own hand when he grovelled and begged for release.

The kitchen clock had ticked off fourteen long seconds, and Pepper, not Than, had time on his side.

He countered a lightning flurry of handcuts known as the stings of the hornet, left his right flank open to draw Than's brilliant use of the scythe and the morning-star, and pinched the base of Than's thumb as it withdrew; a returned arrow that pierced the quiver of nerves in Than's elbow.

Than skipped away rolling a shoulder, flowing from mantis to dragon, from crab to spider; a constant shift of threatening postures almost too fast for the eye to follow, stalking Pepper's passive pillar of serenity with the speed of a snake. His hydra threw out seven heads to sting pressure points in Pepper's forearms, and drew back when Pepper's trident beheaded them with hand-blocks to strike at his chest. Than's left pectoral grew a red crescent and spurted blood. Pepper's nails had cut deep into the muscle to echo the bite on Donna's breast.

Than spat phlegm, and curds of saliva spattered his chin as he taunted Pepper with a mimed erection, and made a woman's shape in the air with eloquent hands. Pepper drew a pig with Than's face, turning the insult back with a greater one. Than countered with a scissor-kick and had the soles of both feet kissed before he was turned in the air by the ankles and slammed to the floor. He rose faster than he went down, pirouetted, and scraped Pepper's temple with his right heel. Than landed on his toes and blood exploded from his mouth from a blow he never saw. He reached down into his core to rise two more planes, covering the move with a fast series of threat postures.

Pepper's cold anger kept his heart from labouring as he watched the transformation. Than Nghu's blood would be simmering just below boiling-point on the Twelfth Plane. He shed sheets of sweat with every violent move, dehydrating himself to stabilise his dangerously high metabolic rate.

The clock marked thirty-seconds as Pepper rose to the Eighth Plane with no outward show. The Master in Kyoto had taught Pepper well. He would exhaust Than Nghu with the Two Hundred Coils of Vapour.

Pepper sank to his knees and dared the Japanese to attack.

'That's 1122 Dexter Drive. A live one on the roof and a prostrate in the driveway. The SWATs are three minutes behind us. That's a 10-4 and out, Central.'

The black detective added 'shoot' as the windscreen shattered on his turn into South Dexter, a block from Dexter Drive. He slewed to a halt and the rock caught Maycroft in the lap hard enough to make his eyes water.

Taylor saw running black youths outlined in the helicopter's searchlight. Just eyes and teeth and the sheen of satin jackets. The yells of 'Pigfuzz' and worse faded as they scattered to lose themselves in the night. The detective brushed glass from his hair and reported his position and status over the radio.

Taylor hefted the rock onto the front passenger seat.

'You okay, Chuz?'

Pain turned Maycroft's accent to crystal.

'For a chap hit at the centre of equilibrium, I'm extraordinarily cheerful – so long as I put my socks on sitting down and don't try for the bloody high notes.'

'He's okay,' Taylor told the detective.

'Well we sure ain't. Three minutes is a long time to wait for a taxi in this town. Watch the roofs.'

'For what?'

'Snipers, damn it.'

'And I booked the Universal Studios Tour,' said Taylor. 'Move this pukey heap, will you? Punch a hole so's we can see where we're going, and move it.'

'Works for me,' said the detective. 'Let's get where the light is. Just keep your noodles below the sill.'

'And certain other commodities,' Maycroft tried not to groan as the Plymouth accelerated away.

For twelve long seconds, Than Nghu had been the tentacles of the octopus, the bee swarm, and the twenty-five kicks of the emperor's horse. All the attacks had foundered in the sea of Pepper's defence.

Each tentacle had plunged into still water to be sucked into slams of undertow. Chopping wavelets swamped his bee swarm, and the kicks of his horse drowned in the eyes of surfing waves, needled by stinging spray that agonised his nerve-endings.

141

Retreating from a tidal wave of aggression, Than gathered himself for the final assault.

There were open weals on his back and shoulders, and deep scores on his buttocks. His tongue was too big for his mouth, and he breathed with difficulty through dry nostrils. Only his right pectoral was unmarked. It was the clue he had been seeking, and now was the right moment to exploit Pepper's weakness.

Than feigned a clumsy mantis to draw Pepper's twisting lance into his chest, parried it with a short trident, and dropped into the curl of an eel. Wriggling under Pepper's high defence, Than uncoiled to slash at the exposed ribs with a converging double-sword. He felt the shock empty Pepper's lungs, and axed the tanned neck with the heel of his right hand. The fatal blow snapped Pepper's head aside and threw him across the couch in an untidy sprawl, his legs scissoring weakly. Blood burst from his left ear, and Than saw his black aura lose power.

Than crossed the room to fork Pepper in the throat before killing his brain with a finger-spear to the carotid artery. That done, Than could descend to the First Plane and break the body to pulp for the pleasure it would afford him. For all his strength, Pepper should not have telegraphed his need to take revenge for the sake of a mere woman. The foolish extravagance had destroyed him.

The Plymouth hit the approach to Dexter Drive at ninety and burned rubber breaking through a cordon of black youths. A tall one turning to throw a garbage can skidded off the hood and was bounced away into the gutter. Controlling a speed-wobble the detective said:

'That's one El Tigre won't limbo worth a damn this side of Labour Day. Down, damn it. Rounds coming in.'

The snap of smallarms fire followed the Plymouth, and a ricochet chipped the dashboard. Taylor measured the hole in the rear window and knew the ·22 bullet had missed his skull by centimetres. Maycroft just held his crotch with a stoic smile.

'Coming your way, Skyball One. Keep that beam steady.

We're the cream Plymouth heading south on Dexter. You copy?' the detective said into his mike.

'We eyeball you, Mobile One. Target vehicle, black panel truck, coming up on your left. You copy?'

'Copy. Parking alongside for a two-vehicle fort. Out.'

'Roger, Mobile One. Our prostrate now inside subject building. No other movement front or back.'

The detective made the tyres smoke when he braked, stopping the Plymouth dead alongside the panel truck, and a door's width from it. 'Now we've got the truck between us and the house, and our vehicle between us and the local hostiles. Neat, huh?' He threw his door wide and it took paint from the side of the panel truck as it jammed open. 'Even got us a secluded patio when you open the rear door. You wanna peek at the house, lie in the road and look under the truck.'

Taylor had rolled out into the road before the detective had finished speaking. He could see the empty path and the lower half of the front door. Rourke's sweat still spotted the cement, and there were blood smears on the porch. The flat snap of a Tunnel Weapon came from inside the house as Maycroft pointed his Ruger at Taylor.

'Look but don't touch, Corny.'

Taylor put his finger against the bore.

'Says who, Chuz?' he said, and rolled away under the truck. He had sprinted up the path and hit the door with his shoulder before Maycroft or the detective could react.

'What kind of a meatball . . .?' said the detective.

'My kind,' Maycroft sighed, falling after Taylor.

'So leave me with a race riot, you limey loonie-tune.'

The detective opened his mike and talked rapidly, watching for snipers.

Than Nghu drove his fork with the full force of his body. His stiffened fingers went into Pepper's neck and fractured with the snap of breaking biscuits. Rearing back in disbelief and pain, Than saw Pepper's eyes open and gleam like cold blue stones. His neck was unmarked when it should be blackened dead tissue, and Pepper came up from the couch like a lazy cat.

143

No living man could turn that blow, Than thought. Least of all an American. Only the Master in Kyoto was said to know the secret of such inner control, and took only one student a year from the hundreds who were invited to apply. And only four of them had survived the course. The rest had succumbed during training.

This was not happening. Could not be happening.

Pepper wiped blood from his ear and flicked it into Than's face.

'Kyoto water,' he said. 'The red of your sunset.'

Than broke for the stairs with fear eroding his core. By killing Pepper's woman he would at least die in defiance. He cleared the living room with a single leap and got his hand to the banister rail for the turn. His smashed fingers had no grip and he began to fall. His legs turned to mush from a stab to the base of his spine, and his good arm snapped above the elbow as he collapsed with Pepper astride him.

Twisting to face Pepper with the last of his strength, Than tried to bury his teeth in Pepper's jugular vein. His head was jerked sharply, and paralysis killed all the feeling in his body.

Lifted by the hair, Than was carried to his rush mat and propped there supported by cushions. He was a paraplegic with useless limbs, forced to watch Pepper smash his shrine as if it was just a cheap fairground novelty. The pieces were thrown into his face, and he heard himself sob when Pepper ground the Bowl Of Serenity to powder under his heel.

'Kill me, One of Four,' Than demanded weakly. 'It is my *right*.'

Pepper's face was as unyielding as cement.

'You have no rights, One of None,' he said softly. 'I'm leaving you to justice. To *them*.'

'No, One of Four.'

Than saw himself strapped to a hospital bed in prison. Fed by tubes, his body-waste draining into plastic bags. Sucked dry of all he knew by truth-serums for a show trial that would put him into a tiger cage on Death Row whilst an army of lawyers argued the ethics of commuting his death sentence to imprisonment for life. How they would execute him would occupy the legal system for years; by the electric chair, in a gas chamber, or by painless lethal injection. Their medics would keep his useless body alive, and his will would atrophy like his wasting muscles, leaving his failing mental powers locked inside an unfeeling chemical machine he could no longer control.

Than longed for death and saw Pepper deny him that release.

There was a soft dragging on the stairs and Than smelled the woman. He could not turn his head to look at her, but he saw Pepper's face change as he watched her move towards him. Saw his eyes softened by loving compassion as she swayed over to stare down at Than's broken body. Her eyes were ants on Than's skin and he hated her for seeing him brought down.

'The gun . . .' she said. 'Give *me* the gun . . . Matthew . . .'

Than's heart thumped with hope. Better to die at the hands of a woman, he reasoned, better by far than lingering in the mortification of captivity. Daring Pepper to deny her the right to finish him, Than found his voice to goad the American.

'See what I did to your woman. See how I used her forty ways and forty ways more. First, the twelve ways of bestiality . . .'

Pepper's expression choked Than into silence. He could turn Than into a blind mute in constant agony by touching his face in five places.

'Give me the gun . . . Matthew . . .'

Pepper drew the Tunnel Weapon and weighed it in his hand.

Her right, Than projected mentally. *Give it to her, Pepper. Give it to her NOW!*

Than saw the gun pass from palm to palm. Saw the woman take it from Pepper and out of Than's sight. He tried to turn his head to see the flash that would kill him. To embrace that final flare with his eyes opened, but he commanded dead nerves. There were only the shards of the bowl to stare at, and Than concentrated on bringing the bowl back to wholeness, seeking a momentary oneness with the void that might take him whole into the beyond.

The woman's voice was wind stirring dried leaves.

145

'I waited and waited. I knew you'd come . . . Matthew. Better . . . if you . . . hadn't . . .'

Than had achieved a pinpoint of white light when the gun went off with a light snap. He smelled the bloom of smokeless powder and the sweetness of fresh blood, and felt no pain. The bowl broke apart again and he was still propped up on the rush mat. Pepper was a wax effigy and the gun smoked in a small hand at his feet. There were blood freckles on his face and the woman had hit the floor with a gentle thud.

Without the need to look, Than knew the woman had cheated him of death by putting the gun into her own mouth.

The front door smashed in as Pepper kneeled to weep over the body, and the smell of another man was in the house. His voice was rough with shock as he took in the scene.

Fear came to Than and would never leave him. He grew old just thinking about how long he might live.

CHAPTER EIGHT

The room on the seventh floor of the Hall of Justice where Maycroft met with the Captain of Detectives was painted green and smelled of green cigars. There were bowling trophies on the brown sideboard where the District Attorney leaned, the two detectives seconded to Maycroft sat in leather chairs with worn arms, and the Medical Examiner drew his conclusions from the double-autopsy he had just performed over the amplifier attached to one of the six phones on the Captain's desk. When the report ended, the Captain of Detectives grunted his thanks, smoothed his walrus moustache, and favoured Maycroft with his friendliest glare. Maycroft didn't know him well enough to know the difference.

Captain of Detectives Beau Grimwald was a political animal with his eye on the Governor's Mansion. He had been known to smile for the cameras at fifty-dollars-a-plate benefits, and had once kissed a baby that commented by barfing over his suit. Mostly he growled at his people, wrote scathing memos to his underlings, despised deputies and convenience-foods, autopsies and coroners' reports, the narcotics and vice squads, the 'glamour boys' from homicide, all ranks below captain, and the ethnic minorities who shot, raped, knifed, strangled, mugged or burgled their neighbours. In short, most of the inhabitants of Greater Los Angeles, the men who policed them, and anybody lacking the wherewithal to boost his political aspirations.

Only multiple murderers brought a gleam to his eye; catching and convicting one of them always caught the media's attention, and the smell of one had Grimwald reaching for the phone to set up one of his infamous 'Task Forces', when the usual team of two detectives working methodically under a homicide lieutenant achieved more certain results.

Grimwald was more than usually unhappy. This left-field Maycroft character had been foisted on him with the tacit blessing of the FBI, double-talk from some CIA Boston cream-puff, and an ambivalent directive from some anonymous cubicle down the hall from the Oval Office.

To confuse him further, Grimwald had been assured at fourth hand that the present White House incumbent expressed the 'confidence' that 'California's finest' could expedite this matter with 'bold and delicate sense of purpose', whatever the hell *that* meant. Grimwald knew a shaft when he saw one.

The Los Angeles County Sheriff's Department might boast the seventh largest airforce in the world, have the best forensic facilities outside of Washington, and be capable of swarming any pool-hall within its jurisdiction with seven thousand highly trained officers, ranging from sharpshooters through criminal psychologists to deputies with Phds, but handling these inter-national terrorists like local urban guerillas in order to flush out some bedwetting-pinko-liberal-deviant-bedbug Grimwald had never heard of was exactly the kind of politics he wasn't ready to play without his arm being wrenched out of its ambitious socket.

They had done that without raising their voices or a mild sweat. The sheriff had handed him a phoney smile and the phone, and pretended not to listen as the three voices took turns telling Grimwald what was expected of him. Grimwald's refusal to co-operate would have caused them quiet sorrow, and necessitated their seeing Grimwald didn't even sport a campaign button for dog-catcher in Toledo, let alone have his own dogs pee on the governor's lawn whilst his photogenic wife trimmed roses for *Time* magazine photographers.

The sheriff ushering Grimwald out of his office with 'That sucker really sucks' before the door closed properly, made the shaft a longer, pointier stick than it needed to have been. Grimwald needed to dip all the apples in this barrel to come last in the Justice Building's monthly popularity poll. He glared at Maycroft through cigar smoke and said:

148

'You sure know how to start a war, Chuz. Cadavers ain't dog-doody you shovel into a pail, you know. They have to be accounted for, like the office paper clips. We operate in a goldfish bowl around here. Every call made or received by phone or radio goes onto the master tape at Central. I even call the valet service it's logged at Central. A thousand years from now, some joker'll know I went to dinner with pressed pants, even if my shorts got lost in the wash. Sweeping crud under the carpet leaves you with just one thing, a lumpy rug. This ain't Boondock County, and I ain't Judge Judas H. Beedlebaum selling favours and moonshine from the trunk of my police car.'

Maycroft saw the District Attorney yawn at what had to be a stock speech, and looked attentive when he really wanted to pull Grimwald's fleshy nose.

'I recognise that, Captain,' he said, and would have continued if Grimwald hadn't bulled on with his seething diatribe.

'Then recognise this: One fragged Black Panther pulled out of a gutted house in La Crescenta. One dead Caucasian Irishman and a female suicide in the middle of a race riot in Watts. One paralysed kamikazi kook you say needs a brain laundry, pulled out of the same house. This Taylor character on ice downstairs for jaywalking, and this other mastermind Pepper, suffering from self-induced catatonia in a rubber room at State Memorial Hospital. The dead woman is Pepper's wife. You want her logged as a Jane Doe until, or even *if*, this Pepper character mends enough to take a hike. *And*, you want us to tell the media the two dead guys were housebreakers who got unlucky when they resisted arrest. The black got swatted at the scene of the crime, and the white perpetrator got as far as Watts where he took a woman hostage and killed her before breaking his neck trying to escape. The Japanese is no Japanese. He's a neighbour who got himself all busted-up trying to help the woman the Irishman had a gun on. This Pepper wasn't there, nor was Taylor, and I've never even heard of you. You do recognise that as the scenario you want me to peddle to the media?'

'Crudely put, but essentially correct, yes.'

149

Grimwald glared at the District Attorney.

'You hear this, Fred?'

'Using British legalese, Without Prejudice, I did. Which means this is all off the record. And my comment for what it's worth is: No sweat, Sherlock. Do what the man asks, Grimwald. John Doe the bodies and the wounded Japanese. Tell the media he's in protective custody for his own safety, needs extensive surgery and is on a life-support machine so he can't be interviewed; that his testimony isn't crucial to your investigation, and that no further arrests are expected. Wear your pressed pants for the cameras, look wearily exultant, and make sure you're flanked by deputies who weren't involved but have nice smiles, and you're home and dry. Captain Beau has made the world a cleaner place to live in, cut to commercial and count your column inches.'

Grimwald's cigar crackled between his knuckles.

'And what about the El Tigres and Honchos knocking heads with fourteen teams of our deputies down there in Watts? You want I should say that was a neighbourhood barbecue that got a *leetle* out of hand?'

The District Attorney shrugged.

'It's happened over less. Law Enforcement Officers in hot pursuit of a felon were attacked by social deviants of a Negro persuasion. That's what Angelenos expect as the norm in the ghettos of our imperfect society. They'll shake their heads over their morning flakes, reach for another cup of breakfast-blend and wait for the daytime soaps to start. The news is just another TV show, and their attention span is notoriously short, as you well know from your own attempts to milk the media for your own ends. No offence there, Grimwald, but if our British friend here needs a certain unnamed person to know his people are out of the game without really knowing how, then this has to be the best way. And doesn't this give you the opportunity to shaft the media for all the times they've jeopardised an investigation by blabbing details you'd rather have kept back? This is your chance to get back at them on behalf of all your fellow officers, right? And what would *that* do for your image around the Justice Building?'

Maycroft watched Grimwald begin to enjoy the prospect. His face would go national and might even get picked up by the European agencies for their international telecasts. And *they* might just fund a documentary about Captain Beau of the LAPD. Grimwald felt much better as he composed an impromptu speech for Eyewitness News.

'Anything else you need here, Maycroft?' he asked.

'Enough men for a twenty-four hour surveillance on Pepper and the Japanese. That unnamed somebody might be tempted to silence them.'

Grimwald glared at his detectives.

'You heard the man. Get Lieutenant Jenson to re-roster his "Bulldogs". His homicide "glamour boys" can form this Task Force. And have him get back to me to rubber-stamp the paperwork. Dismissed.'

'Breakfast,' the District Attorney ushered Maycroft after the detectives. 'These fellows can take us to the Greek's joint. I hear he makes the best hash-browns this side of the tracks. We'll collect Taylor on the way out and let him visit with Pepper.'

The door hissed closed and Grimwald was too busy thinking to make his goodbyes. There might be violets at the bottom of the manure heap after all. He phoned his wife to make sure she taped the morning news for his video library, and went off to shave for the cameras. The sun would be up soon and it ought to be a nice day.

The day was only an hour old yet the Nevada desert was already baked white. The highway running north to Beatty and Death Valley was a shimmering ribbon swept by chorus lines of dust devils, and joshua trees spiked the liquid air, patient green aliens lost in an ochre wasteland. The only building for thirty miles in either direction was a low stucco oblong inside a storm fence, and the sign above it read: Bella's Bordello. Girls 20 Girls. Whirlpool. Waterbeds. Eats. The banner pasted on the bar window said: Closed for Renovations. Watch for Grand Re-Opening.

Cassie, a blonde whore in a kimona, sat on the side porch

to watch the quails' morning promenade. It was too hot to sleep, and Cassie wished her menstrual cycle wasn't so erratic and painful as she peeled and bit into an orange. Juice ran down her chin to spot the bluebird tattoo on her right breast, and she let it dry there, sulking because she'd been left behind to play nurse to the bandaged man in Bella's private rooms. All the other girls hostessed a business conference in Las Vegas for Bella's partner, and would come back with stories of high-rollers with juvenile perversions and expensive gifts they actually got to keep. All Cassie had for company was Bella's Modoc, the bandaged man, and the quail.

Cassie sat very still when the first scouts came in a rush, calling an all clear to the main group. Then, their plumes bobbing, and gossiping in their hundreds like old ladies on a shopping expedition, the flock scuttled across the compound to disappear into a dry wash, leaving Cassie alone with the crashing heat. She yawned and stretched and spat a last pip into the dust, bored by her own company.

Like all Bella's girls, Cassie was handpicked, had a five-year contract, neither smoked, drank or used drugs. The one girl who'd developed a secret heroin habit, and had a trucker smuggle the stuff in, went out into the desert with Bella's Modoc and was never seen or mentioned again. The trucker jack-knifed his rig and burned along with the gasoline he was hauling, and Bella wore black for a day to prove to her girls she took sudden death seriously.

Modoc emptied trash, hosed the yard and stocked the bar as if nothing had happened, but he only had to look at any girl throwing a fit after that to make her toe Bella's line.

Cassie rubbed her tender stomach and idly wondered who the bandaged man might be. He wasn't the first to use Bella's rooms to recuperate in, there had been others, but they were mob guys who smoked, drank and took their pick of the girls whilst their cosmetic surgery healed, and were generous with their money. This one was strictly celibate, only spoke to Bella or the surgeon who came to check him over every second day, and made Cassie feel like a nun under a vow of silence when she took his meals and changed his linen. When he wanted something, he wrote Cassie notes with a gold pen, and tore them up when she had read them. Although he had only undergone facial surgery, he wore linen gloves at all times so as not to leave prints, and only used the TV to watch the news. All his calls were outgoing, and he made them on a cordless phone mounted in a special attache case he kept by his bed. At night, Cassie heard him pace the floor, and use an inhaler to clear his nasal passages as he dictated long speeches into a tape-recorder. Cassie had never made out the words, but his tone made her think of the sermons she'd suffered through as a girl in Aspen Falls. The same tired angel-dust the Reverend Kelley had droned from the pulpit when he wasn't abusing his prepubertal parishioners, and threatening them with Hellfire if they told their parents. Cassie's turn had come when she was twelve, and she'd bitten half-through his pecker before running home to be disbelieved. She and the Reverend Kelley had left town in opposite directions that same day; Cassie to her Aunt Mildred in Medford, the Reverend Kelley to oblivion with pills and wine in a Eugene motel room . . .

Cassie was jerked from her reverie when the surgeon's Jaguar swung off the highway in a veil of dust. Bella's Modoc came out to take him inside, and returned to thrust a fold of paper into Cassie's hand, his eyes blobs of grease in his flat brown face.

'Bring the man back his note with his breakfast tray,' he said. 'With an extra coffee cup for the doc. And cover up that damned bluebird, Cassie girl. Bella says the man don't take to it.'

'Don't take to much, does he?'

'About as much as you'd take to a walk in the desert. You talking that way's as useful as an undertaker giving his customers an early morning call.'

Cassie paled and clutched the neck of her kimona.

'I meant nothing by it . . .'

Modoc grinned with gold teeth and wiped a skinning knife on a horny palm.

'The desert's bigger'n your mouth, Cassie. Swallow you whole.'

'Don't scare me no more, Modoc. The man inside does that enough for both of you,' Cassie pleaded. 'He's Christmas Day in July and Alaska in Nevada all rolled into one. Two years I've been here, and you never even had to squint at me mean one solitary time, did you?'

'Always a first time, Cassie girl.'

'Not with me, Modoc. Honest Injun.'

Modoc grinned his golden grin and sheathed his knife.

'Take your bluebird inside afore I teach it to fly, Cassie.'

'Yessir, Modoc.'

'You still here?'

'Nossir.' Cassie hurried inside to heat the oven.

The lithe Indian stared out at the desert, hands on his hips, his face without expression. Bella told him most things between the sheets, but she had no words for him about the bandaged man. He was a hole she talked around as if he was bigger than Uncle Joe Bananas himself. That meant big bucks in Bella's stocking-top, which was fine with Modoc so long as he went away soon and never came back. Him and his eight-week nose-job were giving Modoc an itch he couldn't scratch. Bella had never closed the bordello before, not even when the man from Palm Springs stayed for a month, and that was one mother who was connected with all the five families. Bella wouldn't even turn the jukebox down if the president himself came calling, but she walked on razor blades around this solitary mother. Modoc shook his head out at the desert, smelling trouble instead of rain.

'If whores was mules,' he told himself. 'I'd be a crackerjack teamster with petticoats for reins.' He threw a stone to show a lizard he knew where it hid, and went off to feed the guard dogs with a frown that wouldn't go away, hoping Bella knew what the hell she was doing.

Maycroft had a fourth cup of coffee with the District Attorney when the detectives left the Greek's to meet their lieutenant at the Justice Building. The diner was almost empty, and the Greek argued horse racing with his short-order cook at the far end of the counter. The District Attorney lit a menthol

Kool with a paper match and yawned smoke at Maycroft.

'You're an original, you know that?' he said with suddenness.

'Am I to be congratulated, or do I sense animus, Fred?'

'A smidgeon of both maybe. Whatever. I've got seventeen hundred cases pending on my desk, ranging from misdemeanours to murder one. My office is bursting with eager-beavers and time-servers learning law at the county's expense, and at a guess, my conviction rate is around the 17 per cent mark. We're run so ragged we plea-bargain and go for the lesser charges to make even that low rate viable. Our crazy constitution favours the black hats, and the white hats rate zilch if they're the victims. Our courts hardnose state witnesses, adjourn time and again over some technicality or legal nicety, and lean over backwards to give the accused a more than fair shake. Okay, so we're in a war, and we're losing. I can just about live with that. But what I can't stomach is how an out-of-towner like you gets to turn citizens into grease-spots on the sidewalk with the tacit blessing of those above. I mean, why you, Maycroft? Off the record, and for my own private satisfaction.'

Maycroft creamed his coffee and added sugar.

'Aren't you making much of little, Fred?'

'Don't patronise me, friend. I'm not some toytown lawyer just out of Harvard. I did three years in Military Intelligence before I passed the California bar exams and got to fly my desk. That gives me a pretty good idea of what's going down here, and it doesn't smell of Chanel. I believe in the law, even if it is imperfect. Your way means we'll be machine-gunning illegals crossing the Rio Grande instead of sending them back so they can try again. For every Mexican with a green card there are ten to fifteen illegal wetbacks. One day down the road the official language in California could be Spanish. What then, huh? Do all us smug white Protestants head back east to talk Yiddish-Bronxese as an alternative to border Chicano? Or do we stay and see it through? Work to see some sense come out of all this chaos.'

Maycroft held a cigar without lighting it.

'Nothing stands still, Fred. Remember the Alamo and don't

forget your own revolution against the Union Jack. That's why your coffee's so good and your tea is so awful. Or would you like us to come back and try again?'

The District Attorney almost smiled.

'Only if you wear those pretty red uniforms, they made a hell of a good target.'

Maycroft winked.

'We're more devious now. We oil in one at a time to grab off the odd Oscar.'

'You won't get an Oscar for this, pal.'

'Officially, old son, I'm an observer. A liaison officer advising on terrorism.'

'And you want I should swallow that along with the Greek's hash? Pull another scenario out of your coat of many sleeves, Maycroft. This is Fred Dempster you're sloughing off here. I know your bird flew the Washington coop, and it's pretty clear he was allowed to. *They* were all of a dither in case he got himself dead on their official carpet, right? The guy had files, lots of files, and they have to be recovered or destroyed. Why? Because nobody wants another J. Edgar Hoover haunting the next several administrations from the grave, that's the "why" of it. And I do believe I could give you a name to go along with his gold pen and malformed proboscis.'

Maycroft lit a match and blew it out. The Greek brought more coffee with the check and went back to his horses.

'Best you don't do that, Fred. That would be desperately indiscreet, and you a self-proclaimed hotshot legal-eagle too. Tut and double tut. No, you must think of him as Mr Anonymous, and of me as the scapegoat if it all ends in tears. Just a foreign agent involved in a bad-tasting domestic issue your people want buried. Your Hoover analogy was quite perfect, except that our Mr Anonymous will go to his maker as a private citizen, and without any unseemly scrambles for his files or his chair of office. Langley and Washington have already shredded all reference to him and the Executive Bureau. And should anything untoward happen, I'll be declared *persona non grata*, and leave the country under a cloud of adverse publicity, much to the relief of all interested parties. Job done. All forgotten.'

'And Pepper, the guy in the rubber room. He's your bird dog?'

'I rather hope so. Mr Anonymous has quite disappeared.'

'Who selected him, you?'

'Circumstances did that for me. And you do have a long history of individual crazies gunning for the famous, don't you? Two Kennedys, Luther King, Lennon, Reagan. All in the best American tradition, so who am I to go against tradition?'

'You're a cold bastard, Maycroft.'

'Be grateful then. It allows people like you the right to feel both superior and nauseated.'

'Maybe I deserved that, but what if Pepper fails?'

Maycroft lit his cigar with a shrug.

'Nobody lives forever, Fred.'

'Meaning good old reliable Maycroft's on hand to finish the job. It stinks.'

'Doesn't it just. But there is another element you may have overlooked whilst wallowing in justifiable wrath.'

'Like what?'

'A small boy called Max who's lost one parent to these bastards and may just lose a second, always supposing the poor little beggar's still alive.'

'That really stinks.'

'That it does,' Maycroft fanned dollars onto the counter. 'Shall we watch Grimwald delude the world and himself on the morning news?'

'I know a local bar with a TV, you smooth-talker,' said the District Attorney. 'Kidnapped orphans at breakfast deserves a snort.'

They went out into a morning as pink as a barmaid's blush.

Cassie wore a swan-necked shirt and black skipants when she took the breakfast tray through the bar. She checked her hair in a Budweiser mirror with the air-conditioner clattering and dust motes dancing in the slatted light from the windows. Without lipstick she looked about as wanton as a seed catalogue, and her small hazel eyes were myopic buttons in her plain oval face.

157

'Cassie,' she told her reflection. 'Monroe you ain't, but you got yourself a trick pelvic-hold Harry Houdini couldn't wriggle out of. Not that he wouldn't have had fun trying. Three-years from now, you could be selling bibles to Mormons in Salt Lake City with no one the wiser about all them peckers you've rode. 'Cept you and the Lord, and He ain't been in Salt Lake since the talkies came in. Your momma said that, and she knowed the bible like I know the *National Enquirer*, only better.'

Cassie pushed through mahogany batwings into the main parlour with its loungers and scatter-cushions shaped like pink breasts with red button nipples, pink mirrors engraved with erotic poses from a Japanese Pillow Book, and a fitted shag carpet alive with static electricity. A reclining plastic nude aereated a wall tank of angels with bubbles from her vagina, and an illuminated phallus pointed off to the 'Studs' comfort station and the back bedrooms. Bella thought sex should be fun, and constantly refurbished her parlour and bar from a specialist warehouse in Atlantic City. Her favourite homily: Dull Bawd Don't Bank Bucks, hung over every girl's crib, and was printed in gold on the complimentary ashtrays she gave her 'come again' clients. Bella's taste was as loud and as brash as her personable laugh, and the bordello was a morgue without her.

Cassie trotted down the passage. A red light glared over the door painted up as a bare-breasted Queen of Hearts with Bella's face, and Cassie's discreet knock turned it green.

The room was chintz and diffused light. The dark blue carpet turned the mirrored ceiling into a night sky, and the white four-poster bed was an ark floating in space. The bandaged man lay on the rumpled counterpane like a dead crusader, and the surgeon larded a lint-dressing with cream salve. Neither man spoke whilst Cassie was in the room. She put the tray on a side table, handed the bandaged man his note, and went out, glad to escape until it was time to bring his lunch. The bandaged man waited until her footsteps died away before taking the last dressing from his face and turning on the TV.

The surgeon studied his handiwork with a satisfied nod.

'You'll pass for forty,' he said. 'And more skingrafts are unnecessary. The bruising will be gone in a week or so, but you'll need to keep out of the sun for a while longer. Then you can toast yourself all you want. With your skin, you could go as black as that Indian outside and pass for Mexican.'

'Or Panamanian, Cuban, or Brazilian, eh?'

'Whatever your pleasure.'

The surgeon gave the bandaged man an enlarging shaving glass. The face staring back was square and florid and had the same hairline. The eyes were old friends that had shed years, but the straight and patrician nose with its fine white scars was a complete stranger. He was somebody he had never met before. Somebody who had stolen his eyes.

'My God,' he whispered. 'Great God in Heaven . . .'

'You're pleased,' said the surgeon. 'That's payment enough for an artist. You're my masterpiece, and my only regret is that you're a portrait I can never exhibit in public. A pity, but the money will compensate for my loss.' He laid the pads of salve onto the tender scars, and watched his patient settle the surgical balaclava over his head to stare up at him through the eyeholes.

'I know of a clever fool who once said something similar to one of the Medicis, a goldsmith who had made Medici the most perfect dagger in the world. When Medici asked the goldsmith if he could make an exact replica, the fool boasted that he could make as many as the great Medici could want, all of them identical. Medici killed him on the spot with the very dagger that had taken him three years to craft. "Now," said Medici, "Now I own the only one of its kind in the whole world". Isn't there a lesson in that for you, my medical friend?'

The surgeon went pale and smoothed his necktie.

'How long d'you think I'd last without discretion, for chrissakes? I didn't get connected by flapping my jaws, you know.'

'Palm Springs will be glad to hear that. I'll expect you at the same time two days from now. Coffee before you go?'

'I'll grab a cup at Indian Springs on my way through to Vegas. Thanks all the same, but I have to make a meeting there at four.'

'The whore makes good coffee . . . for a whore.'

'I'm sure, but no thanks.'

'Goodbye then.'

'Yeah . . .'

Sweating before he reached his car, the surgeon turned his Jaguar into an ice-box with the air-conditioner full-on as he drove south. 'Cold sonnabitch,' he muttered. 'Cold sonna*bitch* . . .'

The bandaged man turned his attention to the TV news. The Watts fires burned under the captions and a sonorous voice-over announced the main headlines of the morning. American warships cruised off Libya, Florida orange-growers had lost another crop to snow, there was civil war in the Yemen, and violence had flared again in Los Angeles.

The bandaged man bit into his sandwich and forgot to swallow when Grimwald fielded questions and made his statement. According to Grimwald, two armed burglars had been disturbed during a robbery north of Foothills. One had died resisting arrest on the premises, and the other gunman had been pursued to Watts where he took a woman hostage, and badly injured a neighbour coming to her assistance. The woman had died from gunshot wounds, and the fleeing perpetrator had fallen to his death attempting to escape. Strongly maintaining that the civil unrest in the area was unconnected, Grimwald smiled when it was suggested that the gunman had orchestrated a fire-fight between local gangs and the LAPD to cover his escape. He could, however, confirm that several alleged members of the El Tigre gang had been taken into custody on firearms charges, and would appear at the Juvenile Court later that day. He would take pleasure in updating his media friends at a future moment in time.

The bandaged man pushed his breakfast aside and punched out a Boston code on his portable scrambler when Grimwald was replaced by Aden refugees boarding the Royal Yacht *Britannia*. He waited for an answer through models drinking Coke in bursts of spray, the space-shuttle iced-up on its gantry, and shots of frostbitten oranges. He killed the connection during the weather forecast to work his fists open and closed, open and closed.

Having failed to neutralise Maycroft and Taylor, Kolki must have gone into hiding.

'I'll find you, Felix,' he promised. 'I'll find you . . .'

Felix Kolki saw the metre maid approach his convertible a split second before Taylor came out of the Justice Building between two deputies. Kolki pulled away to avoid a citation for illegal parking, and circled the block for the seventeenth time since first light, his car-radio tuned to a news channel.

Kolki had reached La Crescenta in time to see Tibbs brought out in a bodybag, and had cruised Watts until two darkened ambulances left Dexter Drive for the Harbor Freeway. When they parted to take different offramps, Kolki had trailed one to the Coroner's Building and watched the paramedics offload two more bodybags. Who had been in the second ambulance now concerned him, and Kolki nosed into the traffic behind the black-and-white carrying Taylor north.

Kolki drove with no outward sign of tension. He had slept soundly on the flight from Boston to San Francisco, and catnapped on the shuttle up to Portland. Gaining access to the hospital where Torreo recuperated had been simple, and an injection of scopalomine had made Torreo talk without the need to inflict pain. The first-hand account of how Cash had died, and how Pepper had been involved, had brought Kolki directly to Los Angeles just too late to witness the annihilation of the team Kolki had taken six years to forge into a weapon. Still shocked by Charlotte Stoller's death, Kolki missed her bright mind and hard body, and knew he had let things slide for far too long. As the only survivor, he must act with speed to redress the balance. The man with two noses had betrayed them all.

Kolki hummed at the wheel as he kept three car-lengths behind the black-and-white, his anger warming with the brightening sun.

Taylor shivered in sub-basement chill as he followed an orderly and two deputies past rows of steel doors to room 11D. The deputies looked too young to be in uniform, and the orderly looked bored as he checked door numbers against his clipboard. He worked keys in two locks and had Taylor look at Pepper through a peephole before releasing the security bar.

'You may know this guy real well, Mr Taylor, but he sure won't know you. You have to be prepared for that. He's under restraint in case he comes out of his catatonia and hurts himself, but he ain't medicated. We only use narcosis for violent or disturbed intakes. This man's a cabbage, and our world doesn't exist for him. Wherever he is, it ain't down here with us ordinary folk. He could be flying north with the greylags, or be getting born again. Any time or place he's chosen to hide in, in fact. We've cleaned him up and catheterised him, and we'll keep him that way until he decides to come back to us. This may look a dump, and it is, but we take real good care of our people. Real good. Now, you sure you wanna go in and visit close-to? Like I said . . .'

'I'm sure. Open up.'

'Okay. These guys going in too?'

'No,' said Taylor. 'Just me. You all come back here in about fifteen minutes.'

'I dunno. I'm supposed to stay close, Mr Taylor. Like be in there with you in case . . .'

'In case he eats the buttons? Pulls my hair and calls me dirty names. Just how'd he go about doing that, son? Trussed up that way he can't even scratch his own crotch.'

'Okay, but I have to lock you in. There's a microphone in the ceiling. Kind of baby alarm we use to hear if they get outta hand? You just yell out and we'll hear you.'

'Leave it off and come back in fifteen minutes. You got that?'

The orderly's look of appeal earned shrugs from the deputies.

'We're just the delivery boys,' said one of them. 'I could use some java and a Twinkie, how about you, Ray?'

'Coke. Where's the commissary?'

'Up on Mezzanine One,' said the orderly. 'Fifteen minutes?'

'Fifteen minutes.'

Taylor walked into plasticated sponge and the door clanged shut.

'Hullo, kid,' he said.

Pepper sat in a foetal curl with a blank face, his chin on his knees, his arms buckled inside a white strait-jacket. He had been shaved and his hair smelled of hospital soap. His eyes were vague scraps of sky that saw nothing, and his toenails had been trimmed hard back. The bullet wound in his right foot was a dark blue pucker, and his knees were still scabbed from going over the falls in the Blue Mountains.

Taylor kneeled to sit crosslegged, and Pepper didn't respond when his hair was ruffled. Taylor took cigarettes and matches from inside his shirt and lit up, watching the smoke he blew drawn into a grill.

'Least we can do is break their no smoking rule, kid,' he said. 'Us and the rules were always strangers, eh? Corny Taylor and Pepper san, the guys from left-field. Well, The Company worked the shaft to us this time, and I should have seen it coming. It's confession time, and this has to be as good a place as any to get it said. And when I'm through telling you what I know you can't hear, I'm gonna wind you up, and send you back out there to finish it.'

Taylor held Pepper's face close to stare into the vacant eyes, and smoke from his Marlboro whipped in long blue curls against Pepper's cheek.

'The Company should have left us in retirement, kid. Sure I gave them the big razzoo when they came knocking, but I should have figured they'd never take ''no'' for an answer. I should have told you right off what they had in mind, but you were playing happy families and all that domestic wonderfulness, so I let it slide. Not that they wouldn't have used us anyway, they wanted the man with two noses more than they gave a small hot-damn for us. They had our files marked as ''expendable'' from moment one. They knew us better than we knew ourselves, and they pushed the right buttons to put us back into the field. With you it was your wife and kid. With me it was owing you for hauling my sorry ass out of the Iron Triangle. What the hell if we got wasted by ''friendly fire'', the shots had been called anyway. They bit you. They bit me. Now we bite back, kid.'

Taylor rose to lean against the grey padded wall.

'You know how we do that, kid? We do what they wanted in the first goddamned place. We nail this Felix Kolki to the wall, and then play grabass with that bastard with two noses. We terminate him, and we get all his taped files. We get them, not The Company. Us. And we make those Langley mothers dance to our tune all the way to those numbered Swiss bank-accounts the man with two noses opened. All the money in the world, and it's ours.'

Taylor wrote a dollar sign in the air with his finger.

'It won't bring your Donna back, you poor bastard, and Max is probably in some shallow grave someplace, but we'll have the power money brings. And I'll by God settle for that.'

Taylor's laugh was a tear in old fabric.

'The Master in Kyoto always knew I had a weakness for the folding green. That's why he denied me the final initiation. I was sore about that, you know. Still am. I love you as much as I can love anybody, kid, but that don't mean I don't plan to use you. I'm gonna press your buttons like the Master taught me. He made us One, remember? Gave us the key to each other's minds to bring serenity when pain became overwhelming? I used my key when I found you with Donna's body. You were shook green, kid. You were reaching for that Tunnel Weapon to finish yourself. You'd forgotten Max might still be out there somewhere, and I couldn't let you do that, could I? I want that money so bad I can taste it.'

Taylor's eyes were wet and angry. He drew smoke deep into his lungs and snorted twin plumes from his nostrils.

'Sorry, kid, but Max is all that keeps you going.'

Taylor crushed his butt against the sole of his shoe and crouched to pass his hands across Pepper's face.

'We are One, and you are with me,' he said to bring Pepper out of the void. 'There is only the pain of living, all other pain is of no consequence.'

Pepper's eyes focused and his shoulders squared inside the heavy canvas strait-jacket. Taylor grinned and cuffed his chin.

'You want out of that thing?' he asked.

'Go for it.'

'Think you can handle a couple of deputies and an orderly?'

'Uhuh.'

Taylor undid the buckles and began stripping off his clothes.

'My threads honk, but they'll get you outta here. There's money in my wallet, enough to get you to the wheels you've got stached. You'll maybe have an hour's start, I'll give you what I can, kid. Here, feed me into this thing, and make it look good. Sit me where you were, but I'll do without that bag and tube you got taped to your pecker, okay? Hey, not so tight under the crotch there. Okay, I can handle that. Man, Maycroft is gonna blow his tiny pointed stack. Guess he'll pick up his marbles and go home. Pity those tapes of Cash's didn't get through though, they'd have given old Chuz chapter and verse on the Executive Bureau.'

Pepper zipped himself into Taylor's trousers.

'They will. I sent the real ones from Klamath. The ones I sent from Portland were copies.'

'Now *that's* hustling pool, Matt,' Taylor wiggled his naked toes. 'There're some telephone numbers in my wallet. Bars I'll hang around in at the times I've written down. You just call when you're ready to meet, and I'll bring whatever armoury you want, okay?'

'Sure,' Pepper checked the wallet and the time by Taylor's watch. 'Five minutes to go. Hide this damned catheter behind you.'

'Time flies when you're having fun. Spit, but this thing itches where you can't . . .' Taylor broke off to blink up at Pepper. 'You . . . couldn't know that . . .'

'That you allowed yourself fifteen minutes, Corny?'

'Yeah, you were . . .'

'I was what?'

'Christ, kid.'

Taylor watched Pepper's eyes blank and come alive again. He swallowed hot, sour bile and said, 'You can do that at will?'

Pepper ignored the question and squatted on his hams to lace Taylor's shoes.

'After twelve long years you figure me for a *suicide*? That endows you with the emotional depth of a muddy puddle, Cornelius. And isn't so surprising, coming as it does from

165

a guy who can say, ''I love you, kid, but I'm gonna use you''. I was about to shoot that Japanese psychotic, not *me*.'

'I just wanted to stop you, Matt, we're . . .'

'Buddies, pals, brothers?'

'Sure. All those things.'

'Horsefeathers. We're divorced, pal. Looking at you I see another Luther Cash. He at least had the grace to be boozed to the gills when he tried to use me. You're trying it sober in the cold light of day, and your motives stink the more because of it. You're just another taker in a world of takers, Cornelius. Just another Playboy stud who talks love when he only has the ability to fuck. Women are trophies, and friends are cyphers to be used. I preferred Luther's approach, and he's dead.'

'Jesus, kid, you ain't thinking of . . .'

Taylor choked off as Pepper lifted him like a bag of helium and held him off the ground at arm's length.

'Of killing you?'

'Don't do it, kid. That's crazy . . .'

Pepper held Taylor suspended without a tremor.

'The Master had me hold an iron pot out like this. Must have weighed a good 120lb. I lasted seven hours before I fainted. Passed out at attention like a cadet on a summer parade. Took them an hour to prise my hand open. You lasted how long? Twenty minutes?'

'About,' Taylor licked his mouth.

'You want me to tell you about love, Cornelius?'

'Sure, kid . . .'

'Love is giving your wife oblivion when she asks for it. That's right, stud. I *let* Donna put that gun into her mouth and pull the trigger. She was just a shell. Nothing left but the will to end it. All she had ever been was already dead, and she had nothing left to come back with. All her colours had burned to black, and she hated me for seeing her like that. She wanted Max and me to remember her the way she was, not as a hollow . . . *thing*.'

Pepper mourned with dry eyes, a nerve jumping in his cheek.

Taylor felt nothing for him. He just wanted to live. Wanted

the deputies to come back. Wanted to say the right thing to make Pepper let him go.

Pepper said, 'I couldn't commit my Donna to a place like this. Bring flowers on Sundays. Visit with a corpse resembling someone who was once precious to me. Have Max grow up knowing his mother's a vegetable locked away in a rubber womb. No trees, no sky, no . . . feeling . . .'

Pepper let Taylor fall as if he'd forgotten he was there.

'That's love, Cornelius.'

Taylor scrabbled away to get his back to the wall.

'Okay, kid,' he said. 'I get how you feel. But you need me. Going it alone is like trying to hide the sun with your fist, you won't make it. So I'm a barracuda hungry for money, so what? They owe us both. You collect your way, I'll collect mine. And I'll back you come whatever, that you can rely on.'

'If you don't hear from me, Sultan's in the Katz'N'Dogz Hotel in Portland. He gave you your life, give him a good home.'

'Screw the mutt, what're you handing me here?'

'The goodbye shaft, what else?'

'Wrong move. Happens I can find the bastard with two noses where you can't. I ain't just a bird aturding, kid. One thing I know how to do, and that's check land-titles. And you don't have the time to beat it outta me. So deal, Matt. Old Corny had a touch of the smarts and hit paydirt, so I ain't coming along empty-handed.'

Pepper was reminded of Cash again.

'I'll find him through Kolki.'

'After the morning news hits his TV? Not a chance, Kolki'll be long gone. We killed off his army, remember? He'll either cut and run, or come back with a new army. Either way, you're crapped out without me.'

Pepper cocked his head and his nostrils flared.

'They're coming.'

Taylor's returned confidence made him waggish.

'Gong me, or Come On Down, Matt.'

Pepper's face was as bleak as a winter beach.

His hand whipped into Taylor's temple too fast to be seen, and he crouched with his back to the door, his head lowered to hide his blond hair. Taylor went limp with twitching toes.

'I love you too, buddy,' Pepper whispered, rising to the Fourth Plane.

Felix Kolki made himself invisible with a white coat, palmed a bleeper-unit from duty-reception, and eavesdropped on the orderly and the deputies as they took the elevator up to the commissary. In the coffee line, the orderly asked the deputies to call him 'Fletch', said he had been in Psychiatric for two years, and could diagnose mental ailments just as readily as the resident shrinks who rotated faster than their patients.

'All gung-ho for private practice. Never around long enough to know our patients as people. There's a table by a window in the smoking section, guys. No light down in The Tombs, and I like to grab some rays when I can.'

Kolki waited until they were settled, tripped his bleeper as he passed their table, and asked if they minded if he left his tray with them whilst he took his call.

'Never a dull moment,' Fletch hardly paused in his monologue.

Kolki had an imaginary conversation with a dead wallphone and slid in beside Fletch as he said:

'Law enforcement is my special bag. A lot of your guys come here suffering from career-related stress. And they get to ear-bend with me a whole heap more than they do with the guys with diplomas. With me they can really talk, you know? Not get wheeled in for a sharp thirty minutes of "uhuh" and "hohum", and significant nods over their potty training years. One of your homicide guys came in here tired to the bone. Too many bodies and autopsies, too much whisky-drinking to keep himself going around the clock. He flipped one morning. Took a service ·38 to his back lawn.'

'He did say what?' asked a deputy midsip.

'Shot up his grass,' said Fletch. 'See, how it was, he'd just had his whole yard returfed by a landscaper for over eight hundred bucks. He comes home after thirty-eight straight hours of duty, looks out into his yard, and sees this mole-run carving up his new turf. He does no more than goes out to lay for the mother. Gets him too. Blammy. Wakes up the whole neighbourhood. He's left with a pair of pink paws, an itty piece of tail, and windows going up all down the block. His bride's going screwy in the kitchen, and there's him with a smoking piece and enough moleskin to upholster a thin dime. Turned himself in for reports before he got to seeing pink pachyderms in the wallpaper. He was in and out of here for weeks, and me and him talked up a regular storm. He just needed the right ear to give himself a sense of perspective. He's fine now he's getting eight straight hours of sack-time, and has quit bourbon breakfasts.'

Fletch wiped donut jelly from his mouth and took the Camel Kolki offered with a light. Both deputies refused curtly.

'You have to be Fletch, right?' said Kolki. 'Nobody else knows Psychiatric that well. I'm Eddie Duquayne. Came down from Quebec about a year ago. That call I got? Admin. Means I'm in The Tombs with you guys starting next month. Glad to know you, Fletch. You're the guy to show me the ropes, if you've a mind to.'

'Eddie you say? Meet Ray and Gene. You been assigned, or did you put in for The Tombs? I don't want nobody who's been drafted.'

'Volunteered,' said Kolki. 'Heard of the good work you guys do down there. And it sure has to beat yo-yoing for the primadonnas up in Surgical. I heard your name dropped when I was wheeling linen and taking limbs to the incinerator. You got a great rep around here, Fletch.'

Fletch's sallow face glowed. This Eddy looked a dope with his thick glasses, cropped hair and Quebecoise accent, but he made the right noises, and had the build to handle the violent patients.

'What'd I tell you guys? You need a dedicated ear, is all.'

Ray narrowed his eyes at Gene.

'You said it, Fletch. You ready to roll, partner?'

'Has to be that time again.'

Gene crushed his Twinkie wrapper and rose squaring his gunbelt. All this talk of dingy cops going ape from pressure was getting to him.

Kolki kept smiling at Fletch.

'I'm on a long break. Mind if I tag along?'

'Come ahead, Eddie.'

Fletch continued his lecture in the elevator and down into the grey corridors of Level D. He was explaining about the patient in 5D who thought he was in Hanoi, and that Fletch was Ho Chi Minh, when he opened the door to Pepper's cell.

A blur in Taylor's clothes threw Fletch aside, dropped Ray with a neckchop, and had put Gene down with a straightarm to the solar-plexus before Fletch jarred his spine against the cold floor. Eddie had jumped back and spun an ugly handgun from inside his white coat. It coughed and bucked, and a gas pellet exploded against the cell door. Fletch inhaled bitter chemical and started to retch. His eyes burned, and the misty figure in Taylor's clothes had turned on Eddie.

Eddie was no longer pleasant. He had lost the thick glasses, and his white, pocked face trembled like crusted whey. The handgun was trained without a tremor.

'You can't reach me before I fire, Pepper,' he snarled. 'You either walk out with me, or I carry you.'

'Kolki,' said Pepper. 'Felix Kolki.'

Eddie bared yellow teeth and nodded.

'And it's truce-time, right?'

Pepper was in the air and the handgun coughed twice. Gas burst in Pepper's face and a second pellet hit Fletch between the eyes. Fletch fell into a twilight sea and drowned in pleasant nothingness trying to see what happened to Pepper. He laid his face on Gene's thigh and lost consciousness in a wave of melancholy.

Grimwald's moustache straggled and he needed his second shave of the day. He stabbed the air with a meaty finger, and gave Maycroft his furious 'you're in shit-alley' glare.

'I got me two deputies down-and-dirty at the State Memorial, a junked orderly talking like he's Ho Chi Minh, Pepper's long gone, and your jaywalker Taylor's babbling like he's got a handful of hot molasses. You want to tell me about that, Chuz?'

'Hardly, I wasn't there.'

'The first medics down there got woozy from some kind of gas.'

Maycroft shrugged that aside.

'Did Pepper make for the rental he left on Foothills, do you know?'

'The local station's checking, but that don't tell me zilch . . .'

'It doesn't, does it?'

Maycroft started for the door.

'You can't just walk . . .'

'Have to. We've a homer on that rental with a twenty mile range. Won't do to let Pepper get too far ahead of us. Good afternoon.'

'MAYCROFT!'

The door sighed closed.

Grimwald crushed a sheaf of reports his secretary had taken all morning to type up for his signature, balled them up and threw them across the room. His creative use of foul Anglo-Saxon rose in pitch when he realised he must apologise to his secretary instead of taking a bone-saw to Maycroft's skull.

The Sheriff paused on his way to the elevator to listen and smile his avuncular smile.

'Old Beau's still sucking like a champion,' he said. 'Eight-to-five he has a stroke before he's fifty.'

'No contest,' said his aide, punching the button for 'down'.

CHAPTER NINE

Pepper tasted the night with a gummy mouth.

Consciousness had crawled back like an anxious child to nudge him for reassurance. The moonlit arroyo was sage and warm earth, and a stream purled over stones somewhere below. Kolki was a black hole in the starscape, and lassitude kept Pepper on his back. Kolki threw him a Doctor Pepper.

'You've been talking. Scopalomine makes a man thirsty.'

Pepper worked the ring-pull with rubbery fingers and spilled carbonated flavouring over the plastic charge taped to his chest.

Kolki had the detonator in his hand.

His face was pitted chalk when he looked up at the moon to mutter something in gutteral Russian made musical by grief. He kicked a pebble over the drop and said:

'Now we've both lost our women.'

Pepper drank to stop his tongue running away with him. Spat the aftertaste of gas and oversweet bubbles onto scorched winter grass. Thought, *words are only words*, and said:

'You think that gives us something in common? Howard Johnson hotels are all the same inside, but the view from the windows are different. You look out of your window, I'll look out of mine. Don't compare your dead bitch with my wife, Kolki. I saw your woman's corpse, and was only sorry I couldn't kill her again.'

Kolki's outline seemed to grow taller and darker.

'I saw her too,' he said. 'I saw her too . . .'

Pepper laid still to listen, drained of energy.

'I can see how you'd feel that way about Charlotte,' Kolki said. 'My alley-cat of a woman was no Barbie doll like your mousey little hausfrau. She was something else, unique, and

172

I was the only man with the balls to have her. She learned everything from me without the complications of emotional dependence. Charlotte must have been hiding behind God's door when they handed out emotions. She felt nothing inside. She took pleasure from my pleasure, and she balled my brains out trying to feel what I felt. She was as thorough in bed as she was in the field, and she made love like she was stripping down a machine-pistol. By numbers, straight out of the manual. Never a headache, always willing. Killing and having sex were all one to her. Just things she did to please her Felix. She was a kind of perfection for a man like me.'

Kolki toed pebbles into the arroyo, and some skittered into the stream below.

'She was the only kind of woman a man like me could afford to have around. She didn't make nests, and she didn't want a kitchen full of brats and shiny gadgets. In this business a man needs to be an outsider looking in. Well separated from the sheep we cull when they stray. You know that now you've crossed all the way over to our side of the fence, Pepper. You have to be singular with no ties. And you also know a lush like Luther Cash couldn't have taken my woman out. Not without an edge and a lot of help. You know what I'm telling you here?'

But Cash did take her out, thought Pepper, grinding his teeth as his limbs tingled with returning life.

Kolki paced the slope and talked on as if Pepper was just another moonlit rock.

'She died protecting your kid, Pepper. Not from some perverted maternal instinct, but for two million dollars in cash money. We doubled the ante after we got out of Belfast with nothing but our tails intact and your wife and kid in tow. But they were willing to pay us a million apiece for them. The dough was to be delivered to the Clayton place, and Cash was supposed to swing by to collect the kid the following day. Then we'd release your wife somewhere in downtown LA, and be long gone. But it didn't go down like that. Somebody from left-field took a hand. Don't that put a twist in your mental shorts?'

Pepper washed his hands together to ease the pain of

173

returning circulation. The Doctor Pepper rolled away to empty itself, and Kolki kicked it after the pebbles.

'My Charlotte was still warm when I got to the Clayton place, Pepper. I went all over that house, the outbuildings and the grounds. And I found this.'

Pepper squinted up at a broken string of rough brown beads. They meant nothing to him. Kolki walked away to twirl them on a finger.

'I found these little beauties trodden into a flower bed. There were sandal prints all over the place. Some barefoot prints too. I guess they'd have been rained out before you got there, but you went down into that cellar, right? What did you see?'

Pepper fought sudden nausea to speak.

'They'd been dead going on three weeks. What would I see, apart from the Bravo playing cards on their chests?'

Kolki lost the beads inside a fist. Pointing a long forefinger.

'They'd have been all puffed up and wormy by then. A serious autopsy job. You couldn't have seen and smelled what I saw and smelled.'

Pepper rolled into a ball with stomach cramps.

'Make your . . . *point*,' he muttered, fighting for breath.

'The whole place reeked of soporific gas. The same stuff I put you down with. My woman and the old man had been shot in the cellar where they were dumped. Unconscious and helpless. Now d'you see where I'm leading you?'

'No . . .'

'The beads, Pepper. The goddamned beads. When you were humping the bush in 'nam, most of San Francisco was decked out in this hippy crap. When screwing strangers with flowers in their hair was the prime national pastime, and the whole world was on an LSD trip. But things have changed some since then. Nowadays you have to look in communes out in the boondocks for items like this, right? So what were these mothers doing on your father-in-law's place, huh?'

Pepper shook his head and held his stomach.

'Frigging hippies, Pepper. I figure there must have been twenty of the mothers tramping around up there. Swarming

174

all over the Clayton place. Tinkling their bells and flapping their robes. Maybe another crazy sect like the Manson Family. They must've gotten Charlotte to the door somehow. Panhandling for handouts or whatever. Must've hit Charlotte in the face with a gas-pellet as she was handing out crackers and milk and stuff. Thrown her and the old guy down in the cellar, and boogied off with your kid. Maybe it was them brought the money. Decided to stick to it, and left Charlotte and old man Clayton there for Cash to find. That was the edge that lush would need. Them out cold when he blew them away.'

Pepper broke wind. A long throbbing vibrato. Knives of fire torched his stomach as he gaped at the ground. The painful spasm passed, and he laid back against a rock to furrow his brow at Kolki.

'You're making a hell of a lot out of a few beads,' he said.

Exasperated, Kolki punched a thigh.

'I had them analysed, asshole. Right down to the trace-elements in the clay, and what kind of glaze was used to shine them up. The closest those beads got to the Hindu Kush was a canyon in Colorado. They were made right here in the US of frigging A. In dinosaur country where even the Indians don't live any more.'

Kolki sat on a boulder and turned his white face to the moon.

'Out there somewhere is a bunch of religious crazies with your kid and our two million. My team is dog-meat, Cash got his in Portland, you ain't giving me nothing but headshakes. What's the matter, you don't believe in the greater justice of coincidence?'

Pepper eased himself onto his side to help his breathing. The cramps were lessening in intensity.

'About as much as I believe the Executive Bureau hired a bunch of Hari Krishnas to deliver your blood-money. Or that the man with two noses would pay you a wooden kopek for my wife and son. Take your beads and shove them, Kolki. Next you'll be telling me they coughed up with your dough anyway. With apologies. And that you made the hit on Maycroft because all was forgiven.'

Kolki's laugh rattled off into the arroyo.

'That's exactly what I *am* telling you. The dough Cash bribed you with was meant for us. You don't think you just waltzed into the Bank of Nova Scotia – got Poon to cough up without that deal wasn't already set, do you? Cash was tapped-out, you prickhead. He was paying *you* off with *our* money. And I want it back. One press of my thumb and you're just another blood spot in Angeles Forest. There are more dead bodies in these hills than there are *schwartzers* in the whole of Watts. You wanna join them, say the word.'

'I'm dead anyway, right?'

Kolki almost looked shocked.

'I'm *trading* here, doody-brain. Why else weren't you dead back there at State Memorial, you clown? You get the beads, I get the dough you got from Cash. Go get your kid. Go hit the man with two noses. Me and two mill will get along real well back in Italy. I need to buy me some new soldiers before I can make a move. Then, if you fail, I'll come back and flush old double nose down the toilet. That'll maybe take me a year or three, but I'll get him if you don't. Nobody can hide forever. Sooner or later they give themselves away. They pay taxes, take out a library book on their favourite subject, buy on time payments, or get themselves on an electoral role. A man can change his name, appearance and location a thousand times, but his habits stay the same. I found one guy because he liked to grow a particular variety of rose. Only one grower propagated them. I got his list of mail-order clients, and found my guy planting the little mothers in his yard. Planted him right beneath them. And know this, Pepper, I can find you again, any time I want.'

Kolki's grin was ugly with game humour.

'Know how?'

Pepper just looked at him, killing a yawn of pain.

'Through that dog you left in Portland is one way.'

Pepper nodded. Massaged his thighs.

'Sultan always was a worry,' he said. 'Okay, Kolki. The money's in a Hertz rental parked outside a rib-joint on Foothills. No keys though.'

176

'I'll manage.'

Kolki threw Pepper the beads and the detonator, and a gun jumped into his hand. Capped teeth shone in moonlight as he grinned his ugly grin.

'You planning to come after me if you finish your beef with that two-nosed bastard?'

'What for?' said Pepper.

'Meaning you don't have to, huh?'

'That gets it said.'

'And old Felix gets to guess what's waiting for him out there?'

'Would you have it any other way?'

Kolki shook his head.

'Hell alive, no,' he said, melting away in a rattle of loose shale.

Pepper lay back to yawn at the stars, unable to move.

An engine fired and headlights swept off toward the highway.

A coyote yipped and the stream chuckled in whispers.

Pepper fell asleep thinking about Max.

The Hertz rental was outside the rib-joint where Pepper said it would be, no other vehicles near it. The shops were all closed and showed no lights, unlike the big Lucky's behind Kolki. Kolki checked out the Vista intersection and panned his night-glasses to his side of the boulevard. A cream Plymouth was parked near the Wells Fargo Bank on the far side of the shopping mall, and one of the men in the front seat had glasses on the rental. The one at the wheel stared Kolki's way, white eyes in a black face.

Salt and pepper team, thought Kolki. *Detectives, or I'm first cousin to the Widow of Windsor.*

Kolki lost his binoculars in his lap and flipped on his internal light to make himself visible. Pulled a route-map from the glove-compartment and pored over it like a lost tourist. The Plymouth stayed where it was and traffic from La Canada accelerated west. The lights changed twice and the boulevard stayed empty. Kolki looked around for help and pretended to see the Plymouth for the first time.

'Okay, mountain, here comes Mahomet.'

Kolki reversed out of his parking bay, swung around an abandoned supermarket trolley, and drove in alongside the Plymouth waving his map.

'Hey, guys,' he called. 'You know which way I turn for Angeles Forest? Seems there's a way up there, but I got turned around so many times . . .'

The black detective rolled his window down to memorise Kolki's face.

'Nothing to see up there this time of night. Where you headed?'

'Steerwater in the desert? I was up there one time last year. Thought I'd take the same route, but it's surely different at night.'

'Never heard of no Steerwater,' said the black detective.

Kolki held out his map.

'Right here,' he said, and fired his gas pistol through the car window twice. Both men reared back and went limp, and Kolki drove for the exit without hurry. 'Never heard of no Steerwater,' he mimicked, waiting for the lights to change in his favour before crossing the boulevard.

The Foothills Pizza Parlour smelled of freshly-baked pastry.

Maycroft had lost the toss for who bought dinner, and waited in line to be served, glad of the opportunity to stretch his legs. A small boy rocked on a mechanical elephant, his parents yawned under a giant TV screening a M*A*S*H re-run, and a whistling black busboy wiped tables in the 'closed' section as the wallclock ticked up to midnight. The counter-man boxed Maycroft's 'everything-on-pizza-special', filled three styrofoam cups with coffee, and made change for twenty with a flourish.

'Last customer deserves the best,' he said. 'Australian, right?'

'English, actually.'

'Asked some Aussies if they were Brits and they got all bent out of shape.'

Maycroft smiled wearily.

'Tender egos. Colonials are like young wines, they don't travel well.'

'If you say so, brother.'

Maycroft backed into the night balancing the coffees, sugar and creamer on the pizza box, knowing he must have sounded the perfect pompous ass. Tiredness had taken the banter from his tone. Analysing and transmitting the tapes Pepper had sent from Klamath had taken most of the evening, and sharing the surveillance of the rental with the two detectives for the last hour seemed only fair. When they were relieved at 1 a.m. he would go home to sleep. Chilled by hunger and exhaustion, Maycroft hid a yawn in his cheek and stepped out across the mall. A grey convertible was pulling out into Foothills, and the Plymouth seemed a long walk away.

Maycroft skirted a Lucky's trolley and yawned wide enough to crack his jaw. Taylor had acted predictably when he helped Pepper escape from the secure cells at State Memorial, and confirmed Maycroft's suspicions that he was motivated by more than loyalty to either Pepper or his former masters in Langley. Where Taylor had been for the four weeks before he turned up on the Snake still had to be explained, and Maycroft planned to keep him on a loose leash until he knew the truth of the matter.

Maycroft smelled the gas the moment he kicked the Plymouth to be let in. Both detectives were unconscious with contorted faces. Maycroft dumped the pizza, and scalding coffee spattered his shoes. The gas could be lethal in a confined space. He hauled both men out onto the tarmac and left the doors open, not daring to lean in to use the car-radio. He was already dizzy from the toxic fumes. The grey convertible had crossed the boulevard and was turning into the parking lot near the rental.

Maycroft drew his Ruger and broke into a run, cursing himself for not using a second mobile. The gas teared his eyes and made him clumsy. He jumped the boundary wall, skidded to a halt on the sidewalk, waited for a Mack truck to clear the lights, and used it as cover to cross the broad boulevard. Angling right, Maycroft sprinted for the forecourt of a hamburger stand, and rolled through privet into shadow. Crouching close to the wall, he closed on the rental, trying to keep his breathing quiet.

The man in the convertible wasn't Pepper.

Kolki walked around the rental twice before touching anything.

The open glove-compartment held nothing but hire-documents and a courtesy map, and the seats were empty. Kolki took the magnetic homer from the wheel-arch above the rear offside wheel, and grinned as he slapped it on the side of a Chamber of Commerce waste-bin.

Let the LAPD swarm that, he thought, ready to tackle the trunk.

He sprang the lock with a skeleton key, held the lid down as he crouched to the side, easing it open enough to use a penlight on the interior. The attache case lay on the spare wheel behind a red wheeljack held upright and steady by elasticated cord under tension. A spring-loaded Criterion paper-clip was mounted near the head of the jack behind two stainless-steel cartridges, two nails epoxy-resined to the open jaws. A wedge holding the jaws open was fixed to the trunk lid by a steel wire, and acted as an efficient trigger.

Kolki raised his mental hat to Pepper's skill, fed his steel haircomb into the gap behind the cartridges, and let the trunk fly open. The wedge released the jaws with a loud snap, and the nails dented the spine of the comb instead of striking the priming caps.

Kolki wiped sweat from his nose, disassembled the car-jack, and lifted the attache case out, keeping it dead-level, knowing Pepper would have prepared a second booby-trap inside it. He had just straightened up when he heard the cock of a double-action Ruger behind him.

'As still as a mouse, Mr Kolki.'

The mother knows me. Kolki's mind raced. *But that accent goes with English muffins and tea at the fireside. And he sounds breathless. Got me an old Brit pussy cat with too many years and cigars and port at the club. A ten minute constitutional in Hyde Park and off to an early night with a large whisky in milk.*

'In the back, Englishman?' Kolki said.

Maycroft's sigh was laboured.

'Lay the case on the ground, spread your arms out to the side, and walk backwards towards me.'

'Take 'em alive, that your bag?'

'Move now. Very slowly.'

'Sure, cap,' Kolki went down at the knees. 'What's this case boobied with? A gravity primer? Sulphuric-acid, a wax-ball and three-ounces of gelignite? Or is it chemical fertiliser and a thermal lance?'

'Just do it. And leave the gas-pistol in your waistband.'

'Know all the tricks, huh, cap?' *But not this one.*

Kolki swivelled at the hip and shied the attache case back at Maycroft's voice with all the strength in his powerful shoulders, judging Maycroft to be about twenty feet away. Saw the case scale in at waist-height, and threw himself on to his back, ready to roll under the rental to shield himself from the explosion that would take Maycroft's head off. Fully expecting Maycroft to duck or jump aside.

Maycroft did neither. He batted the case away with his left fist and let it skid away across the forecourt behind him, the Ruger still levelled in his right hand.

Kolki faked a roll toward the rental, kicked himself away from it, drawing and firing his gas-pistol in one fluid movement. Saw he had aimed high, and corrected for a second shot.

Maycroft stood very straight and calmly shot Kolki through both kneecaps, flipping him onto his stomach. The gas-pistol skittered off somewhere, and Kolki felt shock without pain. Closing his mind to it, Kolki reached for the hold-out Airweight strapped to his right ankle. Writhed in simulated agony to cover the move, and fired a double-cluster at the spot where Maycroft had been. His first shot furrowed the blacktop, and the second hit the attache case. A fountain of red dye shot into the air and an alarm wailed.

The usual bank security system, Kolki through drearily.

Maycroft had skipped left and still had Kolki covered, his lined face shining with sweat.

Kolki got a third shot off into nowhere and shuddered as

red flame hammered along his forearm into his shoulder. He drooled bile and watched his shattered gunhand jerk as it reached for the smoking Airweight. Maycroft toed the revolver away and leaned Kolki against the rental, humming something by Bach. A siren sped up Foothills from the La Crescenta station, and Kolki swore in Balt, unwilling to lose consciousness.

'Not with a bang, but with a whimper,' Maycroft quoted, mopping his face with a very white handkerchief.

Kolki's world spun, dimmed and fragmented. Then a paramedic worked on him in a speeding ambulance, the two gassed detectives took oxygen on the opposite stretcher, and Maycroft played with his handkerchief. Kolki butted a pain-killing injection aside and grabbed Maycroft's sleeve with his good hand.

'Pepper traded . . . so should you,' he said with weak ferocity.

Maycroft stopped looking sleepy.

'You're wanted in five different countries. Save your strength.'

Kolki elbowed the paramedic away.

'Get that crap outta my veins . . . My ass safe in Algeria for the man with two noses . . . Deal, limey?'

'I'm listening. What're his chances, doc?'

'Zilch going on zero if I don't staunch that blood.'

Kolki gripped Maycroft's wrist with all his strength. Fought to keep his thoughts unravelling like sinuous red yarn. Maycroft's face melted and reformed as he leaned in to listen.

'Convince me.'

'Algeria . . . Deal?'

'Deal,' Maycroft lied smoothly.

'Okay. I was with East-German Intelligence in Cuba when the Bay of Pigs invasion went down . . . Interrogated the survivors we didn't execute outta hand . . . Scooped some real sweethearts. One of the mothers was connected to the mob in Palm Springs . . . The Mafia wanted back into Cuba to control their casinos again . . . This guy was there to make the deal work with the new regime when Castro was eliminated . . . except he wasn't . . . right?'

'I'm with you.'

'The guy's name was Juan Melixto . . . And he turned into a pussycat when he watched his people face a firing-squad in Laurel Ditch. I turned him around and sent him back to Florida . . . Only now he worked for me . . . We helped him get more raw opium base into Miami than any fifty Columbian families . . . It was beautiful . . . In one year we screwed up more American kids . . . earned more US dollars than Castro's whole sugar crop earned roubles . . . And Melixto put our agents anywhere we wanted . . . And that included *inside* the Mafia . . .'

'Where's this going, Kolki?'

'All the way to home base . . . We wanted anybody rubbed without using our own agents . . . Melixto made the call. We wanted plastic-surgery on a guy . . . Melixto fixed it. That's how I know where two noses is . . . We gotta deal or don't we . . .?'

Maycroft's 'Yes' was as firm as his grip on Kolki's cold hand.

Kolki bucked against the straps holding him. His face was whiter than his teeth and oily sweat spiked his cropped hair.

'Two noses asked me about Melixto and facial surgery, right? Like it was idle curiosity . . . except it wasn't. I could see where his questions were going . . . With his nose fixed he's invisible . . .'

'Where is he, Kolki?'

'Algeria, limey . . . Algeria . . .'

'Enough,' said the paramedic.

Maycroft ignored him.

'Algeria, Kolki. Hold on to Algeria.'

'They'd cut him in Vegas . . . but he'd rest up in a whorehouse on Route 95 . . . south of Death Valley . . . Bellaaaaas . . .'

Kolki's mouth sighed sour breath. Worked on new words that emerged as disjointed grunts.

'Try, Kolki, try,' Maycroft urged, crushing the limp white hand.

Kolki reared to stare at nothing.

'Watch out for them hippy mothers,' he said, falling back.

The paramedic shoved in to feel for a pulse.

'If he makes it, it's surely no thanks to you.'

Maycroft let the cold hand fall.

'Probably not,' he yawned, not caring one way or the other.

Juan Melixto was a dead FBI file. He had fallen sixteen floors during a drugs bust in Miami. At least, somebody who was supposed to be Melixto did, which probably meant nothing if that was the price he extorted for the man with two noses' operation. All Maycroft could see was a mountain of deadly snow being pumped into young veins, courtesy of Felix Kolki, as the ambulance turned into a hospital.

He followed the stretchers into Casualty and fell asleep on a hard wooden bench.

For the second day running, Taylor woke up in the cramped room with powder-blue walls, a rotten view of the Hollywood Hills, and no handle on the inside of the door. The black nurse with no conversation had cleared Taylor's breakfast tray and locked herself out, and Taylor was ready to climb the walls for a smoke. Taylor would have set fire to his bed to relieve the crashing boredom if he'd had the matches, and yelling for Maycroft and Grimwald had only resulted in two beefy interns administering a sedative that left him too weak to bounce his plastic chair off the shatterproof window. He'd dozed off during his morning press-ups, and climbing back onto the steel bed had left him drained. He barely struggled when two deputies fed him into his clothes, threw him into a black-and-white, and followed Grimwald's limousine to Maycroft's safe house.

The gutted wing had been boarded up and some of the eucalyptus trees were scorched black. Taken through the three-car garage into the annexe where Maycroft enjoyed the sun, Taylor was sat in a garden seat and waited to be told what was going on. Grimwald told his deputies to wait outside and laid airline tickets in Maycroft's lap.

'You and the jaywalker here are booked on the afternoon flight to Las Vegas,' he said. 'That makes it a wrap and alveda-bye-bye from the Sheriff's Department, Chuz.'

Maycroft's expression would have poisoned hemlock.

'And I thought we were such special chums,' he said.

Grimwald smoothed his walrus with a brown hand.

'Go kiss a cottonmouth, Chuz. Nevada's loss is our gain. With Kolki on ice and knowing he's gonna make it through the night has the FBI sweet-talking us like saccharine salesmen. That makes me and the Sheriff real cosy. In twenty-four hours from now we go public with his capture and tie him to Tibbs, Nghu and Rourke. When we give that ball-breaker to the media all our previous fiberooneys will get lost in the scramble for headlines.'

'Featuring good old Beau Grimwald no doubt.'

'Sheriff's need to get re-elected, and I'm on the ticket.'

'Congratulations,' Maycroft lied.

Grimwald ignored the sarcasm.

'Just a pity this didn't go down during LA Olympic Year. We'd have gone coast-to-coast for weeks.'

'The shame of that underwhelms me,' Maycroft sneered, smiling up at Grimwald's glare. 'Just remember that twenty-four hours is a lifetime in politics, Beau.'

'Come on, Chuz, we've all gotten what we wanted out of this thing. Being number two you'll just have to try harder. Come back and see us, you'll find this a hard town to get a taxi in, that's all. And there's forty-nine other states in the union to visit before you have to repeat yourself. I'm off, don't wanna be the cause of you guys missing your plane now, do I?'

Grimwald went away grinning and Maycroft threw Taylor a pack of Marlboro, chasing it with a book of matches and a cold chuckle.

'That man,' he said, 'must have been something spectacularly unpleasant in his previous life. The sort of crawling thing that got serpents a bad name.'

Taylor hid his face in tobacco smoke.

'Yeah, like Rin Tin Tin's dialogue coach. Could be he taught Quasimodo deportment and introduced Charlie Manson to Sharon Tate. You took your own sweet time springing me from hospital.'

'Miles to go and promises to keep, Cornelius. You haven't been exactly "up-front" with me either, have you?'

'Which means what, Chuz?'

185

'Nothing and everything. Unless you have something to tell me about land titles?'

Taylor swallowed what felt like a cotton boll.

'Say what?'

Maycroft looked at the ceiling for divine guidance.

'God, how I hate tautology. Land. Titles. Shall I shout?'

'Means you've seen or spoken with Pepper, right?'

'The telephone is a wonderful invention, yes.'

'So is your word of honour. Give me that and we can deal.'

'Exactly what Pepper said you would say.'

'Not for me to make Matt a liar, is it?'

'Not when you're such a consummate liar yourself, no.'

Maycroft's quiet fury could have vaporised mercury.

Taylor stared owlishly and thirst roughened his voice.

'Come on now, Chuz?'

'Come on nothing. You've treated me like some addle-pated avuncular primate for the last time, Cornelius. I'm no monkey's uncle, but I am completely out of patience, and you aren't moving from here until I get some answers.'

Taylor lit a second Marlboro from his stub.

'These butts taste of yuk. After two days without, my tongue-buds must be shot. And is it cold in here?'

'A pleasant seventy-five. Must be the drug taking effect. For which I make no apology. Let's go back to Belfast, shall we, Cornelius? Back to your first work of mendacious fiction, and the resentment you harboured for the man who brought you out of the Iron Triangle? You really must have hated Pepper to do what you did to him.'

Taylor's stomach bubbled and lurched. He threw the Marlboro away and his heavy face slid down onto a cushion printed with faded blue roses. He tried to stand and the garden-seat swayed his feet from under him. Without moving, Maycroft zoomed off into a sunlit tunnel and left his face behind to talk with soft venom.

'You couldn't even bring yourself to tell Pepper the truth when you thought he was under your control. All that old buck about how the CIA moved in on BelTech without so much as a "by your leave". How your conscience pricked you for not telling Pepper about their initial overtures. The truth is rather more unsavoury, isn't it?'

Taylor pushed himself upright, but his head would not support itself. All he could do was sit and listen, hating Maycroft's didactic manner.

'Our late friend Sean Collins had been skimming the company for the IRA, that's true, but not to the degree you had for your own selfish ends. And Felix Kolki turning up must have been a real godsend. By acting as Kolki's inside man you were home and free, weren't you? You got paid for the prototypes, you could make certain Sean Collins died during the ''robbery'', and that Matthew Pepper took the blame for everything else. But Collins made sure that safe didn't open, didn't he? Which, using your own colourful parlance, caused you to come completely unglued. You'd have killed Collins with your bare hands if Pepper hadn't done the job for you, *and* came damned close to taking your face off with his ''unloaded'' ·38. That meant nothing for Kolki, and you out in the cold without a brass farthing. You had to make the rendezvous at the Clayton place with the prototypes to get your cut, didn't you? And that was the point where this theory foundered, because you didn't have the prototypes, did you?'

'That's . . .' Taylor started.

'Except you did,' Maycroft's floating head leaned closer. 'You'd already taken the prototypes from the safe in plain sight a week before. Left dummies in their place. I had my people play back every foot of video-tape from the automatic cameras in Pepper's office, and there you are, as big as life and twice as ugly. A beautiful palming job, I must say. As soon as you got out of hospital and had fed Pepper enough nonsense to take him off on the right tangent, you took yourself off to Oregon, and arrived just too late. That's when you went up into the Blue Mountains where you thought yourself safe until you could make a deal with Cash or the man with two noses. But neither of them were in the mood to make a deal, were they? They earthquaked the whole area and planned to take those prototypes from your dead body. You only got out of there by the skin of your teeth, and due again to Pepper, the man you never forgave for being all that you are not. You really are a rather poisonous specimen, Cornelius.'

Taylor rolled his eyes and head. Words boiled out of his mouth.

'Everybody takes care of Number One, it's the American way. I couldn't breath in that guy's shadow another minute. Luther Cash had already marked Pepper for a fall, and me with him if I didn't tag along. They got the prototypes, you moron, they were gonna put Matt down and dirty anyway. I had a gun up my ass from the moment Kolki and his team hit Belfast, I had to play along, play dumb, play any damned game they wanted to stay healthy. I went up to the Clayton place to try and get Matt's kid back, I had nothing they wanted any more, but I thought I could do that much for him. When I couldn't I took off to Flo's ridge. There was nowhere else to go.'

Maycroft's head nodded and went away to join the rest of his body in the sunlit tunnel.

'I believe you,' he said.

'Who gives a damn what you think? Being a hero's no full-time thing, you know. Courage comes and goes like shadows. One second you've got it, the next it's gone. Like a fist turning into fingers. Could be Matthew Pepper's the exception that proves the rule. If he'd bent just a little out there in Indochina, maybe none of this would have happened. Without Pepper they didn't want me, and that suited this kiddy just fine until now. He's still stainless steel, but I'm all rusted up like I got left out in the weather. Try living with *that*, you superior bastard. One day you wake up and you ain't seventeen and immortal any more, you're just a guy who used to be somebody tall, straight and had balls like an elephant. My hair went white in the tunnels, but the rest of me came home to die by inches. That's the only truth anybody ends up with. The rest ain't worth squat.'

'Self-pity will get you absolutely nowhere.'

'Yeah? Where did wearing a white hat get me? Blow it out of your ear, Maycroft.'

'Once you've told me about land titles.'

Taylor's resistance dissolved as more of the lysergic-acid derivative seeped into his bloodstream from the doped cigarettes.

'I had a lot of time on my hands lying around up there with Flo Cordova and his bikers. Did some serious thinking, and got to talking to one of the bikers about all kinds of stuff. Turned out this biker was really into computers, and balled some broad over in La Grande just so he could hack on her console. He figured he could break into anybody's mainframe. I told him "bulldurham" enough times to make him show me what he could do, and we went over to La Grande for a weekend so he could win the fifty dollars I bet him. Once he'd relaxed the chick enough, and had murdered a dozen six-packs, he got to hacking, and I gave him the codes I knew for a certain mainframe in Washington. He got into it all right, but he came up against some security blocks that got him spitting nails. I laid another fifty on him, and he hacked away until he got himself off into a real labyrinth of numbers and stuff that went to infinity and back. We was up there a week, and I ended up laying this real homely woman of his so he wasn't distracted and could keep hacking. On day six he cracked it by hooking up some electronic auto-searchers that can take on a zillion numbers a second and scan for what he called a "repeater-binary-feedback". I never knew what that meant, but it got him all excited, and before I knew it, there was me feeding my name into it, and up came my service file with a cross-reference that we went after, which in turn showed my white CIA file. We danced all over that thing, and somehow slid off into some files that were grid references to a whole bunch of property deals . . . I need a drink. My throat's as dry as camel-doody . . .'

Maycroft leaked orange-juice into Taylor's mouth and wiped the drool from his chin. Propped his head with a cushion and went back down his tunnel to listen. Taylor coughed and said:

'There were files on everybody at Langley, Virginia. Old two noses really had it in for some of those guys. One file on a previous director read like a handbook on marital aids. I had real trouble keeping my guy outta that crock of nothing. Something about those property deals rang weird. They'd

189

been made over a lot of years from '67 through to '82. Bought up in small parcels at random it seemed like, until I got me an atlas and began putting them all together. The whole tract came out to being one great block forty miles square. Can you believe it? Forty square miles of rock and sand.'

'Where?'

Taylor's drugged grin was sloppy and oddly feminine. A coy ingenue needing a shave. He tried to bring a finger up to his nose and failed.

'I'm telling you, Chuzzy old Chuz . . .'

'So you are.'

'Sure I am. This stuff give you a hangover?'

'No.'

'Chuzzy thinks of everything,' Taylor told the blue roses. 'You know where all that land was? Was in Colorado. Right inna middle of nothing. No water. No 'tricity. No roads. I mean, worthless. That's when I thought mineral rights. Oil, gold, uranium, y'know? Went all the way over to the County Recorders' Office in Portland to check it out. Nothing turned up worth a chicken scratch. All that's down there are fossil beds and solitude. Solitude's the thing, right? Worth more than a million bucks and a nickel. Seeing as how that's what he'd want more than anything, right?'

'How much more hacking did you do?' Maycroft asked.

'Never got the chance. My guy had taken off when I got back to La Grande. I had a crack at going back into that mainframe to get some printouts, but the whole frame had been wiped clean. Nothing left but dead air. Two days later, we got hit by the men in white. You know the rest.'

Maycroft thought of solitude and a broken string of rough brown beads. Of dinosaur tracks and Hari Krishnas with gas-pistols. Of a small boy named Max in the middle of forty miles of nothing but bleached rock. Of Matthew Pepper listening over the intercom in the upper bedroom.

'Got any more o' that juice, Chuzzy? Maybe with a straight-ener in it?'

'Drinking alcohol on top of . . . certainly,' said Maycroft. He laced orange-juice with a liberal shot of vodka and fed it to Taylor in three long pulls. Taylor went to sleep and was a dead weight when Maycroft laid him out like a dead crusader. He would sleep for twenty-four hours and wake up in the powder-blue room with little recollection of the meeting.

'One hour to flight-time, Pepper,' Maycroft told the intercom. 'Time this circus left town, and bags I the window seat. I've never seen Las Vegas from the air.'

'You hear something?' Cassie asked Modoc.

Modoc turned off the yard hose to listen.

His guard dogs had cocked their heads to the south, growling at the chime of bells drifting out of the rippling heat haze. Modoc faced into the hot wind to catch the elusive fragrance of burning incense. The monotonous drone of a bass chant. Saffron robes billowed in the shimmer, and Modoc counted off at least twenty shaved heads coming down the highway.

Modoc wiped off his face with a horny palm.

'The sights you see when you ain't wearing a gun,' he said.

CHAPTER TEN

Las Vegas wore her afternoon face when the shuttle circled to land. Crossing town to the north loop of Highway 95, Pepper and Maycroft were disenchanted.

A manmade scar in the dun wastes, Las Vegas was a carnival queen scrubbed of charm by desert sunlight. Litter blew in her streets and dust scummed her fountains. Without the night to cloak her raw bones, she was a huddle of fanciful concrete shapes overwhelmed by heat, sky, and baked ochre sands. Only at nightfall would her electric necklaces sparkle, her face soften in dancing waterfalls of light, her neon rainbows advertise star attractions in vivid primaries. In daylight she reminded Maycroft of a naked whore with too many yesterdays, and he accelerated into the desert as Pepper cleansed and stripped their guns.

Stained by drifting sand, Tonopah Highway arrowed north between folds and hummocks of grey-white boredom. Distant brown hills ran with the lower edges of the sky, and a long white marlin of cloud pacing the car turned pink and salmon as the afternoon purpled down into evening. A creeping veil of shadow grew out of the western hills to kill the glare, and a fat blood-orange sun sank in a blaze of crimson fingers. The desert became part of the night and the highway shrank to the length of the headlights. Grit rattled on the hood, the tires hummed, and the stars were numberless holes in black lignite.

The lights of the first brothel showed thirty miles out from Las Vegas, a winking oblong of coloured bulbs. A neon girl bounced on a waterbed and the sign read: BEDS BROADS BOOZE *Cards Welcome*, above a crescent of tired-looking trailers and a cinder-block bar.

Maycroft gave it the thumbs down with a drawled:

'Could you see my accountant's face if I charged an evening of bliss in there against my Visa card?'

Pepper worked the action on his Savage.

'Never felt the need to pay for it. You?'

'Not after all those compulsory hygiene lectures the army made us sit through – or seeing the line of "pork swordsmen" waiting on sick-parade for the "umbrella-man". No young subaltern went without nice female companionship in my regiment, so I was never tempted.'

Pepper loaded his Savage and fed it into his shoulder clamshell. Drew it fluently a couple of times and started work on his Tunnel Gun.

'I could never separate the body from the mind – use a woman as a piece of equipment like there was nobody home when I called. There had to be a world more to it than that.'

'Men are the true romantics. Probably why my pubertal acne lasted until I married,' Maycroft said. 'And to express one's finer feelings without going into clinical detail is impossible. Like that famous chap who, when asked about his sex-life, replied with a frown, "I *hate* Saturdays, old boy. *Hate* them." '

Pepper's laugh was sudden and abrupt.

'You get the feeling this conversation's getting nervous?'

'A car at night becomes a perfect confessional. You could tell me about your last days in Vietnam with the man with two noses?'

Pepper loaded the Tunnel Gun with his eyes closed. Smiled with lowered lids.

'Lights ahead on your side,' he said.

'And a good three miles off,' said Maycroft. 'One of the wonders of zero humidity, but it doesn't answer my question.'

'Where does it say questions rate answers? Mostly they earn lies, Chuz.'

'There's nothing idle about my curiosity.'

Pepper holstered his Tunnel Gun and shucked the shells from Maycroft's Ruger.

'Nor Charlie's. The VC knew all about questions. There's

193

this West Pointer named Rowe. Got scooped up by Charlie with four other members of our Special Forces, and was force-marched off into the jungle. Rowe told Charlie he was an engineer and kept to his story through brain-washing, torture, and a starvation diet. Charlie shot Rowe's captain, and the others died of disease, but Rowe survived five years in a tiger cage he couldn't stand up in by living inside himself. At night, the mosquitoes would come to feed on him in their thousands, and he'd kill them by the handful until he passed out. Days would go by when he was too weak to do anything but lie in his own body-waste, but he stayed alive.

'The only times he left that cage was for interrogation. Charlie stood Rowe on a log. Tied his arms behind his back at the wrists, elbows and biceps. Threw the end of the rope over a branch and tied that off so Rowe couldn't do anything but try and keep his balance. Then the questions would start. Too many wrong answers that log was kicked away. Rowe was left hanging there until his shoulders dislocated and his arms were torn out of their sockets. One of their medics would cut him down, reset his arms, let him rest up in his cage, then take him out and start all over again. For five solid years.

'In the end it was all just a crazy black dream, and Rowe kept his mind straight by designing the ultimate luxury hotel in his head. Right down to the waiters' jackets, the colour of the drapes, the size and shape of the swimming pools and the glassware in the bars. Every day in that cage he went to work managing that hotel, hired and fired staff, and decided the menu every morning. He had Charlie fooled, and he survived.

'Then some anti-war characters back home blew his cover. They published Rowe's true particulars in a protest magazine, and made damned sure Hanoi got ahold of some complimentary copies. With their tame engineer turned into a Green Beret, Rowe's interrogators lost face with their bosses in Hanoi, and they had to turn Rowe into jello and fast. They worked him over day and night, but he had their measure, and he wasn't about to die betraying himself. He was just ready to die, and to hell with their by-the-book political claptrap. Finally they

sent Rowe north with five guards, hoping they'd find somebody to order Rowe's execution.

'Then some Cobras came along looking for trouble, saw
Rowe and his Charlie guards, and went in for a strafing run.
Them VCs and Rowe were all in black pyjamas, and must have
all looked the same from the air. Rowe separated himself from
all but one of his honour-guard, and waved his mosquito net
in one of them clearings they have between the dykes. But
if that strafing run hadn't missed, and if one of the brass hadn't
decided he wanted a live Charlie, Rowe would have been mown
down right there by his own people.

'Rowe took out that last Charlie with a stump up the side
of the head. Ran for the nearest helicopter about the time
the sidegunner figured no VCs sported American beards and
held fire. When Rowe climbed into that Cobra he was home
and free, and ten short minutes after takeoff, he was talking
to an old class-buddy over the radio.'

Pepper loaded the reassembled Ruger and passed it across.
Maycroft nodded his thanks.

'That story is relevant to what?'

'To this: Rowe lasted five years. Luther Cash was a basket-
case after two weeks. And to this day I don't know if I'm a
Rowe or a Cash. How about y'self, Chuz?'

Maycroft reduced speed to coast past the next roadhouse.

'That's no kind of question to ask yourself or anybody else.'

'And that joint ain't Bellas,' Pepper said, knowing his point
had gone home.

Harriet's Whorehouse had red window-shades and orange
bulbs chased around the long fascia board. A jukebox thumped
Willy Nelson down the highway, and a patrol car was parked
in amongst the pickups.

Maycroft accelerated away, checking his road-map with
suicidal bugs smearing themselves all over his windscreen.

'All the real-estate to the right of us is one vast nuclear
testing site. You'd think that the thought of that would shrink
the gonads of the sexually active, but Bella's has to be this
side of Indian Springs.'

'You want I should spell you at the wheel?'

'I'd prefer answers I can use. You can't play the clam forever. All veterans have the same arrogance. Their war was different to everybody else's. The stock phrase is: "You weren't there, so you can't know how it was". My Uncle Charles was a prisoner of the Japanese from the surrender at Singapore to VJ-Day, and he never ever talked about it. But he was a conscripted duration-of-hostilities soldier, not a regular like us.'

'What difference does that make? He went through it, not you. He had to find his own peace, his own answers. Talking to himself, not to anybody who'd listen, like a wife or a shrink. When a man is coming to terms with himself, talking gets to be a whole lot of words going nowhere. The talkers are the ones who never make it, Chuz.'

'Like Cash? Or Taylor?'

'Corny Taylor never had Cash's problem. He went with the flow and came out the way he went in, only more so. About issues of morality or conscience Corny couldn't care less, and never will. The only motivation he has is a permanent erection that leads him from bed to bed to bed, and making money is something he does to feed his habit like any sexual junkie. Making bucks to make the broads. Ten minutes after you let him out of that hospital, old Corny'll be sneaking quail from bar-stools without a second thought for you, me, or World War Three.'

'Well,' said Maycroft. 'Cynical old you.'

'Sensible old me. A friend is somebody who knows all about you and still likes you. Knowing your friends as well as you need to know your enemies saves a man a whole raft of unpleasant surprises.'

Maycroft swung out to avoid a dead smear that had lost an argument with a passing truck.

'Talking to you is like peeling an infinite onion. The more layers I peel away, the more there are underneath. And all I end up with is tears in my eyes.'

'Hold it down there, Chuz.'

Pepper dismantled the interior light and put the bulb in the glove compartment.

'We just passed a place in darkness. Don't want the light coming on when we open the doors. Kill the heads and pull in here.'

'I saw nothing,' Maycroft complained.

Pepper cracked his door, ready to roll out.

'Too many onions,' he said.

Maycroft crouched in starlight.

The desert was black on black. Night sounds sweated up the Ruger in his hand and wind played the storm-fence like a harp. His scalp crawled with the long minutes Pepper took to let him into the compound.

'Leave your stomach behind, Chuz. The bastards have killed like once wasn't enough.'

Pepper played his flashlight over a mutilated Dobermann on the stoop, then swung the beam to the remains of a bitch sprawled beside a red Jaguar with opened doors. Her blood soaked papers spilled from a looted briefcase, and somebody had walked across them barefoot, leaving perfect brown sun-dried prints. Maycroft picked up a business card and read it aloud by torchlight.

'Simeon Keller. Cosmetic Surgeon. Tropicana Medical Centre. Las Vegas.'

'The car's registered to that name too. He's inside.'

Pepper stepped over the dead dog and followed his flashlight across the stoop. A broken screen-door opened onto a wrecked kitchen with lewd graffiti scrawled on the walls, and the two men crunched through broken crockery into a bar heady with the fumes of spilled alcohol. All the mirrors and bottles had been smashed, and the floor was frosted by broken glass.

The blinds had been torn from the windows and laid out as a makeshift bed. Two figures were entwined on it. A man and an inflatable doll posed in indecent display, locked together at the hips. The man's bare rump was deeply lacerated, a bloody double moon rising from the trousers puddled around his crossed ankles. Lividity had reddened his face after death, and he and the doll outstared each other, their faces almost touching. Any one of the knife thrusts through his shirt could have killed him. The cleaver in the back of his skull had been driven there for effect.

'Meet the late Doctor Keller,' said Pepper. 'I found the keys to the Jaguar in his pants pocket. There's another guy on exhibit in one of the back rooms. Back past the cribs.'

He and Maycroft went down the long corridor to Bella's private rooms and pushed into the blue and chintz bedroom. The body on the white four-poster leered at its reflection in the mirrored ceiling. The olive face showed no surprise, no resignation. A face that had left life and pain behind without much regret. The milky eyes stared blindly, and the crooked lips sneered enough to bare two very white teeth. The hands clasped the haft of the ham-knife rising from the naked chest, and the slashed throat was a second red sneer. The tiny hearts on the rumpled shorts were redder than the blood trailing down the plump thighs.

'I figure they butchered this one in the bar then laid him out in here. Maybe to make it look like the work of Columbians. It's the way they like to turn a hit into a butcher's shop. And with this being a Mafia house, the Columbians would make a real meal of it.'

'But we know different, don't we?' said Maycroft.

Pepper pointed his torch at the dead olive face.

'D'you make him?'

Maycroft nodded without lighting the White Owl he wanted so badly. Hoped the strain in his voice didn't show in his face.

'He matches up to the candid shots in Juan Melixto's FBI file. According to Kolki, Melixto was our man's contact with the Palm Springs Family. And through them, to this place and Keller's services. Looks like Melixto fell a long way from that window in Miami, and Keller would have been the only person in the whole world to have seen our man's new face. He's still one step ahead of us all the way, Matthew. I could cheerfully break down and weep.'

Pepper's laugh was as dry as wind in mesquite.

'Not this time, Chuz. Not this time.'

'How d'you mean?'

Pepper left the room without answering. Led the way back

198

outside and walked across to the rear of the compound. Flashed his torch at the disturbed sand near the storm-fence. The overlapping footprints and crusted dimes of blood.

'Sandals . . . bare feet . . . and moccasins, right? Read the sign, Chuz. Our Hari Krishnas caught up with somebody right here. Two somebodys, and had a hell of a brawl. And look out beyond the fence there. One high-heeled shoe. There's another just like it in one of the cribs. And right beside that shoe, the same moccasin prints as inside the fence. Whoever it was those characters came up against got a woman away over the fence. Held them off until she was clear, then went over after her. There's blood on the wire near the top of the fence, so he's maybe hurt, but he got away into the desert. And they went after him on foot. Four, maybe five of them in pursuit. If he's an Indian, and that's what I'm betting, they've got their work cut out. That's his turf out there. Not theirs. And that's a break for us.'

Maycroft's night-vision was too poor to make out anything but dark nothing under the stars.

'They've got eight, perhaps ten hours start on us, Pepper. And there's at least five hours to daylight. Just what good would I be out there to you?'

Pepper narrowed his eyes with a lopsided grin.

'None. But don't tell me our friend Keller didn't photograph his handiwork. That kind of nose-job would come up once in a lifetime. He couldn't let it go without some personal record. And Las Vegas never sleeps, so back you go, Chuz. I'll contact you at the motel down the street from Circus-Circus.'

'And what's a piddling burglary to us, that it?'

Maycroft should have been prepared for Pepper's quiet savagery of tone and expression.

'Nothing is all. The man with two noses used Bella's bedroom, Chuz. He watched the news on that wall-mounted Zenith, and laid on that four-poster where the Krishnas left Melixto's body. I could smell him through that boar's nest of blood. But I still need to know what he looks like.'

Pepper went over the fence and jogged toward the distant Funeral Mountains. His flashlight was a bobbing glow-worm until he slid into a downsloping draw. Maycroft rolled a White Owl in his left hand and listened to the desert listen back.

Wind drifted sand over the woman's shoe and the sign above the bordello creaked like an arthritic joint. Maycroft lit the cigar for company and went back to the rental with a million dead eyes chilling his spine, the smell of a charnal house in his nostrils as he drove south along the deserted highway.

Three hours later, he had set off a silent alarm in Keller's office at the Tropicana Medical Centre, and waited to see who would turn up.

Four hours into the Toiyabe Desert, Pepper went to ground to wait for first light. The trail of sandals had petered out in a dry wash below a broken wall of low buttes that fell away into a maze of crisscrossing arroyos. The wind had scoured the high ground of fresh sign, and going on by torchlight would have been senseless. Pepper felt something brush his mind as he squatted in pungent sage with a mouthful of pebbles. It came out of the darkness as a dark and silent bird, circled him and glided away, always at the very edge of his vision. Something vague he couldn't look at directly.

Pepper shivered when it returned a short time later, just as a deep rumble came from the pass he had refused to enter. The ground shook under his feet, and the dragging roar of a rockslide went on for long moments, grinding into silence as if a stone beast had shrugged under the earth's crust. The black bird-shadow skimmed the corners of his eyes and flew into the paling night.

Pepper stamped life into his feet as the wind dropped and the stars dissolved in pre-dawn violet. Streaks of green and rose bannered the eastern horizon, gilded the Funeral Mountains to the west, and washed earth colour into the rolling flatlands above Lee Canyon. Quail chipped from the brush and thirsty burros brayed from an isolated hogan.

Pepper backtracked into a forked draw where the five sets of feet and sandals had milled around to talk to a larger group from the north. One of them had drawn in the sand with a knife, there were dips where rifle butts had rested, and dry pocks marked the dribble of a passed canteen.

The sandals had split after their conference. The original five took off into the high ground, and the larger group followed the false trail that had worried Pepper, trotting directly into the rockfall he had heard. Without the need to investigate, he knew what had happened to them.

Quartering the ground as he went, Pepper took the north fork and jogged for a half-mile before he found the sagebrush broom he and the sandals had missed in the darkness. It had swept the ground for fifty yards on either side of where it lay, and had bounced before settling in the sugary pink sand. No tracks led away from it, and meant it had been thrown down from the western rim of the draw, a sheer limestone butte with high bellies of overhang.

Pepper scanned the heights with a grunt of disbelief.

'You may have gotten up there, Indian,' he said aloud. 'But the lady sure as flying didn't.'

Pepper moved down the twisting draw until he found the clump of sage the broom had been cut from. The raw scar had been camouflaged with spit and sand, but still showed to his experienced eye. Pepper bored into the dense growth and found it concealed a deep slash in the rockface that opened out into a natural chimney studded with fossil shells and amonites. He squeezed into the vertical fissure and climbed the spiralling fault to the summit, pausing for breath below the rim, sensing wrongness.

Cold coils came into his mind.

Fangs hooked into his upper lip.

Freeing his flashlight, Pepper gingerly probed the last handhold without raising his head to look, felt the snap of powerful jaws on the hard rubber handle, the pull of squat power straining his wrist. Black and yellow diamonds squirmed in the dark cleft, and venom drooled from a purple mouth.

Pepper rose on a one-armed lift, kicked himself out onto the upper shelf of rock, and lifted the gila monster from its lair with a grunt of effort. Rolled into crashing sunlight holding the reptile at arm's length, more than arid heat sweating up his face. The gila hung from the torch with a thrashing tail until Pepper threw it from him. Hissing and furious, the gila backed away, taking the flashlight with him. Gone with a flick.

Crawling away, Pepper lay on his stomach to take in the view.

The sky was as blue as a Boston stocking, the Funerals had turned the horizon to sepia, and the wastes below his vantage point ranged from dull marzipan to the high gold of Jamaican rum. With the sun at his back, Pepper could see for miles in the clear morning air.

Shadowing his eyes, he traced the broken foothills of the Springs down past Lee Canyon to the washes and arroyos cutting the ground below him. The fresh landslide was a bright crimson scar to his left, and about two-miles north-west of him, small saffron figures toiled out of a canyon the cream of flaked almond.

Charting the route the Indian and the girl must have taken away from the butte where he lay, Pepper figured the sandals would cut their trail before noon. The barefoot girl would be completely lame long before then, and the Indian would have to fort her up. Out of the sun and near water. Then the Indian could use the desert to his advantage.

Pepper dribbled sand through his fingers. Working on a way to get between the sandals and the Indian. Deciding it would be a close-run thing, he picked his way down to the flatlands through limestone slides with his eyes peeled for water-bearing cactus.

Maycroft had shaved and breakfasted in his cell when the lawyer he requested was locked in with him. A tall Sicilian with a tan and a stoop, he leaned against the grey wall until the deputy had gone. He bared ivory teeth and shot a white cuff from a heavily jewelled gold watch.

'You got ahold of my name how?' he asked.

Maycroft smiled without warmth.

'From Simeon Keller's files. You're listed as his legal advisor, so I ran you through Washington before I called you at home. You made colourful reading, Mr Salvatore, and with you representing me I face the future with confidence.'

The lawyer looked at Maycroft as if he was just another

roach in the cell. Said: 'You steal medical records from my client's office, and you expect me to defend you? I'm giving you one short minute, Mr John Doe.'

'You'll give me as long as I want, Salvatore. Keller's dead.'

'How? According to the uniforms out there, your piece hasn't been fired.'

Maycroft's smile was as thin as Detroit chrome.

'Juan Melixto is also moribund. The name I breathed down the phone at you? The reason you're taking a closer look at me.'

'Juan Melixto died in Miami a while back, smartass.'

'And managed to die again yesterday. *Here*. In Nevada.'

'Forty seconds left, Mr Doe.'

Maycroft crossed a knee. Smoothed a seam and stopped smiling.

'Then I'll talk more slowly. You get to think a good deal faster. Upset me and you upset Washington. Washington will in turn upset Palm Springs. You leave me to the tender mercies of the local law and Las Vegas will simply swarm with Federal agents. Making waves and the wrong kind of headlines. It's you who's on a time-limit, not me.'

The lawyer thumbed his tanned nose and looked bleak.

'And you want what exactly?'

'To walk out of here with my Ruger, the medical files from Keller's office, and blissful peace of mind. Nothing on the police blotter, and none of your people on my tail.'

'For which you exchange what?'

'The location of the bodies in question, my silence, and no FBI.'

'For pictures of some nose-job?'

'You have it in one.'

The lawyer leaned off the wall. Hung a thumb in his waistcoat and looked at his ugly expensive watch.

'You could have called me direct, you know. Saved me all this chicken shit hassle with the local law.'

'Ah, but can you think of a safer place for us to talk? Would you have been so amenable on some quiet desert road? You Mafiosi fellows tend to act first and think second. I wasn't about to take that chance.'

'Hey, Limey, do I look to be into that kind of garbage?'

'To paraphrase: You can't tell a crook by his cover.'

'You get it said, don't you?'

'I've seen your file, remember?'

The lawyer puffed his hollow cheeks.

'OK, smartass. OK. Palm Springs will want to know how this nose-job connects with Keller and Melixto ending up on a slab. Just out of curiosity, you understand. No way does either guy connect with Palm Springs.'

'Of course not. Melixto knew a guy named Kolki from the Cuban days. When Palm Springs tried to reopen the casinos in Havana. Kolki told the nose job Melixto could arrange discreet plastic surgery and secure after-care for a price. The nose job was the kind of Washington connection Melixto dreamed of – even compromised his own connection with your people to fix it, and ended up extremely dead for his pains. A calculated risk in these troubled times when your people in Palm Springs are having all kinds of trouble keeping control of their traditional territories. Melixto was losing ground in Miami against the Cubans and Colombians, and he must have thought an ''in'' with a high-ranking Washington official could only be beneficial. He was wrong and got dead, and the last thing Palm Springs needs is the FBI swarming in to despoil Las Vegas's laundered image. I'd say that discretion on your part would please them. As to the nose-job, your people can safely leave him to me.'

'You being who exactly?'

'Me and the Washington numbers you checked out.'

'Hands off with a smile, huh?'

'Again in one.'

'And if you accidentally-on-purpose got dead in the desert we could expect a whole raft of government seersuckers swarming The Strip?'

'Even your breakfast grapefruit would be working for Uncle Sam.'

'No wonder Phoenix sounded bemused. The FBI down there never even heard of you. That puts you left of left-field, Mr John Doe Maycroft. Means you go as high as a certain Admiral with an office a spit and a jump down the corridor from the Oval Office. Right?'

Maycroft said nothing with a cocked eyebrow.

The lawyer sucked an ivory tooth.

'Don't race your motor, Maycroft. Let's just say that certain government guys are as shook about those mothering Cubans as us, and we're riding the same posse until they're neutralised. After that, the old battle lines'll be redrawn. Enough said?'

'Yes, I'd say so.'

'Off the record, you wouldn't like to tell me how a Limey got his ass into all this, would you?'

Maycroft just smiled his meaningless smile.

The lawyer sighed with mild reproof.

'Time was everybody knew who the opposition was. Now? Zilch.'

'Blame television,' said Maycroft.

The lawyer banged on the cell door.

'I'll make some calls and get back to you. Get your necktie and shoelaces back. You said Melixto and Keller were where?'

'I didn't. Try looking about seventy miles up Highway 95.'

The lawyer suddenly had whites to his eyes.

'They didn't hit on Bella too, for Chrissakes? Best damned madam in Nevada.'

'Not that I saw. It was nighttime.'

'And Modoc? Bella's Indian?'

'He was hurt, but he made it into the desert.'

The lawyer punched the steel door again.

'Then somebody's gonna be staring at the sun without eyelids. You want I should send you some coffee?'

'And my wristwatch. I'm dashed if I understand how you people can live in a town without clocks.'

'I'll get back to you.'

'I'll be here.'

Maycroft lay back to worry about Pepper with faint amusement masking his inner feelings.

Cassie gave Modoc her red dress and lay in the trench he had dug for her. He had rubbed cactus juice into her swollen

205

feet and left her five cubes of pith to chew on when she needed to slake her thirst.

The sand under her back was surprisingly cool, and she watched Modoc haul a joshua tree into position over her supine face, jamming it upright between two rocks. He had cut an airhole up through the core of the plant so that she could breathe when he covered her with a slab of limestone, and slow joshua sap dripped onto her cheeks as Modoc hauled the rock into position.

The slab slammed down over the trench and sand dribbled onto her naked body. The sudden darkness made her gasp, and she fought panic until her eyes became accustomed to the vague spill of light coming down the airhole in the joshua tree.

If Modoc spoke whilst he made the slab and the joshua blend with the landscape, Cassie didn't hear him, but his orders had been clear. If he didn't come back for her, she was to wait until dark before digging herself out. Then, avoiding any traffic, she was to follow the highway to Pahrump, and find Modoc's sister-woman at her hogan near the 372 Interchange east of the Nopahs. Old Mary Threehands would know what to do, and Cassie ought to cover the twenty miles in a single night's march if she used her strength right.

The way Modoc had said that had Cassie believing he wouldn't be back, and her fear of the taciturn Indian was replaced by real concern for his survival. The machete wound in his side hadn't had time to scab properly because of Modoc's exertions to send the landslide down on their pursuers.

A last handful of stones clattered across the limestone slab and the quietness drew out into silence. Modoc had gone, and Cassie refused to weep as she waited for night.

The sun had climbed into white glare when Pepper found the cactus Modoc had cored for the water in its pith. His moccasins angled heavily as he supported the girl, and her prints were dragging hops. Both sets wound through scattered shale and old stumps below the razorback ridge overlooking Highway 160, and Pepper damned the Indian for not getting the girl to cover when he'd had the chance.

The trotting sandals had cut the trail a mile back, and three sets of prints had veered off into the high ground before reaching the dissected cactus, leaving two sets to follow the Indian and the lame girl. And if, as Pepper suspected, the sandals had the right kind of support vehicle on the highway, outrunning a hurt Indian and a footsore girl would give them no trouble at all.

Pepper crouched over the tracks and knuckled his chin. Grinned and stood up.

The trail was another phoney the Indian had laid out on his own. Only one person had made for the highway over the high ridge, and the Indian had split the sandals up by superior craft. Pepper kept a low profile as he climbed, his outline lost in heat haze. Lizards flicked away into the boulders and a nest of young horned vipers reared as he passed. He went up through a slide of pitted rock and dropped into a hollow with the two sandals who had pressed on after the Indian. Taken from behind, they had fallen with their weapons in hand. One had ploughed up the sand with his face, and the other one had sat down hard to hold his throat together. Both had machetes, pistols and surprised expressions.

The bark and flutter of a ·30/30 rifle came over the ridge, and confused echoes chased down the arroyos to Pepper's rear. He kneeled up to listen, and tyres hummed on the road long before he picked up engine noise.

Pepper climbed without drawing his guns. His work would have to be silent and at close range, and he watched for a lookout as he worked upward.

The day got hotter and his sweat dried in his pores.

Pepper lay flat to blend with the crest of the ridge.

The paved highway cut the desert a hundred yards off, and a mustard dune-buggy carried four saffron figures out of the northern shimmer. Something that could have been the red skirt of a woman's dress fluttered in a dip between the ridge and the road, and must have drawn fire from the ·30/30. Pepper sniffed the wind to locate the source of the gunfire.

A rising thermal rolled human scent up into Pepper's face.

The smell of cartridges and the feminine musk of sour perfume and unwashed hair. The man smells of leather, sweat and oriental body-paint. A rifle-bolt worked a fresh shell into a breech, and a call-sign came from a two-way radio in a burst of static. A woman answered, and Pepper judged her to be about thirty feet below him.

He wormed down into a shallow gully of sand and inched out onto the lip of a glass-smooth overhang hot enough to burn through his clothes. Ignoring the discomfort, he lay still to listen.

'Yo,' buggy,' said the woman. 'This is Moonlady. Brother Wind here just nailed himself an whore to the cross. But that aborigine pimp is still running free down there. He cost us six brothers in that rockfall, and we can't raise Steelhead or Brother Orange. Now could be their radio's out, but we're taking no chances. Wind and me plan to slice his hide personally. You come on in easy, and we'll flush that Navajo no-account into Wind's sights.'

'Got the bitch twice, tell him,' said Wind the rifleman.

'Boasting is blaspheming, Wind,' the woman scolded. 'Get that stock back in your shoulder and cover us. Me and Blue are going down there. You read that, buggy?'

'Come ahead,' said the radio.

'Stay outta my crosshairs, Moonlady,' said Wind. 'You make one swell target.'

'In your dreams, Wind.'

Shale rattled and Pepper watched a man and a woman emerge from the shadow of the overhang to angle down towards the red dress.

Blue was scrawny and his head was shaved. Moonlady carried a machete and a radio, and her saffron robe billowed around meaty thighs like a cinema curtain. Her hair was tightly beaded and braided, and several strings of brown beads bit her thick white neck. When she glanced up and back, the kohl around her eyes had run down her cheeks to smudge her chin.

For a blinding moment Pepper saw her at the Clayton place. Reaching to smother Max against her huge bosom. Stinking him up with her cheap perfume to the sound of bells. Jabbing him with her machete to teach him fear.

'Max wouldn't have cried,' Pepper muttered. 'Not for *her*.'

His hands met around a fat and invisible neck to squeeze on nothing. Moonlady's eyes rolled to white and became part of the sky. Pepper spread his fingers against burning rock and forced himself to stay where he was.

Blue had reached the red dress and pointed down at it with a small black pistol. Yelled something at Moonlady and slid into the dip to roll the body over. Held it aloft with a scrawny arm to scatter twigs and shout sarcasm at the rifleman.

'Here's your whore, Wind. You done killed yourself a mess of tumbleweed real dead.'

Pepper heard Wind damn his luck and Moonlady took a small landslide into the depression with her. She knocked the stuffed dress from Blue's grasp, hacking it apart with her machete, big breasts rolling under soiled saffron as she worked off her manic frustration.

Wind laughed, and Blue grinned until the machete hacked sand into his face. Momentarily blinded, Blue knuckled his eyes as the red soil behind him surged upright. Spitting out a gritty expletive, Blue stepped back into the embrace of a man in brown deerskin, and Modoc cut Blue's throat before he could cry out.

Wind breathed out to steady his aim when the Indian came up out of the ground, unable to fire with Moonlady's bulk blocking his shot. Pepper hung over the rim of the overhang. All he could see was the tip of the rifle running out of a cleft some fifteen-feet below him. Wind would be hard to take by surprise.

Held upright, Blue jerked in terminal dance as Modoc walked him toward Moonlady. Wind's hard whistle brought her head up and she saw Pepper outlined in glare a moment before Blue spat blood at her.

Rearing away with a violent double-take, Moonlady lost her footing and fell heavily, fending off Modoc's skinning knife with wild swings of her machete. Scrabbling along the trench on heels and buttocks she lost the radio, and Modoc crushed it with a hard stamp as it tried to ask what was happening.

Wind grunted and the rifle steadied.

Modoc heaved Blue at Moonlady and went flat. A heavy slug tore a hole where his heart had been and Moonlady screamed a warning at Wind that was half-lost in clattering echoes as she went down under Blue's jerking body. She threw Blue away and his last kick spun a sandal into Moonlady's face.

Pepper took the incline in a slide, braking his descent with his feet. Grit and shale showered ahead of him, alerting Wind. Kicking himself out from the overhang, Pepper turned in the air, and landed facing into the cleft.

Wind was squat and brown, and his face was a tiger mask of black and gold paint. He swung at Pepper and worked the rifle-bolt for a close snap-shot. The concussion was deafening in the confined space, and the bullet tore rock splinters from between Pepper's feet. Blew chippings back into Wind's painted face and snapped his shaved head back into the low limestone roof.

Pepper used the swivel-kick of the emperor's horse, slamming Wind on to his back in a loose sprawl. The rifle leaned itself against a dying thigh and brass shells spilled from a fringed leather bag. Pepper scooped up both rifle and ammunition and checked on the Indian.

Despite the wound in his side, Modoc moved well. He backed Moonlady out of the dip with darts and feints of his skinning knife, countering her machete cuts like a dancer.

'I gut you, woman,' he promised. 'Like you cut me and gutted my dogs.'

'In your dreams, Indian.'

Moonlady thought she could keep Modoc at bay until the buggy arrived. She stood her ground daring him to come at her.

Pepper settled himself to cover the dune-buggy. It had swung from the highway and was coming fast in a boiling cloud of pink dust. An Uzzi burped from the front passenger seat. Sand dollies ripped along the trench. Chopped up the ground at Modoc's heels, forcing him onto Moonlady's machete.

Modoc blurred into motion. Shouldered in under Moonlady's guard and pinked her in both arms with quick lateral cuts. Forearmed her across the throat and spun her between him and the Uzzi.

'No dreams, woman.'

Moonlady screamed her mantra as Pepper loaded and fired the ·30/30.

The buggy driver sat up very straight.

Pepper reloaded and fired again.

Punched sideways, the driver folded outward from the waist. His head hit the sand and he was flipped free as the buggy slewed. The front wheels carved through a dune and the buggy turned on its axis, throwing up dry waves of sand. Bodies tumbled and the buggy showed its undersides, churning to rest in a long and lazy drift of swirling dust. The engine cut out as the carburettor flooded, and the silence was as abrupt as a slamming door.

One of the saffron figures came out of a final bounce on rubber legs and tried to find the Uzzi. Staggered a few steps and fell on his face. The dust settled and the others lay where they had fallen.

Pepper threw the rifle as far as he could, draped Wind's body over his shoulder and started down the slope.

Mute with shock, Moonlady swayed on the spot. She was just a fat woman with a big knife and nowhere to go. She let Modoc take her machete and sank to the ground to stare at her blood spotting the sand.

Modoc squatted on his haunches turning the machete to catch the light as Pepper carried Wind down to where he waited. Modoc had no need of questions. The way the blond man looked at the fat woman told Modoc all he needed to know, and when Pepper had thrown Wind into the trench beside Blue, Modoc spoke.

'You want this woman I think.'

'If all the others are finished.'

Modoc glanced at the buggy and off toward the pass.

'These are. The desert took the rest.'

'With your help, Navajo.'

'The woman is yours. I go over there aways.'

'Yeah, that little gal won't stay buried forever.'

Modoc looked away at nothing and everything.

'You see pretty good,' he said softly.

'I *guess* pretty good.'

'Same corn, different husk.'

Modoc rolled Moonlady onto her stomach, and she mewed when he wiped his knife off on her exposed buttock. Modoc sheathed the knife, stuck the machete into the ground, and stood holding his ribs.

Pepper offered to bring the first-aid box from the buggy, and Modoc didn't sneer out of politeness.

'Your medicine is not my medicine,' he said. 'And I'll take nothing from these half-people. They use the magic cactus to make their minds fly, but their feet are dead sticks in the earth. No roots. By dark, this woman would eat glass for a taste of their drink. I saw them share a flask last night before the rocks fell. When she needs that drink she'll talk good. No need to cut her too much I think.'

'Thanks for the advice.'

Modoc's forehead creased. Being thanked for the obvious only diminished the gift. He held Pepper's eyes without staring.

'I felt you out there last night. Once before the rocks fell. One time more when they did. You felt me I think.'

Pepper nodded and let Modoc's eyes slide away.

'I took an owl for a shadow. If it was your owl it came twice.'

Modoc allowed thought to show in his brown face. The blond man knew about spirit owls, but not enough to avoid talking about them. But he was a white eyes and that figured.

'Listen,' Modoc said. 'When you kill this woman you will kill burned sand. Her heart is a black pebble, and her soul was never alive. She was born lost, a mud ball without breath. All these others in robes were the same. All their thoughts were borrowed things of no value. Planted stones they carried for another man stronger than them. They're soldier bees from his bad hive. They must be buried deep where the desert things can't eat the taint in their flesh. Their dark dreams must not pass into the desert things. Friend coyote has enough madness to share with the moonlight.'

'This hive you see, is it close?'

Modoc's grandfather had known how to live with the Something Else that came in dreams. Talking of the old ways was

212

not easy, even alone on Big Mountain, and making the words for this white eyes was impossible. But Modoc needed to give Pepper something. Not to would be very bad. He scuffed the sand and tried not to smell the woman. Finally he said:

'It is the place of this woman. It is in her now, and it is far away where nobody goes. Only the feet of the big lizards have walked there. Until these half-people stole the place for their own. Beyond the Rio Grande and the mountains you call the Rockies. Cut the rest from the woman.'

Pepper asked his big question with a dry mouth.

'Do you see a boy?'

'There is a boy,' said Modoc. Knowing without knowing how.

Pepper's sigh was a torn thing. His eyes watered yet he grinned.

'I'll start digging. You mind if we use their shovel?'

Modoc hid a rare smile behind his hand.

'Use it. I'll be back in two graves time.'

Moonlady mumbled a song from childhood, blind to her surroundings. Modoc loped away and Pepper searched the buggy for a shovel, thinking of Max. Alive.

Moonlady came out of her stupor to fight stomach cramps.

Still blindfolded, she rolled into a ball to gasp for air, needing a curative drink from Wind's phial. Without it there was no focus to her thoughts. There was a vague remembrance of crawling through narrows of living rock as the day lost heat and light. Of being thrown down to fight withdrawal symptoms with a running nose and shaking limbs as pemmican simmered in grease with squash and herbs.

Shivering against a floor of smooth stone, Moonlady smelled water in the still air as wheatcakes baked over a chipped kindling fire. Voices and the small sounds of cooking threw flinty echoes into far reaches, and the woman with the two men had to be the whore in the red dress who had turned to twigs under the machete.

Moonlady's mind jumped from the bordello dogs to the crushing rockfall, flinched when Blue kicked his sandal at her, and froze when the buggy spilled the last of her brothers into the sands of the Toiyabe. Wind and Blue were shovelled into the ground, and the Indian's knife cut into Moonlady's arms. Now they throbbed under their dressings of vegetable paste and wild honey, a sure sign that she was to live long enough to give them what they wanted to know.

Moonlady turned her blindfolded face toward the heat of the unseen fire and asked for water. If one of them came close enough she knew how to kill with her teeth. Then they would have to finish her without the chance of her betraying the commune.

A calloused hand came out of nowhere. Lifted her chin as she bit on the gourd put to her mouth. Bitter liquid stung her parched lips and numbed her swollen tongue. It was like the brotherhood drink, but somehow subtly changed. Added to in some odd way. Moonlady's jaws were clamped shut when she tried to retch it up, and her throat was stretched taut until she took the whole draught. The familiar euphoria came with suddenness, but the singing strength was missing. Moonlady went limp and blinked slowly when the blindfold was stripped away.

Modoc left her to sit between Pepper and Cassie, and Moonlady couldn't hate them as she should. All she felt was childish curiosity.

The cave was a shadowed mustard womb big enough to house a navy blimp. A natural limestone shelf ran off into darkness above a pool of fossil water the black of oiled silk, and wall niches held human bones. Above these burial chambers was a vast panoramic wall-painting in blacks, browns, creams and whites. Rare earths had been pounded to make reds, jades and singing blues, and hammered sheets of silver formed auras around gods from the Lost Time of the Old Ones. Their Sky World dominated the four sacred mountains of The People who came after, and were now the Navajo and the Hopi. Father Sun and Earth Mother sent The Twins to earth down the rainbow ladder; Monster Slayer to twist cloud into tornadoes, Child-of-Water to stir the air into hurricanes.

Elk men made crude medicine in forested hills and tracked game through snowfields under dying glaciers. Hunters of many totems ran bison from a cliff and speared them in pits. Blue corn grew under the cliff dwellings of the three mesas, and green parrots marked all the desert springs. The feathered figures of kachina dancers made the sacred circle of the rain dance under arrows of lightning, and the animals of the great annual hunt made a frieze between the Door to the Western Gate and the Circle of Knowing. The all-seeing lawgiver Massa'u held the stone tablet that showed The Way to the True White Brother, and the Breath-Giver blew life into mud figures to bring The People out of the earth. The colours had become part of the stone, and the figures writhed with life borrowed from the fire.

Dread stole Moonlady's breath. The Indian wouldn't have shown her these secret things if he meant her to live, and she was helpless, even her hatred had been stolen by the poisoned drink. The magical picture-writing seared her mind like a bad acid trip, and tearing her eyes away took the last of her resistance. Moonlady stared into the black lake as the questions started, and her tongue rolled away from her teeth when she tried to bite through it.

Pepper's voice was as pleasant as any shrink's, but Moonlady wasn't fooled. She knew the way they asked questions to fill their notebooks. Made tests only they understood and walked through her brain like a public park. But telling the difference between what she thought and what she was telling Pepper was impossible.

Plunged back into time, Moonlady left Yuma by Greyhound as Debra Houseman, and hit San Francisco when Candlestick Park was all self-proclaimed gurus, flowers and mantras, hard rock and free dope. Spontaneous love-ins where strangers shared their bodies and roaches with equal abandon, and free-wheeling Debra graduated from muggles to hard tabs in a frenetic brawl of Beatles, Stones and Alice Cooper. She popped speed and snorted coke, sang protest songs and danced naked, and it was Moonlady who clawed her way to the surface after weeks of craziness into the cold light of psychosis.

Strung out beyond recall, Moonlady rose from a sea of bareassed hippies sleeping off the long nights of carnival in an apartment she had never seen before. Her money and previous fragile identity long gone, she remembered balling girls and guys without caring which was which. She held on to being Moonlady, and made for the street in clothes picked at random from a general heap. Debra Houseman was dead, and Moonlady fell through the sidewalk into a cockroachy public hospital where they let her scream through thirty days of cold turkey.

All hollowed out, she saw herself in a mirror. Fat and down and dirty. In a shapeless numbered gown with stringy hair plastered around an empty face with emptier eyes. When she had finished smashing all there was to smash she tried to peel her face from her skull until they held her down and sedated her into oblivion.

That was the grey time and she never knew how long it lasted.

Kept outwardly placid by soporific drugs, Moonlady screamed inside her head and willed her heart to stop beating. But it pumped on through tests and questions as she matched wooden shapes to the right holes, said ink blots were butterflies raping enchilladas or mafia guys making a hit on a loan shark, and smiled sweetly until they let her out with a change of underwear, ten dollars, and the address of a halfway house.

Boarding with do-gooders who said prayers at every meal and told Moonlady who she ought to be, she worked a diner where nobody cared what the help looked like so long as the short-orders hit the counter fast and all the tips went into the manager's bean jar.

Moonlady went along with all that until Elmo and Sadsack swung by the diner to push tabs at the Berkeley students who hung out there. Elmo tagged Moonlady as a strung-out white momma with unravelled seams, and slipped her a jolt of happy-powder on the cuff. Moonlady hit the restroom, the tab hit Moonlady, and she hit the road with Elmo and Sadsack after giving the manager the finger in lieu of notice.

Higher than the Sky World on the wall painting, Moonlady lost the next seventy-two hours chasing her thumbs across a motel bed as Elmo and Sadsack romped all over her. Then she serviced all the tricks they fed her. They set her up permanently, and Moonlady's crib made money until she was busted by the vice squad.

Moonlady drew ninety days, dried out writhing through all the bad dreams Debra should have left in Yuma, and came back to the outside world looking and feeling like a female blimp. Elmo and Sadsack had drifted down into Mexico, and Moonlady worked the bus station without turning a single trick. That night she slept rough, and crazy for a fix, she held up a liquor store with a borrowed gun in company with a chippy from Salinas. Capping off rounds into the owner and his wife after rifling the cash register was something she did without thinking. And wasting the girl from Salinas instead of splitting the eighty-nine dollars and change made a kind of sense when she got around to thinking about it after dropping acid. Debra had knifed her stepfather for busfare out of Yuma, and made it easy for Moonlady to follow suit.

When her head was straight, Moonlady moved on to banks, and lucked out on her fifth solo robbery, a new Savings & Loans on Market Street. The instant she showed her gun, the counter grills slammed and the door to the street locked fast. Choked by CS gas pumped in from the street, Moonlady emptied her gun at nothing and gave herself up to half the blues in California.

After seventeen months of medical and psychiatric reports, interim hearings and delays, her case was thrown out of court on a legal technicality, and Moonlady was back in business the following afternoon. She hit a bank on closing with nothing but her thumb in her coat pocket, and walked out with $78,000 in used bills. Taking the night shuttle to Los Angeles, she lost herself in the marijuana clouds of Long Beach, partying on bennies and horse until she found herself strapped to a bed in a psychiatric ward.

Found unfit to plead to murdering an old gay pusher and his pedigree terriers, she was committed to an institution for the criminally insane for the duration of her natural life, and from day one she was kept in isolation.

For months she never saw another patient or the nursing

staff, and her gown and bed linen were changed whilst she lay in drug-induced twilight. Then a board of solemn doctors with military tabs put her through some kind of programme that involved swirling lights and electronic sound, and she was moved to a concrete building with no windows.

There were dark rooms filled with whispers, bright and blank rooms so acoustically perfect she deafened herself with her own breathing, and quiet days in a garden room where all the plants were behind safety glass. For long periods she couldn't distinguish between sleeping and waking, and the Important Voice came to her out of the walls. Told things about herself that opened her to the bone, authoritarian rhetoric chased her into the greyness of not knowing. Brought back by the Important Voice, she met Debra Houseman as a third person, and relived her childhood like a fly on the wall of her own mind. Told what she must become with clinical precision, Moonlady became what the voice wanted. There was nothing else to do.

She was let out into a real garden after that, but the Important Voice was always with her, guiding her new persona. In the end it was right inside her head, a wordless compunction she could not defy, and she thought what it wanted her to think

The garden changed with the seasons and Moonlady was nothing without the Important Voice. On the days it didn't come, she sat still and did nothing, and would have starved without being told to eat.

An enclosed vehicle took her on a long drive and let her out into desert sunlight. Blinking and disorientated, Moonlady was shy of the silent brown beads who came across the plaza to meet her. They took her to a bath house where she was scrubbed and oiled, had her hair braided and was issued with a saffron robe. Forbidden to speak, she was led to eat in a communal dining area where the hundreds of wind chimes reminded her of Shangri La.

After the vegetarian meal, a bitter drink was served as a toast to the Coming One, and the Important Voice came from hidden microphones as the company linked hands to listen. Moonlady slept on a cot in the newcomers' dormitory, and id what she was supposed to do without the need for orders. The Important Voice had prepared her, and the bitter brotherhood drink made sure she never forgot.

Like all newcomers she drew water from the well, prepared ice and vegetables in the kitchens, dyed cloth in stone vats, nd learned to raise blue corn in the Hopi manner. She lost her allor and her flaccid limbs hardened. She spoke only when he was spoken to, and learned not to see the doctors in white who came amongst them from time to time. They took people way when they were due for initiation, and those who came ack wore the brown beads, gave orders to the newcomers, nd moved into one of the four brotherhood dormitories.

A full year passed before Moonlady's turn came to go with he doctors in white, and she came out with no memory of hat had happened. She wore her brown beads and attended losed sessions of the Purity Council where the Important Voice spoke of the need for leaving the commune to purge hose on the outside. Moonlady knew what that meant, and he waited for the call, anxious to prove herself to the mportant Voice.

Seconded to Wind's group, she passed months in weapons raining and patrolling the commune lands by buggy or on foot. Moonlady became Wind's equal in tracking, and they spent nuch of their time following the petrified dinosaur tracks cross the eastern basin. At the next Purity Council meeting he learned what happened to the ones who failed the tests f the doctors in white. Expelled into the desert without food r water, they were told to follow the rising sun. Wind and Moonlady were sent after a girl found unworthy. They let her un until she was exhausted, then buried her where she fell. There were others like the girl, both men and women, and Moonlady hunted them down just as the Important Voice vanted.

Soon after the corn harvest, Wind led a group to Oregon a the enclosed vehicle to take money to Kolki's woman in xchange for a boy. The old man there had tried to stop Moonlady taking the child, and Kolki's woman said the brotherhood must wait twenty-four hours before doing so. Wind had lost patience. He gassed the old man and Kolki's woman, and brought the money and the boy back to the commune.

The Important Voice made no judgement on that, and the doctors in white took the boy to the Coming One's temple below ground where none of the brotherhood had been. The doctors in white went away soon after that, and no more newcomers came to the commune. The Important Voice said the Coming One would soon be amongst them, and the Purity Council of forty was ordered to make the commune secure against the outside. The brotherhood was four hundred strong and self-supporting, and the time was near for bringing about the new generation. Celibacy was soon to be a thing of the past.

Called to council with Wind and Blue, Moonlady joined the Purity Council to hear the Important Voice order a last purification of the outside. To cleanse a Nevada bordello of evil, and to bring the Coming One back to the commune. He would be known by His Covered Face, and all the others there must be liquidated. The Coming One's danger made the council savage, and there was anger amongst those not selected to join Wind's band of fifteen . . .

Told to sleep by Pepper, Moonlady stopped talking mid-sentence.

Just when she was ready to say how it had been to hear the Important Voice come from the bandaged man. How his hand on her head had felt. How good it had been to help him step up into the enclosed vehicle when the dune-buggy had been offloaded, knowing He would be waiting at the commune when their work was done. How the red tail-lights had been His eyes when he drove off and the brotherhood deployed in the Toiyabe, but the command to slip into grey mist was too strong, and Moonlady began to fragment. All spooned out like melted sundae, she fell into the greys without the Important Voice to mend the frail seams of her mind. Unravelling as she fell into a dark vacuum alone.

'Dinner is served, Mr Doe.'

A grinning deputy wheeled a lot of restaurant silver into Maycroft's cell and backed out with a wink. The Sicilian lawyer flashed a capped smile between champagne buckets, popped the first cork and poured with a flourish.

Maycroft bowed over the chipped handbasin, washed sleep from his eyes with lukewarm water and dried off with a linen napkin from the tray. Handed a crystal tulip of vintage Bollinger, he sat back on the hard bunk to yawn.

'The last meal before the kiss and the garlic bullet?' he asked.

The lawyer snorted down his nose.

'Nothing so sinister. Fresh sole and asparagus, prime Scotch steak and three out-of-season fruits. The bubbles are imported, and the cigars are way finer than the brown sawdust comes out of Havana these days. You get to eat. I get to talk.'

Maycroft forked the sole, sniffed, shrugged, and began eating. After twenty-one hourse in custody he was hungry.

The lawyer lit a long white cigarette with a gold lighter that tinkled a tune, kept the smoke down for a long beat, and let it out through an ivory smile.

'And he fell upon the victuals with the gusto of a hound-dog,' he said as Maycroft savaged the fish. 'You've given me a busy day. Our laundry-service cleaned up at Bella's. A real butcher-shop of a hit, according to the foreman on the job, and he's seen the elephant more than once. He took Polaroids for Palm Springs and flew them up there with a Xerox of the nose-job medical file. That took some time, and I got word to come see you an hour back. Thought I'd throw you a private dinner to take the edge of the sting.'

Maycroft took the head from an asparagus spear.

'And the sting is?'

'You don't get to walk alone.'

'Well, I am taken aback,' said Maycroft.

'Except you ain't. You wouldn't change expression if your shorts exploded. Palm Springs figures you wanted us in on this from the start. Otherwise you'd have boogied with the file without bothering to make sure we noticed your presence here in entertainment city. You've played both ends, now you want to play the middle, right? So now I get to tell you what goes down here.'

221

Maycroft held his glass out for more champagne.

'And that is?'

The lawyer poured and sighed.

'Why do I get the feeling you know ahead of my saying it?'

'Can't imagine. Chuz.'

'*Salut*, you limey ding-dong. Palm Springs wants the Executive Bureau tape-files the nose-job boogied with.'

'Absolutely not.'

'Not to use. To destroy. Erase. Burn. Whatever. Just so long as they *don't* get back to Washington or Langley. It's too damned sensitive to let those seersuckers get their hands on it. That material goes bang, but nowhere near Palm Springs. And you don't trust Washington any more than we do, which brings us neatly to you coming out of left-field into this boar's nest of dirty dealing. Like I said, nobody, but *nobody* trusts nobody no more. Not the FBI, Langley, the Senate or Congress. Too many empire-builders out there. Too many private armies. All dying to dip their beaks into all that dangerous dirt the nose-job gathered. So, somebody had the bright idea of using an uncommitted nation, namely you. Somebody real high-up sees you as Mr Clean. You may look and sound like a movie butler, but that somebody knows a whole lot different, and Palm Springs plans to go along with that somebody's decision. Like trust you.'

Maycroft wiped butter from his chin.

'And I reciprocate and trust Palm Springs.'

'Only far enough to get the job jobbed. Sure Palm Springs toyed with the idea of keeping all that good shit to use, would've been against nature if they didn't. But maybe we've all gotten that much smarter with the years, and owning the ultimate weapon makes the holder too rich a target for the have-nots. Not just from the outside, but from the inside too. Our internal security would get top-heavy. We'd be so damned busy watching our own people we'd never get around to taking care of business. You hear what I'm telling you?'

Maycroft savoured tender steak. Swallowed and winked.

'Assuming I'm convinced, what's your proposition?'

The lawyer eased a long ash into a side plate.

222

'We join forces. Smear that mothering nose-job with maximum force and minimum noise. We've got everything you need
in the way of fire-power, from fast choppers to ex-vets with
Green Beret training. Name it, you've got it. Well?'

Maycroft's eyes veiled in thought as he weighed prob-
abilities, not least of all his own survival.

'Thirty men with high-altitude parachute training,' he said.
'A night drop from a high-flying aircraft so there's no engine-
noise heard on the ground. Silenced weapons and compact
charges. Withdrawal on foot to waiting ground vehicles. Yes,
that should work.'

'That's gonna take some putting together,' said the lawyer.

'That's it. Take it or leave it.'

'We'll take it. One thing though, Palm Springs gets to handle
the nose-job personally. Some things don't change my British
friend, and that's one of them.'

'Tell that to Max's father.'

'Say who?'

'Chuz,' said Maycroft, chinking glasses.

Modoc let Cassie snuggle for comfort as he watched Pepper
tie Moonlady up with rawhide strips.

No way would Bella have made it across the Toiyabe like
Cassie had, and if Bella hadn't kept the girls in Las Vegas for
that extra night, they'd all have been massacred by the half-
people. Now it was Bella or the bandaged man. No contest,
thought Modoc. He would go into lizard country with the
blond man.

Pepper tied a last knot and spoke without turning.

'No way, Navajo. He's mine.'

Modoc felt no surprise. Pepper had the power of knowing,
but he was blind. Just as Moonlady and the others had been
blinded. Like all whites, they saw revenge as an end in itself.
They killed their own like their dams killed the river and the
fish, and their machines ripped the hearts from the sacred
mountains for coal and aluminium. Raping the earth until it
screamed and died. Always taking without putting anything
back. Covering beauty with concrete and destroying what they

should preserve. They had conquered the land without becoming one with it. They had no inner peace, so living in harmony
with the earth was beyond them.

The prophecy was right. Their own black rain would sweep
them away when it drowned the earth, and from the mud
would come new things. Then Man, like the old lizards, would
have had his day. Modoc knew Pepper sensed these things
but he didn't feel them, which was a sadness of great size.

He had courage and the gift of sight, but he refused to see
the obvious. The bandaged man had a hive of 425 more like
Moonlady, Wind and Blue. One man was just one man for all
his craft, and if Pepper's fingers were knives that killed twice,
there would still be five Moonladys left to kill him back.

Modoc eased himself away from Cassie and cleared his
throat.

'Mister,' he said. 'You and the woman at your feet are the
same now. You've both run the path this man wanted you to
run. Killed them he wanted dead. And now you know this,
you think to kill this man in his hive. And if you do this thing
what then? Can you stop being what you've become? What
will you have left to give the boy?'

Modoc's words thundered in Pepper's mind, paralleling
what he had been thinking himself. He wheeled to look at
the Life Plan Rock behind Modoc, close to yelling.

'Listen yourself,' he said. 'Thinking of going home before
going into combat means a man don't *get* home. For a buck
who left the reservation to swamp floors in a whorehouse
you've got a nerve pushing my buttons.'

Modoc just grunted.

Cassie had stiffened beside him, and her small hand stroked
his arm. She like Modoc could feel Pepper's hurt, but only
on the emotional level. Pepper hadn't looked at her nakedness
directly, but Cassie was conscious of him being conscious of
her. This one really was different. He was no trick to trade
empty smiles with, no loudmouthed rabbit whoring because
he hadn't the emotional equipment to hack it with a waitress.
If Pepper wanted her it was for a lot of reasons she didn't
understand, and there was no way he would make any first

moves with Modoc putting knives into his head. Cassie just wished she had a pretty dress and some ribbons for her hair like she was out on a box social.

Modoc spread his hands over the fire and grunted again. 'Can't push what ain't there, mister.'

'Doesn't mean you've the right,' Pepper sighed.

'Maybe. But the man watching sees more than the man doing. That's if he knows how to look. And you, d'you see all you *can* see? You may see them spirits of mine, but you sure don't feel 'em. That makes you like her at your feet. Just another dead stick in the earth.'

Pepper's bark ran off into the shadows.

'You figure you can explain you to you, Navajo? You're just as lost as any of us. When did you last look at all that picture-writing up there? I mean *really* look at it?'

Modoc touched a solemn brown hand to his heart.

'It's here,' he said simply. 'What've you got there?'

'A ten-dollar bill and a picture of my mother,' Pepper snarled. 'What the hell d'you think?'

'You won't like what I think.'

'Won't stop you thinking it.'

'Nope.'

Modoc rolled makings into yellow paper, pinched off the ends and lit up.

'Spit out what's choking you, Navajo. Ain't no never-mind to me.'

Modoc made smoke from a burning splinter.

'That's the dead stick talking. You're a goddamned liar. Not to me, to yourself. Can't say that in my language, ain't no word for it. Can only say you talk off both sides of your tongue. Asked Bella about that one time. Had her look in her books for all the words for lying. Found fifty-seven before I had her stop. All them ways of saying a man don't know the truth tells me a whole lot about you people. If lies was lice you'd all be busy. A dog-fox gets chiggers in his tail, he backs into a stream until they're all on his nose, ducks under and drowns 'em. Whole world of truth staring at you, but you go right on down the pike with them lies biting on your tailbone. Makes

that old dog-fox smarter'n you, don't it? See, I told you yⲟ
wouldn't like it.'

'That's prejudice, not philosophy,' Pepper shrugged.

'Another ten-dollar word Bella read up for me. Meaⲛ
common-sense. I can live with that.'

'And prejudice?'

'Why not? Hating what's bad ain't too shabby.'

Pepper found himself laughing until the tears came.

'Well, looky,' said Modoc. 'If the sun don't shine at midnighⲧ'

'You're something else, Navajo.'

'If you can see that, whyn't you see the rest?'

'In time perhaps.'

Pepper sobered and climbed back to the fire, trying not ⲧ
see Cassie's bluebird tattoo. For the first time since Oregⲟ
he wanted to smoke, and he distracted himself by staring ⲟ
at the fossil lake of black water. The Indian, the girl, and thⲉ
strange and magical cave had somehow combined to melt hⲓ
reserve. Nobody had got this close to him for a very long timⲉ
and the dark waters reminded him of his loneliness.

Modoc read his mind again.

'Safe to swim there, but cold. And the water's good fⲟ
wounds. This Cassie likes you I think. Not like you like heⲓ
but good enough. Swim. Help each other sleep. This one goⲉ
outside to watch.'

Pepper found himself blushing with too many fingers ⲧ
make fists.

'Damn your eyes, you mothering . . .'

'Sonbitch?' Modoc asked comfortably. 'Been called worsⲉ
by deader sticks'n you. You got a name I can use?'

Pepper looked up as Modoc flowed to his feet.

'Matthew. But I figured you'd get around to calling mⲉ
something fancy like: He-who-walks-far-with-a-dead-stick-uⲣ
where-the-sun-don't-shine-weekdays-or-holidays.'

Modoc's eyes twinkled through chill.

'Matthew. Good strong name. It mean something?'

'I guess so, it's from the Bible.'

'And you dunno what which figures. Even your religion
stolen. Don't you people have anything you ain't borrowⲉ

or stole out from under somebody else? Your God from them old-time Jews, our land from us. If thieving's got a god, you people are all priests.'

'Well this priest plans to take that walk outside with you.'

'Best you don't,' Modoc said. 'If your friend went where you said, the man from Palm Springs will maybe happen along. Jim or his gorillas. You they'd maybe kill. Me they'll maybe talk to. Maybe.'

'That's a world of maybes, friend.'

'Maybes make the world. Fancy words won't change that.'

'You talk white for a Navajo,' Pepper teased.

'Maybe it's the sameness makes the difference, you ever think of that?'

'Couple or three times, yes.'

Modoc's grunt had humour. He hefted the ·30/30 and Wind's ammunition bag. Touched Cassie's head and paused by the hidden entrance.

'I don't come back, Cassie'll get you to the sister-woman over to Pahrump.'

'You sure I'll be here?'

'Hell, Matthew, even iron rusts in the sun. A man rots the same way without he rests up regular. It'll be three-four days afore them communers get to worriting 'bout Moonlady and them others being overdue. And without wheels you ain't going no place. You've figured that, and nobody lies to the desert but the once.'

Modoc left a curl of tobacco smoke in the air when he tucked from sight. It swirled up into the soot stains of a thousand fires and warped to nothing.

With the Indian gone, the cave belonged to nobody.

One day it might fall into the hands of anthropologists and the tourists who came in their wake, but they would never own it. A spur would grow from the highway, restrooms would be thrown up alongside a coffee shop selling postcards and souvenirs, and the desert would retreat from blacktop parking areas.

Pipes would drain the fossil lake to flush public toilets, the old bones would end up in some university basement, and

227

the picture-writing would be protected by glass panels. What had been a secret splendour of native heritage would become another scenic halt on AAA road maps, even more lost to its true owners by being discovered.

Shy and painfully aware of the naked girl, Pepper washed his hands over the fire. She was beside him, in the fire, in the lake. Fine hair tumbled and tangled and roughly finger-combed. The bluebird and freckles on skin the gold of freshly baked biscuit. More freckles across her cheeks and snub nose. Small eyes as brown as glazed chips of Mexican pottery, shyer than his in the guttering flames. The pout of a mouth, unpainted, pink and vulnerable. Tiny hands with scuffed nails, all the more appealing for being roughened by desert sand. One covering her breasts, the other at rest on the smooth and fine grain of demurely clamped thighs. An whore trying to be a little girl.

Or was it the other way around? Pepper wondered.

If she would only say something dumb or crude he could forget the whole damned thing. Be off the hook with no need to make a moral decision. Widowed for less than a week, and wanting to touch girly softness for the comfort it would bring. And if he did, what words would he use? There had to be words, didn't there?'

Donna wouldn't come when he summoned her. There was just an aching void where she used to be.

'Donna's dead,' he said aloud to see if it was true.

And it was. His eyes stayed dry and his chest didn't tighten. Nothing left but the icy stone of loss.

Cassie's touch made his neck tingle.

'But you ain't,' she whispered. 'Unless you want it that way.'

And somehow it was enough.

High on the ridge Modoc grunted softly, attuned to the night things that guarded him. Only the shrinking black pebble of Moonlady's dying struck a discord in the symmetry of his starlit world. When she was in the ground they could all move on.

CHAPTER ELEVEN

Cassie and Mary Threehands waved until Modoc's pickup was out of sight. A black Dobermann paced the truck to the spur onto the highway then stopped to water the rocky verge.

'That's a dog knows his business,' Modoc grunted. 'Pees out his territory and goes home for some shade. Had that old boy up to Bella's until he took to bushwacking the tricks on the way to the john. Got himself a few peckers afore Mary bit him back. Now he sleeps with the mares and don't truck with the stallion. He'll make stew he don't mind Mary real close.'

'Mary's somebody to mind.'

Pepper grinned at the thought of Modoc's leathery old sister and dove back into the black lake with Cassie at his side. Held her by the dying fire as she brought him erect inside her with shy confidence. Setting his body alight with clever hands and liquid moves of her pelvis. The long and slow climb to union that lasted and lasted and was over too quickly for both of them. The second swim of shouts, splashes and echoes, and coming together with gentle urgency for a final ascent into snuggled calm with sparks snapping from a fresh log.

Modoc took a curve and gave Pepper a sideways glance.

'And he asks why I swamp a whorehouse.'

'The mind-game works both ways, Navajo. Bella's fat and forty, and you keep yourself for her. You think more of her than you do that damned dog. It's coming out of your ears.'

Modoc's eyes disappeared in crowsfeet.

'You sleep. I drive,' he grunted.

'Well, Hallelujah,' said Pepper, still stiff from carrying Cassie twenty miles and digging a deep hole for Moonlady. 'And we both take a bath when we reach Utah, my man.'

'I'll think on it.'

'A hundred and fifty miles should be enough.'

Pepper closed his eyes under his hat.

'A man smells, but soap stinks. Ain't natural like dunking in a river,' Modoc grumbled.

He took the pickup over Mount Springs summit and barrelled down to the Route 15 Interchange, touching ninety all the way. The finely tuned engine purred and warm winter air sighed in the quarter-lights. He crossed the Nevada–Arizona border at Mesquite, and the evening cooled when he drove up into Utah. Night came on when he gassed-up in St George, and Pepper came awake as if he'd never been asleep. He gave Modoc money for a sack of groceries and called Maycroft from a public booth.

The motel nightman's voice was wind creaking a hinge, and electronic cicadas chirped on the line before he made the connection. The clicks became a bugged hum when Maycroft answered.

'Room two-two-three.'

Pepper's knuckles whitened around the receiver. He looked out at the neon reds of the gas station canopy and the misty yellow spill of the general store. Counting off the forty-five seconds it would take to trace the call, he said:

'Sounds like you made some new friends, Chuz. Friends from Palm Springs. And that means you'll be coming in like the Seventh Cavalry.'

Maycroft just listened, and Pepper heard ice chink in a glass.

'Also means we part company. For a man who says he likes quiet, you sure invite the crowds. Your new playmates won't be on my team, and means you ain't either from here on in. Should be that surprises me, but it don't.'

Maycroft said nothing as he sipped whisky.

Pepper frowned at the eloquent silence.

'Just remember what happened when Custer blew his bugle, Chuz.'

'Joshua did rather better outside Jericho, Matthew.'

'Yeah.'

Pepper cleared down dead on thirty seconds and pushed out into cold mountain air.

Back at the truck Modoc said, 'You got the look of a man knows who his friends ain't.'

'You a drinking man, Navajo?'

'Only alone or with somebody.'

'Let's you and me go hurt a bottle or three.'

'That instead of taking a bath?'

'Whatever.'

'First white who ever got his priorities right,' said Modoc.

Pepper made for a blue Michelob sign.

'Know what you are, Modoc?'

'Sure, why?'

'Saves me telling you, is all.'

'Let's you and me and that old dog-fox drown some chiggers.'

'Tell me about it,' said Pepper.

The Sicilian lawyer listened to his man on the desk tell him there was no chance of making a trace on Pepper's call and sat on the edge of Maycroft's bed.

'One smart bird dog,' he said.

Maycroft sipped whisky with a broad smile.

'Isn't he just?'

'You know he's a target when we go in?'

'More importantly, my legal friend, so does he.'

'He's still only one man.'

Maycroft drained his glass and reached for the Glenfiddich.

'So I've been told,' he said. 'Often.'

The lawyer gnawed his lower lip with even ivory teeth.

'Ain't you sucking the sauce a mite heavy for a guy making his first high-level practise jump at first light? Don't want you so crocked you break your neck.'

'Englishmen don't get drunk, they get even,' said Maycroft. 'I was leaping from aeroplanes when you were chasing your first ambulance, and a little malt relaxes the knee-joints. Known medical fact, old boy. Now go away and let me slide into the arms of Morpheus. I'm sure your garlic-smelling heavies will see that I don't abscond through a window.'

The lawyer shook his head.

231

'Why choose now to end a dry spell? The only crop whisky waters is a field of hangovers.'

'And the harvest is self-disgust. That's one commodity I can flood the market with, my friend. Old Chuz needs to turn off his mind for a few short hours. Draw a veil of amber liquid over that still, small voice we call conscience. Hide in the fridge with the light out. You do understand, I hope.'

'That you're sauced? Sure.'

'Not just yet. But I'm working on it. Good evening.'

The lawyer went out into the hall to snap fingers at his men.

'Two inside at all times,' he said. 'He don't go to the bathroom without one of you sits on his lap. Anybody sleeps he loses his nose. That guy's holding a wake like he's lost a kid or his mother or something. Something he had to let go of and can't handle what it cost. Weird.'

'You want him worked over maybe, Mr Salvatore?'

The lawyer stroked his upper lip.

'You want to eat your own gun, Moose? That old mother could feed you your head. Just babysit him and take him out to the airfield when it's time.'

'You got it, Mr Salvatore.'

The lawyer went downstairs to stand in the glare of casino neon. Lit himself a long white cigarette and waited for his limousine to glide into the kerb.

'What got to you, Maycroft?' he asked the brilliant night. 'Who'd you shaft when you threw in with us? Wasn't just the bird dog.'

He was still puzzling over it when he reached his suite at the Sahara.

Maycroft responded to the slap on his shoulder by jumping for the oblong of sky beyond the dark hatch. Snatched away in a surge of vertigo, he fell through rushing blueness that turned his lungs to solid lead. The apple-green Dakota elevated away from him in a drone of lazy engine-noise and he spiralled out and down through hard wind-rush. There was too much light and his eyeballs felt sandblasted.

He picked up the count at five and cleared his throat with

232

a gummy cough. His ears popped, spit flew away in a streamer, and the ground turned under his face when he remembered to spread his arms.

Mannikins in blue helmets and coveralls fell below him, swimming for position above a bullseye target the size of a tackhead. The desert was a crumpled tablecloth between low jaundiced hills, coming up at him with inexorable slowness.

'Ten!' he yelled, counting a beat. 'And eleven . . .'

There was nausea in his ankles and his stomach was a knee under his chin. Trying to look at his wrist-altimeter made him tumble and fall faster.

'Thirteen, Christ . . . Fourteen, Jesus . . .'

Eighteen was a million digits away at the far end of an infinite abacus. He kicked into a shallow-dive and felt gravity and air-pressure cave his gut in against his spine. But he could see the ground again, and the dropping zone was only a thousand miles off to his right. He dove towards it and kicked himself in the rump without meaning to. A comic figure plunging to earth, his grey hair belying his teenage stupidity. Captain Nonsense saving the world for no good reason that hungover fool Maycroft could think of.

'Fifteen, stupid . . . Sixteen, mindless . . .'

The whisky left him, and he was alone with unkind clarity. A middle-aged Icarus falling out of the sun with nothing but dark conscience for company. Wondering which number came next as the men below him grew bright canopies and came up past him like opening blooms.

Get to eighteen and punch the release, he told himself. *Go ahead, live with what you've done to Max and Matthew. Or just keep falling and buy the farm. Plough into the sand north of Lake Mead and be a splash of British strawberry jam on the nicotine-stained scree that passes for countryside in this sandheap of a state.*

'Seventeen, bastard . . . Eighteen, coward . . .'

Nylon cord and silk streamed out as he punched the release.

Slammed to a halt, he hung suspended as the yellow earth circled between his feet, not a single blue mannikin in sight. He hung on his harness to swing himself over the bullseye

233

target, sideslipping too far to the right. Correcting with the ease of past experience, he dropped into a descending pattern of ever decreasing circles, and checked he wasn't taking another skydiver's air. The others were far above him, and Maycroft realised he had deadfallen the farthest. He dredged up a grin and swallowed tainted saliva.

The target came up in a big hurry, and Maycroft's heel touched the inner bull before he walked his parachute off with the slight easterly that kept the canopy full. Gathering the red and white silk as he walked, he killed its lift, and sat down to watch the others come in around the target with varying degrees of accuracy. Then he lit a White Owl and thought about breakfast.

'Ten for courage, zilch for style. Where d'you get off playing Superman, you crazy mother?'

The instructor threw his tall shadow over Maycroft, smiling and angry.

'You could've bought the whole damned farm.'

'But I didn't, did I?'

'Not for want of trying, goddamn it.'

'Excuse me a moment,' Maycroft said politely, and threw up on the sand. 'Boyish excitement,' he added, wiping off his mouth. 'So sorry.'

'The guy's a pixie,' said the instructor. 'With the pecker of a goddamned rhino.'

'How kind,' said Maycroft, wondering if another drink would straighten out his eyesight.

Modoc came out from under his hat to look at the day. He had slept crooked, somebody with a grudge had slept in his face, and his mouth was too puckered to hold his tongue and teeth. The pickup jolted through a high mountain pass flanked by knobcone pines and spruce, and Pepper's face vibrated too hard to be looked at. Clenching his skinned knuckles brought Modoc's memory back.

Quiet beers in a booth had become fast shots of Jack Daniels, and Modoc came out of the mensroom to find Pepper gone. He had almost made the door when a spilled drink

234

erupted into swearing and milling and breaking bottles. That had suited Modoc just fine, and he hit faces until he went down under a lot of hot bodies equipped with boots and teeth and fists. Then Pepper was holding the door for him, and telling Modoc he shouldn't have stripped the rotor-head to disable the pickup. Modoc told Pepper he wouldn't have known that without trying to drive away on his ownsome, and if he wanted to fight about it that was just dandy. Then they got busy all over again when the brawl spilled outside, and Modoc fixed the pickup with Pepper knocking heads together until the police cruisers arrived. That meant hiding in a bar down the street where they decided tequila with salt and lemon was the drink to clear their heads, and leaving there was a hazy thing of falls and staggers and remembering the words to 'Sweet Betsy from Pike'. In a motel room Modoc took a bath in his clothes and fell asleep singing in suds. Now he was somewhere else and Pepper was driving as if he'd never taken anything harder than sasparilla.

'You wanna tell me about this?' said Modoc.

'You mean it wasn't your idea to drive through the night? It wasn't you said you could take this heap anywhere drunk, asleep, or just dozing? Must've been two other fellows.'

'That was me, huh?'

'Or a reasonable facsimile. It was that or have you curled up under the hood cuddling that rotor-head of yours. We did the first ten miles with you holding the wheel and me working the gears. Then you needed a nap and just rolled over.'

'That was one good drunk.'

'That was *two* good drunks.'

Modoc squinted at the milometer.

'You've covered nigh on four hundred miles. Where we at?'

'You slept through Shonto and Cortez, and we just left Mesa Verde. Eleven miles to Durango and brunch, and you get to take the wheel all the way to Pueblo. You want some Scotch tape for your eyelids?'

'Maybe some whisky for my eyeballs. Tell me about it in Durango.'

Modoc went back under his hat to snore gently, and Pepper

let the pickup follow the road, thinking as little as possible. One night's sleep away from his son and the man with two noses.

It was the time of the long shadows when the gong summoned the Purity Council to the round table. They came in ones and twos to take their places as the sun sank into the foothills of the Rockies across Black Squirrel Creek. The lamps guttered and brightened as the evening chilled into night, and the council sat in silence, waiting for the Important Voice to express their collective anger. There were fifteen unlit black candles before fifteen empty seats, and after a fitting eulogy of remembrance, the brotherhood would exact retribution on the outsiders responsible.

CHAPTER TWELVE

The terrain of El Paso County was a cauldron of tallow heat.

A prehistoric river wound north and south through crumbled terraces of Mesozoic rock, its wide, faulted bed warped and crazed by land-slips and dehydration. Deep fissures writhed through broken pallets of grey marl, and skipping lizards scurried away from Pepper's mansmell in puffs of white talc. The sun was a ball of glare above the tumbled fret of the eastern shoreline, and long hummocks of smooth claybank rolled west between squat buttes of petrified rock, dipping into a far basin where high upfalls of liquid shimmer boiled the distant Rockies into streamers of pale haze.

Pepper swallowed his last peach in a dribble of syrup, and buried the can with care. Modoc had gone off with a bundle from the pickup, expecting Pepper to understand his need for privacy without explanation. They each had their own way of preparing.

Seeking calm, Pepper spread his arms and kneeled to chant an ancient *shin tao* verse that opened the door to profound mental grace. Blanking off all outer stimulus, he saw his inner-self with inverted eyes, and the shale under his knees became the black teak of the secret Kyoto shrine. He smelled the flames of the dried candle fish, the heat from the charcoal braziers, and the delicate fragrance of green tea on the Master's breath; the fresh jasmine in its bowl, and warm rain in the cherry orchard outside the barred window. Serenity came like a flurry of windborne snow, swirling Pepper into the white perfection of oneness. Lit by the brilliance of his own core, he savoured a long moment of tranquillity before expanding through his body to rejoin the outside world.

237

To his enhanced senses, the naked landscape held a raw and rare beauty. The sun was a friend warming his back, and Lake Meredith was a water-smell off to the south-west. The eighty-mile meander of Pond Creek was a sluggish brown snake wriggling north to south, and he could taste the ferrous metals trapped in the primordial rocks. The great Jurassic rock basin across the dead river was a lifeless bowl of heat where the rocks sang as they absorbed the sunlight and, closer to hand, Pepper became aware of miniature circuits feeding low wattage to electronic sensors buried along the rim of the western shoreline some two miles off. He flowed upright and traced the alien network from horizon to horizon, knowing it was the outer defence of the commune. He had come to the right place.

Modoc's aura brushed him then.

His devotions complete, the Navajo came out of the eastern glare as a hard sear of indomitable self. Having shown himself naked to the cardinal points of the compass, he had scattered dust to the four winds to see where his future lay. When it blew west, he prostrated himself to make union with Earth Mother, and kneeled to offer smoke to the blue face of Father Sky. Sure it was a good day to die, he dressed in clean buckskins and took his weapons to join Pepper. He had Wind's rifle and ammunition, his skinning knife, and a sling made of leather thongs looped through his belt. In his pouch were five skystones Mary Threehands had given him, iron meteorites her grandmother's grandfather had found on Big Mountain, and silently deadly at fifty yards when slung by an expert. Where the rifle or the knife failed, the skystone sling would not.

'Call it.'

Pepper flipped a nickel and Modoc chose heads.

'Buffalo,' said Pepper. 'I carry you.'

Modoc creased his forehead at the two miles of crumbling alluvial river-drift and broken limestone of the prehistoric waterway.

'The hell you don't.'

'Sensors,' said Pepper. 'Me carrying you means we cross as one man. That makes you a big surprise on the other side.

238

Modoc's puzzlement became a wide grin. He turned Pepper to jump on to his back.

'Lucky for you I ain't spurred, horse,' he said.

The nightmare was vivid and disjointed.

Movie clips assembled out of sequence by a devilish cutter.

Plaguing him in the sweating dark until he surged bolt upright in the cool and humming silence of his sleeping chamber, safe under forty feet of rock and lead and concrete and steel. The phantoms of the past lingered in his mouth with the aftertaste of night as he staggered from his bed.

The cold religious fervour of parents who prayed over his 'Mark of Cain' without offering comfort. The nuns who educated him in the closed wing of the convent with the crippled, mongoloid and mentally bewildered. Discovering books held the world between their covers. Hiding with them in the barn loft whilst his father forked hay to the beasts, making the sign of the cross when he saw his son's face in the shadows. The doctor who recognised untutored brilliance and got him to college on a scholarship. The sniggering students who apple-pied his bed. Called him the 'Ugly Mandarin' behind his back but in his hearing. Loathed his appearance and envied his grades. Girls who shuddered when he passed. A small laughing boy pointing at him in the street, wanting his halloween pumpkin carved that sardonic. Him hiding behind his split-nosed mask, seeking weakness and vanity in others to be used for his own ends. His rapid rise through the lower echelons of The Company and the posting to Vietnam when his views and personality became thoroughly unpopular.

He pressed his hot forehead against the full-length dressing mirror. Misted it with his breath and wiped it off to see himself. The new face was still a novelty, but the same old knowing eyes stared back. They reminded him of the ugliness no longer reflected in the multiple surfaces. The hurt had gone too deep for too long to be softened by a patrician nose and a new silver beard. The eyes knew his history. Sent him on the field-trip when a zonked black marine had peeled away from stretcher cases awaiting the medivac chopper to ask how many ugly sticks whitey seersucker had been hit with back there in Whitesville.

'Ain't no air-conditioning out here inna boondocks, fool,' he'd added, slamming his automatic weapon to spurt. 'Only US hamburger's on them stretchers, my man. Less'n you gives this chile one itty-bitty 'scuse to zap your hide. Have you join the brothers on the cemetery chopper for the last flight to glory.'

The insolent grin as he swaggered away from the jeep after urinating against the offside wheel with: 'Salute that, you CIA mother.' An empty and untouchable shell, brutalised by covert missions and drug dependence, saying aloud what all volunteer Grunts felt about Company Snoops who turned up along the Cambodian border.

Many such incidents burned in the knowing eyes.

They saw. They catalogued. Remembered and never forgave.

Gave him Pepper and fifteen black candles to ponder.

Pepper. The only man ever to hold his gaze, look deep and break eye-contact when he had seen enough. A sponge with a hard stone core who saw all there was to see in the knowing eyes, and was impervious to psycho-neuro-probes and sleep deprivation. Feigning breakdown so brilliantly he suckered the PsyOps shrinks into writing him off as a mental derelict with a sunny smile. Seemingly aimless when released, Pepper played the backwoods nomad until they lost sight of him. Just another crazy Vet turned recluse in the wilderness. Hiding his bruised psyche in the thick green canopy until he was ready to emerge.

A sleeper who should have been left to sleep.

Awake now. And coming. All according to plan.

Our plan, said the knowing eyes. *One final vanity. Our last act of personal revenge before giving Ourselves over to the commune. Pepper stared Us down. You and Us. Saw too deeply and would not bend to Our will. He was too strong for Us then. But not now. No, not now . . . The Purity Council will take Pepper alive. Bring him before The Arrived One. Us. Then We shall have Our . . .*

A tolling bell broke his concentration.

Reaching out, he closed the folding mirrors.

Shut his new face and the knowing eyes away.

Hurried from the cool marbles of his private sanctum and crossed the lower temple where genuine basalt dragons from Ankor Wat guarded the staircase of a thousand steps that led up to the main temple and the main air-lock. Pausing for a moment, he admired the rare finds he had made during his final excavations on the site. A fossil pteradon with an eighty-foot wingspan spread in full flight, better than any found in Texas, and a complete Apatosaurus that measured sixty-five feet from head to tail, and would have weighed some thirty tonnes in life. Imbedded in yellow Upper Jurassic rock, the prehistoric saurians flanked the staircase and hid the leadlined walls, adding their own air of menace to the huge vaulted chamber. Once, they had ruled the swamp and forest where there was now desert, and now he owned them, absolute master where they had enjoyed joint sovereignty.

He moved on, finding the right key on his belt.

Army engineers had built the main underground labyrinth during the nervous fifties. Complete with diesel generators, fuel bunkers, water-cooled aeration units, filtration screens, and a vast underground reservoir fed by pipe from Lake Meredith, it was secure against all but a direct nuclear strike.

Sealed and abandoned upon completion, the huge complex remained a 'blue file' secret until he discovered its existence in the early sixties. Approaching the Pentagon through inter-mediaries, and using a clandestine PsyOps programme as a cover, he employed his secret 'slush' funds to reopen and refurbish the facility as a covert research unit rehabilitating brainwashed veterans. Knowing the Pentagon mind as well as he did, he furnished them with nothing but highly convoluted data requiring analysis they were unequipped to implement, and kept the more sinister and useful aspects of his findings to himself.

Careful to rotate the staff assigned to him before they became too involved, he was able to defend his considerable budgets without publishing the true nature of his work. After five years, others in the field took on his 'psywar' research along with the kudos attached, and 'closing' his unit had been a simple matter of referral to these more overt and prestigious facilities. By 1975 nothing remained on record apart from some obscure numbered files deep in the Pentagon vaults. Complex Alpha-X ceased to exist.

Using his electronic key, he passed through three self-sealing doors into his command room, and sat at the main console to study the gridded wallboard showing the commune and the surrounding desert area. The outer eastern perimeter had been breached at a point six miles north of the Ordway highway. He killed the warning bell and punched up a computer analysis of the intrusion: a single man weighing some 352 pounds. Weight distributed evenly on both feet. Walking speed: 3·4 mph at point of entry. Travelling due west. ETA at commune perimeter: 4 hours 17 minutes.

On a whim he keyed in Pepper's code and the green figures laid themselves on the screen without a pause.

PEPPER Matthew: AKA: Pepper San.

Codename: ZULU ONE.

Height: 5 feet 11 inches.

Weight: 182 pounds. (When last known)

Weight inc. combat equipage: 293 pounds.

Discrepancy: 59 pounds.

FURTHER ANALYSIS REQUIRED?

'Required,' he said.

More green figures lined the screen.

(A) Weight gain in ten years probable 50-60 lb.

(B) Carrying more equipage: (Possible weaponry filed).

(C) Hostile incursive *not* subject.

(D) Hostile incursive carrying light equipment and second hostile.

(E) Walking speed lower than PEPPER average: 4·72 mph. Suggests weight-gain/combat equipage + anno domini. ANALYSIS ENDS.

'Along with my patience, you cretinous web of circuitry,' he said aloud. 'Anno domini, for heaven's sake? That's no butterball out there, it's him. Him!'

The screen blanked to a sulking black and went to Red Alert when he keyed up the warning gong to summon the Purity

Council. Then he sat back to watch them hurry to the long table on the wall monitor, washing his long hands together in anticipation.

Pepper kneeled and shed Modoc like a backpack. Flopped on his face to get his breath and watch the western horizon for movement. The Rockies could have been painted on glass by a special-effects artist, and the distant flatlands wriggled in the middle air as eels of undulant opal above the monotonous sandstone basin he had to cross. There was no cover and, caught in the open, the Purity Council would run him down like an exhausted hare. Once he made the run of buttes on the far side the odds would swing in his favour. Just.

Pepper stood and looked down at Modoc.

'Keep to the plan, Navajo,' he said. 'Cover me and follow out of sight.'

Modoc grunted and wiped grit from his bared teeth.

'If they don't blow your knees away from minute one.'

'They do that, you get to play havoc on your own.'

'That,' said Modoc. 'You can rely on.'

Pepper set his guns and holsters more comfortably and went down the crumbling slope, digging his heels in to make a clear set of tracks. Slid down onto the vast pan of heat, jumped a boulder and began jogging west.

'Brave ain't always smart,' said Modoc, sighting along the rifle.

Maycroft had one sock on and was blowing on his coffee when the door slammed open. Moose came in ahead of Salvatore and caught the hot java in the face as Maycroft backflipped across the motel bed, scooping up his Ruger before hitting the floor. Moose yelled something obscene and the Sicilian lawyer spread his hands in placation. The Ruger was aimed at his nose and Maycroft's grey eyes were anything but sleepy.

'All *right*, so we didn't knock. Does that earn a double-cluster?'

Maycroft stayed where he was, letting the gun talk for him.

Moose ripped a curtain from the window and wiped off his

243

face. Steam whisped from his hair and coffee eclipsed the sun setting behind palms on his necktie.

'We're making nice here, limey. What's with this cluck, Mr Salvatore?'

'Ask,' said the lawyer. Then to Maycroft: 'Anybody'd think we'd caught you with dew on the lily, Chuz. Will you dress and move it, for chrissakes? We need to speed things along here.'

'Why?'

'Why? Why is simple. The pilot made a high reconnaissance pass over the target this a.m. . Took photographs. Your bird dog and some A.N. Other are already down there for chrissakes. A whole day ahead of your reckoning. They get in there and start whatever, we're down the toilet.'

Maycroft stood to scratch his naked stomach.

'Or make a perfect diversion. Have you alerted the field?'

'Does heroin come in tabs? Dress will you? Typecast as one of life's born naturists, you ain't.'

'Unkind but true,' said Maycroft. Fully awake.

'We can make the drome in seven minutes.'

'Only if your tame moron stops trampling my shorts,' said Maycroft.

The first dune-buggy showed as a bouncing mustard smudge less than a thousand yards out from the first run of buttes. A second and a third swung from the dusty pall as buttery blobs of hot yellow, as busily shapeless as daubs of fat in a hot skillet.

Quelling his natural instinct to move into a higher plane, Pepper walked steadily, watching them come. Whitened by the dusty marl he kicked up, his outline was diffused by the shining sandstone he walked across. A shifting ripple in a sea of ripples, he was invisible until they came closer.

Pepper choreographed Modoc's moves since he had left him. Moving north, he would have kept to the bank of the ancient watercourse, then swung west along the rim of the basin to parallel Pepper's course, leaving no tracks on the baked ground.

Two more buggies showed to right and left of the leaders,

converging on Pepper's position. The first buggy cleared the heat distortion, and Pepper picked out big speakers mounted on the hood, whipping radio aerials, and the men aboard. One of them stood to point, and the cock of automatic weapons rattled with the first purl of engine noise. A Tannoy pinged as it came alive, and the command to stop came as a distorted brawl of echoes.

Pepper threw his head up in feigned surprise. Cast about, feinted left and darted right, sprinting for a boulder the shape of a sleeping horse. A warning shot whacked the air near his face and he made a meal of tripping and falling. Rolling when he fell, he came up running and sprawled behind the rock as Uzzi rounds gouged its upper surface, snarling away as spiteful ricochets. Hornets glancing from hard mica.

Pepper drew his Savage and fitted the stock as he hugged the ground. A buggy brawled past, throwing up dust in a choking cloud, losing him in a stew of blindness and spits of invisible gunfire. He fired a wild shot that would carry to Modoc's vantage point, and moved in a scurry, using the dustcloud as cover.

The ugly buttes seemed farther away than ever.

The wheels of a second buggy threw grit and shale into his face as it passed. Pepper put a shot into its tank. A second through a meaty shoulder. Gasoline spurted like erratic rain, spattering him with high octane stink. He rolled back the way he had come. Made himself small in the overhang of the stone belly. Braced his arms behind the Savage for a clear shot to present itself. Another buggy sped through the thinning dust veil too close and too fast. Bombarded by churning grit, Pepper hid his smarting eyes behind a forearm.

Incoming rounds chewed the ground. Stitched holes close to his thighs, galvanising him upright. He kicked himself over the boulder followed by lead splinters and shards of exploding rock. For a split-second he had a clear view of the circling buggies, and he fired a double-cluster before he hit the ground with a shoulder.

Gears clashed and somebody squealed in high falsetto. The dust rolled in again and he made himself move.

Getting his feet under him, Pepper ran blindly west until the ground around him attracted jumps of shale and sand. Angry spits of close misses. Folding at the waist as though he had been gut-shot, he flipped and bounced, let his legs fall where they would, rolled onto his side and squinted back the way he had come.

The buggies stopped weaving and formed a semi-circle to face him.

Kneeling up fast, Pepper shot the nearest driver in the face and the hammer hit an empty chamber. Throwing the Savage away he drew the Tunnel Gun, knowing he hadn't the range. Three guns opened up on him in concert. Tensing himself to take the shock of multiple wounds, he felt nothing as cartridges erupted all around him. The world turned a stinking white and he choked on gas with nowhere to go but down.

Down was a long way to go with no sensation except a singing chime of unmelodic sound. The single note hit him in the face with hot desert sand and numbness came as black on black on nothing.

The nothing lasted a long time.

Modoc jogged to a halt when gunfire came out of the basin as wingbeats of distorted sound. Climbing into the buttes to play chase, the echoes died away like lost applause.

Modoc shaded his eyes to stare south, seeing nothing but the dancing heat.

The thin cut of the Savage came then. Cut twice more and was swamped by the rapid clatter of Uzzis. After a long pause, the handgun emptied itself, and the dull coughs of exploding grenades walked up through the buttes with the measured tread of finality. Stomped north and kept going until they were swallowed by the returning silence.

Modoc grunted and hefted the rifle. Followed the basin west, intent on covering ground.

Pepper had proved it was a good day to die.

Surrounded by men in black, Maycroft had a feeling of déjà vû as he checked his equipment. They had the same look of cool competence as the ill-fated SWAT team he had accompanied into the Blue Mountains a few short weeks before, and he prayed the outcome of this expedition would be very different.

The long-range Boeing Vertol 234 cruised at 165 knots and maintained its maximum ceiling of 15,000 feet as it crossed the Sangre de Cristo range between Red Wing and Blanca Peak. There was a long yawing jog of turbulence on the turn above Farista where the foothills levelled out into the desert, and there was little lift in the thin overheated air rising from the desert flatlands. The pilots followed the Cucharas River north, monitoring air-traffic control from the airport at Baxter to avoid incoming commercial flights, making for Crowley before swinging north-west to approach Black Squirrel Creek.

The No Smoking sign flashed to signal depressurisation, and Maycroft swifted to oxygen from his backpack tanks. The temperature in the forward cabin dropped, and Maycroft's flying suit heated itself automatically. He raised a thumb to show the instructor his personal systems were 'go'.

The view from the ports was blue-violet cloudness nothing, and although Maycroft couldn't hear what the pilots were hearing, he knew they were now monitoring radio-traffic from Colorado Springs. Once they had made the drop, they would turn the 234 east, swing below the radar umbrella, and feather in on the dirt road south of Truckton until called in to bring the task force out of the commune. Two medics were ready to convert the after cabin into an emergency surgical unit when the heavy equipment had been jettisoned by parachute.

Maycroft shook his head at the bleak thought and fed a full clip into his silenced Sterling-Pachette. Where the Sicilian lawyer had picked it up from was a mystery Maycroft hadn't pursued, nor did he worry about where the phosgene grenades had come from. He had five clipped to his belt and, used judiciously, they'd poison the underground complex for a decade. A chill wind swept the cabin when the side doors were battened open, and he struggled to his feet to plod aft.

The slipstream wailed in the open ports and the pitch of the wide-chord glassfibre rotors changed as the helicopter turned in a tight circle to maintain its ceiling for the drop, 5,850 feet too high to adopt a hover mode.

As third man through the door, Maycroft went out and down in a hard ball, bulleting out to clear the rotor wash, hitting the silk on the count of seven. The black canopy snapped open with the crack of a high-velocity bullet, and Maycroft was slammed to a halt in midair. Other chutes cracked open all around him, holding their circular pattern until the air thickened enough to supply lift for manoeuvring.

When he was sure none of the chutes had failed, Maycroft concentrated on the ground below. At that height, the desert was a chrome and lemon patchwork of rumpled folds, marbled by milky drifts of talc. This time there was no bright target to zero in on, and the laser-sight in his helmet visor was useless in daylight. He hung in the straps, watching his wrist-altimeter spin off the first long mile of descent.

Haze and upthrusts of turbulence rose to engulf him, buffeting him with hot roils of turbid air. For long moments all detail on the ground was lost in distorted refraction, and he leaned on his left strap to keep close to the two canopies below him. They had started a committed spiral, and Maycroft went in on the same curving path.

Visibility cleared suddenly, and tiny details jumped up at him in hard focus.

The commune was an open U of stone buildings with flat roofs and lean-to stoops of timber and palm built around a plaza of smooth limestone slabs. A herd of white goats grazed a penned hillside where steel air-ducts rose from the surface of a rocky outcrop with a sheer face. A wide columned entrance had been cut from the face, and steps led down to the northern end of the plaza. Long dormitories had their open sides draped with white canvas sun-blinds. Saffron figures crowded the plaza, moving around a structure bright with flowers and fire. Yellow dune-buggies were drawn up line abreast on a swept area between fields of Indian maze. Sweet unguents and burning incense rose on the warm thermals with the smoke from charcoal and oak chip fires.

Maycroft turned off his airtanks and opened his facemask,

248

raning to see what the central structure was. Long balks of timber formed an oblong pyre for a deep bed of hot coals, and a wooden cross of St Andrew was erected at one end. The man hanging from the cross had yellow hair.

Sound came then. The continuous and overlapping boom of a gong. The sharp tremolo of hundreds of handbells. The long OMMMM of a bass mantra coming from the swaying crowd. The slow clap of wind in the sun blinds and the crackle of flames. The amplified words of a sonorous address coming through speakers. A perverted version of the sacred words Maycroft remembered from Sunday School.

Maycroft turned away from the man hanging from the cross to see his shadow creep through the maize fields towards the plaza. Leaning left to swing himself away from the sun, Maycroft signalled the men above him to follow his example. His shadow drifted into an elliptical curve south of the commune as he spilled air from his canopy to lose height.

Dropping below the two men ahead of him, Maycroft saw the other shadows follow his line of fall as he curved in to the west of the long dormitories. Landing there would give perfect cover for a sudden assault. Keeping to that safe angle, he picked out the assembled Purity Council deployed across the steps of the columned entrance, and tabbed it as the way in to the underground complex. A man in white robes stood in the shadow of the column, beckoning to a small figure behind him.

Maycroft yelled in recognition. Called himself a bloody fool for such an outburst. Said thanks when none of the painted faces craned in his direction, intent on watching the flames rise in the plaza. The man in white beckoned again, and Maycroft knew with sick certainty who he must be bringing out to witness the execution.

Maycroft made his decision when he saw his first two men land in kicks of dust to the rear of the dormitories. He tilted his canopy hard. Spilled air and dropped like a stone. Braked at the last moment, and went down through a palm and tinder roof with the sound of an exploding breakfast cereal. His parachute snagged on a roof joist, and he smacked down

through a trestle table, scattering earthenware dishes before
turning an ankle on the hard stone flags.

Yelling in pain, he punched his chute release and blew holes
in a row of water jars with a burst from his Sterling-Pachette
giving himself a clear view of the funeral pyre.

Then he rolled for cover, hoping his diversion had been
effective.

OMMMMMMMMMMMM . . .

Pepper erupted from black nothing to vomit.

OMMMMMMMMMMMM . . .

Popping rosettes of nausea burst inside his head like
maroons.

A hammer punished a vibrating metal surface, hurting him
with hard resonance.

OMMMMMMMMMMMM . . .

A bass chant made his ears ring.

He tasted sour bile and spoiled peaches as his stomach
revolted.

OMMMMMMMMMMMM . . .

The sea of black nothing had beached him. A last black wave
lapped his mind and ebbed away.

OMMMMMMMMMMMM . . .

There was no rest. He was lifted and carried face down.

Mauled by a thousand pairs of hands, he was rolled on his
back. Spreadeagled across rough wooden beams. He squinted
drearily, his mind fogged by soporific gas. Dark figures worked
over him. Fretted against the brilliant sky. Chanted down at
him as they tied off his wrists and ankles. Spat at him until
his face ran with their saliva.

OMMMMMMMMMMMM . . .

Ropes creaked and he was lurched forward as the thing he
was lashed to moved. The sky tilted and the faces dropped
away as he rose into the air. Up into the face of the sun.
Hanging from his arms.

OMMMMMMMMMMMM . . .

Something greasy smeared his jaw. Hot animal fat dribbled
down his chest. Basting him as his stomach knotted with

leaving contractions. Dripping into hot coals it burned his legs
with spits of fire.

OMMMMMMMMMMMM . . .

Shocked fully aware, Pepper arched his back.

The sun at his back was hotter than the sun burning his eyes.

A voice as cold as gin came from speakers, cutting through
the chanting. Talked of flesh of my flesh. Blood of my blood.
Who shall eat of this man shall eat of My . . .

Pepper reared against his bonds and opened his eyes on
a sea of chanting faces. Men and women swaying in trance.
The third eyes painted on their foreheads staring where their
own eyes were glazed stones. Their monotonous chant a dull
drone of hatred.

OMMMMMMMMMMMM . . .

Girls larded Pepper with rancid goat fat. Another showered
him with rose petals. Yet another dusted him with saffron.
The petals stuck to his greased torso. Hung in his dripping
hair and clung to his face. Fatty pills of unguent gave off cloying
fumes as they burned away in wire braziers. The plaza was
strewn with red petals, and thousands of sticks of incense
perfumed the air with pungent blue smoke. Sullen heat
climbed Pepper's back as a man with a painted face stirred
the coals of the pyre with a rake.

OMMMMMMMMMMMM . . .

Pepper blanked off the mounting pain.

Sent out a mind probe.

The massed brotherhood had closed in on itself. A negative
psychic field he could neither touch nor penetrate. Shielding
the mind he sought. A wall of black stones without life. Without conscience. Linked by the dark skein of the brotherhood
drink.

Pepper tasted the first pang of defeat. Knew he had placed
too much reliance on his considerable gifts. The minds around
him were darker than any tunnel he had fought in. The fire
was draining his strength, and he would be unconscious long
before he and the cross were lowered into the flames. A new
emotion welled inside him. More acid than anger, and he was
shaken by its intensity. Pepper had discovered hatred.

251

He hated the crowd. Their mindless herd instinct. Their communal stink. More than that, he hated the cold amplified voice and its pernicious control of the commune.

Pepper looked beyond the crowd to see the video cameras mounted in the eaves of the building facing him. Recording his end on tape for the man he had come to find. He might even have Max watching . . .

Max.

Galvanised, Pepper turned in on himself. Turned his ankles inside the hemp ropes. Used the goat fat as lubrication. Braced his shoulders and *thought* his legs free. Felt movement and sensed something different coming out of the sky. Looking up as he tensed his whole frame, he saw a black butterfly pass across the sun. Trailing a man beneath its faltering wings. Beams tore apart as man and chute went down through a rustic awning. Brittle palm fronds showered across the plaza and into the crowd. The chanting faltered and the fire crackled as a run of fronds fell across the hot coals.

Pepper's left foot came free. Bracing it against the strut he pulled steadily, bringing his right foot upward. The hemp parted with a snap. The cross lurched out of alignment and tilted closer to the fire. Swung Pepper to face north, all his weight on his right arm. Hanging there, he saw the columned front of the temple. The Purity Council on the steps. The man in white robes with his arm around a small boy.

Hatred drained away and Pepper's mind was filled with singing whites. The boy's face leaped at him. Yellow hair alive with sunlight. Donna's freckles on his temples. The snub of a nose that tilted. The bluest blue eyes and the knees that always looked like they needed a wash. He was thinner, but he'd grown a good inch.

Know me, Max, thought Pepper. *Know me*.

But the eyes were as vague as scraps of sky. Seeing only what they were told to see.

Pepper looked at the man in white robes then. Saw mockery and perverted triumph there before the cross lurched a second time. Teetered and dropped closer to the flames. Pepper's left foot kicked white-hot embers, and he bawled with pain.

One of the women beat up at him with her basting ladle. The others leaned their weight against the base of the cross. Pepper ignored them, his mind on the man and the boy. His left hand squirmed free as silenced gunfire cut into the left flank of the Purity Council. Two men went down like logs and a woman sank to the ground holding her stomach. Rounds sprayed across a column and made the man in white robes duck to gather the boy in his arms. Shadows swallowed him as he retreated into the temple.

Pepper reached for his son, and with infinite slowness the cross fell into the fire in a brawl of smoke and sizzling goat fat.

Modoc had the commune in sight when he heard the thin crack of chutes opening. A trick of acoustics that made him pick up his pace. Following the upwardly shelving outcrop, he vaulted a dogwood fence, scattering goats when he landed on the far side.

A ram stood his ground. Mad yellow eyes full of malevolence.

Modoc let him charge. Leaped over the short butting lunge and kicked back stiff-footed. Caught square in the rump, the ram went over in a furious tumble. Came up dizzily and bullied some nearby she-goats in a show of thwarted temper. Shook his head, bleated, and stalked off downwind.

Modoc grunted and loped on through cairns of stone built around huge steel air-ducts. Reaching the brow of the outcrop, he ran into the stink and noise rising like a wall from the plaza below. Crouching low, he approached the sheer face and sprawled flat to orientate himself.

The plaza lay directly below him.

A brawling mass of sweating bodies, discordant percussion and heat, and he was repelled by the collective persona searing his mind with perverse negatives. The reality of the hive was blacker than the distant dream-views he had seen in Moonlady's mind. More evil.

The gathering was a vast soulless thing. Individual notions of self subservient to the greater will of one dark mind whose recorded voice fed hatred to the commune like tainted carrion. Focused that unnatural and pathological emotion on the man

hanging above the fire. Hatred for Pepper had been multiplie
four hundredfold. One man's need to burn Pepper to ash ha
become their collective frenzy, and they were amplifiers fo
his driving madness.

Modoc stared up at the sky. Counted off thirty parachute
spiralling down. Flakes of sooty vinyl only seconds away fror
deploying their massive fire-power around the commune.

Modoc grunted in frustration and tossed the rifle aside
Stripped off the ammunition pouch and threw it back at th
goats. Hauled himself to the very edge of the drop and peere
over, deciding his route to the ground. Planning to smell ou
the man under the overhang before all hell broke loose. Th
man in white robes smelled of desiccation. The boy gave o
the fresh tang of a sunwarmed apple.

Modoc started down as Maycroft hit the awning.

Pepper held Max safe in his mind.

Took his image with him as he rode the cross down int
the fire.

Jarred to a halt when the cross struck and slewed, Peppe
was pitched aside when it went through the wall of th
pyre. His right arm freed itself with a painful wrench and h
dropped awkwardly. Landing with a stagger, he bored int
bodies shrinking from the tumbling scree of white-hot ash
His hair and eyebrows crisped. Mad fists beat at him and robe
caught fire.

Rising to the Eighth Plane, Pepper became the Tw
Hundred Coils of Vapour. Saw the panicking crowd in the re
spectrum, and was fluid oil running through frozen statues
Racing ahead of the fire, he cut through a dormitory, and mad
for the western fields where canisters hit the ground unde
spent parachutes.

Clawing and spitting with mindless venom, the women cam
in at Maycroft from three sides. An earthenware crock scrape
his forehead before smashing across his shoulder, and bitte
nails raked his chin. A kitchen knife skidded on his airtank
and a kick to his sprained ankle made his head balloon.

'That, ladies,' he said conversationally, 'cuts it.'

He hit a face, kicked a kneecap, and buried a fist into a heavy stomach. Hit across the chest with a wooden faggot, he fired a high burst. Showered himself with stone splinters from the dormitory wall, and found himself alone with three unconscious bodies. Appalled by feminine savagery, he looked out into the plaza.

The fire-tender with the painted face helped the women to topple the cross. Hooking his rake into the crosstree near the small of Pepper's back, he leaned on the long haft, grunting with effort. The crowd's mantra picked up tempo and urgency, drowning the silenced breaking out along the western perimeter. They surged forward to throw flowers and aromatic dust, oblivious to the brawling heat.

The cross swayed, turned on one foot and teetered before falling to hit the pyre sideways on. Ploughing up the coals, it shed flame and sparks into the crowd, losing Pepper's twisting body in a rolling gout of sparkling flame. Shuddering, the cross rolled onto its face, taking one wall of the pyre with it.

The crowd milled and fought itself as the heavy balks spilled a landslide of glowing ash across their feet.

Maycroft shot the fire-tender through the spine. Blew him head first into the pyre and hobbled from cover. Fired a high burst to keep the crowd back, afraid of hitting Pepper in the sudden burning fog.

Fire ran up into the nearest awning. Flashed along its length and boiled smoke down into the plaza. Caught a run of sunblinds and turned them into a waterfall of orange light before crisping them to drifting tatters of canvas stink.

Blinded by smoke, Maycroft replaced his facemask and dropped his visor. Turned on his airtanks and set his Sterling-Pachette to single-fire. A burning torch of a man blundered past and spun off shedding flame and screams. A stun-grenade stopped an Uzzi stuttering near the temple.

Maycroft skirted the pyre as close as he dared. Crunched through a sea of glowing charcoal to the spot where he'd last seen Pepper. Felt along the smoking cross and touched rough timber where Pepper should have been. Felt his boots and coverall begin to smoulder as he lingered long enough to find the empty loops of hemp. Only then did he hobble toward the temple, assuring himself he had done his level best to put humanity before professional expedience.

Knowing it had been a poor effort.

Modoc eased down the sheer face until his toes found the roughly-knapped ledge above the columns. Teetering on contact, he scrabbled for a handhold, and got two fingers into a hairline crack. Laying in against the rock he sidled left, working towards a capital carved with acanthus leaves, his heels hanging over the void.

The seconds he hung there lasted forever, and the boom of the gong seemed to come from the rockface he clung to. Inching on, his foot touched the wider ledge above a capital, and he rested there until he was ready to negotiate the deep overhang.

Crouching with infinite slowness, he lowered his arms and made a bridge, balancing on the heels of his palms. Taking his weight on his forearms, Modoc eased his cramped legs out over the edge and lowered himself until he hung from his fingertips.

The chanting became more frenzied. Rose in pitch and tempo as some of the women ullulated a high and chilling warble of anticipation.

The Purity Council cocked their weapons and silenced rounds popped. Stone chipped from the column below Modoc and hard ricochets stung the air around his ankles.

Modoc reached down and felt carved leaves. Let go of the capital and dug his fingers into the deep fluting of the column.

Incoming rounds met a broadside of answering fire.

A man went down hissing through a hole in his throat.

A woman said 'Oh' very quietly and her machete skittered down the stone steps.

Modoc went down fast. Hand over hand, braking himself with his feet. Touching down on stone flags he lay flat as soft-nosed bullets chewed up the fluting where he had been. A Purity Councillor trod on his hand as he backed for cover. Rounds blew his robe to tatters and he went down. Hit the round with his knees and pinned Modoc to the ground.

Modoc glimpsed the man in white robes hurrying the boy way through the hard shadows of the upper lobby. Only pausing to punch at a wall panel, he scooped the boy up and made for the stairs.

Machinery throbbed under Modoc's chest, and heavy steel doors grew from the walls of the portico.

Modoc twisted up on an elbow and heaved the slack body way.

Came up running and launched himself at the closing doors.

He was less than five paces from them when his world turned to thunder and smoke and abrupt silence as his eardrums were cannoned by hammers of sound. The stun-grenade threw him through the closing gap, slammed him across the lobby, and rolled his unconscious body down a long staircase.

He flopped on cold marble and lay still, unaware that the second set of security doors ground closed behind him. His buckskins smouldered and blood leaked from one ear. The concealed lighting flickered and died. Red safety lights cut in and the air-conditioners stopped humming. The air grew hot and stale as oxygen was diverted to the lower levels, and the atmosphere poisoned itself with carbon-dioxide.

Modoc lay on his face without knowing he was slowly but surely being suffocated.

Maycroft stumbled out of the smoking pall and sprawled up the temple steps. His sprained ankle had ballooned inside his boot, and he lay where he fell until his vision and thoughts unscrambled.

Most of the buildings were alight now, and the communers had scattered into the maize fields where they stood around like lost zombies. The rising column of black smoke would be visible from the air, and it could only be a matter of time before it attracted attention. Time Maycroft didn't have to waste.

He levered himself to his feet and climbed to the temple. His men had cleared away the bodies and deployed half their number as a defensive screen overlooking the burning commune. Two squads were bringing the heavy equipment in from the drop-zone, and the rest lounged around the steel doors. The explosives expert tipped Maycroft a sloppy salute and banged his weapon against the dull silver surface.

'Titanium plate,' he said. 'Back of that'll be laminates of sheet-lead and honeycombed-reinforcing somewhere around eight feet thick. They built 'em way back then, boy, and it'll take all we've got *and some* to lance through that mother. Best thing is, concentrate on one area. Take out the bottom three-four feet of one door, and *hope* it brings the top-section down when it blows. See, them doors have gotta be set back into the concrete ten or twelve feet on either side, right? Now, they just warp out of alignment without we blow one of 'em loose first crack, we've got ourselves nothing but a buckled door going nowhere.'

Maycroft leaned on his Sterling and raised his visor.

'You fail, you get to tell that to Palm Springs, old son. You sold yourself to them as the best. Took their money and shook hands. Just tell *me* how long this is going to take. That's *all*.'

'Tops? One hour.'

Maycroft made a show of looking at his smashed watch.

'Let's say thirty minutes, shall we?'

'Saying it won't get it done. We got one shot is all.'

'Then go for it,' said Maycroft. 'That is the expression?'

'Will you guys move it with that stuff?' yelled the explosives expert. 'Man here needs to work.'

Maycroft raised his hands to the heavens and went off to light a mashed White Owl with hands that no longer shook. Hummed some Bizet and blew smoke into the pall rising from below. He stopped humming when one of the squad bringing up the heavy equipment reported that one of the canisters had been broken into. A set of breathing gear, detonators and hand-charges were missing.

'Mice,' Maycroft told himself. 'Clever Matthew Mice.'

'That guy's nuts,' the man told the explosives expert.

'Ain't it the truth. But d'you wanna look in them crazy

grey eyes and tell him? Face to face?'

'Lemmee help you here,' said the man.

Pepper lay with the goats and worked fat into his blistered thighs. A serious ropeburn circled his right wrist, and his shoulder muscles still ached from hanging from the cross. Landing badly, hot ashes had spilled across his crotch before he could throw himself into the crowd. By the time he had stolen a robe from an empty dormitory and cut into the western maize fields, the men in black had converged on the commune and weren't looking for strays outside the plaza. Picking what he wanted from the canisters had been the work of moments, and nobody but the goats had seen him climb the western slope of the outcrop.

A bristled mouth nuzzled Pepper's shoulder and he looked into the mad yellow eyes of the ram as it licked fat from his deltoid.

'Cupboard love, friend,' he said. 'And as close as you'll ever come to cannibalism. This fat's probably all that's left of one of your wives.'

The ram butted the air. Wrinkled his nose at the smoke rising from the commune, and walked off, flicking his stub of a tail.

Pepper laid out the five charges he'd lifted, and fitted the timers and fuses with a familiarity he'd forgotten he had.

'Like riding a bike, goats. You never ever forget.'

Saying that reminded him of punishing Max and his face hardened. He'd confiscated Max's BMX a couple of weeks before he and his mother had been abducted. All because he rode through a row of glass cloches.

'Not for the damage you *did*, son. For the damage you could have done to yourself. You hear me?'

Pepper cocked his head to listen. Heard goats and the drone of an aircraft descending towards the north-west. Punched the ground between his thighs. Hurt his rope-burned wrist and brought his mind back to the work in hand.

Shrugging into the breathing gear, he tucked four of the

primed charges into the blouse of his belted robe, used the fifth to blow the armoured security cowl from the main air duct, and lowered himself into the humming darkness.

The blast brought the explosives expert to his feet with sweat running in his eye sockets.

'I'm still breaking wind, so it wasn't me kissed my goofed up butt alveda bye-bye.'

Maycroft flicked his cigar stub away and crooked a finger at the nearest man.

'Take two men up there and report back. No shooting unless fired upon. Clear?'

'Quicker if we take one of them there buggies.'

'Then do so. How's it coming there, expert?'

'Close as June is to July, cap.'

'How very precise,' Maycroft murmured with heavy sarcasm.

Pepper cut through the first protective grill thirty feet down the shaft and found his way blocked. The titanium and rubberoid baffles below the grill were pneumatically sealed, protecting the filtration and cooling units from nuclear flash. Demonstrating that the command levels were sealed off and relied on reserve tanks of air, independent of the surface until they were exhausted, a matter of weeks rather than hours.

Balked for a moment, Pepper felt around the walls of the shaft and located the radiation sensor panel that controlled the dampers throughout the upper filtration system. With that neutralised or destroyed, the baffles might open to restore air-intake for analysis until an override countermand came from central control. That could take milliseconds or minutes, but Pepper had to trust to providence if he was to penetrate the purifying chamber. There, tons of dry-ice super-cooled the inducted air before pumping it down to the command levels for re-filtering and consumption. By blowing out the walls of the cooling chamber he would gain access to the air shafts, and they would lead him down into the heart of the underground complex.

Pepper clamped a quarter-pound charge to the sensor panel

and set it to detonate after a six-minute delay, enough time for him to return to the surface. Then he linked his three five-pound charges and laid them along the seal of the baffle, positioned so that they would drop through when the baffles opened. Setting them to fire ten seconds after the primary charge, he wormed out through the grill and climbed back up the shaft.

Standing on the stone cairn, Pepper was enjoying a long stretch when he heard a dune-buggy snarl up the eastern slope. He hugged the ground and listened to the men whoop as they scattered goats.

The first charge went off with the sound of all the jack-hammers in the world drilling at once. The cough of pneumatic release was almost lost in the racketing echoes. The dune-buggy changed course with a swerve, and the baffles gaped with their motors running in neutral as the pumps cut in. Pepper heard the triple clang as the charges dropped. The roar of air being sucked into the shaft, and the solid click of gears engaging to close the baffles when the pumps cut out.

'Keep going, pumps,' Pepper prayed. 'Keep going . . .'

The whole shaft shuddered as the cooling tanks ruptured. Pepper fitted his face mask and fed himself air.

The cairn shook and shed rocks. Air punched upward, followed by a solid column of vapourised carbon-dioxide that ate all the breathable air for fifty feet. Bowled flat, Pepper turned onto his face with dry-ice bouncing down like golf balls of sleet.

The dune-buggy swerved to a halt in a carbonated rain storm that stopped almost as quickly as it had started.

'Whole place smells like a club soda,' said the buggy driver. 'Damn, but look at them goats run.'

The men in the buggy watched the herd mill in panic and didn't see Pepper climb back into the shaft.

'Fire in the hole, cap. Thirty-eight minutes ain't shabby.'

The explosives expert lay beside Maycroft and punched keys on a detonator board the size and complexity of a word-processor.

'Very impressive,' said Maycroft. 'All that to make a bang?'

261

The explosives expert grinned and drew a diagram in th[e]
sand.

'Things have moved on since your day, cap. This gizm[o]
thinks in sequence, blows those charges with precision. We'[re]
gonna take a piece out of the left-hand door the shape of [a]
wedge of cake. Thermal charges cut the section out, the[n]
the main charge blows that wedge of cake inward. Leaves u[s]
a hole like this.'

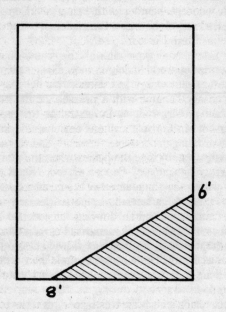

'You wanna do the business, cap?'

'I?' said Maycroft. 'To me, shoelaces are machinery.'

'Just press that red button, watch all the green light tur[n]
white, then kiss the ground. Don't look at them thermals blow[,]
they'll burn the retinas out of your eyeballs, OK?'

'Fire in the hole,' said Maycroft, and tapped the red butto[n.]

Sunlight burned on sunlight, bleaching the air itself. Th[e]
thermal charges hissed like lightning hitting the sea, an[d]

he main charge went off with the sound of a boot against a
arbage pail.

'That's it?' asked Maycroft, his eyes squeezed closed.

'Open sesame,' said the explosives expert. 'Is that a hole,
r is that a hole?'

'That,' said Maycroft, 'is a hole.'

he freezing darkness dripped as Pepper felt his way down
nto the cooling chamber with sensitive fingers and toes.
Ie needed no light to know the chamber had grown a belly
efore the blast had torn the floor seams away from the
anting floor. Wading through slush, he squirmed through
he gap and lowered himself on to a maze of twisted piping,
eeling for the nearest ventilation shaft. Ragged edges
wayed under his foot with a metallic groan. Its moorings
orn from the wall, the vertical shaft was unsupported until
t formed a junction somewhere below in the inpenetrable
;loom.

For a scalding moment Pepper was back in the tunnels of
Cu Chi.

The darkness came alive with saucer mines and trip-
vires. Fire ants and bamboo vipers. Stinking water traps
nd the smell of Charlie smelling him back. The grave-
ard odours of latrine pits and caches of rotten rice. All
he nightmare things that came back when sleep made him
ulnerable. When Donna used to hold him until he could
old her back. Their warm snuggle taking the threat from
he night.

Pepper shook it all away. Unstrapped his tanks to hold them
it arm's length. Balanced on his toes and made a racing dive
nto the shaft with the tanks held ahead of him.

Gravity slammed him into a bend and slowed his fall. Skidded
im around a second bend into a horizontal run where inertia
lowed him to a halt. Light bled from a grill many yards on,
nd Pepper crawled toward it, knowing no Charlies waited to
mpale him on poisoned punji stakes. A quickening draught
tirred his greasy hair and cooled the sweat on his face. Sniffing
he air he found it cold and breathable, and he crawled on,

263

holding the tanks so they didn't scrape against the metal sides
of the shaft.

Unknown to Modoc, the atmosphere around him stabilised.

He fell trying to rise, and clawed his way to his feet using
the base of an Ankor Wat dragon. Red service lights had
turned the upper temple to a bloody monochrome, and he
made the sign of peace at the stone lizards. Fought to stay
awake in the bad air, and let instinct guide him down to the
lower temple where the veil of carbon-dioxide had yet to
sink. A colour-coded wallplan gave him the layout of the lower
levels, and he traced the access points with a shaking brown
finger. Tapped a down-shaft with a grunt, and went to find
it. Striding through glue with labouring lungs, he came to
the elevator, punched the button, and heard the cage rise in
the shaft.

Loading his sling with a skystone, he waited for the doors
to open.

Maycroft and the explosives expert climbed over fallen rock
to study the inner security doors by flashlight.

'How long?' Maycroft asked.

'Using the same pattern? Fifteen-twenty minutes. Don't
rush me, cap. I don't get these charges dead-dee-right, this
whole lobby will cave in. Then you got yourself a stone quarry
with no way through.'

Maycroft gave the expert a long grey look.

'You make me a hole, my friend. In my book, you are the
best.'

'Cap, I'll do her in twelve.'

Maycroft walked away to kill time with another White Owl.

'He ain't so bad,' said the expert. 'Man knows quality when
he sees it.'

Pepper kicked the grill from its housing and dropped into a
concrete passage. The air was good. Deodorised by excessive
filtration it smelled of nothing, reminding him of the BelTech
plant. The red service lights gave his greased limbs the look

264

of melted wax. He leaned the air-tanks against a wall and padded down a slope, reaching out with his enhanced senses.

The complex spoke to him.

Micro-switches opened and closed, triggering slave mechanisms in a memory-retrieval bank, and coolants chuckled from humidifying units. Fans circulated at the intersections, and servo-motors panned surveillance cameras.

Pepper ignored them. Reached out for more than the mindless sounds of machinery. Caught a flicker of fear cloaked in chemical depressant. The tart jangle of nerve-induced sweat-pricking frightened skin. The warm apple smell of Max. Pepper soothed him with a bolt of compassion and moved on.

Then there was something different. Something other. An aura shielded by wrongness. A snapping field of psychic energy churning in on itself. A persona absorbed by self. The core was a black spin of inverted force. An implosive boil of oneness incapable of bonding with anything outside itself. The outer surface was a mad web of hatred for anything outside of self.

It knew Pepper was coming by mechanical means. Took perverse pleasure from the fact. An unholy glee colder than starburn. More glacial than Antarctica, it waited. Feeding on triumph.

Pepper homed in on the aura keeping to the threshold of the First Plane. Not enervating himself more than necessary. Leaning on the emotional strength Donna had given him, Pepper saw Max as a totem without human ties, and he rose to the Fourth Plane to destroy the metal door facing him. As he reached for it, it slid open with a pneumatic hiss to show him two more doors irising open on an area bathed in cold white light.

The two auras waited for him. The black of carbon. The sweet white of innocence.

Pepper went forward on the balls of his feet.

Ready.

The elevator dropped three levels and opened on a vault of blue light. A huge underground reservoir aerated by submerged pumps. Phosphorescence shone in the dark waters where blind cave fish swam in transparent shoals. There was no mansmell. Modoc had gone too deep.

He prowled the concrete walkways and found the feedpipes to the upper levels. The sophisticated governor that controlled the upward pressure of delivery to storage tanks throughout the complex. The filters that took alkalides and natural salts from the water.

Modoc grunted to himself and stroked the lobe of his deafened ear. Thought for a long moment, then smashed the governor with a steel rod he found on a workbench. Pushing all the switches to manual, he sent water upward at top pressure, figuring he'd blow every valve in the place.

'That,' he said aloud, making echoes. 'Should back up a few toilets,' and he took the elevator up to the next level.

The doors opened on humming generators. Gigantic machines that would have filled his secret cave. Modoc put the elevator on 'hold' and stepped out into crimson light. He didn't like the coffin in a shaft. There had to be another way up to the last level where the man who wanted Bella dead lived with his thinking machines.

Fifty yards along a steel gantry he found a metal staircase and went up fast, his footsteps drowned in engine-roar.

On the first landing an automatic camera swung his way.

Modoc tore its eye out and threw it away. Took the next flight two at a time and blinded another camera. Then there was a plain steel door without a handle. Modoc ran his hands over the surface, wondering how long it would take him to tear through it. He slapped his hands against the metal surround, broke a beam and watched the door slide open.

Beyond it was hard white light and the murmur of computer banks. He went through with his knife drawn and his sling wound around his wrist.

There were three smells, and he moved toward them, listening hard to pick up words.

'Matthew Pepper.'

The mocking gin-cold voice rolled the years away.

'Pepper san the Zulu.'

That brought the smell of Saigon into the command centre.
The memory of a constantly scratching gold pen.

'Close enough, I think.'

Pepper halted in a pool of light fifteen paces from the raised
podium where the man in robes lounged. Where Max made
himself small against the side of the swivel chair. His eyes
empty and his thumb in his mouth.

'Max?' said Pepper. 'Max . . . ?'

'He can hear you, Pepper. But he can't answer. I've had
him long enough to achieve that miracle.'

Pepper looked at the man in the swivel.

The eyes were the same cold chips of mica. The mouth
tasted itself with flicks of the same pink tongue. The thick
wirewool hair made crisp waves around the same square forehead. The same long hands hung over the arms of the padded
chair. Stroked the controls set in the leather arms. Only the
nose was a stranger. A jut of cosmetic perfection that changed
nothing. He was still the same man.

Pepper met the mocking eyes. Calculated distance and
metabolic rate. Flinched when the man in the swivel laughed.
A sound that was just a sound. No humanity in it.

'Let me save you the trouble, Pepper. It would take you
exactly two and four-fifths seconds to reach me. Much too
slow. By then I should have killed the boy's brain with a single
word. Oh, he might live long enough to die in your arms, but
that spectacle could only enhance my pleasure. And there's
your dilemma. Do you embrace your son, or do you waste
time trying to kill me? Never certain that you could, even if
you could reach me.'

'I'd reach you.'

'I *should* let you try.'

The laugh clawed the air.

'But that would end things too quickly. I have yet to see
you grovel. And you will grovel, I promise you.'

Pepper closed his eyes. Cut eye-contact to lay the room
out in his mind. Found the singing web of invisible light
between himself and the raised podium. Found it formed a
perfect screen from floor to ceiling.

A third clawing laugh opened his eyes.

'You've sensed it. And now you know you've lost.'

'Then we've all lost,' Pepper said.

'You mean those cretins out there? Blowing their way in
In the hope of destroying me and all this? They won't get pas
the upper temple. Have you ever seen what liquid nitroge
does to the human frame, Pepper? It turns men to froze
glass. In a trice. When I pump that into the upper chambe
they're finished. And you with them, unless you give yoursel
to me. Are you prepared to do that to save your son? Los
all sense of identity and become just another finger on m
right hand?'

Pepper pushed the thought away.

Talked to keep things going.

Probing the laser shield he said:

'What have you done to Max?'

'Mind control through drugs. Nothing that cannot be reversed
If you have the technique. And I have. In a week he coul
be just another snot-nosed brat in a schoolyard. Learnin
swear words and how to use a computer. Being told by hi
contemporaries that he's retarded if he hadn't made it wit
a girl by the time he's fourteen. How to get a fix with hi
lunch money. How to compete in mindless games with chee
leaders and brass bands. The entire ballyhoo. If you want tha
for your son you must pay the price. My price.'

'You're sick if you think that that's all that's out there.'

'Different, yes. Sick, no. Don't try to goad me, Pepper
The laugh was as dry as the de-humidified air.

'You're different, all right. Others will come. I made sur
of that.'

'Perhaps, but I'll have *you* then. And I shall be elsewhere
This experiment has run its course. A hobby I'm prepare
to give up. But not you, Pepper. You're mine. Now kneel. O
your own volition. Not out of a sense of coersion.'

Pepper allowed his shoulders to droop. Shook his head an
feigned defeat. Willed Max to see his father under the greas
and filth. Heard the sick laugh as he sank to his knees
Something synthesised by a machine.

'You can't kill me, can you? That act of revenge would leave your son crippled by psychic scars he'd carry all his days. I'd make certain of that.'

Pepper felt something dark sweep the edge of his eyes. A vague brush of wings against his face.

The man in the swivel licked his white smile.

'Convince me. About Max,' Pepper said, holding the cold eyes.

The man leaned forward. Gave off a glow of pleasure that smelled of rot.

'With the boy returned to the society you approve, you wouldn't fight me. Knowing he was back to "normal" you'd bow to the inevitable. You see?'

'No. Convince me, you bastard.'

Pepper willed Max to look at him. To focus those lost blue eys. The lids fluttered. A visual yawn.

The chamber shook as blast rolled down from the upper level.

'That ain't Avon calling,' Pepper said. Needling the dark ego.

A klaxon started to wail and the man in the swivel killed it as he brought console screens alive with pictures from the upper temple. Men in black ran through chemical vapour, their voices tinny through the speakers.

Max blinked at Pepper. Saw him and tried to smile.

'Stand away from him, son. Down on the floor,' Pepper ordered, controlling his voice. Controlling emotion.

The man in the swivel turned from the console, hissing.

There was a soft swish of leather. The sharp cut of disturbed air. Sparks flew from the invisible screen as a skystone ripped through it to smash through the robed man's hand. Ripping into the command console. The man in robes bawled as the console threw sparks and electrical stink from smashed circuits.

The defensive screen flickered and blinked out.

Max crawled away from the raised podium, his eyes on Pepper's face. Pepper went to meet him. Took him in his right arm, his left stiffened for the Naked Kill. Swung it across his face as shorting electronics spun electric fire from the console to sear the swivel with spits of fire.

The man in robes was backing away. Had his good hand on

the elevator button. Pressed it and backed into the cage, taking breath to say the word to kill Max's brain.

The leather sling snapped and sang. A skystone blurred and buried itself in the robed man's face. Spattered the perfect nose apart. The head slammed back against the elevator wall as the eyes bulged and the cheekbones caved in. Dead blobs of phlegm staring at nothing as the gaping mouth blew a blood bubble and sighed out the last breath of air. The doors closed and took the body down the shaft.

Pepper swung to face Modoc.

'You took him from me.'

Modoc grunted and spun his sling around his wrist.

'You have your son, fool. That dead thing was never yours. Finishing him would have destroyed you. One day you'll see that.'

Pepper held the boy. Smelled his hair and felt his throat contract as Max snuggled.

'Home, poppa . . . To mother . . .'

The boy went to sleep holding tight.

'You got the strength to be both parents, Matthew?'

'I don't know.'

Water spilled across the floor to surf around the computers. Shouts echoed down the corridors.

'You wanna be here when the others come?' said Modoc.

Maycroft was first through the door of the command centre. The swivel chair was empty and Modoc sat cross-legged on the dead console, chewing on a strip of jerky. The machines behind him spun their tapes and the floor was already an inch deep in water.

Maycroft showed as little surprise as the Navajo.

'You'll be Bella's Indian. A very busy Indian.'

Modoc waved a laconic hand.

'You mean all this? Nothing is all. Hell, if you can keep a '65 Pontiac onna road for twenny years, this ain't so much.'

'And flooding the place was just a matter of pressing the right buttons?'

'Pumps is pumps. No big trick.'

'And you didn't get a smidgeon of help from a fellow named Pepper?'

'Say who?'

'That's the fellow. And the boy?'

Modoc looked at Maycroft long enough to decide he was as good as any whiteyes could be that sounded like an uptown pimp.

'If there was a boy, guess he took his daddy's hand and trotted off home. *If* there was, and I don't know.'

Men in black crowded in with levelled weapons.

'Where's this guy Palm Springs wants, Limey?'

Modoc jerked a thumb.

'Try the elevator.'

One of the men summoned the lift. Maycroft offered Modoc a White Owl as the tapes deleted themselves. They lit up as the cage came up the shaft to swill water and a soaked corpse out into the command centre.

'How would you like to fly in a wingless white bird back to Nevada with this old white father, Navajo? Soar away and never come back?'

Modoc looked solemn.

'That nice-looking 234? Seems a neat enough machine. There's this new chopper the man from Palm Springs has. Now that's really something else . . .'

Talking like old friends, the two men waded through the rising water and made for the stairs. Both of them hoping that Pepper would make it to wherever he was going.

THE END

A SELECTED LIST OF FINE TITLES
AVAILABLE FROM CORGI BOOKS

THE PRICES SHOWN BELOW WERE CORRECT AT THE TIME OF GOING TO PRESS.
HOWEVER TRANSWORLD PUBLISHERS RESERVE THE RIGHT TO SHOW NEW
RETAIL PRICES ON COVERS WHICH MAY DIFFER FROM THOSE PREVIOUSLY
ADVERTISED IN THE TEXT OR ELSEWHERE.

*All these books are available at your book shop or newsagent, or can be ordered direct from the publisher.
Just tick the titles you want and fill in the form below.*

Transworld Publishers, Cash Sales Department, 61-63 Uxbridge Road, Ealing, London, W5 5SA.

Please send a cheque or postal order, not cash. All cheques and postal orders must be in £ sterling
and made payable to Transworld Publishers Ltd.
Please allow cost of book(s) plus the following for postage and packing:

UK/Republic of Ireland Customers:
Orders in excess of £5; no charge. Orders under £5; add 50p.

Overseas Customers:
All orders; add £1.50.

NAME (Block Letters): ....

ADDRESS ....

....